D0982440

Early Acclaim for *My Gun Has Bullets*

"Lee Goldberg's *My Gun Has Bullets* is a wonderfully funny romp through television land, and its band of merry—and not so merry—homicidal maniacs may be the greatest cast ever assembled. It's hilarious, suspenseful, action-packed. . . . There may be a more entertaining book published this year—but don't hold your breath waiting. This is the real thing."

—Warren Murphy, two-time Edgar winner, coauthor of *The Forever King*

"In *My Gun Has Bullets*, Lee Goldberg proves himself the Quentin Tarantino of novelists, with riveting, hip, original prose that is savagely funny, and a story that accelerates with eccentric characters bent on violent solutions to 'business' problems. Best of all, *My Gun Has Bullets* is written with the unmistakable authenticity of a television-industry insider."

—David Neuman, Former Vice President of Comedy for the NBC Television Network

"*My Gun Has Bullets* takes aim and hits the bull's-eye of all good satire—the truth."

—Howard Gordon, Producer of *The X-Files*

"Lee Goldberg has wonderfully captured the insanity of the state of our industry."

—Gerald Sanoff, Executive Producer of *Matlock*

My Gun Has Bullets

MY Gun Has Bullets

LEE GOLDBERG

St. Martin's Press
New York

This is a work of fiction. All the characters and events portrayed in this book are fictitious, and any resemblance to real people or events is purely coincidental.

Production Editor: David Stanford Burr
Designer: Sara Stemen

LIBRARY OF CONGRESS CATALOGING-IN-PUBLICATION DATA

Goldberg, Lee.
    My gun has bullets / Lee Goldberg.
        p.   cm.
    "Thomas Dunne book."
    ISBN 0-312-11862-7
    I. Title.
PS3557.03577M9   1995
813'.54—dc20   94-47821
                                                      CIP

First Edition: March 1995

10 9 8 7 6 5 4 3 2 1

To Valerie, the star of my show

Acknowledgments

This book could not have been written without the support and encouragement of Zachary Klein, who sets a fine example, and my screenwriting partner, William Rabkin, who never lets me take the easy way.

A special thanks to William Robert Yates, for starting my television career and inadvertently dooming me to write this book. But without Michael Gleason and Ernie Wallengren, and everything they taught me, I wouldn't have lasted in "the biz" very long . . . and would've missed out on all the bizarre experiences that inspired this story.

And finally, my sincere appreciation to Mel Berger, who knew me first as "Ian Ludlow" and has inexplicably stuck with me ever since.

Teaser

....

Eddie Planet pressed his face against the cold, tinted glass and looked ten stories below at the jerks on the Las Vegas Strip, standing around waiting for the Mirage volcano to erupt. Cheap Hollywood spectacle. Some flash and dash to lure 'em in to lose their money. Just like television, he thought. Give 'em enough ass, laughs, or bullets to hold 'em to the commercial.

He shook his glass, oddly reassured by the tinkling of the ice cubes. How many times had he told the sound guys to "jack up the cubes" when one of his characters carried a drink across a room? Hundreds. Maybe thousands. Tinkling cubes are very important to a scene. Whether it's make-believe or real life. He checked his watch again. A Cartier. The Renault of fine watches. Two minutes until the volcano outside erupted—who knew how long until the one behind the closed master-suite doors blew.

He felt like one of the hick tourists, having their picture taken in front of the steaming fake fissure. Maybe he should hire somebody to take a snapshot of him, pacing in front of the bedroom door with his bourbon and water and tinkling cubes, waiting for Daddy Crofoot's schlong to erupt.

There was a time when the roles would have been reversed. When schmucks would have been waiting for *him*. When *he* would have had the grand Vegas suite and some bimbo welding his beam. Back when *Saddlesore* was riding the top ten, and the network begged him for more. When studio heads would've shined his shoes with their tongues for the privilege of financing his next TV pilot.

But *Saddlesore* was ten years, two wives, six flop series, three production deals, and eight busted pilots ago. Back when he had a Palm Springs house and a Maui condo, three Cadillacs and a yacht, and bowels that moved so regularly he could set his Rolex, the Mercedes-

....

1

Benz of watches, by it. His lawyer was wearing the Rolex now, in lieu of fees. That sonofabitch was probably shitting like a bird. Planet had to borrow money against his *Deputy Ghost* residuals just to keep the Studio City house and the Seville. Which was, oddly enough, how he ended up here.

Eddie glanced out the window as the volcano burst, all lights and smoke and jets of water. Flames shot into the clear night sky. The funeral pyre of losers. Look close enough, he figured, you might see bits of charred polyester wafting up into the stars.

Suddenly the doors of the master suite banged open and out strode Daddy Crofoot in a white terrycloth Mirage bathrobe and leather slippers. His wet hair was combed, his skin was taut and tan, his eyes sparkled with youthful exuberance. Eddie was momentarily startled. In his mind, he had cast Charles Durning or Danny Aiello for the part. Something about the name Daddy Crofoot. But this guy was James Woods, maybe. Or that guy Marty Scorsese cast as Christ. Thin. Edgy. Dangerous.

Crofoot flashed a smile and offered Planet his hand. "You must be Eddie Planet. Thanks for waiting."

His voice spread across the room like an oil slick. Planet forced his cringe into a smile. "It's pronounced Plan-*A*. It's French for hyphenate," he chuckled, but all he got from Crofoot was a blank look. "As in writer hyphen producer."

Crofoot knew how to pronounce the guy's name. But he liked to needle people. Gave him an edge. Not that he needed one with this guy. "I see you've already helped yourself to a drink—is there anything else I can offer you?"

"No thanks, I'm fine, Mr. Crofoot," he said, thankful the man didn't ask him to call him Daddy. That would have been too much.

Darla came out of the bedroom in her backless evening gown that accentuated her large, authentic breasts. Crofoot watched Eddie drink her in like another bourbon as she walked to the door and, with a smile, left. Eddie Planet was hungry, and hungry people are vulnerable.

Crofoot knew all about Eddie, knew the difference between the paunchy, too tan guy in the rumpled suit who stood in front of him now, and the titan of television he once was. The difference meant everything. Crofoot went to the mahogany bar and took an Evian out of the refrigerator.

"I just came like Vesuvius," Crofoot said casually. "How many times have you come today?"

Eddie Planet's third wife, Shari, didn't think sex was a good idea so soon after her latest breast implants. That was six months ago.

"I've lost track." Eddie nervously shook his glass, but his ice was melting too fast to tinkle.

"That was my third," Crofoot said. "You got to have three a day, minimum, just to keep your balls working, the testosterone pumping. If there's no one around, use your hand. But why am I telling you? You know what I'm talking about. You're a producer."

"Aren't you?"

"I'm an investor, Eddie." Crofoot joined Eddie at the window and looked out at the neon night. "I'm just creative with my money."

When Bugsy Siegel came to Vegas, he stood in the desert and saw casinos. When Daddy Crofoot came, he stood in the desert and saw Bill Cosby. A two-bit comic worth two billion thanks to off-network syndication. Crofoot wanted in.

"I understand that you've got an investment opportunity for me, Eddie."

Eddie downed what was left of his drink and set the glass down on the table.

"I've sold a pilot to MBC, and that's like a miracle," Planet said, winding up for his pitch. "You got any idea how hard it is to sell a pilot these days?"

Crofoot knew exactly how hard—he'd been camping out in Vegas for two months, reading up. The network guys hear thousands of ideas, buy hundreds of scripts, and make a couple dozen mostly doomed pilots, sample episodes of wannabe TV series or, as Crofoot saw it, million dollar bets with a slim chance of return.

"You were lucky," Crofoot said, though he had no intention of relying on chance. The best gamblers cheat. Television was a fool's bet otherwise. And Crofoot was no fool.

"It's not about luck, it's about relationships—who you know. And Morrie Lustig and I go way back, back when he was the network exec on *Hollywood and Vine*."

Eddie was referring to the infamous, short-lived series about the busty fashion model teamed with a photosynthesizing, green-skinned detective who could communicate with plants—*Half-man. Half-plant. All-cop.* Morrie Lustig was now MBC's head of programming. It wasn't so many years ago that Lustig was a network liaison, the skinny kid with the clip-on tie nervously giving Eddie script notes like "What's the potted palm's motivation?"

"Morrie called me up a couple months ago, said it was time to do *Frankenstein* as a series, and that I was the only man in this business who could pull it off." Eddie's hands were beginning to move now, underscoring each point with a gesture or a sweep of his arm. "Morrie wants to do the classics, but updated. Sophisticated. Hip. Pulsating with the mood of the streets. So I came up with something."

And then Eddie Planet was off, building up to what he did best, what he enjoyed most. The pitch. Sometimes it felt better than sex. He certainly did it more often.

"Nick Stryker is a rogue cop who doesn't play by the rules, he just makes 'em up as he goes along. He's an undercover cop who finally went so deep into the bowels of organized crime it took half the L.A. police force to get him out." Eddie was feeling good now, getting caught up in his own momentum, building his pitch. "And when the smoke clears, and the blood dries, there are seventeen corpses on the floor. Ten of 'em are mobsters, seven of 'em are cops. One of 'em is Nick."

Eddie's hands were moving now, as if grabbing ideas out of the air and thrusting them into the hungry maw of his voracious pitch. Crofoot watched with a poker face. Eddie didn't care whether Crofoot liked it or not; the pitch had a life of its own, it couldn't be stopped.

"Then a black Corvette pulls up and out steps Dr. Francine 'Frankie' Stein, a scientist with a badge, a black-belt beauty with more dangerous curves than Mulholland Drive. She picks up Nick's decapitated head and clutches it to her heaving bosom. He was her lover, the best she ever had, and damn it, she's going to bring him back, somehow, someway." Eddie was feeling the rush, carried by the energy of his idea, of his vision, of what had to be the best fucking idea ever.

"She takes his head, and the corpses of the dead cops, back to her secret, high-tech, underground lab where, using the latest advances in surgical engineering, cybernetic organs, and computer imaging, she makes medical history." Eddie was in the homestretch, the finish line in sight, the prize money and the fame his for the taking. "She builds a man. He's got Nick's head, and the best body parts and healthiest organs from the seven other dead cops. He's also got a gun. And a badge. He's no ordinary man. And he's no ordinary cop. He's *Frankencop,* and he's serious about fighting crime. *Dead* serious."

Eddie stopped then, a broad smile on his face, waiting for the rousing applause. Crofoot nodded, taking it all in.

"Are we talking a two-hour pilot?" Crofoot asked.

Not exactly the enthusiastic response Eddie had hoped for, but at least he was showing an interest. "We can shoot some sex scenes and sell it overseas as a big, wall-to-wall action movie—on the slim chance MBC is stupid enough to pass on a sure thing."

Crofoot tapped his fingers on the arm of his chair, adding up the figures on an imaginary calculator.

"It's going to cost two million dollars, and what's the network coughing up, maybe half?" Crofoot didn't need an answer, he could see it on Eddie's face. "So that leaves a million dollar deficit. How much is the studio kicking in?"

Eddie instantly plummeted from his postpitch high. "I think I'll have that drink now."

Crofoot motioned to the bar. "Help yourself." He knew where this conversation was going, but it wasn't fun unless Eddie squirmed.

Eddie took a handful of ice cubes and crammed them into a crystal glass, then liberally splashed them with Jim Beam. "I've worked with all the studios, and made each of 'em a fortune. We're talking millions on millions. But executives have no loyalty, no respect. You have a couple near misses, and they forget you exist." He gently shook the glass as he walked back to Crofoot, the tinkle of ice cubes making him feel like an important character in a meeting rife with human drama. Suddenly, he felt like he actually had some control over the situation. He sank into a leather chair.

"I did a half-dozen ambitious, high-concept series that were too innovative, ahead of their time kind of stuff. The networks didn't have the guts to stick with 'em. So the studios lost a few bucks, but not nearly as much as they've made off of me in my time." Eddie settled into a seat opposite Crofoot, who was staring impassively at him. "There's still a *Saddlesore* stage show on the Pinnacle Studios tour. But, can you believe this, no studio will give me a cent for this incredible pilot, just because they lost a couple dollars on a couple shows."

Crofoot smiled, but Eddie found it anything but reassuring. For the first time in days, his bowels wanted to do aerobics.

"The shows were toilets, Eddie. Everyone shit all over them and the studios had to flush twenty million bucks down the drain." Crofoot's fingers were doing their tap dance and so was Eddie's stomach. Crofoot's choice of metaphor verged horrifyingly close to mind reading. "No one can afford you. The big studios are too smart now, and the little ones are too poor."

Eddie sat up so quickly some of his drink sloshed out of the glass onto the black leather. "Look at *Saddlesore*, look at *Deputy Ghost*, look at *Beyond Earth*—those shows made ten times what my other shows lost!"

"A decade ago, Eddie." Crofoot handed Eddie a napkin and motioned to the wet spot. "In Hollywood, that's the Stone Age. You're extinct. You've had to mortgage everything you own just to keep up the appearance that you're still alive."

Eddie wiped up the tiny puddle, then unconsciously dabbed his brow with the wet napkin. "This is your chance to get into the television business big time, to start as a player. You know how hard it is to sell a pilot? You don't let opportunities like this slip away. It's brass ring time. You understand what I'm saying? They don't come along every day."

And in Eddie's case, might not come along ever again. But Planet was right about one thing, it was the perfect opportunity for Crofoot to buy into the exclusive network television game and get a coveted seat at the high rollers' table.

"You're asking me for a million dollars just for the pilot, and maybe three hundred thousand an episode to cover the deficit if it goes to series," Crofoot said. "That's a big risk."

"*Frankencop* is gonna sell and it's gonna be a hit, I can feel it," Eddie said. "I'll stake my career on it."

"If I give you a million bucks, more than your career is going to be at stake. You do understand that, don't you, Eddie?"

Eddie swallowed some Jim Beam and mulled the implications. If he couldn't deliver on a pilot commitment, for Christ's sake, he was dead in the business anyway. What difference did it make if he was dead all the way around? Better to be six feet under than to face the humiliation of waiting for a table at Morton's.

"Sure," Eddie said.

No contract. No deal memo. No handshake. One tentative word was all it took for Eddie Planet to strike a coproduction deal with the mob, otherwise known as Pinstripe Productions International, Daddy Crofoot, president and head of production.

"I own the negative," Crofoot said, "and I call all the shots."

"I want the final card, at the end of the show, executive producer credit." Eddie hoped the bathroom was close by. He was going to need it.

"You can call yourself Grand Poobah of the Realm, I don't care, as long as you remember you work for me."

"Gotcha, Mr. Crofoot." Eddie downed the rest of his drink. "Could you point me toward the bathroom?"

"Call me Daddy." Crofoot walked to the desk, opened a drawer and pulled out a manila envelope. "I want you to meet the star of *Frankencop*. Flint Westwood."

"What's his TVQ?" Eddie had never heard of the guy, much less his popularity quotient with the public.

Crofoot opened up the envelope and tossed Eddie an eight-by-ten photo. Eddie looked down at a picture of the biggest hard-on he had ever seen. Crofoot grinned.

"That's his TVQ."

A stream of cold air was aimed at Sabrina Bishop's nipples, and eighty-three people were waiting around impatiently for them to get hard. But her nipples just weren't team players.

Maybe if she had spent all those years in all those acting classes pretending to be erect nipples instead of a tree, or an old woman, or a dog, she wouldn't be sitting topless on a pool table, while a stringy-haired makeup lady dabbed Sabrina's face and a gum-chomping special effects man wearily aimed a tiny air hose at her breasts.

Her cinematic lover, Thad Paul, who had already managed to become a has-been TV star at age thirty-five, was huddling with the shaggy young director, just out of USC. They were watching the video playback of Thad's close-up, taken while he lay on top of her and mimicked orgasm.

Being a method actor, Thad had thought they should *experience* the orgasm rather than *act* it, but she wouldn't go for it, despite his fervent protests. After all, he claimed, Mickey Rourke did it in *Wild Orchid,* so why couldn't they? She didn't care if Ronald Reagan did it in *Bedtime for Bonzo,* she wasn't going to prostitute herself for a direct-to-video, erotic thriller—another *Postman Always Rings Twice* meets *Double Indemnity.*

In this epic, *Scorching Passion,* she was playing a sexually frustrated woman in a bad marriage who falls for a mysterious loner—and then becomes the target of her murderously jealous husband. This time she was a frustrated sex therapist, last time she was a frustrated city councilwoman. Sometimes she killed the hubby and framed the lover for it—but it always ended up with her writhing around naked with William Katt, or Andrew Stevens, or Jack Scalia, or Thad Paul, or some other refugee of series television.

Sabrina was born with genuine acting talent, but she was also born with perfect breasts—the kind women bought for themselves and men dreamed of groping. Big without being large, well defined and firm, sloping into soft, smooth curves that led the eye down to her flat, taut stomach and narrow waist.

They were terrific, she had to admit. And combined with her long blond hair, blue eyes, quick wit, and vivacious personality, they had gotten her far. She was momentarily a journalism major at the University of Chicago (where she had successively been an art major, French major, communications major, and English major) when *Playboy* offered her five grand to take off her shirt in their "Stop the Presses" spread on collegiate cub reporters. She found a new major. Playboy Centerfold. And then she graduated. To Playmate of the Year.

That got her $50,000 and a red Corvette convertible. And it got her noticed in Hollywood. First by sleazy porn producers, whom she ignored, and then by television casting agents looking for something pretty to sizzle up the hundredth episode of their tired detective shows. It wasn't much, but her brief bounces across the screen got her into the Screen Actors Guild, and gave her enough money when her *Playboy* prize ran thin to keep her nice little Venice house, maintain her gas-guzzling Corvette, and enroll in all the major acting courses.

She eventually graduated from TV bit player to a guest shot as a bikini-clad *Baywatch* lifeguard killed by a ferociously horny jellyfish. And that led to her first direct-to-video thriller, *Torrid Embrace*, and that led to another, and another, and now, if she wasn't careful, she was on her way to being the next Shannon Tweed or, worse, Tanya Roberts.

It's a living, she told herself. And she *was* the star. But deep down she knew that if it were at all possible, she would get second billing behind her breasts. All she wanted to be was a serious actress. And all anybody else seemed to want from her was a stiff pair of nipples.

The director, in desperation, had already dropped the temperature in the soundstage to near freezing, but complaints from the crew and the foggy breath of the actors made him reluctantly give up on that approach.

Satisfied that his writhing and wincing were Oscar caliber, Thad Paul tore himself away from his celluloid orgasm and looked up from the monitor. "Are you ready yet?"

Sabrina glared at him, a man she detested, a man who would soon be nuzzling her cleavage like a baby and getting paid for it. Is doing porno any different? The writing is much better, she told herself, and she's working with real actors.

She glanced at Thad again. Okay, the writing is better.

The special effects man studied her breasts. "The soldiers are still at ease."

"We need 'em hard enough to cut diamonds," the director said. "The audience has to know she's hot and bothered, and spraying her cleavage with sweat isn't enough."

She closed her eyes. I'm not doing porno. This is an *erotic thriller*. Porno is all about the sex. These movies have a plot. There's murder, there's passion, there's angst. Even the big studios are doing movies like this, so it can't be porn, right? Look at *Basic Instinct*. Was that porno? Hell no, it was an *erotic thriller*. Like this. It's not just about sex. Click your heels together, Dorothy, and repeat after me: It's not just about sex. It's not just about sex.

"How about I stick an ice cube in my mouth and caress her boobs with it," Paul asked the director. "We could even work it into the scene."

"It's been done," the director said. *"9 ½ Weeks."*

"How about a frozen Tater Tot," Paul suggested. "I've never seen that."

Sabrina opened her eyes and came to a realization. Tater Tots weren't going to do it. Neither were Eskimo pies, frozen peas, or a couple of waffles. Her nipples were trying to tell her something.

She abruptly got up from the pool table, startling the effects man, and grabbed her shirt, pulling it over her chest.

"It's a wrap," she said.

"But we haven't done the close-up of your heaving breasts," the director said.

"Steal a shot from *Passion Play,* no one will know the difference," she said, heading for the exit and the safety of her trailer.

"You walk out of here, babe, you'll never work again," Thad called after her. "You'll be finished in this biz."

She should be so lucky. She didn't know what tomorrow would bring, but it wouldn't be more of this.

Sabrina Bishop was going to change her life. But she had no way of knowing that if she wasn't extremely careful, she stood a good chance of losing it.

One Adam-12, a 211 in progress . . . One Adam-12, a 415 man with a gun . . . One Adam-12, a 415 fight group with chains and knives.

Twelve years as a cop, and Sergeant Charlie Willis still thought of Officers Reed and Malloy when he saw a black and white. Even when it was his own. That's what you get growing up in front of a television set.

He could also thank his mother. Married four or five times (the validity of the Tijuana ceremony was still being hotly debated), and each new hubby was a bigger deadbeat than the last. If they weren't beating on his mother, they were making moves on Zoe, his early-blooming younger sister. So Charlie found himself unwillingly cast in the role of family cop. By the time he was eighteen, he had subdued so many drunken stepfathers, wife beaters, and would-be child molesters, it seemed like a natural career move to actually make it a profession.

Besides, it looked pretty good to him. At least from what he saw on TV. When he wasn't defending the family from predatory stepfathers, he found solace observing the orderly world of television. Everything made sense, and good was always noticeably different from evil. And the people who seemed to have the most control over this orderly world, who led the happiest lives and had all the answers, were the kindhearted, clean-cut police officers.

Boy, did TV have it wrong.

Charlie zipped up his fly and stepped out from behind the large bush he was using as a combination speed trap and urinal. The sweltering Santa Ana winds were sweeping through Los Angeles on this sunny afternoon, kicking up lungfuls of hot-baked, free-floating muck. Which made his throat dry and sore. Which made him drink about a quart of cola every hour. Which made him make a pit stop five times a shift.

The clean-cut officers of *Adam-12* never parked for hours at a stretch on Coldwater Canyon, keeping the homeowners of the $4-million-plus mansions safe from the evils of loud mufflers, casually flung fast-food wrappers, and the occasional speeding European car. And not once did Reed and Malloy ever have to take a leak, Charlie thought as he slipped back into his trusty black and white Impala cruiser. Come to think of it, they never sweated, had a runny nose, or stomach cramps—each a particular joy he had experienced during this all-around rotten day. Then again, Reed and Malloy never got laid, either. Reality occasionally had its advantages.

Not that Charlie was notching his bedpost into sawdust. He was obeying a self-imposed oath of celibacy since Connie ended their six years of blissful cohabitation. She cut out his heart, and his libido, when she packed up and ran away with the gardener. If Charlie was a better detective, he would have suspected something when she started taking Spanish courses and waxing poetic on the virtues of

Atilano's green thumb. At least she dumped him right away. Another three months and he would have been stuck untangling himself from a common-law marriage. This way, at least he got to keep his gym set, his collection of John D. MacDonald paperbacks, and all his NFL glasses.

Thank God for small victories.

Charlie was making a mental note to check on Atilano's immigration status when he heard a screech of tires, followed by the sight of a white Rolls-Royce convertible whipsawing around the turn and charging past him.

He flicked on the lights and siren and pulled out, shredding an ice plant in a spray of gravel. His car skidded onto the street right behind the Rolls. If the driver noticed, he didn't give a damn. The Rolls sped downhill, closing in tight on a Range Rover and, just shy of ramming it, swerved into oncoming traffic, forcing a cellular-toting boytoy in a Jeep to make a sudden right, jumping the curb onto a front lawn and plowing through the Statue of Liberty and Michelangelo's David.

The Rolls returned to the proper lane, cutting off the Range Rover, which skidded to a sudden stop, eating about a thousand bucks worth of brakepad. Charlie swerved to the right, deftly avoiding a rear-end collision with the Rover, choosing instead to mow over a perfectly manicured juniper and a mailbox with a wood-shake roof.

He bounced back onto the road behind the Rolls as it barreled toward the intersection, making a right-hand turn, south toward Wilshire. Charlie surged into the opposite lane, overtaking the Rolls and cutting it off as it rounded the corner.

He took a deep breath and glanced into his rearview mirror to catch his first glimpse of his adversary. She was in her sixties, her face tight with plastic surgery and anger, a string of pearls around her neck the size of gumballs. Not exactly what he had expected. If he factored in senility, old age, respect for elders, maybe he could cut grandma some slack. That's when she leaned on her horn.

"This is a street," she yelled, sticking her head out of the window, "not a doughnut shop parking lot."

So much for Officer Friendly. Charlie got out of his car and strode to the driver's side of the Rolls. "Let's see your license and registration."

"I don't have time for this nonsense," she said. "We just wrapped an hour ago and Neiman Marcus closes in fifteen minutes."

Charlie sighed. Without knowing a thing about her, he knew everything. For one, she obviously lived in the Beverly Hills zip code, which meant she was not of this earth.

"License and registration, *now.*" Reed and Malloy would have added a "ma'am," but Charlie figured he was doing her a favor by not dragging her out of the car, slapping her into consciousness and, perhaps, returning her to our world.

She reached into her purse and thrust her license out at him. He took it from her and glanced at it. Her name was Esther Radcliffe, and old Esther had scraped her birth date off with an Exacto knife and replaced it in ball point with a new one that would make her forty-seven.

"Now that you know who I am, move that boat," she said firmly, "or I'll have your badge on my charm bracelet."

Enough of this shit. Charlie opened the door and motioned to the street. "Step out of the car."

She glared at him, her eyes flashing with fury. "Perhaps you don't understand the severity of the situation. The Neiman Marcus once-a-year sale ends at five P.M. If I don't leave now, I will miss it. Do you get it now? Is any of this sinking in?"

Oh yeah, Broom Hilda, it sure is.

"You can get out yourself, or I can remove you," Charlie said. "Your call."

"No one talks to me like that," she seethed, turning her back to him as she reached for her purse on the passenger seat.

"Then you'll get a real thrill when I read you your rights," said Charlie, who was preparing to do just that when she turned around, aimed a .38 Special squarely at his stomach, and fired.

Charlie felt as if he'd been impaled by a ballistic missile and carried into the stratosphere. His last thought, in that split second before blackness completely overtook him, was that there had to be a better way to make a living.

Esther Radcliffe tossed the gun on the passenger seat, drove around the police car, and managed to make it to Neiman Marcus before they closed the doors. The only thing on her mind when she left the store forty minutes later with her $11,000 in purchases was whether to tip the two salesmen helping her to the car in cash, or to put it on her charge.

The whole incident on Coldwater Canyon didn't cross her mind again until later that evening, when two plainclothes detectives drove up to her gate with a warrant for her arrest. She didn't let them in, of course. She made a telephone call instead.

The first thing Charlie Willis saw when he opened his eyes at the UCLA medical center were two men in tailored Armani suits standing at the foot of his bed. One was a William Morris agent. The other was a network executive.

ACT ONE

Network Primetime Schedule for Thursday and Sunday

MBC — Monumental Broadcasting Company
UBC — United Broadcasting Company
DBC — Dynamic Broadcasting Company

Thursday

	8:00	8:30	9:00	9:30	10:00
DBC	Adopted Family	My Wife Next Door	Young Hudson Hawk		Blacke and Whyte
UBC	Boo Boo's Dilemma	Rappy Scrappy	Broad Squad	Smart Alec	My Gun Has Bullets
MBC	Johnny Wildlife		Dedicated Doctors		Frankencop

Sunday

	8:00	8:30	9:00	9:30	10:00
DBC	Red Highway		Movie		
UBC	Miss Agatha		Movie		
MBC	Honeymooners: The Next Generation		Sheriff of Mars		Sleepwalker

Chapter One

· ·

Eight Months Later

It was a dark alley. Somehow, it was always a dark alley. The sole light came from a distant moon, which was about as far away from the dead end of the rancid-smelling alley as Charlie Willis wanted to be.

The alley was bathed in shadows, silent except for the death rattle and dark chords of a menacing soundtrack only Charlie heard. Something wasn't right here. He wasn't sure what. Just that the music in his head told him something was wrong.

Then three shadows seemed to peel off the wall and take the form of men—stern faced, young, angry, their gang colors vibrant even in the near–pitch blackness of this endless night.

One of them carried a crowbar. Another wielded a nunchaku. The third flicked open a knife that caught the moonlight and reflected off his cold, dead eyes.

Charlie smiled grimly. "Nice night for a stroll, don't you think?"

That's when he heard the clatter of three more men rising from the trash bins and garbage cans behind him. He was caught in a shrinking circle of death. One of them held a gasoline can. From the way the others deferred to him, it was clear he was the leader.

"You shouldn't have come down here tonight," the gasman said. "I'm in the mood for BBQ pork."

His minions snickered at his marvelous wit. Charlie sighed. "I know you've got the ambassador's daughter stashed somewhere in this neighborhood. If she doesn't get her insulin in the next hour, she's dead. I was hoping we could work this out without you getting hurt."

Now they really laughed, until a sharp glance from the gasman cut off their guffaws.

"You got the million dollars?"

Charlie reached into his pocket and everyone tensed up, ready to blow him away at the slightest provocation. His hand came up holding some lint, a ticket stub, and a couple of crumpled bills.

"I stopped for a burger on the way over," Charlie said. "I'm afraid I'm a little short. What do you say we settle for a buck eighty-five and call it even?"

Gasman unscrewed the cap on the gasoline and shook it so Charlie could hear the liquid swirl inside.

"First I'm going to douse you with gasoline, light you on fire, and watch you burn, and then I'm gonna do the same to the ambassador's daughter." The gasman grinned. "They're gonna call this Gasoline Alley in your honor."

Charlie shrugged. "I guess that's a no." Charlie's hand closed on the money. "Then I've got no choice but to place you gentlemen under arrest."

The gasman wasn't laughing, so neither were his cronies. He took a deliberate step forward, flicking his Bic, the tiny blue flame casting an evil glow on his hawklike features. "You're alone, outnumbered, and a second away from having your rotting flesh burned right off your bones. What makes you think you're gonna walk out of this alley alive?"

"Because," Charlie said, his handful of money disappearing into the fold of his jacket, *"my gun has bullets."*

And out came his hand again, grasping the biggest gun the gasman had ever seen and the last thing he ever saw. Blammo! The first bullet burst the gasoline can and suddenly the gasman was a human fireball. Charlie pivoted on his heel and fired off three more rounds, taking out half the gang members like ducks in a shooting gallery. The two survivors dropped their weapons and held up their hands.

One of them quivered in the sickening glow of the gasman's crackling corpse. "We'll take you to the girl, just don't hurt us."

Charlie glared at them for a long, triumphant moment until a voice cried out, *"Cut!"*

A shrill bell echoed through the soundstage, the lights came up, and out rushed two men with fire extinguishers, covering the flaming rubber dummy in foam. The gasman, safely offstage, stepped forward and pumped Charlie's hand.

"It was a pleasure working with you," the young actor said. Charlie smiled politely. "I'm doing a little equity waiver thing down in Santa Monica, a Harold Pinter play. Maybe you could come down and see it?"

"Maybe," Charlie said, walking away and handing his gun to the propman. He was eager to get away from this week's bad guy. Actors made him nervous. For one thing, they knew what they were doing, which was one up on Charlie. For another, every actor he met was psychologically ill. What other kind of person would spend their days pretending to be someone else? Then again, what did that make Charlie? After all, he did spend his days pretending to be supercop Derek Thorne, the laconic hero of the UBC series *My Gun Has Bullets*. But Charlie knew he wasn't an actor. His badge was plastic now, but deep down, he was still a cop.

What the hell difference does it make? Charlie asked himself. No one gave a damn about the distinction—why should he?

The director, Seth Bruce, caught up with him. Bruce was known as the denim director. The man wore nothing but Levi's top to bottom. Probably even had stonewashed underwear.

"You just out-easted Eastwood," Bruce said. "And, between you and me, you gave the scene verisimilitude that was nowhere on the page. You have verisimilitude coming out of your pores."

Charlie had no idea what Bruce had just said, but he figured it had to be a compliment. In Hollywood, he learned, people were always complimenting you, even when they thought what you just did was dogshit, which was most of the time.

"Thank you, Seth," Charlie said. "I think you're full of verisimilitude, too."

That stopped Bruce in his tracks. He didn't know whether to be insulted or flattered. Charlie kept on going, hoping to make it out the door and into his trailer before Bruce came to a decision.

A harried assistant director, fiddling with the walkie-talkie on his belt, came up alongside Charlie, handing him palm-size copies of the script pages for the next scene. "We're in the cop shop next, scene 47D, interrogation of the Hasidic Jew. You got a half-hour to change into the gray suit."

Charlie nodded and headed out the door, momentarily blinded by the harsh glare of the morning sun over Pinnacle Studios, nestled in the far corner of the smog-choked San Fernando Valley. Somewhere in the distance he could hear the screams of several tramloads of tourists as they were attacked by a giant squid made famous in the movie *Terror Tentacles,* its three sequels, and the Broadway musical.

He squinted against the glare and made his way toward one of the mobile homes that lined the alleys between the soundstages. That meant passing the row of extras, the dayplayers with nonspeaking parts waiting to be called to populate the crowded precinct scenes. He tried to ignore them, because like the actors he worked with, they made him feel uncomfortable.

The extras were lazing in the shade of the soundstage, sitting in folding chairs, leaning against the wall, lying on the asphalt, doing whatever they could to ease the crushing boredom between scenes. They were taking naps, playing solitaire, practicing acting class roles, reading dog-eared paperbacks, or writing their million dollar spec scripts. They were waiting for their $50 a day and two square meals and paying their dues, something Charlie Willis never had to do.

He got gutshot by the star of a hit TV series instead.

Esther Radcliffe was known and loved by millions of viewers as kindly *Miss Agatha,* the deceptively mild-mannered widow who solved perplexing murders and still found time to bake chocolate chip cookies for all the suspects. Only the people Esther worked with, and the cop she gunned down, knew her for the bitter, paranoid, utterly self-absorbed hell bitch that she really was.

Miss Agatha was going into its fifth smash year, the unshakable foundation of the United Broadcasting Company's Sunday night schedule. The show attracted the Geritol set in droves. The old codgers were less desirable to advertising agencies than free-spending yuppies, but there was no arguing with *Miss Agatha*'s consistent ranking in the top ten shows. The audience flow from *Miss Agatha* went right into the UBC movie, making even the most insipid true-life potboiler a ratings powerhouse. UBC owned Sunday nights. Retirement homes around the country were glued to UBC from eight P.M. right on through to the local affiliate's evening news.

In an era of shrinking audience shares and cutthroat primetime warfare, UBC could not afford to have Esther Radcliffe sent to prison for gunning down a Beverly Hills police officer. The adverse publicity would be horrific. The network would be forced to cancel the show, kissing off the night and losing millions of dollars in advertising. And the eighty-eight episodes already in the can, which Pinnacle Studios conservatively figured would bring $200 million in future off-network syndication revenue, wouldn't be worth the celluloid they were captured on.

Clearly, this catastrophe could not be allowed to happen. Esther's network, her studio, and her talent agency were mobilized in minutes. Deal memos were drawn up, careers were made and ruined, and primetime schedules were juggled over sizzling fax machines and crackling cellular phone lines, culminating in the critical moment when Sergeant Charlie Willis regained consciousness to find two executives standing at his bedside. He was so out of it he actually thought one of them had pubic hair on his head.

And now he was here. As Detective Lieutenant Derek Thorne, the man behind the catchphrase that was sweeping the country—*my gun has bullets.*

An extra who hoped to be the next Demi Moore was sitting against the soundstage just outside his trailer. Her police officer uniform had been discarded and neatly folded beside her so she could sun herself in the scant bikini top she wore underneath. Her eyes were closed, so Charlie made the mistake of glancing at her. Instantly her eyes flashed open and met his. He averted his gaze too late. No backing out now.

"You were terrific in the bar scene yesterday," she said.

"Thank you," Charlie replied, turning his back to her as he unlocked the door. "You were terrific, too."

"I bet you didn't even notice me," she said, a bit too coyly, unable to hide the hope in her voice. It was something about the softness of her voice, more than anything, that made him turn around.

"You were waitress number three." He shot her one of his Officer Friendly smiles. "You delivered the beer mug I broke over the mobster's head."

She grinned. "Thank you for noticing."

Charlie shrugged. "You're hard to miss, ma'am." Sometimes he couldn't help himself.

He stepped into his trailer, and would have closed the door behind him, but it was like walking into a warm towel. The air conditioner was on the blink. The air trapped inside the tin box that was his "dressing room" was so hot he figured he could throw a handful of Jolly Time into the air and have a bowl of popcorn when it landed.

Charlie peeled off his shirt and was reaching for a clean one when she tentatively came in, though there was nothing tentative about her. Everything, Charlie suspected, right down to her bikini top, was premeditated. But what the hell.

"I'm Alice." She had put on her uniform shirt, but left it open to show off her résumé. "Alice Doss."

"I'm a thorn in the side of organized crime," Charlie replied, offering his hand. "Or, as I'm known to my friends, Charlie."

"I thought big stars had air-conditioned dressing rooms." She stayed in the doorway, where at least she had some fresh air.

"That should tell you something." Charlie pulled on the fresh shirt, and faced the mirror. He could see her behind him, admiring his body, which still showed the positive effects of regular workouts. There was only one thing not quite right about his body, though. There was a scar that looked like an extra bellybutton, a lasting memento from the slug that passed through his stomach, miraculously weaved past vital organs and vertebrae and, eight months later, became an attractive acrylic paperweight on his coffee table.

"Were you really a cop once, or is that just hype?"

"I was a cop, but I wasn't Derek Thorne." Charlie buttoned up the shirt. It was clear from her expression that that wasn't what she wanted to hear. So she sure as hell wouldn't want to know how he sold out. How he "forgot" who shot him. How he claimed he got the license number wrong. The face wrong. The name wrong. How he agreed to cover the whole thing up in exchange for their generous thirteen-week series commitment and $15,000-an-episode salary.

Now he really was like the cops on *Adam-12*. He had become make-believe. At least it beat being shot at.

"Where did you get the scar?" she asked.

He thought about that for a long moment. She looked at the pained expression on his face and thought he was reliving a painful experience. It was actually the first acting he had done all day. Perhaps all month.

"I walked into a burger joint in the middle of a holdup. I ended up digesting a bullet instead of a hot meal," he said. "The four scumbags sent me to the hospital. I sent them to the morgue."

That was what she wanted to hear. She looked at him with an appraising grin, the grin of someone admiring something they wished they could own but couldn't afford.

"Did you ever take an acting class?"

"To survive undercover, you have to know how to be anyone, anywhere, anytime." Charlie had no idea where this was coming from, or more worrisome, why it came so easily. Perhaps he really was Derek Thorne. Or maybe he simply wished he had been half the cop in reality that he was now.

"I bet what I've been learning in acting class for the last five years isn't half as valuable as what you learned on the street," she said with forced innocence, proving she needed more acting classes. "I can't imagine what I could learn from you in an hour."

"Imagine what you could learn in an evening. Do you think it would be against department policy for a detective lieutenant to have dinner later with"—he tipped up the badge on her uniform—"a lowly parking enforcement officer?"

She smiled and he smiled back. As long as he was going to sell out, he should go all the way. He left his trailer without looking in the mirror again.

Chapter Two

Eddie Planet always read the trades on the toilet, which was a good thing, because the headline in *Daily Variety* scared the shit out of him.

Boo Boo Fetches Audience; *Frankencop* D.O.A.

UBC's Boo Boo's Dilemma *has proved his bark is as big as his bite, chewing on a 40 share of the Thursday night audience and tossing a big bone to the shows which follow.*

The spin-off Rappy Scrappy *is the cat's meow, holding 75% of* Boo Boo's *lead-in, and leaving DBC's* My Wife Next Door *and MBC's* Johnny Wildlife *to fight over the litter box.*

The two sitcoms which follow, Broad Squad *and* Smart Alec, *are performing so strongly, sources say the web's programming whiz, Don DeBono, is considering moving the successful skeins to shore up an ailing night elsewhere in the sked. DBC's* Young Hudson Hawk *isn't likely to grow much older, while the venerable* Dedicated Doctors *are on life support after five seasons as MBC's primetime prescription for ratings malaise.*

DBC's Blacke and Whyte, *beaten black and blue at 10 P.M., is being pulled and will reportedly return mid-season with a new title and a new format.*

My Gun Has Bullets on UBC is loaded with a strong lead-in, but it's misfiring, dropping off a disturbing 10 share points from Smart Alec. *This presents MBC with a real opportunity to blunt UBC's Thursday night dominance, but producer Eddie Planet's* Frankencop *is lumbering along a distant second, despite improving 25% on its* Dedi-

cated Doctors' *lead-in. If lightning doesn't strike soon,*
Frankencop *will be dismembered fondly.*

It used to be that Eddie would shrug off a story like this. The vicissitudes of the business. It wasn't as if his life was riding on it.

That was before he signed with Pinstripe Productions.

After only six weeks on the air, *Frankencop* had tallied over a million dollars in deficits and its ratings were eroding. But it wasn't cheap to do a sci-fi action show these days. And going up against UBC's strongest night was a kamikaze mission. All in all, *Frankencop* wasn't doing badly.

Figure in that dickhead Flint Westwood, and it was a miracle the show even got made. Flint's real name was Huey Krupp, and he was Crofoot's cousin. His previous acting experience consisted of being a dick double in porno films financed by Crofoot. Luckily, playing a hulking, undead cop stitched together from corpses didn't require a lot of range.

Flint's unique approach to a scene was to ask himself "What's in it for my dick?" If his dick didn't have a motivation, Flint couldn't move. The same was true for Flint in real life.

Eddie had his hands full just thinking of reasons for Flint's dick to chase down bank robbers, kidnappers, and terrorists instead of jamming buxom Dr. Francine "Frankie" Stein. Simply telling Flint his dick was dedicated to truth, justice, and the American way wouldn't fly. Coming up with new dick motivations ("You've got a hard-on for the Statue of Liberty, and if the terrorists blow it up, you could become impotent") took more creative energy than thinking up stories.

So between the powerful competition and Flint Westwood, Eddie should be congratulated for even putting a show on the air. Even Crofoot could understand that. And if he didn't, fuck him.

The phone jangled. Startled, Eddie reached for the toilet paper instead, unspooling the roll all over his knees.

Cool your jets, he told himself. You're the executive producer. You're a powerful man in this town. Remember that.

He took a deep breath and picked up the phone, mounted just above the toilet paper rack.

"Eddie Planet," he said decisively.

"Have you read the trades, Eddie?" Crofoot's voice poured into his ear.

"Yeah, but I wouldn't take 'em too seriously," Eddie's knees clacked together nervously.

"I do," Crofoot said softly.

"We're in a suicide slot, everybody knows that. Coming in second is a major accomplishment. You should congratulate yourself."

"I'm not losing three hundred thousand bucks a week to come in second," Crofoot snapped.

Eddie wanted to say *Take it easy, Daddy, have your daily jerk-off and leave me the fuck alone.* What he said instead was:

"You wanted in the television business. No one said it would be cheap, and no one said it would be easy. It's out of our hands."

"You promised me the show would be a hit, Eddie."

"It is, it's a terrific show, the concept is fucking brilliant, but I'm not running the network. They put us in a rotten slot—you can't blame me for that."

There was a long silence on the line. Each nanosecond was torture for Eddie. Had he said the wrong thing? Had he said the right thing? It was enough to make his sphincter twitch. He willed himself to stay calm, to live up to the executive producer card at the end of the show.

"Every time I read a bad review, you're insulting me. Every cent the show loses, you owe me," Crofoot said. "If the show is canceled, so are you."

Eddie's stomach cramped so severely he almost lurched off the toilet seat. He wanted to whimper but instead he forced himself to laugh, to show he knew Crofoot was just being a funny guy.

"Don't worry, my shows are never canceled, they're just put on *permanent hiatus.*" Eddie coughed out a couple of uproarious guffaws, nearly choking. "All kidding aside, Daddy, you know it's not my fault. The networks control everything. It's the way the television business is run."

"Then it's time it was run differently." Crofoot said it so coldly Eddie's ear went numb. "In my business, you don't wait for someone else to take you out."

"What do you want me to do?"

"Whatever the new co–executive producer tells you to do."

"You got it, Daddy." Eddie was actually relieved. Fine, let one of Crofoot's goons take the heat. But there was one big, terrifying drawback. "I'm not gonna share a card, am I? I won't share a card."

"You'll have your own card," Crofoot said. "And if the show doesn't start winning its time slot, you'll have your own tombstone."

"That's classic." Eddie laughed, but the tears rolling down his cheeks weren't joyous. "Great stuff. Incidentally, does this guy have any television experience?"

Crofoot hung up.

Eddie lost the connection and the control of his sphincter all at once.

He managed to slit Rodrigo Lincoln's pale, thin little throat without getting a single drop of blood on his rubber surgical gloves.

And when Rodrigo fell on the marble entry hall floor, spilling blood like a dropped carton of milk, not one speck of red landed on Delbert Skaggs's brand-new Nike running shoes. That's because the shoes were sheathed in plastic bags that were cinched to his ankles with rubber bands.

Delbert had been waiting in Rodrigo's immaculate Cape Cod–style home for only twenty minutes, and it took less than five seconds to do the job, without getting dirty and without leaving a single fiber or particle behind for some forensics specialist to track him with.

Delbert calmly walked back into the kitchen, rinsed the steak knife carefully, dried it with a paper towel, and returned it inconspicuously to the knife drawer, whistling while he worked, something he'd learned from Snow White and never forgotten.

He opened another drawer, took one of Rodrigo's ziplock bags, dropped the damp paper towel into it, then pocketed the bag in his sweatsuit for disposal a long distance away from the scene of the crime.

Delbert sprinkled some Comet in the sink and carefully washed it down. It was his policy to leave a crime scene cleaner than it was when he arrived. Unless, of course, it would call attention to his presence. Then he just wiped away anything that might, even in the most obscure or microscopic way, point to his existence.

Attention to detail. All the best craftsmen had it. Delbert was no exception.

He headed for the back door, pausing for a moment to admire a child's crayon drawings and finger-paint masterpieces taped to the fridge, and the picture of Rodrigo's wife, striking a self-consciously silly pose in a bikini on some Hawaiian beach. Mixed among the pictures were notes, grocery coupons, and postcards, all held in place with plastic fruit magnets. This could have been a fridge in any middle-class household in America. But only the Angel of Death knew the whole picture . . . that Mom occasionally "explored her sexuality" with another woman from the car pool, Daughter enjoyed crushing snails while walking home from school, and Daddy laundered money for the mob—when he wasn't shoving it in his own pocket, that is.

That *was*. Past tense. Delbert Skaggs had seen to that. He was good at what he did, but he was growing bored. He wanted a new challenge, yet something that took advantage of his unique people skills and his experience in the organization.

He went into the backyard and took off his rubber gloves. He slipped the bags from his shoes, stuck them all in his pocket, and ran in place for a moment, consciously keeping his gaze averted from the dead Golden Retriever. Nothing pained him more than killing an innocent animal, but there were unpleasant aspects to any line of work.

Once he worked up a sweat, Delbert hit the street, just another lean, healthy, clean-cut jogger in his mid-thirties. Seattle was full of them, but not many of them killed for a living.

He jogged down East Laurelhurst, every so often catching a view of Lake Washington between the formal houses fronting the shore, and leisurely making his way the four or five miles to the university, where his rental car was parked. It would rain soon, as it always did in Seattle, and he'd be safely in his Ford Taurus before the first, thick droplets came down. He'd dispose of the bags and the sweatsuit downtown on his way to the airport.

It felt good to run. It cleared the mind, opened the pores, and gave him a chance to get some perspective, away from the pressures of his workaday world. He was strictly a contract worker now, which suited his need for independence. But he was growing tired of seeing only small pieces of the big picture, tired of being a vital cog in a larger machine.

It was time to get noticed, to get himself on the fast track and into middle management. Maybe run an operation that would get him noticed higher up. He started sending out some feelers a few weeks ago, but all he got was more of the same, doubleheaders and groups. Sure, killing paid the bills, but it didn't tap his real potential.

He jogged into the cement parking structure and scaled the stairs to the third level, where his car was parked in a dark corner. As soon as he was inside, the cellular phone in the glove box began to trill. He picked it up.

It was his travel agent. His trip to Baltimore was being canceled, and there would be a new ticket waiting for him at the airport.

"Where am I going?" he asked her.

"Los Angeles."

"What am I going to do?" he asked.

"Produce."

He didn't know what that meant, but he had a feeling it was what he had been waiting for.

Chapter Three

∙∙

The three-bedroom house on a quiet, tree-lined street in Reseda did not impress Alice Doss. Neither did Charlie's 1992 Camaro.

It was bad enough when he picked her up in a late-model, American car. She had been expecting something sleek and European. That was the first surprise. When Charlie cruised off the Reseda boulevard offramp, she was clearly stunned when he turned right, heading north, rather than left, heading south and across Ventura, the wide thoroughfare that cut across the valley at the base of the Santa Monica Mountains. She was expecting some stunning hillside mansion. Everyone who was anybody lived *south* of the boulevard.

Now came surprise number three.

He lived in a typical valley neighborhood, *north* of the boulevard, that is. Dozens of small, boxy houses that were hurriedly snapped together in the deafening reverberations of the baby boom.

The boom had long since ebbed. In its wake, crickets fought to be heard over the sounds of MTV, barking dogs, and people fighting over the bathroom. Each house had only one.

"This your house?" she asked.

Charlie pulled up to the curb and glanced out at the overgrown grass, peeling picket fence, and the clump of weeds strangling his juniper hedge. He couldn't bring himself to hire another gardener. This one might run off with his dog.

"Home sweet home," Charlie replied, pocketing the keys and getting out. Always the gentleman, he walked around the Camaro and opened her door. For a moment, she seemed reluctant to get out, but then she forced a smile and politely took his hand.

"It's so . . ." She searched for the right word as Charlie negotiated a path for them through the weeds to the front door. *"Refreshing.* I mean, you haven't let stardom get to you."

Charlie unlocked the door. "Maybe it just hasn't caught up to me yet. When it does, I won't put up a fight." He opened the door to find McGarrett, his Husky, lying on the floor, his tail thumping against the dull hardwood.

"Down, boy," Charlie said, turning on the lights. The dog thumped some more, glad to be noticed, but not enough to get off the floor.

Alice followed Charlie inside, slowly taking in his spartan abode, the Ikea snap-together furniture and halogen lamps, the bare walls, the meticulously clean emptiness. Connie had cleaned him out. He was in no hurry to clutter his life up again.

It wasn't that he couldn't afford it. But every cent Charlie was making was going straight into the bank. The way he figured it, his show could be history after thirteen episodes, and it could be a long time until his next paycheck. If he was smart, he'd have $200,000 in the bank to live on until he figured out what to do with his life.

Charlie tossed his keys on the coffee table, where they clattered to a stop against the clear acrylic paperweight that held a bullet in suspended animation.

Charlie turned to see Alice framed in the doorway, the glare from the streetlight shining right through her thin white blouse. How long had it been since . . . *too long.*

"Is that the bullet?" She picked up the paperweight and held it in front of her eyes. Charlie closed the door and looked at her from the back. Her jeans hugged her so tight he wondered if it would be possible to slip his hands inside without breaking his fingers. He hadn't had a thought like that for . . . *too long.* Suddenly, he wasn't sure if it was his heart he heard thumping or McGarrett's tail.

"That's the one." Charlie came up slowly, deliberately, behind her. "It burnt through my flesh and scorched my heart." Where did this shit come from? But she liked it. He could tell by the way she caught her breath, the way she stood very still, as if listening to a far-off sound.

He slipped his arms around her waist and she leaned into him, warm and soft. "You're holding a piece of my soul in your hands," he whispered.

She arched her head to one side, inviting him to kiss her neck. He did, hungrily, his hands rising up from her waist to her unfettered breasts, rubbing, squeezing, mashing. Reveling in the smell, the feel, the taste of a woman.

Alice moaned, dropping the paperweight on his foot. He didn't feel it. He was feeling too many other things. She rubbed against him, her hands stroking his hips, reaching for his ass, arching her breasts into his hands. He reached under her shirt and pinched her nipples, gently tugging them into stiff points. Alice took in a sharp breath, grinding against him, making him so hard it hurt.

She twisted out of his grasp and pushed him onto the couch. She straddled his waist, unpopped his jeans, and gripped his hard-on like a joystick. Charlie felt the heat radiating between her legs and throbbed in her tight grasp. She stroked him in her fist until he felt like a pillar of cement.

Out of nowhere, she produced a condom, tearing open the packet with her teeth. She slipped the tight latex slowly, achingly over his pulsing erection, and before he knew it, he was coming in sharp, almost painful spasms, his eyes closed against the sudden, explosive pleasure. When Charlie opened his eyes, he saw Alice staring down at him. The condom drooped off his penis like a floppy hat.

Surprise number four, the least welcome of all.

He couldn't tell whether she was confused or frustrated. This night obviously wasn't going the way she planned. It certainly wasn't his idea of a dream date. He hadn't come this fast since high school, when all it took was a slow dance and he was spent.

"My gun *had* bullets," he said.

She laughed, not very convincingly. She was a lousy actress.

Charlie went to the bathroom and cleaned himself up; when he returned, she had put one of his Junior Wells CDs on the stereo and helped herself to a drink. He listened to her talk about acting class, about her aspirations for stardom, about all the meaty roles she knew she could play. And twenty minutes later, when he was sure his gun was reloaded, he took her to bed.

The edge was gone, the urgency, and with it much of his passion. She thrashed around for the audience, but he doubted it was any better for her than it was for him. He wanted sex, but perhaps he needed more. It was the first time another woman had been in his bed since

Connie and, despite himself, he found he missed her, perhaps for the first time. This was their bed. For six years, this was where they'd made love, argued, cuddled, whispered, and kicked off the dog. Alice was a stranger in this bed and, oddly enough, Charlie felt like one, too. He resolved to go to Ikea first thing tomorrow and buy a new one.

When Charlie Willis woke up the next morning, Alice Doss was gone. But she had left him something to remember her by—a picture, a résumé, and a tape.

Boyd Hartnell tooled down the Ventura Freeway to the studio in his Mercedes convertible, automobile exhaust blowing through his hair plugs. He loved the feeling of the wind whipping his hair—it was one of the few joys he had these days and a subtle reminder of the constant terror he lived under.

His hairline had started receding at a steady rate when he was seventeen, a rate that increased tenfold when he became president of Pinnacle Studios, a hundredfold when he met Esther Radcliffe. Meeting her was like being exposed to radioactive waste. His hair came out in clumps.

The old crone was vital to Pinnacle Studios and, by extension, his career. Although the studio had dozens of series shooting on the lot, only three of them were their own; the rest just used the facilities. Pinnacle's laughless comedy *Bonjour, Buddy Bipp*, was doomed. *My Gun Has Bullets* was on the ropes. But *Miss Agatha* was an insanely profitable hit that allowed the Japanese owners of Pinnacle Studios to forgive him for a string of expensive failures.

His one and only mandate was to keep Esther happy.

When she shot the cop Charlie Willis, Boyd nearly went bald with anxiety. After saving her withered butt, he had to schedule two dozen emergency sessions with Dr. Desi for radical hair triage.

Even with all the stress, he still looked better than Burt Reynolds or William Shatner. Hell, he was paying more per strand of hair than even they were. Dr. Desi only accepted a lucky few for his experimental, and highly expensive, procedure.

In the 1970s, Boyd had proudly worn his shirt open, his chest hair fluffing out in vibrant manliness, more than compensating for his ever widening brow. But those days were gone. Nowadays, collars were buttoned all the way up. Boyd was left with nothing to distract from his retreating hairline.

Then along came Dr. Desi and his brilliant innovation. Why should all that bountiful, hairy machismo go to waste, hidden under Boyd's shirt? These days, when people looked at Boyd Hartnell, they still saw a man with a hairy chest. Only now it was on his head.

Now everything was as it should be. Esther was hard at work on a new butt-kicking season of *Miss Agatha*. He had a full head of hair and had even managed to get a new series out of the catastrophe. All told, Boyd considered himself pretty damn remarkable.

He zipped past the stalled lane of cars waiting to turn into the Pinnacle Studios tour and took the next left, cruising under the shadow of the marble Pinnacle Pictures office tower to the executive gate. The guard stepped out of his knockoff Frank Lloyd Wright shack and waved him through. Boyd gave him the grandiose smile of the powerful and sailed toward his coveted private parking spot. He came to a sudden halt.

There was a car in his spot. Not just any car. A 1959 Cadillac convertible, all fins and chrome and attitude. UBC chief Don DeBono was into vintage cars. The bigger and more ostentatious, the better. He wanted to take up lanes, parking spots, entire neighborhoods with the girth of his automobiles. And now the corpulent sack of shit had commandeered Boyd's spot.

Boyd parked in the handicapped spot, got out, and carefully ran a hand through his head of chest hair before heading into the thirty-two story wedge of steel.

The Italian furniture in Boyd's thirty-second-floor corner office had such sharp lines Boyd ran the danger of disemboweling himself every time he slid his chair up to his desk. Don DeBono had unfortunately managed to take a seat behind Boyd's desk without injury.

DeBono was thumbing intently through a *TV Guide* as Boyd came in, no doubt reading every single listing and committing it to memory. DeBono was known for his encyclopedic knowledge of television, his utter devotion to the medium. Not one single iota of trivia escaped his attention. In his own mind, DeBono had programmed every network since he was old enough to spell TV.

DeBono knew what was up against *Bonanza* on every night of its fourteen-year run. He could tell you the ratings for each episode of *Mannix*. He had even memorized Lucy Ricardo's license number.

But it paid off. Ten years ago, when DeBono was a twenty-year-old NYU student, he sent UBC president Guy Chapin a letter. DeBono tore him apart for concocting an insipid primetime schedule and told him how Chapin should have done it, assuming Chapin had any imagination at all.

Fact was, Chapin didn't. Figuring he had nothing to lose, he took DeBono's suggestions, and propelled the third-place network into first. Don DeBono became a junior program executive overnight, stepping right over another, capable executive named Boyd Hartnell, who had been strenuously working his way up the ladder for years. Boyd had even married Chapin's homely daughter in his quest for network glory.

Boyd watched with amazement and loathing as the little shit wormed his way up while his own career reached an inertia matched only by his sex life. Boyd dumped Chapin's hag daughter and took the first studio job he could find.

Now Boyd ran Pinnacle, and wonderboy DeBono made enough money to keep his complete collection of *TV Guide*s in a massive mahogany display case. As if they were copies of the Gutenberg Bible.

"Make yourself at home," Boyd said. "Fuck my secretary, while you're at it."

DeBono glanced up from the *TV Guide* and gave Boyd a wicked grin. "I would, but I've decided to fuck you instead."

"Am I going to like it?"

"Do I care?" DeBono tossed the *TV Guide* onto a pile of scripts and swiveled around in the chair to face Boyd, who was sauntering up to admire his unobstructed view of the valley.

"Have you seen the demographics on *Miss Agatha?*"

"You came all the way down here to ask me that?"

"It was a rhetorical question, butthead," DeBono said. "That *is* butt hair on your head, isn't it? Or did Dr. Desi harvest your armpits?"

The muscles in Boyd's cheeks tightened. Maybe if he gritted his teeth, he wouldn't throw the guy out the window. He turned very slowly to face DeBono.

"The show is a hit. That's all that's important."

"The demographics skew so fucking old, the entire audience of the show could be dead by next season," DeBono said. "DBC's *Red Highway* is snagging everyone who isn't on social security yet."

"*Red Highway* is in forty-eighth place," Boyd said.

"Last season it was seventieth," DeBono replied. "You see a trend here? Of course you don't. That's why you're here and I'm running the network. The right show, with the right demographics, can take Sunday night."

"*We* are already taking the night."

"*We* are sitting ducks." DeBono got up from behind the desk. "So we're going to youthify *Miss Agatha*. She's going to get a niece who wears black leather, drives a sports car, and can do more Ninja shit than Steven Seagal."

Boyd couldn't believe what he was hearing. He had just saved Esther's ass, not to mention his own, rescued the network and the show, and even managed to restore his hairline. And now this jerk was recklessly putting it all at risk again.

"Are you insane?" Boyd marched up to him, practically stammering in disbelief. "You don't fuck around with a hit. You leave it alone and count your money."

"Scrap the episode you're shooting and shut down for a week," DeBono said casually.

"You realize what I had to go through to *save* the show for you?" Boyd exclaimed.

"You saved your own hairless ass *and* got a new series out of the fucking deal, so don't give me that shit." DeBono picked up the *TV Guide* and admired the picture of Rappy Scrappy on the cover. "I want the new character in the next episode, and I want to air it during sweeps."

"Esther Radcliffe won't stand for this."

"Then tell Esther Radcliffe you either shoot the episode I want, or you shoot the series finale."

"You'd cancel a hit?" Boyd asked incredulously. Now he knew for certain that DeBono had actually lost his mind.

DeBono shrugged. "It's been done before."

"We'll take the show to another network." Boyd paced defiantly in front of him. "Let's see how those demos look to you when your ass is getting kicked."

DeBono shook his head. "Check out the contract. You can't shop new episodes anywhere for a year after cancellation." DeBono watched with amusement as the color drained from Boyd's face. "Snuck it into the contract a few seasons back."

Boyd slowly settled into his desk chair and contemplated impaling himself on the edge of the desk. DeBono watched the man wilt.

"If *Miss Agatha* is off the air for a year, most of her audience will be dead when she comes back. You either do it my way, or you don't do it at all."

Boyd could feel his hair losing its footing in his scalp. Another painful session with Dr. Desi was inevitable.

"You have someone in mind for the part?" Boyd asked, resigned to defeat.

"Sabrina Bishop." DeBono said. "You know her?"

Know her? He dreamed of her. Suddenly it all seemed worth the risk. Suddenly Don DeBono was a programming genius. Suddenly he wanted to see Dr. Desi. Sabrina Bishop was going to want Boyd's perfect head of hair as much as he wanted her perfect breasts.

"I've heard of her." Boyd hoped he'd disguised his excitement. At least he was glad he was sitting down. "You realize the risk, don't you?"

"*Miss Agatha* has to go sometime," DeBono said. "Worse thing that happens, you'll get your fucking fortune in rerun money sooner rather than later."

"That's not the worst thing," Boyd said. "She's already shot a cop. You think she'd think twice about killing Sabrina Bishop?"

Chapter Four

There was no way Esther Radcliffe was setting foot in a Winnebago. Even though the studio called it a dressing room, as far as she was concerned it was still a *mobile home.* Economy-size coffins for the living dead. Tin cans for the sardines of humanity. There wasn't a more heinous pairing of words in the English language.

Mobile home. The words immediately evoked images of TV dinners and Barcaloungers. Wink Martindale and Kmart. Fast food and slow death. Trailer parks with names like Sunny Acres, Paradise Pines, and Valley Vista collecting like weeds along the freeways of America. The white-trash Beverly Hills.

She hadn't worked all her life to set herself apart from *them* just to end up in a mobile home herself. That would have been the ultimate indignity.

So she made the studio fork out half a million dollars on her dressing room—a Greyhound bus converted into an estate that just happened to be on wheels. Pity the losers retreating to their Formica and vinyl boxes. Between scenes *she* retired to opulence that rivaled her own home. With her brass fixtures and marble countertops, Persian rugs and mahogany paneling, no one would mistake *her* dressing room for a *mobile home.*

But right now the most noticeable feature of her dressing room was not the Hockney on the wall or the crystal chandelier on the ceiling. It was the plain manila envelope propped up in a chair like a bored guest.

She saw it the moment she came in. She didn't have to open it to know what was inside, but she did anyway. A dozen eight-by-ten photos that could have been a *Penthouse* spread on sexual positions. Or a *Playgirl* tribute to the male sex organ.

Only the limber lass cavorting with the endowed stud wasn't some airbrushed centerfold beauty. It was Esther. Her immediate reaction to the photos was always the same. First came pride. She looked fucking incredible. Was it any wonder this Adonis, thirty years younger than she, was hard enough to cut diamonds? Hell no. She was, and always had been, a spectacular lover and a devastating beauty. Esther was half tempted to ask for blowups. The photos should be published the world over, so men could dream of having her and women could dream of being her. Even Madonna could learn a few things.

After three or four minutes of self-adulation came the deadlier reaction. The one that stayed with her through all her waking hours. The one that gnawed at her like some ravenous parasite. The one that motivated her to do terrible things to innocent people. Rage.

Sharon Stone could be caught giving three guys blowjobs at the same time and it would only make her more popular. Madonna could fuck a horse and it wouldn't hurt her career. But get a snapshot of kindly Miss Agatha holding a man's face between her legs, and civilization would come to an end. Certainly her career would. Other stars could fuck and be admired for it, but not her. It was grossly, horribly, unspeakably unfair, an inequity made all the more unbearable because it had a price tag. Each roll of film cost her another $50,000 in small bills stuffed into a canvas Pinnacle Studios tour bag.

This was the third time the blackmailer had asked for $50,000 and it was going to be the last. She knew damn well who was doing this to her.

Charlie Willis.

It had to be him. The photos started showing up as soon as he arrived on the lot. It wasn't enough the studio gave him a series. He had to soak her, too.

Well, that was going to end. The same way it began.

She was envisioning her revenge when there was a knock on her door. Esther stuck the photos in a drawer and sat down in one of her Pierre Deux upholstered chairs. "Enter," she commanded.

The door opened and Boyd Hartnell tentatively stuck his celery-stalk head in. "I hope we aren't disturbing you, Esther."

"We?" she asked imperiously.

"Yes, I've got Sabrina with me. She's very eager to meet you."

Boyd stepped in, expecting a vase or a knife to come sailing his way at any moment. "You've been her idol for—" He caught himself before he could make a fatal reference to her age. "—for obvious reasons," he stammered. "You're an inspiration to actresses everywhere."

When Boyd had told Esther she was getting a costar, and that there was nothing she could do or say about it, the old crone went crazy—destroyed everything in Boyd's office. He had to hide under the desk as if riding out the Big One. Now he had no idea what she would do. He certainly didn't expect what came next.

Esther broke into the warm, grandmotherly smile that made Miss Agatha welcome in millions of living rooms. "Well, don't leave her standing there in that heat. Bring her right in. Let me give you both a nice glass of iced tea."

Boyd stepped in and motioned outside to Sabrina, who stood a few feet away, staring at the cavernous soundstage as if it were the Vatican. She had finally arrived. This wasn't another crummy refurbished warehouse in Van Nuys or Valencia, this was a real studio where real shows were made. Where professionals plied their craft in an atmosphere of mutual respect. Where nobodies become international stars. Her nipples were already stiffening on their own.

She turned to the Greyhound bus, took a deep breath, and stepped inside. Her agent had warned her about Esther Radcliffe. But could this old lady be any worse than the predatory, drooling pack of producers, agents, and has-been actors she'd survived already?

Sabrina was expecting the Tasmanian Devil in drag—she wasn't prepared for the kindly grandmother who greeted them, pouring two tall glasses of iced tea from an enormous, frosty pitcher.

"Have a refreshing glass of tea, darling, you look positively blanched." Esther handed Sabrina the glass and gave her a quick once-over. All pert and pretty in a short-sleeved, white T-shirt and vest. Long-legged and slim in faded blue jeans. Baring her perfect boobs on film hadn't hurt *her* any.

"Thank you very much, Miss Radcliffe." Sabrina took the glass and smiled. "That's very kind of you."

"I can't have my niece fainting from sunstroke." Esther gave Boyd his glass of tea. "You didn't tell me she was so sweet. Shame on you, Boyd."

There was no way Boyd was drinking anything Esther handed him. He tried to think of a way to warn Sabrina.

"We appreciate the tea, but you know it's not a good idea to drink something so cold immediately after coming in from the heat," Boyd said. "I read that somewhere."

"Nonsense," Esther said to Boyd, her eyes flashing, for just a moment, with the malice he knew thrived in her soul. But when she turned to Sabrina again, Esther was angelic, harmless Miss Agatha. "Next thing you know, he'll say fresh-baked cookies are bad for you, too. I just made a batch, if you'd like some."

What a nice woman, Sabrina thought. It figures. Hollywood is run by men, so naturally they are scared to death of a woman with power, even when it's a gentle lady like Esther Radcliffe. Of course, they *had* to portray her as a queen bitch or face their own fears of impotence. Someday, Sabrina hoped, she'd be popular enough that the men in charge felt so threatened they'd concoct ridiculous stories about her.

"No thank you," Sabrina said. "I'm trying to watch my weight."

I bet you are, you little slut, Esther thought. But she said, "Oh, isn't she darling." She smiled at Sabrina. "I am so happy you're going to be on the show. Finally, I'll have someone to share girl talk with. We are going to have a marvelous time."

"I'm certainly looking forward to it," Sabrina said. "I've been a fan of yours since I was a little girl."

Boyd winced. Sabrina didn't know it, but she had just committed suicide—and without even taking a sip of her drink. It was bad enough Esther had to share the screen with a young beauty, but he knew Esther couldn't stand being reminded she was an old bag by comparison. Esther would ruin her. Then Sabrina had to go and make it worse.

"I can't believe I'll actually be working with you. It's like a dream come true. When I was six, I adored you as *Sally Sweetcake.* I wanted to grow up and live with you, and Santa, and all your cartoon elves," Sabrina said, recalling with genuine fondness Esther's famous role as

Santa's happy-go-lucky, singing nanny in the Disney classic. "And now here I am."

Esther loathed the part, and had been trying to escape it, without success, her entire career. But instead of choking the life out of the little bimbo, Esther surprised herself and Boyd by feigning bashful pride. "I'm so glad."

"Of course, I didn't think I'd be wearing black leather and delivering judo chops." Sabrina giggled. It was an infectious, joyous burst of laughter that endeared most people to her immediately. Boyd was instantly aroused, a fact that didn't go unnoticed by Esther. She saw the pathetic bump in his trousers. A ball of cotton could make a bigger impression. Esther was aroused, too, but in a very different way. Sabrina's innocent laugh made Esther want to grind her thumbs into the bitch's blue eyes until they squished.

"Well, sweetheart, I want you to think of me, on screen and off, as your loving Aunt Agatha," Esther said. "If you have any problems getting settled in, or you just want to have a slice of homemade pecan pie, drop by and see me."

Sabrina glanced down at her glass. Oh shit, Boyd thought. He had to think of a way to stop her from drinking whatever hell brew the witch had cooked up in her cauldron.

"Thank you, Miss Radcliffe," Sabrina said. "I'll do that." Sabrina was bringing the glass to her full red lips when Boyd came up with a solution.

"Well, we'd better run along, the producers are expecting us." He stepped forward as if to set his glass down. Instead, he purposely stumbled, falling forward into Sabrina and spilling his drink, and her own, all over her T-shirt.

Sabrina shrieked as the cold tea touched her skin. The wet cotton became almost translucent, clinging to her breasts like Saran Wrap, her large, round nipples drawing into tight, sharp points.

The view wasn't lost on Boyd or Esther. He wanted to pull her wet shirt off and dry her breasts with his tongue. Esther discovered a body even she had to admit was better than her own. "Oh, Christ." Boyd reached for a towel, but Esther grabbed it first. "I'm terribly sorry." Meaning that he didn't get to the towel first. That he didn't have a chance to use it as a cheap excuse to fondle Sabrina's fantastic breasts. That he wasn't born with a wondrous mane of hair.

"No, don't apologize," Sabrina said. "Miss Radcliffe was right, the tea's very refreshing."

Sabrina laughed again, like a gleeful child, not an ounce of scorn or anger in her. Boyd and Esther had an epiphany just then. Boyd knew he had to have her. And Esther knew Sabrina had to die.

Andre Blauson didn't struggle through Le Cordon Bleu to end up slinging burgers at a movie studio commissary and preparing steaks for Boo Boo, the sitcom dog. Then again, he never foresaw a glut of first-class chefs and a dearth of high-class restaurants to employ them.

The good old eighties were over. Extravagant excess was harder and harder to find. With Reagan gone, Milken in a halfway house, and leveraged buyouts bankrupting America, there were fewer and fewer people who could pay $26 for a dinner salad and $50 for a hamburger. Where trendy French bistros and Italian trattorias once dotted Melrose and Ventura, Burger Kings and El Pollo Locos had taken their places.

So now Andre worked at Pinnacle Studios, merging his culinary creativity with assembly-line food service. And, of course, preparing special meals for the exacting tastes of individual stars. Like the steak tartare for Boo Boo, a particularly finicky eater with a nasty temper.

But rather than feel humbled by his unfortunate position, Andre considered what he was doing a shrewd political move. The people he served here were, ultimately, the people who would make or break a fine restaurant. If he could ever launch another one. Here, he had a captive audience comprised of the rich, the famous, the influential, and, including Boo Boo, the canine. The elite of Los Angeles social life. By dressing up their hamburgers and calling them *Hachis de Boeuf Dijonnais au Saint Amour,* he was making invaluable connections. An investment in the future. Besides, it gave him the opportunity to ogle some of America's most attractive women.

Which is what he was doing right now.

Sabrina Bishop stood before him in only her vest and jeans, a script under her bare arm, her nose crinkled in thought as she surveyed his luncheon offerings. Without a T-shirt, her tan skin and deep cleavage tantalizingly revealed by the plunging lines of the vest, she was positively intoxicating.

"How may I serve you, *mademoiselle?*" he asked her cleavage.

She smiled and surprised him with: *"Mes seins voudraient seulement de la salade verte avec des crevettes, si'l vous plaît."* Which meant her breasts would like a shrimp salad, please.

Red-faced, Andre turned to prepare her meal.

"If you don't want them noticed, you ought to wear some underwear," said a voice beside her. She turned to see Charlie Willis holding a tray.

"You speak French?" she asked.

"No, but I've seen a lot of dirty French movies," Charlie replied. "Want to hear what else I learned?"

Andre unceremoniously dropped her salad plate on her tray with a curt *"Merci."* When he got his own restaurant again, there was one starlet who wasn't going to get a good table, unless she wanted to be seated in the bathroom.

"It was an accident," she mumbled to Charlie. "Boyd Hartnell splashed a glass of iced tea on my shirt."

"I know Mophead, and I guarantee you it was no accident," Charlie said.

She headed for the cash register, Charlie a step or two behind her. But before she reached the machine she turned to face him, a tinge of anger in her cheeks. "But what would be wrong if I was proud of my body and wanted to show it? Does that justify someone talking to my breasts instead of to me?"

Charlie thought about it for a moment. "Yeah."

Despite herself, Sabrina smiled and glanced down at her outfit. So did he. "I suppose you're right." She looked up again and shrugged. "I didn't think anybody would notice. I mean, the lot is full of shows, full of actors. There are people dressed like hookers, Vikings, bums, hideous monsters. What's one woman without a shirt?"

"An eyeful," Charlie said.

When they reached the register, Charlie pulled out his wallet. "Allow me, ma'am."

Ma'am? It seemed to her he didn't even notice he said it. If it didn't sound so genuine, so natural, she wouldn't have found it charming. She would have thought he was a putz. "You don't have to do that."

"It's my way of welcoming you to Pinnacle Studios." Charlie pulled out a few dollars and handed them to the cashier. "Or as the French say, *bienvenue*."

He held out his hand. "Charlie Willis."

She shook it. "Glad to meet you, Charlie." Her skin was unbelievably soft, yet her handshake was surprisingly firm. "I'm Sabrina Bishop."

"You *are* new here, aren't you?"

"My first day." She picked up her tray and sought out a table. Charlie followed, amused and attracted. There was something childlike about her and yet, at the same time, tough and experienced. It was a heady combination, especially combined with that body, her casual sexiness. No need for makeup or special effects to make *her* look good.

"Let me guess," he said. "D girl."

She whirled around, shocked, but before she could cut his head off, he said, "D *girl*, not D *cup*. I knew I shouldn't have said it. I'm kind of new around here, too. Fact is, I just learned the word today myself. It's slang for development executive who happens to be a pretty woman. I saw the script under your arm and took a guess."

"You're forgiven." She sat down at a table by the window. "I just joined the cast of *Miss Agatha*."

Charlie nearly dropped his tray, which would have sent a *Hachis de Boeuf Dijonnais* flying into her bosom, but he recovered just in time. He took a seat across from her as she set her script down on the table. The episode was titled *Agatha's Niece*.

"You must have a death wish." Charlie glanced at the script.

"That's what everybody keeps telling me," Sabrina said. "I don't get it. She's such a sweet lady. I think people are simply terrified by a successful woman."

Charlie picked up his hamburger. "She's a lunatic. Believe me, I know."

"Of course you do," she said good-naturedly. "You're a man."

Charlie was about to take a bite, but suddenly lost his appetite. He set the burger down and looked at Sabrina. The oath he once took to protect and to serve didn't lapse because he'd turned in his badge. At least, it didn't feel as if it had. He couldn't let Sabrina walk blindly into danger. So he reached down and began untucking his shirt.

Sabrina, curious, raised an eyebrow. "You always undress before you eat?"

"I wasn't always an actor."

"I didn't know you were an actor."

"I'm the star of *My Gun Has Bullets*," he said. "But for fifteen years, I was a uniformed police officer in Beverly Hills."

That explains the *ma'am*, she thought. "So you took acting classes at night, did some equity waiver in your spare time, and it finally paid off?"

"No, I just did my job, went home at night, got up the next morning, and did my job again." Charlie pulled off his shirt and handed it to Sabrina. "Here, the shirt off my back."

Sabrina laughed. Charlie's actions were attracting looks from all over the commissary. "I can't."

"You wouldn't be the first woman to take it," Charlie said, his chest bared. "You can put it on later. Truth is, it belongs to the studio anyway. Which brings me to my point."

"This noble act of chivalry wasn't the point?"

Charlie stood up so she could see his stomach. He pointed to the scar. "This is how I became an actor."

She glanced at his body, her eyes pausing on the scar, and then she shrugged. "Don't take this personally, those are nice pecs, but you're not Arnold Schwarzenegger. I'm not even sure you're Don Adams."

She wanted to let more than her eyes wander his body, but she wasn't going to let *him* know that. Sabrina had writhed around with so many perfect bodies on screen, she found imperfection far more attractive. The fact he wasn't hard-bodied, and that he had a scar, only made him more desirable. That, and his surprising chivalry.

Charlie sat down, leaned toward her, and spoke in a low voice. "Esther Radcliffe shot me."

Sabrina just looked at him. "Excuse me?"

"I was on patrol, I pulled her over and she shot me," Charlie said.

"They gave me *My Gun Has Bullets* in exchange for forgetting it ever happened."

Sabrina couldn't believe a person could stoop so low, to slander someone with such a ridiculous story. She couldn't begin to figure out what his motive might be, but she knew she had misjudged him. He was as bad as the others. She gathered up her her things.

"I was beginning to think you were a nice guy," Sabrina said, getting up. "Thanks for setting me straight."

For once, he had told the truth about his gunshot wound and the woman wasn't buying it. And she *had* to believe him. Her life could depend on it. Charlie grabbed her by the wrist.

"Listen to me, Esther Radcliffe isn't going to share the screen with anyone, particularly not someone as beautiful as you," Charlie said. "Your life could be in grave danger."

She yanked her hand free and laughed at him. "Do you have any idea how stupid you sound? I can't believe you're that threatened by a successful old lady. It's pathetic."

And with that, she turned her back on him and stormed off. It wasn't until she was halfway to her trailer that she realized she still had his shirt.

Charlie remained in the commissary, shirtless and stunned, wondering where he went wrong.

"Actresses . . ." he muttered to himself, then took a big bite out of his *Hachis de Boeuf* and tried to imagine what Esther Radcliffe would do next.

Chapter Five

The Wallengren kitchen was known and beloved around the world. It was where the average problems of an average family were solved with equal doses of laughter and understanding—and the wacky hijinks of an acerbic stand-up comic reincarnated as an acerbic mutt.

The dog's name was Boo Boo, and it wasn't easy being a loud, smart-ass, fifty-year-old, cigar-chomping vaudeville comedian trapped in an extremely expressive, four-legged furball. We know this, because all of us could hear Boo Boo's thoughts, and they were absolutely hilarious.

That, as millions of people knew, was *Boo Boo's Dilemma.*

The real Boo Boo, unknown to the network executives, managers, producers, and publicists assembled on the set that afternoon, was almost as smart as the character he played.

He was certainly meaner.

He liked filet mignon for dinner in a silver dish. He liked being followed around by a staff pooper scooper. He liked his air-conditioned doghouse in a private compound on the Pinnacle Studios lot. And what he liked most of all, was human flesh. Particularly baby fat.

There lay the source of the many "creative differences" behind the constant turnover in Wallengren family members. Right now, for instance, Boo Boo wanted to take a big chomp out of Don DeBono's butt.

The only thing restraining Boo Boo was his owner, Lyle Spreen, and the little tranquilizer gun he carried in his pocket. Lyle carried the gun because he knew Boo Boo as well as he knew himself. Like Boo Boo, Lyle was the result of generations of inbreeding. He, too, could fill up with so much hate he'd burst into an orgy of violence. It was like relieving a full bladder. Boo Boo could snap anytime, anywhere. Lyle was more predictable. He only unleashed his hatred doing two things—fucking and negotiating, which were, he thought, more or less the same.

"Boo Boo is very unhappy," Lyle said.

Don DeBono hated this white trash monkey. There was enough hair on Lyle's knuckles to make Boyd Hartnell a toupee. "Too much seasoning on his steaks?"

DeBono had tried to get rid of the two of them a couple of episodes into the first season—unfortunately, there wasn't a dog on earth that looked as ugly as Boo Boo. Now, every season, it was the same thing—Lyle and his pooch wanting more money. More control. More power. It was like dealing with Roseanne, only she rarely dumped a big smelly load at the annual affiliates' meeting.

"He wasn't told the *Rappy Scrappy* episode last season was a back-door pilot." Lyle petted the dog on his deformed little head. His hair looked like greasy straw.

"Really?" DeBono glanced again at the miserable hairbag. Big mats of hair hung from his face, soaked in the rivers of drool that spilled out of his mouth. "Guess he missed the meeting. Must have been the day he mauled the director. In all the excitement, we must have forgotten to mention it to him."

With *Rappy Scrappy*, DeBono proved he learned from his mistakes. The rap-singing cat who lived with a wacky Jewish family looked like any other damn cat, so no one was going to hold DeBono up for caviar catnip or a feline producing credit come renewal time.

"Boo Boo feels betrayed," Lyle said, reminded once again how fucking stupid his agent had been not to negotiate a royalty for spin-offs. Which is why he accidentally let Boo Boo loose in the man's office. Which is why Lefty Leftcowitz was now known as Stumpy.

Today, Stumpy stood a good five yards away from Boo Boo, right near the soundstage door, observing the negotiation, scratching the dry nub where his left hand used to be. He told everybody he lost his hand pulling a fork out of the disposal—because if Boo Boo went, so did the $50,000-an-episode packaging fee that supported his pissant little "boutique" agency. It had always been a small agency; it became pissant after Boo Boo finished lifting his leg on every wall, potted plant, and agent in the place.

"You exploited his fame and good name to create *Rappy Scrappy,*" Lyle said to DeBono. "In fact, he resents not being consulted on the entire Thursday schedule. Whatever programs are put on after him reflect on his reputation as an entertainer."

"Oh, let's cut the bullshit." DeBono leaned back in his canvas director's chair. "He's a fucking dog. How much money do you want?"

Lyle loosened his grip ever so slightly on Boo Boo's leash. Boo Boo felt the leash slacken, but he didn't show it. His eyes were glued on DeBono's gut. Lyle dropped all pretense of businesslike decorum.

"The dog gets twenty-five grand an episode, and I get thirty," Lyle grinned. "For my producing services. And nothing goes on Thursday nights unless I approve it first. I got to be sure it's compatible programming. So you can throw in a series commitment, too. I got a trained ferret that's a lot of laughs."

Stumpy spoke up meekly from his corner of the stage. "Boo Boo also wants twenty-five percent of a hundred percent of the net profits against eight percent of a hundred percent of the adjusted gross profits. For each subsequent season, Boo Boo will vest himself for an additional five percent of a hundred percent of the net against—"

"Shut up, Stumpy." DeBono's glare never wavered from Lyle. "You expect me to give you a million bucks a year?"

"And you can lick my dog's butt for the privilege." Lyle leaned forward, close enough for DeBono to admire the look and smell of his raging gingivitis. "Because if we walk, your network goes from number one to negative integers."

"Negative integers." DeBono smiled. "You've been watching *Sesame Street* again. Let me tell you something Big Bird might have missed. This business is about relationships. *Boo Boo's Dilemma* won't always be number one. Three, four years from now, it'll be gone. And what will you do then?"

"I'll have Boo Boo stuffed with thousand dollar bills." Lyle laughed, purposely letting go of the leash. Boo Boo scrambled toward DeBono, his nails scratching on the floor as he worked up the momentum for his leap.

Stumpy bolted. All the suits scrambled, except DeBono, who calmly watched as the drooling beast lunged for him. Just as the dog was about to reach him, DeBono pulled out a dart gun and fired.

Lyle lurched forward, falling out of his seat to catch his meal ticket before it hit the ground. DeBono stood up and looked down at Lyle and his spasmodic pet.

"You're right—the show is very important to us, and we'll pay the million bucks," DeBono said. "But when talent is that important, we take out insurance. Sometimes the insurance ends up being worth more than the talent. Think about it."

DeBono left, his lieutenants filing out with him, leaving Lyle alone with Boo Boo in his arms. In Boo Boo's narcotic haze, he looked at Lyle and saw DeBono, so he sank his teeth into the nearest flesh he could find, taking a big, delicious bite out of the hand that fed him.

Eddie Planet swallowed a handful of Maalox tablets and faced the Angel of Death, who was wearing a sharply tailored beige suit and stood in front of the schedule board as if he owned it.

The white plastic board was a map of primetime, divided by network, the nights broken down into half-hour blocks between eight and eleven P.M. The board was covered with magnetized plastic strips representing the various series. Whenever a show was canceled or moved, Eddie would have someone rearrange the board. Midseason replacement shows, waiting on the shelf at the network, were stuck on the edge of the board, waiting to be placed on the schedule.

Every producer had a board like this one, mostly as decoration and to look "plugged in" to the industry. Eddie even had one at home, just to cover himself. Of course, he hadn't updated that one since *Saddlesore* was on the air.

When Eddie Planet sauntered into his bungalow office at ten A.M., Delbert Skaggs was already there, standing in front of the board as if he were watching a movie. Eddie's secretary, and occasional mistress, said Delbert had been there since six o'clock. That alone worried Eddie. No producer in his right mind arrived on the lot that early. The unspoken rule was to arrive just in time to make reservations for lunch.

So Eddie ducked into the bathroom, emptied a handful of Maaloxes into his sweaty palm, and prepared to meet his new co–executive producer.

Eddie was about to offer his hand to Delbert, but saw to his horror that his palm was streaked blue with antacid. Unlike M&M's, Maalox isn't guaranteed to "melt in your mouth, not in your hand," so Eddie was forced to wipe antacid off on his slacks as he approached Delbert.

"Welcome to Hollywood, Mr. Skaggs, I'm Eddie Planet." Delbert turned around and looked at Eddie as if he were a misbehaving pet, prompting Eddie to quickly check his palm again before shaking hands with his new colleague. "It's a pleasure having you on the *Frankencop* team. Have you settled in to your office all right?" Eddie had arranged for him to have the tiny one across the hall. He punted the supervising producers, a shaggy writing team splitting one measly salary, to a trailer across from the Pinnacle Studios tour "Land of Muck," home of the mutant superhero Muck Thing.

Delbert looked at Eddie with the dead, flat eyes of a shark. "This is my office."

Eddie covered fast. "Right. That's what I meant. Are you settling in *here* all right?" Now Eddie was really panicked. This was a corner office. He'd *always* had a corner office. How could he be expected to work in a room with only one window?

"Yes, very well. I've been looking at this board," Delbert said. "Explain it to me."

But Eddie's mind was still on more important matters. If he had the tiny office, that meant he'd be sharing a bathroom with the office staff. Well, that was unacceptable. He'd slap an EXECUTIVE BATHROOM sign on there if he had to write it on the door himself with a Magic Marker. They could walk to the commissary to piss from now on.

"It's the primetime schedule." Eddie was thinking it was *imperative* that a phone be installed in the bathroom. That could take a day or two. Until then, he'd have to bring his cellular with him. Damn, he'd need to charge up some extra batteries.

"I know that," Delbert said, trying to be patient. Because if he lost his patience, he could slit Eddie's throat with a paper clip. "Tell me who the players are and what they want. Tell me their strengths and their weaknesses. Don't leave out a thing, no matter how insignificant you might think it is."

Delbert had wanted Eddie Planet removed before he got there. But Daddy Crofoot felt they needed him, at least for a while. Eddie Planet was their legitimate front and a tour guide to the business. Delbert could accept that. But he got Crofoot's personal assurance that once Eddie Planet was no longer useful, he could be discarded in whatever manner Delbert wanted.

Delbert could think of a few right now.

Eddie had no way of knowing how much his life depended on what he said next. Perhaps something in Delbert's dead eyes gave him a hint. Because suddenly Eddie was aware that his armpits were drenched. He approached the board, trying hard to force out the image of the cramped office he'd be inhabiting, and focus instead on the schedule in front of him.

"*Boo Boo's Dilemma* is the most watched show on television," Eddie said. "Everything that goes up against it is dead meat. UBC is virtually unbeatable the whole night. Thursday put the network on top."

Eddie proceeded to quote, almost verbatim, the *Daily Variety* article he had read on the toilet only days before, leaving out, of course, the bleak future they predicted for *Frankencop*. "They're vulnerable at ten P.M., where I firmly believe our show will eventually kick the shit out of *My Gun Has Bullets.*"

"Eventually?" Delbert said.

"I meant *definitely,*" Eddie replied quickly. "Without a doubt. I'm just not one to toot my own horn." The remark reminded Eddie that if he used his cellular in the bathroom, he'd be left without one in his car. He liked to have one in his car even when he wasn't in it. If he didn't, what was the point of having a car phone answering service?

"Continue," Delbert said, his eyes locked on the board.

"UBC fights for time periods the rest of the week, winning more than it loses, but the only other night it really owns is Sunday," Eddie explained. "But *Miss Agatha* is getting tired and *Red Highway* is attracting the kids. Most of UBC's hits across the board are a few years old, they got maybe a season or two left in 'em. Don DeBono's gotta find some new hits, or they're gonna fall to third place as fast as they climbed to first."

Delbert had stalked Don DeBono. He knew where he lived. What he ate. Who he fucked. He could take him out anytime.

"DBC has no fucking idea what it's doing. They are dead last and willing to try anything. I hear they've got David Soul lined up for *Citizen Kane: The Series.*" Eddie continued. "MBC's a strong second on most nights, but their longest-running series, that piece of shit *Dedicated Doctors,* is dead on Thursday. *Johnny Wildlife* is big with the Michael Landon crowd, so maybe it's got a shot if Morrie Lustig, the putz who runs MBC, moves it to another night. And they've got us, which, if you ask me, is their secret weapon and their next big, breakout hit."

Delbert turned to Eddie. "What do you propose we do?"

"Like I told Daddy, it's really out of our hands," Eddie said. "There are a million variables—time slot, audience flow, counterprogramming. We've got no control over any of it, it's all up to the networks."

"Daddy Crofoot isn't going to like that," Delbert said.

"Hey, that's the business," Eddie said. "If he didn't like the rules, he shouldn't be playing the game."

Delbert let it all soak in for a full minute, staring at the board. It was insanity. The producers were taking all the risks, but the networks were making all the decisions. They were spending millions of dollars, and for what? They had absolutely no control over their own fate. What kind of business was that? Why couldn't television be run like any other business? Or even like *his* business?

And then it hit him.

Who said it had to be done their way?

Up until that instant, he had been staring at a plastic board covered in titles. But now it was coming to life for him. He saw it for what it was. He saw the possibilities. The potential. The millions to be made.

This wasn't a primetime schedule. Those weren't television networks. And those little magnetic blocks weren't series.

This was a city. The networks were mob families, all scrambling for a piece of the drug trade. Or the numbers business. Or the protection racket. It didn't matter what the pot of gold was, they all wanted a handful. And the television series—they were the lieutenants, the soldiers, the runners, the small-time hoods.

It was all so clear. He knew exactly what he had to do. How to make *Frankencop* or any other series a hit.

Yes, this was what he had been waiting for—no, preparing for—all his life.

He whirled around and grabbed Eddie Planet by the shoulders, causing the poor man to yelp in surprise and terror.

"You fools," Delbert laughed. "You stupid, fucking fools."

"What?" Eddie blubbered.

Delbert shook the buffoon. "It's so easy!"

"It is?" Eddie felt his bowels seize up.

"A child could do this." Delbert pushed Eddie aside and faced the board again, relishing what was to come. He started rearranging series on the board, moving them across the schedule, rearranging the networks into a new configuration.

"Yes, yes, it must go like this." Delbert was swept up, carried along by something bigger than the two of them. A man possessed by divine inspiration. He had found his calling.

Eddie staggered backward, transfixed by what he saw. It was Beethoven conducting his first symphony, Einstein scrawling $e = mc^2$ across the blackboard and opening up the universe. It was Moses parting the Red Sea.

Delbert stopped for an instant, admiring his creation. "Yes, that's the way it should be. That's the way it *will* be."

He turned to Eddie for confirmation. Eddie's head bobbed enthusiastically, like one of those dashboard doggies. Delbert then turned back to the board, juggling the magnetized pieces around once again. "Then it will be like this," he said.

Eddie's back hit the wall. He watched in awe as the network schedules were turned upside down, as the laws of primetime physics were rewritten, as *Frankencop* went from a struggling show into an overnight hit.

There was no question about it. Eddie Planet was in the presence of a genius.

Chapter Six

The *My Gun Has Bullets* crew was on the backlot, which was doubling for downtown Los Angeles. While the director of photography oversaw the lighting of the abandoned warehouse set, the crew was hanging around the craft services table, killing time and accumulating calories.

The craft services table was a perk devised eons ago to keep everyone on the set. An industry rule, carved in stone somewhere, mandated that there had to be an endless spread of crackers, candy, cheese, nuts, ice cream, chips, dip, sandwiches, fruit, cookies, and brownies available at all times, along with iceboxes of soft drinks, juice, and milk to wash them down.

And the craft services table was only an addition to the catered, four-course, freshly prepared hot lunches served each day of production to everyone in the cast and crew.

Which was why anorexia nervosa hit epidemic proportions in Los Angeles. And why it was all the more unusual that Charlie Willis was absolutely starving. He had grazed at the craft services table between every shot, and had wolfed down a full lunch. And yet his stomach wouldn't stop growling.

Something about the tedium of making a series, of the long waits between shots, of the endless repetition as the same scene was filmed from every possible angle, made Charlie hungrier as each day wore on.

He was also worried. For some reason, he couldn't get Sabrina Bishop out of his mind. Maybe it had something to do with the danger he knew she faced. Maybe it had something to do with the misguided responsibility he still felt to his forfeited badge. Maybe it had something to do with her tremendous body.

Whatever the reason, he knew he had to see her again. He had to find some way to make it very clear to Sabrina that Esther Radcliffe was insane and posed a genuine danger.

So he had another handful of garlic-salted almonds and washed them down with a Snapple before striding back into the warehouse. Along the way, he bumped into Jackson Burley, the showrunner.

"I got a present for you, Charlie," Burley said, in that good-old-boy drawl he had honed to perfection. "Have you seen the overnights?"

Charlie had been forced on Burley, who had lobbied for Chad Everett, but the producer wasn't about to turn away a guaranteed thirteen-episode series commitment. If the network wanted a cop in the part, they could have it. For Burley, pragmatism came before art. That, and his straightforward approach to action adventure shows, had made him quite successful. And truth be told, over the last few weeks, Burley had decided that Charlie wasn't half bad.

"I don't look at them, Jack," Charlie said. "Mainly because I don't understand them."

"Ratings and shares, that's the name of the game, my friend." Burley showed him a sheet full of numbers. "All you've got to know is that the audience is a big cherry pie, and we're getting a bigger slice every week. Last night we left the other shows with crumbs."

For the most part, Charlie liked Burley. Although the man was worth millions, he strived to cultivate the image that he was just one of the guys. Which was why he eschewed designer labels for faded jeans, dirty Reeboks, a polo shirt and a Dodger cap.

The only problem was he wanted you to believe he was just like you. But, at the same time, he didn't want you to believe you were just like him. People who couldn't walk that fine line with him were immediately standing on the unemployment line instead.

"We're snowballing, Charlie," Burley said. *"My Gun Has Bullets* is becoming part of the cultural fabric of this country."

Charlie gave him a look. "It's only a TV show."

" 'Beam me up, Scotty.' 'Go ahead, make my day.' 'To be, or not to be,' " Burley said, as if reciting passages from the Bible. "Those aren't just lines of dialogue. They are a part of who we are. They are etched forever in our collective unconscious. 'My gun has bullets' is going to be there, too. So are you, pal."

"We aren't making a TV show here," Charlie said, as if coming to a revelation. "We're making history." It was the most acting he had done all day.

"And money, hand over fist," Burley said.

Well, at least Burley's head wasn't entirely in the cosmos. Charlie didn't give a damn about history, but his paycheck meant a lot.

That's when the perpetually harried assistant director rushed up, his finger on the walkie-talkie on his belt. "They're ready for you on the set, Mr. Willis," he said.

Jackson Burley clapped Charlie on the back. "Knock 'em dead, Charlie." And he rushed off to coin more catchphrases for the ages.

Charlie followed the assistant director to the center of the warehouse, where the camera crew, soundmen, and various actors-as-mobsters were waiting for him. The director was Elliot Wachtel, wearing spurs and a ten-gallon hat to the set as if he were rustling cattle instead of pointing a camera. He fancied himself the next John Ford. He slid off his canvas chair and sidled up to Charlie.

"This is a big, action set piece and we're running three hours over. So, I'd like to do this bit in one long master," Wachtel said, referring to the wide shot that takes in all the action. "For coverage, I've got a B camera over there." He pointed to a second camera across the warehouse. The B camera would be used to capture footage that could be used for alternative angles on the same action when the film was edited together.

"What do you say we wrestle this shot to the ground and brand it?" Wachtel said. The closest Wachtel had ever gotten to branding a steer was writing his name on a Big Mac carton.

"Let's giddy-up," Charlie said.

Itchy Matthews, the withered old propman, rushed up and handed Charlie the massive gun that was Derek Thorne's trademark. Rumor had it Itchy had handled props on *Birth of a Nation*. It didn't matter that half the time Itchy handed Charlie his colostomy bag instead of his props. The man came cheap.

Charlie holstered the gun and headed to his position behind a stack of wooden crates. He was here to foil the sale of stolen rocket launchers to a terrorist group.

Elliot Wachtel crouched behind the camera, held up his hands to frame the shot, palms forward, thumb to thumb, and satisfied that everything was right, said, "Settle everyone. Background ready. And . . . *action!*"

Derek Thorne crept through the shadows toward the pool of moonlight. Six men were standing around a wooden crate. Lucas Breen motioned to one of his goons, who stepped forward with a crowbar and opened it up.

Akmed Sabib, the international terrorist, grinned as he reached into the box and picked up a hand-held rocket launcher, just the weapon he needed to tip the scales in his private little war with humanity.

"That will be one million dollars," Breen sneered. "Cash."

Akmed held up the launcher and peered down the scope. "I thought you said this location was secure, that we would be absolutely alone."

"We are," Breen said.

Akmed suddenly spun around, taking aim at the exact spot where Thorne stood. "Then I guess that would make you an uninvited guest, Lieutenant."

Breen turned in surprise to see Derek Thorne stepping out of the shadows. "Thorne!" he snapped. "I should have killed you when I had the chance."

"Your mistake," Thorne said.

"Don't worry," Akmed said to Breen, "He's just one man. Nothing can stop us now."

"And that would be your mistake." Thorne said. "You can leave here in handcuffs or a body bag, it's your call."

Akmed laughed. "Perhaps you don't understand the situation. I'm aiming a weapon at you that fires an explosive charge that could reduce a 747 to smoking ash."

"That's sweet and dandy," Thorne sneered. "But my gun has bullets."

Thorne reached for his gun as Akmed fired. Whoosh! Thorne hit the floor. The rocket sailed over his head, slamming into the stack of crates behind him. KA-BLAMMO! The crates exploded in a burst of flaming splinters. Thorne rose up like a phoenix against the firestorm, firing his gun—BLAM! BLAM! BLAM!—the bullets pounding Akmed against the wall.

Thorne aimed his gun at Breen. "What do you want to hear? Your civil rights or your last rites?"

"Cut!" Wachtel sat up. "That's a print."

Charlie lowered his gun, and glanced over at Darren Clarke, a.k.a. Akmed Sabib, who was still lying wide-eyed in an ever widening pool of movie blood. Even he had to immodestly admit the scene had gone well.

"Nice job," Charlie said, brushing cinders off his jacket. "Is this the first time you've been gunned down, or have you been killed before?"

Darren twitched, his body caught in the grip of a pretty convincing death rattle. The assistant director ambled up and stared down at him. "Very nice, but you don't get paid any extra for performing once the camera stops rolling."

Charlie looked into Darren's unblinking eyes. There was a spark that should have been there that wasn't. This man wasn't acting.

Horrified, Charlie crouched over Darren and ripped open the actor's shirt. There were no punctured bags of movie blood underneath, just three massive gunshot wounds in his chest, gruesome peepholes into the man's ravaged internal organs.

Before the words "Call an ambulance" were even out of Charlie's mouth, the man was dead.

ACT TWO

Chapter Seven

The scene at the scene.

That's what this was always called in the *My Gun Has Bullets* scripts. The aftermath at the scene of the crime. The camera would pan across the police tape demarcating the borders, zoom in on the forensics specialists sifting up the most minute clues, then follow the body bag as it was wheeled on a gurney into the coroner's wagon. The door would slam shut on the coroner's wagon and they'd drive off, the camera lingering behind, its angle widening to reveal grieving relatives, and then favoring our detective hero arriving at the scene.

Only now the cameras were off.

An army of studio publicists had descended on the soundstage before the police arrived, briefing everyone on what they saw, whether they saw it or not. Grieving producers and crew members mingled around the craft services table, wiping away tears, certain this meant the end of the series, their jobs, and the return to financial insecurity.

Wachtel had fled and locked himself in his trailer. It was imperative that he be debriefed by a publicist before talking to the police, so a couple of security guards swiped a Jaws of Life from the set of *Emergency 911* to pry him out. Meanwhile, the studio flacks hustled the extras to the commissary, plying the perpetually penniless horde with food and drink until they were too fat and drowsy to remember anything. A couple of PR guys had marched toward Charlie, but he hammered them with the steely gaze Derek Thorne used to stop bullets in midair. The publicists did an about-face and left him alone to face the police without their counsel.

Now, while the forensics specialists were separating the leftovers of real carnage from the aftermath of countless scenes of fake bloodshed, a group of detectives huddled around the video monitor, watching the playback of the fatal moment yet again. Outside, they could hear Wachtel's mobile home crinkling like a beer can as it was torn open by the Jaws of Life.

Charlie sat slumped in his canvas chair, watching two weary detectives scrawling their observations down in their well-worn pocket notebooks, which were curved into the unique shape of their individual buttocks. They could probably tell whose notebook was whose just by slipping it into their back pockets. *Naw, my butt's bigger, this must be Feldberg's notebook.*

He'd killed a man. And yet, somehow, the full force of it hadn't sunk in—or wouldn't. It just didn't feel real. He'd killed so many people in this soundstage over the last few episodes, it was hard to believe this death was any more genuine than the ones before.

But it was.

So why didn't he feel anything?

Itchy Matthews, the propman, had felt something. A shooting pain in his left arm and chest. The ambulance carrying Itchy had screeched out of the studio twenty minutes earlier, almost colliding with the coroner's wagon arriving to pick up Darren's corpse. If Itchy had timed his massive, fatal coronary a little better, the coroner could have taken them both and saved the ambulance a trip.

With Itchy gone, that left no one for the detectives to blame except, perhaps, the fellow who actually pulled the trigger.

"Looks like you're just as lousy a cop on TV as you were in real life," Sergeant Emil Grubb said by way of introduction.

"Are you the investigating officer, or just an asshole?" Charlie asked.

"Both," he replied. "Sergeant Emil Grubb, North Hollywood Division."

"Nice to meet you," Charlie sighed.

"You killed this guy."

"Yes, I did," Charlie said.

"Is that a confession?"

"It's a fact."

Grubb jotted that down. "Did you know there were bullets in the gun?"

"No, I didn't."

Grubb flipped through his notebook. "You sure about that?"

"Yeah."

Grubb smirked. "Funny, I got sixty witnesses who distinctly heard you say 'My gun has bullets' before you pulled the trigger."

Charlie got up from his canvas seat and walked past Grubb.

"Where do you think you're going?" Grubb demanded.

"Home," Charlie said.

Grubb yelled after him, "I'm not through with you yet."

"No, you probably aren't." Charlie turned around slowly and met his gaze. "You're from the North Hollywood division, which means in the hierarchy of police life you rank somewhere between harmless bacteria and gifted amoebas."

Grubb glared at him, but Charlie just plowed on.

"I'm a fuck-up ex-cop from Beverly Hills who makes more in a week pretending to be a supercop than you make in a year being a half-decent one. The way I figure it, you hate my guts, and will do everything you possibly can to make my life miserable. Did I leave anything out?"

After a moment of silence—broken only by the sound of Wachtel's trailer snapping open and the frantic director being dragged out screaming—Grubb shook his head. "Nope."

"Glad we understand each other," Charlie replied and continued out, thankful his trailer was on the opposite side of the soundstage from Wachtel's, which was drawing all the attention.

When he went into his trailer, he wasn't surprised to see Boyd Hartnell and Jackson Burley waiting for him. He was surprised, however, that Boyd wasn't completely bald by now. Boyd was pacing, while Burley sat in a swivel chair, spinning slowly around, lost in thought.

"Hope you're happy." Boyd hurled his words at Charlie like big balls of spit. "First *Miss Agatha,* now this. You're a one-man plague on the television industry."

Charlie stuck his hands in his pockets. They were empty. A fact of life he figured he'd have to get used to. "I guess there isn't enough room on the network schedule to give all those cops their own television series."

Boyd wasn't amused. This had been a very hard month on him. He was undergoing an extremely delicate procedure on the cutting edge of hair technology. Esther Radcliffe, his leading lady on his only hit series, was undoubtedly plotting to kill Sabrina Bishop, a woman he desperately wanted to fuck. The panicked producers of the doomed sitcom *Bonjour Buddy Bipp* actually wanted to retool the show for Dick Van Patten. And now Charlie Willis had gunned down a guest star, a legendary propman was dead, and a hack director was having a nervous breakdown that had reduced a $50,000 mobile home to scrap metal.

"What the fuck are we gonna do?" Boyd asked the heavens. "We're half a million dollars in deficit on this show. This is no time for people to be killed on the set. It's not in the fucking budget."

"Shit happens," Burley observed. It sounded to Charlie like an action hero catchphrase in the making.

"This is a major fucking catastrophe," Boyd said.

"It may not be as bad as it seems," Burley said, eerily serene as he spun. "A killing on the set can reinvigorate a show."

"We've only been on the air six weeks—there's nothing to reinvigorate," Boyd snapped.

"*Venom* was in its fourth episode when Luke Driscoll was supposed to dive outta the way of a hitman's speeding car," Burley said. "Course, he ended up a $30,000-an-episode hood ornament on a $1,500 Nova. Driscoll never could do action. Hell, we needed a stunt double just to shoot him walking briskly. Everyone figured we were gonna be canceled."

The publicity had been enormous. A grand jury indicted the stuntman and the director on involuntary manslaughter charges. The network immediately commissioned a docudrama TV movie on the accident. Meanwhile, Burley and his writers retooled *Venom* to accommodate the tragedy. In the new version, the secret agent, codenamed Venom, was hit by the car and had to go to the hospital for reconstructive surgery. Who would he be when the bandages were taken off? The shrewdly manipulated mystery created a publicity bonanza all its own. All of America, which had largely ignored the show before Driscoll was mowed down, tuned in two weeks later to see Chad Everett emerge from under the bandages.

"Turned out to be a blessing in disguise," Burley said. "Driscoll was no Chad Everett."

"So few are," observed Boyd, momentarily distracted from his woes. But reality abruptly intruded in the form of Don DeBono barging in the door.

"Goddammit, Boyd, can't you keep your stars from shooting people?" DeBono apparently either didn't notice Charlie or didn't care. "I can't mop up the blood with any more pilot deals."

Charlie settled into a seat and popped open a Snapple, content to be unnoticed, which only reinforced his sense of detachment from what was happening. Which, all things considered, was better than having to face the enormity of what he had done.

"Let's not overreact—it's not like the dead guy was anybody. Maybe this could work for us." Boyd was vamping now, trying to luck onto a solution. "In the show, Derek Thorne was supposed to blow away a terrorist and what happened? A guy *really* got blown away. Doesn't matter who he was. Now when people watch the show, they'll never know if the blood is gonna be real or not. It'll give the show an edge, it'll give it—"

"Verisimilitude," Charlie said.

Everyone turned around, shocked, as if he'd just appeared out of thin air.

"I'm told I reek of it," he added, taking a swig of Snapple.

Boyd could feel his hair plugs coming loose from their tenuous moorings, but he turned his attention back to DeBono and forced himself to go on anyway. There had to be a way out of this, short of cancellation. "The point is, let's not panic. We can make this work."

"Sure. What's Chad Everett up to these days?" Charlie asked, his way of showing what a positive attitude he had.

If Boyd had a gun, there would have been a third death on the lot that day. As it was, the only thing dying at that moment were the follicles on Boyd's head.

DeBono ignored Charlie and turned to Boyd. "While you've been harvesting your chest hair, I've been over a spit in front of the FCC. They think TV violence is to blame for every idiot who holds up a liquor store. I got 'em believing it's all make-believe, no harm done—

and you're telling me you wanna create a show where the murders are real?"

"Only one," Boyd offered meekly. "It doesn't have to happen again."

"Oh, that's a big relief," DeBono said. "Have you tried asking Dr. Desi if he'd implant a brain in your fucking head? Frog, newt, cheetah, any old thing would do."

Boyd seethed, but couldn't risk pissing off DeBono at this critical juncture. It still wasn't too late to salvage the situation.

DeBono knew what Boyd was thinking, and it just made the studio chief look even more pathetic. But as bad as the situation was, he couldn't bring himself to think badly of Charlie Willis. Somehow, despite the trouble Charlie had caused, DeBono pitied the poor schlub. When all this was over, Charlie Willis would be forgotten, remembered only as the answer to a trivia question in some meaningless game show.

"I got no idea if this is your fault or not," DeBono told him, "but you're gonna be hung for it anyway, because let's face it, you did kill the guy."

"No way around that," Charlie admitted.

"And by tonight, the phrase *My Gun Has Bullets* is gonna be a sick national joke," DeBono said. "If I keep the show on my network, we'll be a joke, too."

"So we change the name." Boyd desperately turned to Burley and swatted him on the shoulder. "You got lots of 'em, right?"

Burley started rattling them off. *"Thorne of Justice, .357 Justice, Man of Action—"*

"Man of Action, that's a good one," Boyd said. "We put Larry Manetti in there, give the cop a new name, shoot the thing in Hawaii, and finish out the season as if nothing happened. It'll reinvigorate the show."

"As of now, *My Gun Has Bullets* is on indefinite hiatus, pending the outcome of all this shit." DeBono looked at Charlie. "If I were you, I'd make myself scarce."

And with that pronouncement, DeBono left. Boyd immediately chased after him, urging him to reconsider. Charlie found himself alone with Jackson Burley, who rose to his feet and held out his hand to him. Charlie shook it.

"It's been real," Burley said on his way out the door, "too damn real."

It was the most intelligent thing anyone had said to Charlie in his entire television career.

Chapter Eight

The suspects were all in the drawing room. The silver-haired patriarch. His greedy daughter. The stepson with the shady past. The adopted daughter with something to hide. The nanny with a rap sheet. The gardener whose green thumb came from counterfeiting currency. One of them had murdered the blackmailing maid, and Miss Agatha was about to reveal the killer's identity when . . .

Three ninja warriors crashed through the windows, rolled across the floor and came up in fighting stance, ready to dole out death with their swords, silver stars, and lethal hands.

Sweet Miss Agatha's disarming, grandmotherly charm and deductive reasoning wouldn't save her now. But the ninja warriors underestimated the kindly old lady. They didn't know about . . .

Agatha's niece.

A vision in black leather cartwheeled into the room, taking out one astonished ninja with a kick in the face. Another ninja charged her, brandishing his sword. Without even looking back, she ducked, flipped over backward, kicked him in the face, caught his fumbled sword in midair, and with one expert swipe, cut the pants off the third ninja exposing . . .

White boxer shorts decorated with smiling pumpkins.

Miss Agatha whipped the hood off the shocked ninja, revealing that he was none other than the elderly beekeeper. Now the comely maid's enigmatic last words, "smiling pumpkins," made tragic sense.

Miss Agatha had done it again.

Cut together, it looked great. No, it looked spectacular.

Boyd sat behind his desk, remote in his hand, watching the rough assembly of the latest *Miss Agatha* episode on his big-screen TV. Even in the face of disaster, a man has his priorities. And watching dailies, especially ones with Sabrina in skintight leather, was definitely on the top of the list.

As much as he hated to, Boyd had to admit Don DeBono had been right about one thing—*Miss Agatha* had never been so exciting. Sabrina brought new life to the show. The TV room at retirement villas nationwide would be hopping on Sunday nights. A lot of old men would be looking at their nurses in a whole new light. And if Boyd's reaction was any measure, men of all ages would be rediscovering the pure joy of a good mystery. Would Sabrina's boobs fall out of her lingerie as she beat up the murderer? Would Sabrina's shirt be torn by that killer's knife? Would Sabrina peel off her sweater before she went into the freezing meat locker in search of clues? These were puzzlers that would keep men glued to the screen.

Whole new arenas of storytelling had opened up since she joined the cast. Sabrina becomes an aerobics instructor to sweat out a murderer at a health club. Sabrina poses as a Victoria's Secret model to trap a killer with a lingerie fetish. Sabrina goes sunbathing to expose a lethal lifeguard. And inevitably Miss Agatha would come along, with her plate of cookies and homespun proverbs, to sift through the clues Sabrina had uncovered and expose the murderer.

Of course, Sabrina would have to slip into black leather, break some heads, trash a few cars, and fire a couple of semiautomatic weapons first.

Boyd no longer had to endure excruciating hours watching the withering harridan Esther Radcliffe having tea with an endless parade of elderly has-been actors, climaxing in a round-up of senior citizens in a dreary drawing room, where Miss Agatha would deduce the identity of the killer using clues withheld from the audience. Not that the show's loyal audience cared; most of them clapped the lights out and fell asleep before the finale anyway.

Miss Agatha dailies, which he used to dread, had become the highlight of Boyd's day. He'd cancel meetings to jam the cassette into the TV and catch up on the previous day's shooting. Sometimes he'd take them home and watch them again in slow motion, particularly on those days when Sabrina was in black leather, kicking the daylights out of some lucky stuntman.

Even now, sitting in his office high above the Pinnacle Studios soundstages, these indelible images provided him with some measure of comfort as the world collapsed around him. In just a matter of hours, he'd had to deal with two deaths, three if you counted the almost certain cancellation of *My Gun Has Bullets,* and the complete nervous breakdown of a once prolific episodic director. And there was the matter of the demolished trailer, which lay crumpled against soundstage 11 like some giant, discarded beer can.

In an odd sense, Boyd was relieved. He had felt certain that if anyone was going to die on the set, it would be Sabrina Bishop at the withered hands of that insane shrew Esther Radcliffe. In fact, that had been his first, horrified thought when his secretary ran in, frantically blubbering about a shooting on the set. For one terrifying instant, he envisioned Sabrina's perfect body, lifeless on a soundstage floor, passing into the great beyond without once having had the pleasure of Boyd Hartnell.

The thought had been too horrible to bear. He didn't bother waiting for the elevator, but bounded down the stairwell like a man escaping a burning building.

He literally collapsed into the lobby, hyperventilating into a dead faint on the cold marble. In the three minutes of unconsciousness, he imagined himself alone at a windy cemetery, standing over her open grave, hair flying off his head and coating her casket until he was left utterly bald.

Boyd jerked into consciousness, pushed aside the security guards who stood around him, and staggered into the midday sun, grateful to see the ambulance screeching up to soundstage 11, clear across the lot from where *Miss Agatha* was shooting.

He felt relief so strong he nearly passed out again, until a new reality jolted the dizziness away—it was one of *his* shows filming in soundstage 11, not one of the dozens of other series shooting on the lot.

That was this afternoon.

Now, the police were gone, the bodies were in the morgue, and Wachtel had been checked in to a Chatsworth sanitarium, but Boyd's troubles were far from over.

The show's "indefinite hiatus," the TV series equivalent of a terminal coma after fewer than thirteen episodes, was a financial disaster. The episodes would be worthless in syndication, which meant there was no possibility of recouping the considerable deficit.

But Boyd admired his ability to think on his feet. In the time it took to walk from Charlie Willis's trailer back to the tower, he'd come up with a couple of brilliant ideas to turn this tragedy in his favor.

As soon as he was back in his office, he ordered the day's *My Gun Has Bullets* footage, up to and including the killing, edited and prepared for immediate home video release, packaged tastefully as *An American Tragedy*. It was a guaranteed million seller, and at $29.95 it could be one of the division's biggest hits since *Race to Death*, a fast and furious ninety minutes of car racing accidents, and the milestone *Killings of Convenience*, the riveting compilation of closed-circuit camera footage of fatal minimart holdups.

The *My Gun Has Bullets* killing was the lead story on every newscast and would undoubtedly be front-page news in every rag from the *New York Times* to *Soldier of Fortune* by morning. Naturally, the business affairs department, eager to protect the corporate image, was vehemently refusing all requests for footage of the killing.

So, naturally, the suits were stunned when Boyd marched in and ordered them to give the gruesome shots to anyone who wanted them—but to charge twenty times the usual clip fee up front. The media would scream, but they'd pay.

As long as Pinnacle Studios was going to get the negative publicity, Boyd figured they might as well make a few bucks off of it. Still, the Japanese owners would probably shit in their sushi, and behead him to save corporate face.

Yet, amid all this turmoil, two things dominated Boyd Hartnell's thoughts. His hair and Sabrina Bishop which, in reality, weren't mutually exclusive.

For her, he had to have perfect hair. Only moments ago, he'd reflexively run his hand through his wiry locks and was shocked, actually closer to terrified, to see tiny strands between his fingers. Even if, miraculously, the chest hair managed to take hold on his scalp despite the stress this crisis was putting him through, it wouldn't be enough to entice Sabrina Bishop, not when she could have the likes of Thad Paul fondling her glorious orbs *and* get paid for the pleasure.

No, what he needed on his head was something thicker, richer, manlier—something she couldn't resist petting, smelling, and stroking. More drastic measures were going to be necessary. He'd already put in calls to Dr. Desi and his veterinarian.

In the meantime, nothing wrong with enticing the lass with his wit and charm. He rewound the tape for later viewing at home, and certain inclusion in his growing Sabrina Bishop collection, and headed for his private bathroom for five minutes of delicate combing before meeting her.

Esther Radcliffe reacted with surprise to a revelation from someone who wasn't there.

She was standing in front of the Panavision camera, reacting to two characters who were not there and who, in fact, Esther wouldn't actually meet face to face until the last day of shooting. The other actors' side of the conversation would be filmed tomorrow, while Esther was enjoying one of her many days off.

Esther was long past the days when she'd stand around feeding lines to other actors getting their close-ups. She had better things to do.

So now she moved from one set to another, filming halves of scenes that would be completed while she was shopping at Saks Fifth Avenue, floating in her heart-shaped pool, or demanding multiple orgasms from her young lover.

The camera trained on her was covered with so many filters and gels, all carefully calculated to melt twenty-five years off Esther's face, it was a wonder any light at all was passing through the lens and getting captured on celluloid. But those tricks, combined with clever lighting and editing, smoothed more wrinkles than her $120,000 worth of plastic surgery.

Just behind the camera, an overweight assistant director sat in a canvas chair, propping Esther's cue cards on his shelflike girth, while the bored script supervisor read the other actors' parts in her weary, gravelly voice. Esther was long past the days when she'd memorize dialogue.

Out of a seven-day shooting schedule, Esther was only required to be there half the time, and that was before Sabrina Bishop showed up. In previous years, the network tried to scare her by giving her entire episodes off instead, which gave them a chance to try other actors out as potential replacements. Buddy Ebsen, Charo, Bernie Kopell, Jean Stapleton, and even Charlie Callas and his wacky tongue were trotted in and out. But ratings dived when she was gone, and the network quickly went back to letting her have her half weeks.

Now that Sabrina Bishop was in the cast, Don DeBono had made noises about trying it again, but Esther didn't feel threatened. Sabrina Bishop wouldn't be around long enough to be a threat.

Already, Charlie Willis was out of the picture and was probably ruing the day he crossed Esther Radcliffe. Or so she thought as she stood in front of the camera, reading her lines and emoting up a storm. Her only regret was that he wasn't twisted in rigor mortis right now. But she held out hope.

Deaths in Hollywood tend to happen in threes. The way Esther figured it, if someone could get shot on *My Gun Has Bullets,* why couldn't Sabrina get stabbed with a real knife on *Miss Agatha?* Two disasters like that might fluster Boyd Hartnell so badly he might accidentally slip on his hairpiece, crash through his office window, and fall to his death. It would serve him right for tampering in her domain.

The thought amused her so much she smiled wickedly in the midst of a scene where she was supposed to be grief-stricken. The smile was not lost on the director, Dag Luthan, but he wasn't going to say anything. This job was too important to him. Ever since *Gilligan's Island* was canceled, work had been hard to come by.

Sabrina Bishop noticed the smile, too, especially since Esther was looking at her when she flashed it, but she was too absorbed in what had happened to give it much thought.

The idea of Charlie Willis actually killing a man during a scene unsettled her more than she thought it should. Sabrina was dressed in her black leather outfit, the one reserved for action scenes, and she paced around the soundstage, trying to work it out in her mind.

Charlie Willis was just some strange guy who gave her his shirt and told her some wild lies about Esther Radcliffe. Why should she care what happened to him?

Because he called her *ma'am.*

It was silly, she knew. But in that instant, he won her over. It almost didn't matter what absurd drivel spilled out of his mouth after that, the *ma'am* was sincere and true. No one had ever been sincere and true to her in Hollywood, and she treasured that moment, even if it was just that . . . a moment.

But it was the most resonant moment in her first few weeks on the television treadmill. She had never worked so hard. In the blur of days and nights, of dialogue learned, spoken, and forgotten, she'd had little time to reflect on the experience that was dominating her life.

She was in the makeup trailer by five A.M., on the stage at seven, working straight through for twelve hours, except for the odd moment or two grazing at the craft services table. She finally left the lot for Venice sometime around nine P.M. Once home, she had time for a yogurt and banana, and then a hot bath, where she would memorize her lines for the next morning.

But today, the news about Charlie Willis had intruded into her thoughts as nothing else had since she began *Miss Agatha*. She actually gave a damn, and she couldn't figure out why. It couldn't be that Charlie called her *ma'am*, talked to *her* and not her breasts, gave her his shirt, or had a refreshingly ordinary body.

No, it definitely couldn't have been any of those things. She wouldn't be reacting to anything as dumb as that. There had to be a deeper, more compelling reason why, out of all the things to think about, she couldn't stop thinking about him. And couldn't suppress the urge to give Charlie some comfort in the midst of his tragedy.

His shirt.

She suddenly remembered she had it in her trailer. Neatly washed and ironed. She *could* take it to him, and if he needed someone to talk to, she *could* listen. What would be wrong with that?

Her heart suddenly started to pound nervously. She couldn't believe it. Here she was a television star, well, nearly a television star, making $13,500 an episode, with a body most women would kill for, and she was getting all nervous about giving a man back his shirt.

A man she hardly knew. And what she knew about Charlie was that he'd told her a malicious lie about Esther Radcliffe, that he'd tried to tarnish Sabrina's first day on the job. And did she really want to associate herself with someone, at this fragile stage in her budding career, who had just blown away a guy? A man who was going to get thoroughly trashed in the press? Imagine what the media would say about *her* if she got lumped in with him. She could lose her job.

No way, protect yourself, honey, she told herself sternly. Guys like him are easy to come by.

Then why hadn't she come by any?

So she came to a decision. She'd return the shirt. She just wouldn't be seen with him. First, though, she'd have to find out where he lived. That shouldn't be too hard. She was about to go back to her trailer and get her excuse to see him out of the closet when she got sidetracked by the arrival of Boyd Hartnell. The first thing she noticed was that his hair was combed like Christopher Reeve's in *Superman,* a curl conspicuously dangling over his forehead.

"Sabrina, I just had to come down and tell you how fantastic the dailies were," he enthused. "It's your best performance of the season."

"We've only done three episodes," she said, noticing his eyes shift rapidly between her face and her breasts.

"And you're maturing into the role each week," he replied. "The network loves it, and frankly, I think they're going to want to talk spin-off pretty soon." He leaned closer to her, lowering his voice, and using the opportunity to look down her cleavage. "No one is more devastated by the incident on stage eleven today than me, but out of tragedy can come opportunity. The network has an open time period, they have to fill it with something. So . . . I think *we* should be talking spin-off *now.*"

"We?" Sabrina's head was spinning. This was happening too fast. A month ago she was in a warehouse in Valencia, Thad Paul between her legs and a camera between her breasts. Now they were talking about giving her a television series of her own.

"Let's bounce some ideas around," Boyd said, "see if we can find something that fits you, a high concept we can put on the development fast track."

Ideas? No one had ever asked her for ideas before, they just wanted her body, though she had a strong suspicion Boyd wanted that, too. But this was opportunity knocking, albeit panting and drooling, but knocking just the same. If she could play this right, she'd never have to kiss up to the Boyd Hartnells of the world again.

"Sure," she said, taking his arm, "let's talk."

Charlie and his shirt would have to wait.

Chapter Nine

Connie was to blame. If she hadn't run off with Atilano the gardener, Charlie Willis would probably have a working sprinkler system. And if he did, he could turn it on right now and soak John Tesh, who was standing on the sidewalk in front of Charlie's house, addressing the millions of *Entertainment Tonight* viewers, promising them an in-depth look at "The Rise and Fall of Charlie Willis."

It would be a short segment.

McGarrett had been wandering around the house, whining and mewing, ever since John Tesh showed up. The dog had always preferred Leeza Gibbons. Charlie had been hiding in the dark, stealing glances outside through the slats of his Levolor blinds for a week.

Throughout the night and well into the morning, he watched the reporters jockeying for position. *Hard Copy* duked it out with *A Current Affair* for the opportunity to report from his driveway. A cheeky correspondent for *Inside Edition* tried to rise above it all by straddling the fire hydrant, only to topple into the overgrown grass and McGarrett's droppings. *Nightline* went the classy route—they rented the house across the street, and planted Ted Koppel inside, right smack in front of the living room window, where the press scrambling in Charlie's yard became an exciting backdrop for a special report on "The First Victim of Television Violence."

His window had become a television screen. Nothing he saw through it seemed real. He'd killed a man, and there was a horde of reporters out front vilifying him to a nation. And yet, it was so sudden, so hard to comprehend, so big, that somehow Charlie couldn't help feeling it was all make-believe, and no matter how complicated and bleak it seemed, it would end happily with all the loose ends tied up.

That's the way it had always been on *Adam-12*. No matter how much disorder and mayhem there was in his life growing up, no matter how cruel the men were his mother married, no matter how loud his sister sobbed, no matter how powerless he felt, he could always find order on television. There, if nowhere else, he could control his environment. He could be certain good would prevail over evil, and everything would, eventually, make perfect sense.

As much as he wanted it to be that way in real life, it wasn't. He'd certainly found that out in his twelve years on the Beverly Hills police force. Which was one reason why, when given the chance, he gave up on reality and took a day job in the land of make-believe. Where Charlie Willis became Detective Lieutenant Derek Thorne, man of action, a hero capable of bringing justice to a world beset with danger, solving the most perplexing, complicated and impossible mysteries, reducing them to simple problems with one simple solution.

My Gun Has Bullets.

It couldn't be any clearer, or more orderly, than that.

But at the end of the day, Charlie had to return to reality, which had become, since Connie left him, as empty and joyless as the Ikea showroom he had unconsciously recreated in his home. His place in Reseda had become little more than a rest stop on his commute between real life and reel life.

Charlie picked up the acrylic paperweight and stared at the bullet, his ticket from L.A. to Oz, that lay suspended inside it. He remembered Alice, the extra he'd brought home from the set. He remembered her holding it in front of her eyes, staring at it as if it had magical powers, desperately wanting to be transported with it to the make-believe land Charlie inhabited. What fantasy had he seduced her with? Something about getting shot while singlehandedly taking down some robbers.

At the time, he wondered where that voice had come from, why it had been so easy to spin such elaborate lies . . . the fiction she so desperately, and so willingly, wanted to hear. Alice had wanted to sleep with Derek Thorne, not Charlie Willis, and who could blame her? So he gave her what she wanted. Charlie slipped into the role so easily, and so comfortably, that maybe he believed fiction had become reality.

But it hadn't.

Derek Thorne would have remained rock hard all night, sending Alice into an orgasmic delirium. He certainly wouldn't have come while she was slipping on the condom. Charlie had shrugged the experience off, which wasn't hard to do, because the next day he smashed a cocaine ring, found a kidney for an ailing orphan, and seduced an international hitwoman, all before lunch.

Charlie had no real life, so he settled into the fictional one. Was it any wonder none of this seemed real?

It was certainly real for actor Darren Clarke. A TV villain to viewers. A commission to his agent. A loving son to his adoring parents. A sincere and caring lover to his girlfriend. A nobody to Boyd Hartnell. And now, a corpse, thanks to Charlie Willis, cop turned actor, actor turned killer.

Charlie rolled the paperweight in his fingers, the smooth acrylic soft to the touch, belying the harshness of the bullet it encased. He felt powerless, alone, empty. His life was spiraling out of control and he was only an observer.

Suddenly, Charlie felt like sneaking out the back door, screeching away in his Camaro, and reinventing himself somewhere else. Instead, he peeked out the window again.

John Tesh was wrapping up his report, making a smooth segue from Charlie Willis to an inside look at the new $75-million-movie *Titanic*.

Charlie let the blinds flap shut and, for the first time, began to feel the first sparks of anger.

Derek Thorne wouldn't be hiding in the dark, stealing peeks at the enemy outside, feeling sorry for himself and plotting his escape. No, Derek Thorne would holster up his massive gun, stomp outside, and look the camera right in its single, naked eye.

"I don't know who set me up, but I got a message for you," he'd say. "My gun has bullets and I'm coming for you."

Derek Thorne wouldn't have let Connie walk out, either. He would have thrown her ass out, through the plate glass window. And Atilano? Pow, right in the kisser.

Take charge, that was Derek Thorne's way. And if people didn't listen, he'd let his gun do the talking. But this was real life, and Charlie Willis wasn't Derek Thorne.

That's when a thought occurred to Charlie, hitting him with the life-changing, explosive force of Esther Radcliffe's bullet. Alice thought he was Derek, didn't she? Or at least she was willing to believe he was. And if *she* could believe it, why the hell couldn't *he?*

If anyone was Derek Thorne, it was Charlie Willis. He spent most of his waking hours in the role, why not the rest? If Derek Thorne could kick ass, why couldn't he?

None of this was Charlie's fault.

Somebody else put a bullet in his prop gun. Somebody else made a killer out of him. *Somebody else had to pay.*

Charlie hurled the paperweight against the wall. It shattered apart, nearly nailing the dog, who yelped and scampered to safety behind the couch. Charlie scooped up the bullet, stuffed it into his pocket, then glared at McGarrett.

"Stop whining," he snarled, "or I'll blow you away."

The dog didn't seemed convinced, but Charlie wasn't going to let McGarrett shake his new-found confidence. He marched to the closet, found his police-issue shoulder holster and gun, and strapped them on.

He felt better already.

A toothy mannequin from one of the local TV stations was in the middle of a live report from Charlie's front porch when Charlie threw open the door, grabbed the microphone from the startled newsman's hand, and aimed his gun right into the camera.

"I don't know who set me up, but I got a message for you," Charlie said. "My gun has bullets and I'm coming for you."

Chapter Ten

Eddie Planet was having at least two revelations as he nuzzled his wife's saline-filled breasts, the rip-roaring theme from *Saddlesore* blaring from the speakers on either side of the bed. One revelation was that Delbert Skaggs was going to revolutionize the television industry and Eddie would be a major player in the new world order. And, realizing this, Eddie had his second revelation—that he didn't have to coax his reluctant pecker into action with old TV themes from his past hits anymore. That was the revelation he was enjoying most at this moment. And Shari, too, who had thought his hormones had died with his career. Hers certainly had.

But now his schmeckle stood at attention, as if to say, "I'm attached to Eddie Planet and proud of it," rather than shrinking into obscurity in the darkness of his crotch as it had for so many years.

Shari was astonished by her husband's sudden, obsessive interest in sex. He'd paw her whenever she passed, and when he wasn't able to catch her, she had a sneaking suspicion he was actually jerking off alone.

She wasn't sure what had come over him, but she was happy. His ardor was rekindling her own, which she had previously channeled into shopping, spending Eddie further into debt and, in turn, further into impotence.

But something had changed.

Eddie could tell her what it was, but she'd never understand. She wouldn't comprehend the awe—no, the *euphoria*—he felt watching Delbert Skaggs at work on the primetime schedule. It was nothing short of a religious conversion. This was the Coming of the Lord. Delbert wasn't the Angel of Death. He was the Son of God.

The God of Television. The malevolent power behind jiggle shows, Gary Coleman, and infomercials. The inexplicable force that made

The Flying Nun a hit and yet denied stardom to Mark Shera.

Delbert Skaggs showed Eddie the light, and Eddie was an eager disciple. Almost immediately, Eddie's bowels began to move with the regularity of a Swiss timepiece. He resolved to follow his leaders' wisdom, the most profound kernel of which was delivered from the mount by Daddy Crofoot himself.

Thou shalt have at least three orgasms a day. If there's no one around, thou shalt use thy hand.

Huddled in his executive bathroom, his pants around his knees, whipping his schlong into reluctant service, he knew *Frankencop* would be saved.

See, Eddie had faith.

If there was any doubt, the God of Television had given Eddie a sign. Charlie Willis gunned down his guest star. *My Gun Has Bullets* was scrapped, leaving UBC vulnerable and giving *Frankencop* the time period. Instantly, *Frankencop* went from struggling second at ten P.M. Thursday to number one. Eddie Planet was a player again.

Which, in itself, was a certified miracle. Courtesy, no doubt, of Delbert Skaggs or Daddy Crofoot. It didn't matter. He just knew the results. He didn't *really* want to know who was responsible.

When Shari came home from her astrology appointment, Eddie was lying in wait, his erection straining his polyester pants to the breaking point.

Now her DKNY outfit lay in shreds at the foot of their chrome four-poster bed, which was moving to the relentless stampede of *Saddlesore*, Eddie a bucking bronco beneath Shari, who straddled his groin like a saddle, riding him furiously toward her orgasm. She twisted and jerked, shrieking in time with each whipcrack and Frankie Laine *yee-haw*, clutching Eddie's hairy shoulders for dear life until whammo, she climaxed so hard Eddie feared she might pinch off his dick. But his fear passed in a microsecond, as his own orgasm hurled him face forward into the cleavage of sweaty, saltwater sacks, bending his nose so out of shape it bled.

When it was over, she curled up against him, resting her head on one of Eddie's saggy pecs, staring down at his weary tool, throbbing as if it were panting for breath.

After sex, some people light a cigarette. Others quote poetry. Some go on a sugar binge. Eddie reached down for the remote and flicked on the TV.

Charlie Willis suddenly appeared. He looked Eddie in the eye, aimed his gun at him, and said, "My gun has bullets and I'm coming for you."

Eddie's newfound faith evaporated almost as quickly as his erection. He switched off the TV, abruptly twisted out of bed and, clutching his cramping stomach, rushed for the bathroom.

Twenty minutes later, he stumbled out with leaden legs, his toes tingling as the blood slowly dribbled back into his lower body, the distinct impression of the toilet seat ringing his butt. He headed for the phone, dragging one lame, completely numb leg behind him and, although it was after midnight, called the office.

It was the only number he had for Delbert Skaggs, and somehow he wasn't surprised when the Son of God himself answered the phone. No hello, no howdy, not even a questioning "Yes?" Just the sound of breathing greeted Eddie on the line.

"Mr. Skaggs?" Eddie asked tentatively, wondering what the hell Delbert was doing there. Maybe the Son of God didn't sleep. Maybe he wasn't even human.

"Yes, Eddie," Delbert replied, sitting in total darkness, lit only by the glow of four muted television sets. Charlie Willis was on all of them, in one form or another.

"What a day, eh? One minute you're scrambling for anything to get a bump in the ratings. You're ready to drop twenty-five grand on stunt casting, hoping Scott Baio or Tim Conway can steal one measly share point from the dumb-ass show that's kicking your butt and what happens? Some idiot actor shoots his guest star and solves all your problems for you," Eddie said, his way of throwing chum in shark-infested waters. "I love this business, don't you? You never know what's in the script."

"It's a fortunate turn of events." Delbert knew what Eddie was getting at, but like Crofoot, he delighted in letting Eddie squirm. There was something about Eddie's personality that encouraged it. Everybody probably enjoyed it, his wife, busboys, panhandlers. Eventually, he'd watch Eddie squirm in an entirely different way, the kind that only happens when your life is gushing out of your neck. "But our troubles are far from over."

Eddie was relieved Delbert had *finally* gotten the point. For a God-like deity, he could be awfully dense. "You think Charlie Willis is serious about what he's saying? I mean, I'm protected, aren't I?" His legs were still asleep, but as they slowly awakened, they felt like they were covered with ants.

"Charlie Willis is not our problem," Delbert said. "Boo Boo is."

Boo Boo? Charlie Willis was gunning for them and Delbert was worried about a TV dog? Perhaps Delbert didn't grasp the serious-ness of the situation. "This guy is pissed, and if he finds whoever loaded his prop gun with live ammo, he's gonna kill 'em."

"Let him," Delbert said, astonishing Eddie. "It means we can be certain *My Gun Has Bullets* will never return to the schedule. And while that's definitely an advantage, we are vulnerable as long as *Boo Boo's Dilemma* is still on the air."

The man was clearly fearless, Eddie decided. Or completely in-sane.

"Audience flow is like water, Eddie," Delbert explained. "You turn off the spigot, and the water stops flowing."

"Uh-huh," Eddie said slowly, realization seeping into his foggy mind like the circulation returning to his legs. Suddenly, the tingling feeling was gone, replaced by a wave of warmth that brought his legs back to life.

"I want to divert the flow of water," Delbert said, wondering if his choice of metaphor had been too complex for Eddie to grasp. A shoe-lace could confuse Eddie Planet. Then again, in Delbert's hands, a shoelace could also kill him.

"You want to cancel Boo Boo?" Eddie whispered incredulously.

"No," Delbert said. "I want to *kill* Boo Boo."

Eddie's circulation was back, so his legs should have been strong. And yet they suddenly buckled beneath him. He grabbed the counter for support.

Kill Boo Boo?

Without Boo Boo, UBC's Thursday schedule would crumble and, with it, their control of primetime. It would be open season, each network scrambling for domination of the airwaves.

Kill Boo Boo?

Delbert was proposing nothing less than a revolution in primetime strategic thinking. First the advertisers controlled television, and a series stayed on as long as the advertiser was willing to pay the bill. Then the networks got smart, bought the shows themselves, and sold advertising off in chunks, the price tag based on the ratings. As long as Eddie had been in the business, networks controlled their own destinies. They decided when a show was renewed, canceled or moved.

What Delbert proposed was taking the power away from them and putting it in the hands of the producers. Why let your rival make all the decisions? You want to cancel a competing show, you do it yourself. Why fight for ratings with stunt casting, high concepts, and big-name stars, when bullets are so much cheaper? When you could just . . .

Kill Boo Boo.

Good God, it was incredible. Simply incredible. And Eddie Planet wanted to be a part of it. Eddie wanted to become a made man. He tried to speak, but squeaked instead.

Slowly, he forced himself to stand up straight, to summon his voice and take the first, bold step into his future.

"I know just the guys for the job," Eddie said.

Boyd Hartnell's house was a lot like the hair on his head. The one-story glass box had a tenuous hold on Mulholland Drive that defied gravity and was frightening to look at. And, like his hair, it was destined to fall.

The house balanced over the edge of the cliff on four stilts. The perpetually cracked driveway and splintering front porch were the only parts of the house that touched flat ground. The property values of the canyon cottages in the house's shadow plunged with each new shiver along the San Fernando Valley fault. But Boyd wasn't worried. The world could rattle and roll, but the house, like the man who inhabited it, would stand tall.

He was a strong believer in the symbolism of power. His office commanded a view of the valley and the entire studio. He wanted people to know that, at his whim, he could cast his awesome glance upon them and, in that instant, decide their fate. When they were summoned to see him, he wanted them to feel as if they were ascending into the heavens for an audience with the almighty.

And so it went at home. Even at rest, he towered over everything he saw. There was no higher point for a home in Los Angeles; he had looked into it. While other men cowered in vast estates in Bel Air, he rose above them. Don DeBono might run the network, but Boyd Hartnell could piss on his roof. He knew, because he had.

Boyd Hartnell was a powerful man. Sabrina Bishop had to know that from the moment she met him. Her stardom was his to make, or break.

When he came to her on the set this evening, she had to have been giddy with surprise, bowled over that he deigned to spend his dinner with her. He swept her away to an intimate meal at an absurdly expensive bistro, where the price of a glass of bottled water rivaled that of a fine wine. But he wanted her to know money was of no consequence to him. He was above such concerns. He was a starmaker, and he wanted her to know that, for the moment, he had cast his eye upon her and everything else was a distraction.

Now, as he prepared drinks for them both, he could see her standing on his deck, her back to him, taking in his extraordinary view. She said she needed air.

Of course she needed air. She had to be dizzy with the desire to please him, to stand out amid the glittering lights, the uncountable masses of people below, that clamored for his attention. To be in his home, to be so close to the center of everything, had to be intoxicating for her. He envied her the experience.

Boyd couldn't read her thoughts, but he knew what she must be thinking—that she couldn't believe she was actually here.

He had that right.

Sabrina couldn't believe she was standing on the deck, which jutted from the house, which jutted from the cliff, which meant she was just compounding the risk of toppling to her doom.

But the way she figured it, she'd been pushing her luck all night, first when she accepted Boyd's invitation to talk, then his invitation to dinner, then his invitation of a drink. Going on the deck couldn't make things much worse. It certainly put some distance between her and Boyd, a scrub brush in a suit.

I live right by the studio, he'd said. We'll have a couple drinks, talk a couple concepts, and I'll bring you back. And like an idiot, she'd said that sounded great. She was regretting her decision, and thinking of excuses to leave, when Thor, Boyd's buoyant golden retriever, came bounding out onto the deck, shaking every timber.

Sabrina gripped the wooden rail in terror, as if holding on to it would somehow protect her when the whole damn thing went plunging down into the dark canyon. What the hell was she doing here?

Of course, she couldn't say no to dinner. It was good politics. He was, after all, the president of the studio. And if she wanted her own series, he could give it to her. Unfortunately, that wasn't all he wanted to give to her. She'd caught him staring at her several times during the evening. She'd seen the look before. Men had been looking at her like that since puberty, when her breasts took over her body.

The panting dog danced around her, eager for some attention, his eyes bright with enthusiasm. He nudged her with his head, prodding her for a little affection. It was irresistible. Boyd could learn something from his dog—at least the animal was clear, honest, and straightforward about what it wanted. It wasn't until she was running her hands through the dog's unbelievably smooth, clean hair, that she realized she had been gripping the wood so tight there were splinters in her palm.

She went back inside. The dog chased after her, hungry for more attention, then obediently sat at her side when she stopped to look at the photographs on Boyd's wall.

Each one was a picture of Boyd with his arm around another celebrity. Boyd with Dean Martin. Boyd with Sharon Stone. Boyd with Annie Potts. Boyd with Corbin Bernsen. There must have been fifty of them.

"I'm looking forward to adding a picture of us to the wall," said Boyd, walking out from behind the wet bar with her Baccardi and diet Coke.

It was a stupid drink, she knew, but it fooled her into thinking she was sticking to her diet. She turned around to take the drink from him, and was stunned to see that he'd slipped into a red silk smoking jacket.

She took the drink and tried not to stare at his hideous jacket. There must have been a garage sale at the *Playboy* mansion. Five minutes, she figured, was all it would take to finish her drink and call a taxi.

"Is that like having my star on the Hollywood walk of fame?"

"It just means you're one of my special friends," he replied.

Truth be known, he had lots of photos of her. Stacked neatly in the drawer of his nightstand. Right beside the bed.

He covered the thought by flashing a loopy, casually lascivious grin that was supposed to pass for sophistication. But to Sabrina, he looked like a man whose hemorrhoids had just flared up.

"So you had all these pictures taken?" she asked, turning her back to him and studying the pictures. She had a hard time believing any of them were his friends, much less his "special friends." They all looked like they were being goosed by a guy with a dead animal on his head. And the ones that were signed "With love" all seemed to have been written in the same handwriting.

"No, most of them are candid shots, taken of my friends at charity events and premieres, and I just got caught in the flash. They kept sending me the pictures, so I started to stick them on the wall as a courtesy. Got to be a tradition, after a while."

He had a photographer on retainer, of course, just to take candid pictures of him with stars, many of whom no longer ventured out in public for fear Boyd Hartnell would be there, ready to slip his arm around their waists for a photo. But after a while, even Boyd began to believe his lie was the truth.

"Now, whenever I go out, they kind of make a point of shoving me in front of a camera," he laughed.

The dog nudged Sabrina's arm with his cold nose, so she absently reached out and started petting him. It startled Boyd so much he grabbed the couch for support.

"But you said you looked forward to putting my picture on the wall," she said, combing the dog's hair through her fingers. "That sounds premeditated to me."

The sight of her running her hands through Thor's lush, golden mane sent a shiver through Boyd's body that started at his groin and rippled all the way up through each expensive strand of hair on his head. He tried to summon the breath to speak.

"I just meant"—he sucked in more air—"that I hope we'll become good enough friends that we'll have the occasion to be out together and have our photo taken."

"And that I'll send it to you," she said, idly smoothing the dog's hair, "signed 'With love, your good friend Sabrina.' "

It was flirtation. It had to be. She was doing to the dog what she wanted to do to him.

"Yes," he moaned, quietly setting down his drink and dropping silently to his knees beside the dog.

Sabrina was staring at a picture of Boyd with Candice Bergen, trying to discern if her autograph was, indeed, identical to Roseanne Arnold's, when her hand slipped from the dog's soft hair to what felt like a paintbrush dipped in bacon grease.

Disgusted, she yanked her hand away, and was horrified to see Boyd at her feet, his eyes closed in ecstasy. She dropped her drink and backed away, but not quickly enough. He lunged at her, wanting more.

She sidestepped him, grabbed him by the back of his smoking jacket, and flung him into the couch as if he were just another ninja assassin. He slammed into the couch with such force it tipped over with him, covering him with cushions.

The dog, thinking it was a game, jumped up on her, wanting to be tossed around, too. She gently pushed the dog away and glared down at Boyd, pinned under the couch.

"If you want to talk to me again," she said, "do it through my agent."

She walked out and began her long walk down to Ventura Boulevard, the look in her eyes so fierce, no one would have dared assault her.

Boyd lay under the cushions, embarrassed and aroused at the same time. He didn't blame Sabrina, it wasn't her fault.

He glared from under the pillows at Thor, who sat beside him, panting happily, blissfully unaware of the fate Boyd had in store for him.

Chapter Eleven

Charlie Willis could think of only one person who would want to hurt him, and she was passing out home-baked cookies to the crew on a silver platter, a big, warm smile on her face.

She glided through the drawing room set, offering cookies to the gaffers adjusting the lights, the dolly grip moving the camera into first position, the sound guy figuring out where to dangle his boom, and the prop masters as they made sure every doodad was in the right place.

If Esther Radcliffe were auditioning for the part of Betty Crocker, she would have won it, hands down. Of course, it was only a coincidence that a reporter from *Esquire* was on the set that day, a woman who greedily snagged four cookies for herself. The star-struck journalist said she was taking a couple of extras for Annie Leibovitz, who was on the backlot, preparing for Esther's afternoon photo shoot. But judging by the reporter's body, Charlie figured the only place Leibovitz would see those cookies were on the reporter's hips.

Charlie tried to envision how the world-famous photographer would choose to immortalize Esther's charm. Sitting in a Rolls, a smoking gun in her hand, would be his suggestion. Somehow, he doubted Annie would be that perceptive. Esther would probably end up on the cover dressed only in cookie dough.

He caught Esther's eye, and she nearly spilled her cookies, and probably her lunch, on the gaffer. Charlie held the gaze for a long moment, then slipped behind the three-walled drawing room set and headed for the soundstage exit. He knew she'd come after him soon enough.

He paused at the heavy door to slip on a pair of sunglasses, but before he got the chance he was hit by a burst of blinding glare as someone walked into the soundstage.

"You're the last person I expected to see on the lot," the person said softly, with genuine surprise.

It took a long two seconds before Charlie's eyes adjusted enough for him to see that the voice belonged to Sabrina Bishop, whose skin-tight black leather wasn't helping him distinguish her from the darkness. But he wanted to.

"Especially after what happened," she added, as if she needed to. "Shit. That wasn't what I meant to say. What I meant to say was, I'm very sorry."

"So am I," Charlie said, then surprised himself by adding, "But not as sorry as the person responsible for it is going to be."

Sabrina crinkled her brow, confused. "I thought it was an accident."

"A loaded gun is never an accident."

Who says shit like that? Certainly not me, Charlie thought. And yet he just had. It was happening again. Just like it had before. It was as if he had a split personality, Derek Thorne on one side, Charlie Willis on the other. Only this time, he wasn't saying it to seduce someone. He was just being honest. But he never would have spoken like that *before*. Then again, *before*, he had never killed anyone.

"You sound like a man investigating a murder," she said, a tentative smile playing on her lips. He figured what he had said was too silly even for her to take seriously.

"I am."

"Isn't it a little late to be getting into character?"

Charlie shrugged. "I figure it's about time."

Now that he could see clearly, he noticed just how tight her leather jumpsuit was. "How's Miss Agatha treating you?" he asked.

"She hasn't taken a shot at me yet," Sabrina said. "If that's what you mean."

"She will," he said. "Watch your back."

He slipped on his sunglasses and stepped outside. Sabrina trailed after him. "You're really serious, aren't you."

Charlie stopped and turned around slowly. She was squinting at him either because she couldn't make sense out of him or the sun was right in her eyes.

"Is that why you're here? You think she had something to do with what happened?"

"Yeah, I do," he replied.

Sabrina shook her head. "I must be missing something. We're talking about Esther Radcliffe, right? The lady who bakes cookies for the crew? The lady who knitted me an afghan?"

"The lady who shot me in the stomach."

"You're unbelievable," she said. But there was no edge in her voice. He could almost swear she said it with affection.

"I'm not asking you to believe me, Miss Bishop. In fact, I don't care whether you do or not." He met her eyes and smiled. "It's just that I like you, and I would hate to see you get hurt."

And with that, he walked away. Sabrina stared after him, a bit dumbfounded. She couldn't figure this guy out. One minute he was talking tough, like some TV character, and the next, so sweet and polite she could melt.

Miss Bishop.

In a business where absolute strangers and casual acquaintances hug and kiss each other with false sincerity and feigned affection, genuine courtesy was something she was not used to. It was almost, well, gallant. And she liked it. He was a sharp contrast to most of the men she met in the business. The image of Boyd Hartnell sitting at her feet, offering his head for petting, came immediately and sickeningly to mind.

It was only after Charlie disappeared behind the soundstage that she realized she'd forgotten to give him back his shirt.

She would just have to run into him again.

Sabrina was still standing there when Esther marched out, unconsciously banging her silver tray against her hip. "Where is he?"

"You mean Charlie?" she asked.

"Yes, dear, Charlie Willis." Esther forced a smile. "I wouldn't want him to leave before I had a chance to express my deepest sympathies to him."

For an instant, Sabrina thought she was staring at the Grinch Who Stole Christmas. Just as quickly, it passed.

"He went off toward the dressing rooms," Sabrina mumbled. "You could probably catch him if you hurry."

Esther hurried off. Sabrina watched her go. Esther might have been able to hide the fury from showing in her face, but as she marched away, hunched over like a prizefighter heading into ring, her body betrayed her.

And in that moment, Sabrina felt that first cold shiver of realization. Suddenly, Charlie's story didn't seem so unbelievable after all.

Charlie was waiting for Esther in her bus. He was admiring one of her Warhols, his feet up on an antique maple table, sipping Evian from a Baccarat crystal goblet, when she came in.

"No cookies for me?" he said, the first words he'd spoken to her since that fateful day in Coldwater Canyon.

She pulled the door shut behind her and frisbeed the silver platter at him. He shifted slightly to one side, and the tray whizzed past him into the mahogany-paneled wall. It didn't even make a scratch.

"You've got too much from me already," she hissed.

"Bullets are cheap," he replied, swinging his legs off the table and leaning over to pick up the silver platter.

She yanked open a drawer and fished out a pack of Marlboros and a Bic. "You know what I'm talking about." She lit up and blew smoke at him. "You're nothing but a greedy goddamn leech. You took one look at me and saw your meal ticket."

"That's right, I saw you speeding and thought, Hey, if I give her a ticket maybe she'll shoot me and if I don't bleed to death on the street, maybe I can get my own TV series," he replied. "Maybe if I'm real lucky, I thought, they'll dig the bullet out of my gut and I can get an attractive paperweight out of the deal, too."

He set the tray down on the table and met her gaze.

She blew some more smoke at him, her eyes blazing with hatred. "You provoked me, and got what you deserved. You obviously didn't learn anything from the experience."

"So you loaded my prop gun with live ammo to teach me another lesson," he said. "Only this time, you killed a man."

It was her turn to smile. "If it was me, it would've been the day player holding the loaded gun, not you. And you know why."

"Because I didn't die when you shot me."

There was a tentative knock at the door. "The director is ready whenever you are, Miss Radcliffe," a nervous A.D. called from outside.

"I'm on my way, darling," she chirped pleasantly toward the door, then she turned on Charlie, all the rage back in her face.

"Stop playing coy, you're not an actor and never will be." She snubbed out her fresh cigarette on the tray, leaning close enough to him that he was inhaling the smoke that curled out of her nostrils. She looked like a gray-haired bull, ready to charge.

"You'll get your fifty grand," she snarled, "but if you try to take me for another penny, I promise you the next bullet that comes your way won't miss."

She abruptly turned to the door, fumbled with the brass knob, then slammed her body against it in fury. She forced open the door and stormed out, leaving Charlie behind in her smoky dressing room, trying to figure out what she'd meant.

The squadroom set of *My Gun Has Bullets,* known to cast and crew as the "cop shop," was dark and empty, which only added to its authenticity.

Without the artificial brightness of movie lights and the reality of a film crew, Charlie almost felt as if he were walking through a downtown precinct that had been suddenly, inexplicably abandoned in the midst of a busy day.

Signs of life were everywhere as Charlie wandered around the squadroom. The desks were cluttered with bulging files, family photos, and personal mementos. Dirty, unwashed cups cluttered the table by the stained coffee machine. Half-eaten doughnuts were scattered around the room. Mug shots, APBs, and WANTED posters adorned the bureaucratic gray of the walls.

But the official-looking files were stuffed with script pages and fake police reports; fashion models and would-be actors posed for the family photos; and the personal mementos on everyone's desks were scavenged from the prop warehouse. The stains on the cups and the coffee machine were painted on. Dozens of real doughnuts could be bought for the cost of just one of the plastic pastries around the room.

Charlie had learned very quickly that movie magic was all in the details, the little things that barely register consciously, but that tell the viewer that what he sees is real enough to believe, even if it isn't. Jackson Burley, the producer of the show, once went into a rage over a toilet. In the story, the assassin was hiding his gun in the toilet tank. But it was the drainpipe from the toilet going straight into the wall that got the art director kicked off the show and banned at Pinnacle Studios.

The average schlub watching the show doesn't know a lot of things, Burley told Charlie. He doesn't know what dials and gauges are on the space shuttle's dashboard, so you can put as many blinking lights and switches on it as you want. He doesn't know how much $25 million weighs, so you can have your hero carry that in a satchel, even though it would never fit and would weigh about five hundred pounds. But just about everyone knows what a toilet looks like—and they know that the drainpipe goes straight into the floor.

It's one of the details that will pull the viewers out, Burley explained, and once they are out, you can't get 'em to believe the sky is blue. And if viewers can't suspend their disbelief, they can't enjoy the show and will tear apart the entire story, if they bother to continue watching at all.

Charlie thought about that as he strode into Derek Thorne's office, which had a commanding view of downtown Los Angeles, the painted backdrop perpetually sunny and smog-free. Charlie settled into the chair behind the desk and surveyed the room.

Derek Thorne proudly displayed his various citations, degrees, and commendations on his wall. Below them, a bookcase sagged under wide, heavy binders of case reports, books of legal statutes, and bound issues of *Master Fisherman.*

Amid the papers on the desk were a few fishing lures Thorne was working on when he wasn't arresting serial killers and psychopaths. It was an endearing hobby that gave Derek Thorne's character "layers," or so Charlie was told. Once, Thorne had been able to defuse a nuclear bomb with a triple-tease, kokanee-killer fishing lure he had been working on.

Charlie sat in the office of a fictional character, surrounded by odds and ends of an imaginary man's nonexistent life. And yet, he felt at ease. For the first time in days, he began to relax.

He took the bullet out of his pocket and, holding it in front of his eyes between his thumb and index finger, studied it. This was the bullet Esther had fired into his gut, the one doctors dug out of him, the one that had been encased in plastic as a conversation piece. The one that had changed his life.

It was the only evidence he had that Esther Radcliffe had shot him. He had no evidence at all that she was also responsible for killing Darren Clarke, just a strong hunch. Detective Derek Thorne had brought down entire criminal conspiracies on less than that.

But that was television, where reality was shaped to fit the needs of a fifty-eight-page teleplay.

If this were another sizzling episode of *My Gun Has Bullets*, Thorne would send the bullet down to the lab, where Sparks, the cherubic comic relief on the show, would run a battery of tests on the slug. Sparks would then spit out pages of exposition, salted with witty metaphors, that would lead Thorne to his next car chase, mob hit, or ticking bomb.

"The bullet is a semi-jacketed .38. Nice, clean striations, piece o' cake to match," Sparks would say. *"We're just one gun short of a collar."*

Problem was, Charlie didn't have a lab. Or Sparks.

Charlie flipped through the files on the desk. The folders were stamped with subtly altered versions of official LAPD seals and labels. He shuffled through the papers inside the folders, weeding out script pages and studio memos, until he had a file that was filled only with fake police reports.

Then he slid open the top desk drawer and pulled out Thorne's clip-on ID and his badge. They looked as real as the ones he used to have. He stuck them in his pockets, then snatched up Thorne's impenetrable shades from the desk and slipped them on. As he walked out, he stopped at Hewitt's desk, the buxom forensics specialist, and took a couple of ziplock evidence bags from the tabletop, slipping his bullet into one of them.

"I'm gonna run this down to Sparks, see if he can come up with any leads," Thorne would say to Hewitt.

"I'll give you a lead," she'd say, a coy smile on her face as she handed him her home number. *"The question is, when are you gonna follow it up?"*

"I never mix business and pleasure," Thorne would say.

"I promise not to wear my badge," she'd say. *"Or anything else."*

Outside the soundstage, the two "show" cars belonging to Derek Thorne were parked beside a couple of police cruisers and motorcycles. They were LTDs, and like all the cars on the show, were supplied free of charge by Ford in exchange for promotional consideration. Somebody in Detroit actually thought people might buy one of those asphalt-going barges if they saw Derek Thorne driving one.

One of Thorne's LTDs was for typical driving scenes, and had special mounts under the car for the camera rigging. The other car was equipped for action sequences, smashing through storefronts and screeching around curves. Both were the dull blue stripped-down models, with flat vinyl bench seats. Typical bland, city-owned sedans, common in every city in America. Exact, right down to the fake antennas, the fake radio, and the meaningless code numbers on the trunk. Only the red flashing light that the passengers in the front seat could whip out and smack on the roof was real.

Again, attention to detail.

Charlie peered in the window of the stunt car. The key dangled from the ignition. The last thing anybody expected was for someone to drive off with it.

Chapter Twelve

While Otto and Burt prepared for their final *Frankencop* stunt, the rest of the crew stayed the hell away from them. They smelled of death, and no one wanted to take the chance that it was communicable.

The first thing people noticed about Otto and Burt was that there was nothing about either of them that was symmetrical.

The left side of Otto's head was slightly lower than the right, and it seemed as though his elbows were in different places on each arm. His mouth was definitely crooked, and his one, bushy eyebrow was etched across his face at a right angle.

Burt's feet were each a different size, so he had to buy two pairs of shoes. Or, as was his preference, make his own shoes out of bits and pieces of old pairs. Each of Burt's eyes was at a radically different distance from his twisted nose, which curved above his harelip at such a painful angle people winced just looking at it. They couldn't help imagining how agonizing the accident must have felt that caused such a deformity.

What Otto and Burt resembled most were people who, like some malfunctioning machine, had been taken apart and then put back together, with a few things left over on the table. Which was, in fact, not far from the truth.

The *Frankencop* location was out at the farthest edges of Canyon Country, a scorching wasteland northeast of Los Angeles that was so inhospitable it could double for the untamed West and the surface of Mars.

Soon Otto and Burt would be in cars, charging toward each other on either side of a gorge, colliding in midair and falling a hundred feet to the ground below. Otto was standing in for Frankencop, Burt for this week's badguy, Metalface. Frankencop's brilliant plan for stopping Metalface from escaping was to ram into him head on. It would be an exciting conclusion to the episode and, most likely, their lives.

Otto and Burt were renowned in Hollywood for doing death-defying stunts at bargain basement prices. Even more astounding was their willingness to do gags that made even the most experienced, daredevil stuntmen weak-kneed with terror. Stunts of such suicidal proportions that no insurance company would back them, no medical plan would accept them, and no other professional stuntman would work with them.

Which suited Otto and Burt just fine. They didn't want any of their competitors to discover their secret.

But Eddie Planet knew it.

He was the one who discovered them, years ago. They were carpenters, part of a crew he hired just before the '88 writers' strike to add a second story to his house. He always had an impeccable sense of timing.

Unemployed for six months, Eddie had lots of opportunity to see Otto and Burt in action. He watched Otto fall off his roof onto the cement patio . . . Burt drive a nail through his hand and yank it out with a hammer . . . Otto electrocute himself on a power line and fall into the swimming pool . . . and Otto plow over Burt with the tractor, get out to check on him, and get mowed over himself because he forgot to set the brake.

When Eddie carted them off to the UCLA emergency room, he was surprised to see them greeted warmly by name. The nurses explained to Eddie that the inseparable twosome were such frequent visitors, and had been the subject of so many med-student dissertations, that they were treated on the house.

Eddie knew then that these guys had missed their calling. As soon as the strike was over, he began using them as cut-rate stuntmen. Human crash dummies willing to do anything the script or the director wanted. Regardless of the danger.

Otto and Burt's secret to doing stunts was deceptively simple.

They *didn't* do stunts.

Everything they did was real.

Otto and Burt simply had no pain threshold. They'd singed their nerves off long ago.

No one, not even Eddie, knew their last names. Legend had it they were born attached, sharing the same brain stem until they were torn apart. Otto got a slightly bigger chunk, but that was also a topic of much conjecture.

Otto and Burt were paid strictly in cash, under the table, to avoid messy problems with unions, studios, insurance companies, and banks concerned with such niceties as safety and liability. Where Otto and Burt's money went, nobody knew. They lived in a mobile home in Chatsworth and drove cars that looked salvaged from the scrap heap. What they did for fun not even Eddie knew, and few people had the stomach to imagine.

Eddie wasn't on the set this particular day, having no desire to be anywhere around when a public relations disaster might strike. But they were in his thoughts. Very much so.

Everyone on the *Frankencop* set was watching them zip into fireproof suits, strap on their helmets, and check out their steel reinforced Fords. But the check was just for show. The axles could be cracked, the tires bald, and the engine gushing oil—they wouldn't notice. They only wanted the chance to walk behind their cars and, unseen, take a final leak before the gag.

Then they did their ritual dance. An inept soft-shoe, a little pattycake, two jumping jacks, and then a quick spin that finished with John Travolta's pose from *Saturday Night Fever*.

"Too cool for words," Otto said, grinning his lopsided grin.

"Yeah," Burt replied.

They climbed into their cars and roared off in opposite directions. The director cued the four cameras. The cars spun around to face each other on either side of the gorge.

The director picked up a megaphone and yelled, *"Action!"*

Otto and Burt revved in place until their spinning wheels were smoking and then they shot forward, screaming with glee.

The two cars tore across the desert, weaving crazily, mowing over sagebrush, smashing through piles of stone, hurling toward the deadly fissure. The cars surged over the edge, tires spinning, dust hanging in the air behind them like a comet's trail, then smashed together into one crinkled mass of metal and flame that slammed into the ground with such force it pounded out a crater.

The dust settled. The metal creaked and groaned. Steam hissed. Pebbles rained down like hail.

The director called out *"Cut!"* and then there was a moment of apprehensive silence as all eyes watched the cars. After a moment, Otto pulled himself out of his car, with a dislocated shoulder and three broken fingers, and took off his helmet, leaving half his scalp inside. He peered into Burt's car and saw nothing. But then, to everyone's surprise, Burt emerged from behind a sagebrush, his nose at a new angle, a piece of metal lodged in his chest, and his shoes on fire.

Otto stomped on Burt's blazing feet. "I told you not to wear your dress shoes."

"I wanted to look good for the camera," Burt said, heading for the craft services table.

The special effects crew hurried past them to the wrecked cars and doused them with fire extinguishers.

Burt plucked the shard of metal out of his chest and tossed it in with the empty aluminum cans in the recycle bin. Then he grabbed a handful of potato chips with his bloody hand and headed for the stunt trailer.

Otto bent down over the icebox for a Coke, but couldn't get his right arm to work. That's when he realized his shoulder was dislocated. He looked around, finally spotting a solid tree he could use.

He was slamming himself against a cactus, trying to jam his shoulder back into its socket, when an assistant director came up to him with the cellular phone.

It was Eddie Planet inviting them to lunch at La Guerre.

Charlie stopped at a pay phone at the El Pollo Loco around the corner from the North Hollywood precinct and put in a call to Detective Emil Grubb. To his relief, the cop was out.

He got back into his LTD, and took a bite out of a chicken taco, careful to dribble some sauce onto his shirt, which he had already taken off and wrinkled up before leaving the studio.

Charlie had never met a detective who looked too good, except on television. But most viewers weren't cops, so they could buy it. A cop wouldn't.

Satisfied that he looked anything but stylish, he drove around the precinct and swung into the lot reserved for official police vehicles, sliding the car snugly into a space between two other identical LTDs.

Checking himself in the mirror, he snapped on his ID and slipped his badge onto his belt. The sunglasses fit him a little too well, so he took them off and slightly bent one of the arms. He slid the shades back on, pleased to see them slightly askew. The unloaded gun under his arm made a nice bulge under his jacket, and the knit tie was just ugly and dated enough to be unnoticeable. He picked up the thick, ratty file on the passenger seat and took one last look at it. He reached into his jacket pocket for the plastic bag containing Esther's bullet and dropped it among the papers in the folder.

It was all in the details. Now, he just had to be as full of verisimilitude as everyone said he was. Charlie took a deep breath and then heard some unseen director snap, *Action!*

He got out of the car, hiked up his pants, and walked with the same weary, bad-ass swagger as the detectives around him. The key to the walk was imagining your underwear was riding up your ass from sitting too long.

Safe behind his shades, Charlie glided into the station without meeting anyone's gaze and headed purposefully across the faded linoleum floor toward the detective bureau. He could almost feel the Panavision camera on a track behind him, following him into the wide, busy room. A cloud of cigarette smoke hung just below the fluorescent lights, fed by a dozen rumpled detectives, puffing away as they finger-pecked their reports out on heavy electric typewriters that apparently predated plastic or electronics. A city ordinance outlawed smoking in public buildings, but the detectives didn't seem too concerned about anyone citing them.

Charlie went to the back of the bureau, snatched a foam cup, and helped himself to the pot of coffee, setting his file down and using the opportunity to casually survey the room. Everything seemed faded here—the walls, the papers, the faces. The detectives were occupied with their reports, or on the phone, or talking with suspects or victims, who sat in straight-back chairs beside the gray, steel desks.

Charlie wasn't in a hurry and was completely at ease, or so he wanted to seem. Cases often intersected across precinct lines, so it was common for a detective from outside the station to walk in and make himself at home. And that's what Charlie was, just another detective on a case. Only he wasn't the investigating officer, he was the suspect.

No one even seemed to notice he was there. If someone had, and questioned him enough, he could find himself arrested for impersonating a police officer, something he'd been paid handsomely for only a few days earlier. It was also a skill he'd honed for a dozen years in the Beverly Hills PD.

He picked up the file, and coffee in hand, ambled over to the row of filing cabinets. Atop them were the big, thick binders containing the current case files. Black for homicide, blue for robbery, red for vice. It didn't take long to find the binder that contained his homicide report.

The information it contained held only one surprise. The .38 Charlie used that day wasn't his prop gun—it had been switched with a real weapon containing live ammo. Unfortunately, the serial number had been removed, making the gun virtually untraceable. The only fingerprints on the gun belonged to Charlie and Itchy Matthews, the propman. Still, Grubb had the lab boys trying to match the bullet with slugs recovered from other crime scenes.

Charlie was also relieved to learn he was not a suspect in the killing, though Grubb was checking him out to see if anyone might have a motive for setting him up. Charlie doubted Grubb would stumble on the one person with the biggest motive of all. But even Charlie wasn't discounting the possibility someone else was involved.

Esther had implied that somebody was blackmailing her for $50,000 and that it was him. That meant there was at least one other person in the mix, maybe more. And that Esther had a secret she wanted to keep. How it all figured in, he didn't know. But he was going to find out.

According to the report, Grubb had already given up on the possibility that the someone out of the victim's past was responsible for the murder. Apparently, Darren Clarke had led an exemplary life, until he unknowingly sacrificed it for a television show, a soon-to-be-released video, and an *Inquirer* article written by his girlfriend.

Charlie committed the case number to memory, closed the binder, and headed down the busy corridor toward the forensics lab, which meant crossing the front lobby. This was when he'd be most vulnerable, cutting through a crowd of civilians and then past the desk sergeant serving as gatekeeper to the door beyond.

"Hey," someone said to him, "I know you."

The words he'd been afraid of hearing for the last fifteen minutes. He turned to see a ten-year-old boy standing beside a woman with a black eye, who was filling out a report at the front desk. The little boy, in a dirty polo shirt and torn jeans, leaned against his mother and stared up at Charlie with wide eyes. Charlie would have turned and kept walking, but he saw the uniformed sergeant glance up at him, the first time he'd been noticed since he entered the precinct.

Charlie smiled at the boy. "You do?" It was a lame response, but he couldn't think what else to say. With the officer's eye on him, he couldn't ignore the kid.

"I've seen you before," the boy said. "On TV."

"Yeah," Charlie replied, shooting a look at the sergeant. "So did my mother and every drug dealer in town. One second of fame, twelve years as an undercover cop shot to hell."

The sergeant shook his head. "Damn reporters." He tapped a button on the floor and buzzed Charlie through the door leading to forensics.

"You're a thorn in the side of justice," the boy cried out enthusiastically.

"I sure am, kid," Charlie said, closing the door behind him.

Once in the hallway, safe from the kid, he felt relief wash over him, but he didn't dare show it, for fear the cops in the hallway would read something on his face.

He found his way to the forensics department and marched through the door like a man in a hurry. The cramped, windowless room looked like a high school science lab and smelled like a doctor's office. Microscopes and vials lined the long tables and countertops. In the back half of the room, evidence was kept on shelves, safely locked behind an iron cage. Everything from kilos of cocaine pulled from the seat cushions of a teenage drug dealer's Mercedes to the fluffy pillow a Chatsworth plumber used to smother his two-timing wife. And somewhere on those shelves was the bullet and the gun Charlie had used to kill Darren Clarke.

This room was Harry Spinoza's domain, and he was hunched over a microscope looking at a nose hair when he noticed Charlie come in. Spinoza looked like he hadn't seen sunlight in years.

"What can I do for you?" Spinoza asked.

"Detective Derek Thorne, Beverly Hills PD," Charlie said. "I'm working a homicide, happened about three weeks ago. A twenty-three-year-old actress got popped in her apartment. We've got zip, except for the bullet we pried outta the starlet's skull."

He fished the ziplock bag out of the file and dropped it on the counter. "I wanna see if it matches one you dug out of an actor a few days ago."

His story was brushing so close to the truth that Charlie expected Spinoza to start laughing and arrest him where he stood. Instead, Spinoza stood up and pulled a key ring out of his pocket.

"Case number?" Spinoza asked.

Charlie opened his file, as if reading off the number from a piece of paper. "78039845," he replied. Thankfully, Spinoza watched TV even less often than he ventured into the sunlight.

Spinoza walked over to the cage, unlocked it, and disappeared behind some shelves. "You know anything about nose hairs?" Spinoza asked.

"No," replied Charlie, wondering who *would*.

"Take a peek through the scope," Spinoza said.

Charlie did. "It looks like a hair."

"An entire murder case hinges on whether that hair, found in the victim's carpet, matches those taken from the suspect," Spinoza said. "The theory is the killer was standing around, picking his nose, waiting for the victim to show up. That'd show premeditation, too."

Spinoza emerged holding an evidence bag, marked 78039845, containing several bullets, a couple of which were bent out of shape by their travels through Darren Clarke's various organs, bones, and major arteries.

"Imagine going to prison, knowing you were done in by a nose hair," Spinoza said, opening the bag, selecting a bullet and setting it up on a scope. "I once nailed a guy with a piece of lint. It takes real expertise to do that."

Spinoza took Charlie's bullet and put it beside the other one under the comparison scope. He delicately turned the knob that adjusted the focus and brought the two images end to end.

"Do they match?" Charlie asked.

"I'm not sure yet," Spinoza said. "We're still taking nose hairs from everyone who knew the victim."

"The bullets," Charlie said.

"The microscopic stuff, trace evidence, that's the challenge," Spinoza said. "The stuff the perps don't even know they're leaving behind. Bullets are easy, hell, they're practically billboards. They get all scraped up by imperfections on the barrel—the striations on the slug are as good as a fingerprint. Where's the challenge in that?"

"Do they match?" Charlie asked impatiently.

Spinoza glanced up at him, irritated. "You don't need to be an expert to figure that out." He motioned him over to take a look. "See for yourself."

Charlie peered into the microscope. The two bullets were lined up, end to end. They matched.

There was no doubt about it. Esther Radcliffe had switched the prop gun with her own, the one she had shot Charlie Willis with. He had her.

"Looks like a match to me," Charlie plucked his bullet out of the microscope and put it back in its bag. "Thanks for your help."

Spinoza shrugged. "It was nothing. Bring me something tough next time—then I'll strut my stuff."

Charlie shoved the bag in his pocket and stepped into the hallway. He had solved his first murder. Beyond absolving himself of guilt, the revelation would ruin Esther Radcliffe and probably propel the series, and himself along with it, into worldwide popularity.

He was so caught up in his euphoria, he didn't notice Emil Grubb until they were almost on top of each other.

They passed without making eye contact, and then Charlie ducked into the nearest door he could find. When Grubb did a double take an instant later, Charlie was gone. Grubb shrugged it off and continued on his way.

Unfortunately, Charlie stepped into the robbery detail, where the detectives were slipping on Coverall vests and checking their weapons. Lieutenant Budd Flanek tossed Charlie a vest.

"Glad to see you," Flanek said, "we can use all the bodies we can get."

Chapter Thirteen

Charlie sat in the passenger seat of Lieutenant Flanek's unmarked car, weaving at fifty miles an hour through the slow-moving traffic on Lankershim Boulevard toward Noam's Jewelry Emporium. Two other, unmarked units were following close behind.

"I really appreciate the assist," Flanek said, never taking his eyes off the road. "The guys see a uniform, they're likely to start blowing people away."

The silent alarm had come in less than five minutes ago. Anyone crazy enough to pull a jewelry heist in broad daylight was bound to be armed and, more important to Charlie right now, wouldn't think twice about killing a cop.

Especially an unarmed one.

"No problem," Charlie replied. "That's why they pay me the big bucks."

It was just the kind of thing Derek Thorne would say. But Charlie Willis was scared. Which was worse, he asked himself, to go to jail for impersonating an officer, or to get killed pretending to be one? The answer that came back, from deep within his psyche, surprised him.

You are a police officer, Charlie. You always have been.

Flanek pulled up a block away from the jewelry store. One of the unmarked cars passed them and parked another block up. From where they were parked, they could see the two-story brick facade of Noam's Jewelry Emporium. The shades were closed, and people casually walked by, unaware of what was unfolding inside.

Charlie looked for the getaway car, but didn't see any cars with engines running, or anybody sitting in a parked car waiting for something to happen. Except, of course, for the police.

"Did you work the Rodeo Drive thing a few years ago?" Flanek asked.

Charlie had, as a traffic control officer. Two robbers walked into a high-end jewelry store at ten A.M., carrying automatic weapons. They were supposed to be in and out in three minutes. But the manager tripped a silent alarm, and the police were there in two. The police stormed the place, and the robbery turned into a hostage situation. Four people were killed before it was over two days later.

"Yeah," Charlie replied.

"We don't want that here." Flanek took out his gun and checked it, as if the bullets might have mysteriously dropped out of his gun during the drive. "We wait for them to come out, let 'em think they've got it made, then we take 'em down."

"Works for me," Charlie said.

They got out of the car. So did the guys in the car behind them and the two detectives in the sedan up the street. Flanek motioned the two ahead of them to go around back, then motioned to the other two detectives to take positions flanking the front of the jewelry store.

Charlie pulled out his gun and gave Flanek a determined look. "I'll go around back," he said.

Flanek nodded and sprinted up the street.

Charlie hurried around the corner and, once out of sight of the other detectives, holstered his gun, crossed the alley, and kept on walking. He had no intention of pushing his luck. Even if he managed to survive the arrest, he was bound to be uncovered as a fraud once he was back at the precinct, filling out the paperwork. Better to just walk away, hop on a bus, and head back home.

It might have turned out that way, too, if the bus stop hadn't been on the other side of the overpass, which crossed the cement banks of the storm drain.

Perhaps then he wouldn't have seen the three men in Department of Water & Power uniforms crawling out of the sewer pipe, wearing goggles and filter masks, and clutching bulging knapsacks. They splashed across the shallow canal stream and climbed up into a sewer pipe on the opposite side.

He didn't have to be Miss Agatha to deduce they'd tunneled into the jewelry store through the sewer pipes, and that Flanek and his men were creeping up on an empty building. By the time they went inside, the felons would be long gone.

Without thinking, Charlie started to scale the cyclone fence that protected the canal. He was straddling the top when a thought hit him. Derek Thorne would have no problem crawling after the bad guys through the sewage, unarmed, and subduing them with whatever he had on him—his necktie, his badge, and a handful of shit. Charlie Willis, on the other hand, would get himself killed.

There had to be another way.

From his vantage point on the fence, he spotted a tiny hardware store across from the bus stop. He hopped off the fence and ran down the street. Charlie hoped he could run faster than three louts in DPW outfits could crawl through a slick, narrow pipe.

He burst into the mom-and-pop hardware store, pushing his way past customers and clerks to the tool department, where he grabbed a pipe wrench and ran out again, holding up his badge as he passed the shocked cashier.

"Police business," Charlie yelled as he slammed against the doors, back onto the street.

He went straight to the fire hydrant and twisted off the valve. A torrent of water shot out of the hydrant and splashed into the street, streaming into the drain. By the time that happened, Charlie was already running to the next hydrant, a short block away. He twisted the valve off that one, too, letting the water spray out onto the hot asphalt.

Charlie turned to the nearest person he could find, a teenage boy with a curious look on his face.

"You're deputized," Charlie said, handing him the wrench.

"Your gun has bullets," the astonished kid said.

"I wish," said Charlie, wondering if there was a kid in America who went to bed before ten P.M. on Thursdays. "Open every hydrant you can. Don't stop until you hear sirens."

The kid burst into a big smile and dutifully ran to the next hydrant. Charlie rushed back to the overpass, pulling out his empty gun as he ran, wondering what he'd do with it when he got there, out of breath and out of ammo.

Charlie arrived at the overpass railing and was relieved to see he wouldn't be needing his gun, after all.

The three goons in DPW suits had been coughed out of the drain-pipe like a wad of phlegm. They were sprawled on the hard concrete, yelping over their broken bones, and trying hard not to drown in the stream of water that spewed out over them, pinning them down and washing the diamonds from their ripped bags into the cement stream that snaked through the city and out to sea.

In a few days, some lucky beachcomber would find something sparkling amid the raw sewage, soiled condoms, used syringes, and dead seagulls that usually littered the Santa Monica shoreline.

Charlie was hunched over the railing, catching his breath, when he saw Flanek and two detectives jogging his way on the other end of the overpass. Cries of pain from the canal caught their attention before they noticed him. They stopped and went to the rails, where they were stunned to see the three hapless felons writhing and sputtering in the wash.

All the cops would have to do was glance up now and they'd see Charlie.

That's when an RTD bus rumbled to the curb, belching out enough brown exhaust to obscure Charlie from view as he climbed inside. He hunched down in his seat and stayed that way until the bus hit Ventura Boulevard.

Somewhere, in the back of his mind, he heard a director yell, *Cut!*

The shiny brass plaque read RESERVED FOR EDDIE PLANET and was propped between the salt and pepper shakers on a table in the back of the La Guerre dining room, right by the window that looked out on Ventura Boulevard.

Eddie had the plaque made during the *Saddlesore* days, when he could command the best table at the Brown Derby, and wanted the whole town to know it. Since then, he had carted it around to every restaurant that would run him a tab. And there the plaque would stay, until either the restaurant, or Eddie's bank account, went bust.

Over the years, the plaque had traveled to dozens of restaurants, from the Brown Derby to Chasen's, Ma Maison to La Serre, the Columbia Bar & Grill to the private room of the Studio Commissary and, in his darkest days, to the Seafood Broiler down the street from his house.

But now his plaque was back, prominently displayed at La Guerre, the restaurant of the moment. There was a time when his plaque would have been at the table with the best view of the door, where he could see and be seen, but his star had not risen that high again just yet. He had to settle for a window seat, where he could see whose car pulled up, and where, if people pressed their faces against the restaurant's tinted glass, they could see him or his plaque.

The only way people saw his plaque now was if they were heading into the bathroom. Still, everyone, big and small, had to go piss sometime. And they couldn't do it without passing Eddie's name or, if they were lucky enough, Eddie himself.

Eddie paid the maître'd to place the plaque on his table twenty minutes before his reservation, just for appearances, so people would think he was so damn busy he couldn't possibly make it to lunch on time.

Today was no exception.

Otto and Burt arrived early, and were taken directly to Eddie's empty table, where they ate sixteen baskets of bread waiting for him to arrive. They also ordered themselves a couple of steaks, rare.

It was not that Otto and Burt were particularly hungry, but they always had room for food. Whatever was placed in front of them was consumed. If they misjudged the space in their stomach, they'd puke and then eat some more. Otto had read somewhere in a comic book that the ancient Roman aristocracy did that, so if it was good enough for the Romans, it was good enough for them.

Eddie Planet entered the restaurant, listening to a fanfare only he could hear. He swept through the dining room, a schmoozing wind that blew across every table. He clapped MBC chief Morrie Lustig on the back, shook hands with UBC's Don DeBono, shot a grin at Linda Lavin, and aimed a jaunty wink at Bob Newhart before landing at his table, where he found Otto and Burt popping squares of butter into their mouths like mints.

"Sorry I'm late," Eddie said, "but I got caught in dailies."

"No problem," Otto said. "We like this place."

"They have good butter," Burt added, rolling an oily cube in his mouth.

"Some places don't give you the squares unwrapped," Otto explained, "so you end up having to lick it off the paper. These are much better."

"They melt in your mouth," Burt said, "not in your hands."

"You ever see *Last Tango in Paris?*" Otto asked Eddie. "That was a big piece of butter. I would've liked to suck on that."

Eddie looked at Otto for a long moment, reminding himself it wasn't brilliant conversation he expected, or needed, from these two. He had an agenda, and if he didn't stick to it, he might just lose his nerve. So he just pushed on, deciding to ignore anything out of the ordinary they might say or do that would distract him from his mission.

"I'm glad you like the place, boys," Eddie said. "Because this is a very special day for us. It's sort of a celebration."

"What are we celebrating?" Burt asked.

"Moving on to the next phase of our relationship." Eddie reached out and clapped them both on the shoulders. "I'm pretty excited about the whole idea."

"We like you a whole lot, too." Otto narrowed his eyes suspiciously at Eddie. "But we don't buttfuck."

Eddie quickly shushed them and looked furtively around the room to see if anyone had heard them. Thankfully, no one had. He did, however, use the opportunity to blow a kiss to Bea Arthur and shoot an A-OK to Steven Bochco, who pretended not to see it.

"What I meant was," Eddie continued, almost whispering, "your days of risking your necks to make some schmuck actor look heroic are over. Pretty soon, you're gonna be the stars, and some guys will be breaking their bones for *you.*"

Otto and Burt stared at Eddie in shock.

"You guys have what it takes to be stars, and you know what that is?" He looked at their faces. They didn't even know what day it was. "Charisma. Raw charisma. You can't learn it. You can't buy it. It's God given. And I knew you two had it the first time I saw you."

The waiter arrived with the stuntmen's steaks, which were so rare Eddie expected to hear the cow scream when Burt took the fork in his fist and jammed it into the meat.

"We always knew we had the looks," Otto said nonchalantly, looking at Eddie as he cut his steak. "We just never took the time to learn the craft."

Eddie again found himself staring at Otto as the stuntman chewed.

"You certainly look like no other leading men I've ever seen. It leaps right off the screen."

"Son of a gun," declared Burt, then he crammed a chunk of bloody meat into his mouth.

"Hey, don't be surprised. Someone was bound to notice your appeal," Eddie said. "I'm just glad it was me."

"S-U-N-N of a G-U-N-N," Burt said.

"Yes, that would be one possible spelling." Eddie waved at Bob Eubanks and tried to keep his composure.

"It's a little project we've had in mind for ourselves," Otto said, unaware that he was cutting his next piece of meat from his own thumb. "Something that'd capture our understated elegance."

Eddie, horrified, tried not to stare at Otto, nor at the blood spreading from Otto's hand across the steak.

"*Peter Gunn.*" Burt started humming the classic, jazzy theme. "Dum dum dum dum dadada dum dum . . . He's so cool."

"Since we can't both play him, we decided one could be *Gunn,* and one could be *Sunn. Sunn of a Gunn,* get it?" Otto said, pausing to spit out his thumbnail. "You can decide who's who."

Oh Jesus, Eddie thought.

"I appreciate that, I really do," Eddie said, swallowing back the bile rising in his throat. "But there are a couple hurdles we gotta jump first."

Eddie waved over the waiter and ordered a vodka, straight up, then turned back to the guys.

"If it was up to me, *Sunn of a Gunn* would be on the air tomorrow," Eddie said, choosing his words carefully. "But you gotta please the big guys upstairs."

"We can rent a couple tuxedos and do a screen test," Otto said.

"Make all the girls wet." Burt dipped a french fry in what he thought was steak sauce on Otto's plate.

"What I was thinking was more along the lines of doing them a favor," Eddie said.

"We *would* be doing 'em a favor," replied Burt.

Otto and Burt promptly broke into a fit of snorting, nasal laughter that drew the attention of just about everybody.

Eddie was thankful to see the waiter setting his drink down. He abruptly knocked it back, and felt tears coming to his eyes. Why had he brought them here? He could have impressed them some other way without humiliating himself in front of the entire industry.

Then again, what did he care? Soon he'd *own* the fucking industry. And he needed Otto and Burt to do it. So he laughed along with them.

"Wit, charm, sophistication," Eddie said. "You guys got it all."

"Too cool for words," Otto said, noticing his bloody finger for the first time.

When the hilarity died down, and the other diners returned to their meals, Eddie got serious once again.

"You want the big boys to owe you something, so you do 'em a little favor," Eddie explained. "Next thing you know, you got a twenty-two-episode order for *Sunn of a Gunn.*"

"What's the favor?" Otto tied the napkin around his thumb as an impromptu bandage.

"Nothing really." Eddie lowered his voice, making sure no one was listening. "All you got to do is kill Boo Boo."

"The dog?" Burt asked.

"Yeah," Eddie replied. "The dog."

"No problem," Otto shrugged. "It's cheaper than buying beef."

Revised Network Primetime Schedule for Thursday and Sunday

MBC — Monumental Broadcasting Company
UBC — United Broadcasting Company
DBC — Dynamic Broadcasting Company

New shows in **bold**, new time slots in *italic*

Thursday

	8:00	8:30	9:00	9:30	10:00
DBC	Adopted Family	My Wife Next Door	Young Hudson Hawk		The Two Dicks
UBC	Boo Boo's Dilemma	*Energizer Bunny*	Broad Squad	*Anson Williams*	*Miss Agatha*
MBC	Johnny Wildlife		Dedicated Doctors		Frankencop

Sunday

	8:00	8:30	9:00	9:30	10:00
DBC	Red Highway		Movie		
UBC	*Rappy Scrappy*	**It's All Relative!**	*Smart Alec*	*MatchMaker*	**Socially Relevant**
MBC	Honeymooners: The Next Generation		Sheriff of Mars		Sleepwalker

Chapter Fourteen

UBC Disarms *My Gun*, Revamps Sked

My Gun Has Bullets *has been pulled from its coveted slot on UBC's blockbuster Thursday schedule, and in a move that has stunned industry insiders, will be replaced by* Miss Agatha, *a fixture on Sunday nights for years.*

The fate of My Gun Has Bullets *remains unclear, although production has ceased indefinitely. LAPD investigators seem convinced the shooting of actor Darren Clarke by star Charlie Willis was accidental, citing a lack of any clear motive for foul play, though the investigation continues.*

Police are concentrating their attention on the late Floyd "Itchy" Matthews, the property master best known for his work on Birth of a Nation, *who died of a massive coronary the afternoon of the tragedy.*

*UBC has been attempting to shore up sagging demographics by adding sexy femme Sabrina (*Torrid Embrace*) Bishop to the* Miss Agatha *cast, and skewing the storylines to a younger audience. The move is seen as a way to halt any erosion in the Thursday sked as a result of the tragedy. New episodes will begin airing in two weeks. In the meantime, the web will fill the* My Gun Has Bullets *slot with unsold pilots.*

The cops on DBC's Blacke and Whyte *are now* The Two Dicks, *irreverent PIs based in Jamaica, though pundits predict it won't save the skein from* Miss Agatha. *Funeral notices are also expected for MBC's* Frankencop.

The Thursday hits Rappy Scrappy *and* Smart Alec *are being moved to Sundays, where UBC hopes to clone its Thursday success story and steal some momentum from*

DBC's Red Highway *and sound the death knell for MBC's* Honeymooners: The Next Generation.

Rappy Scrappy *will kick off the night, leading into the new McLean Stevenson sitcom* It's All Relative, *about an extended family forced to live in a cramped Miami condo, followed by* Smart Alec *at nine, and the struggling Tuesday night sitcom* Matchmaker. *Buttressed between two hits, UBC head Don DeBono expects* It's All Relative *to be strong enough by season's end to carry a new night next year. The new drama* Socially Relevant, *about a team of caring social workers led by Sharon Gless, fills the ten o'clock hour.* Rappy Scrappy *and* Smart Alec *are being replaced on Thursday by* Energizer Bunny *and* The Anson Williams Show, *a move seen as a last-ditch effort to save the ailing skeins.*

There wasn't a single business in Los Angeles that didn't have at least one autographed photo of a celebrity patron on its walls. It didn't matter how big or small the star, just as long as you had a glossy or two to display.

The vacuum cleaner joint could boast that it regularly replaced Shirley Jones's lint-filled bags. *Lost in Space's* Dr. Smith rented the latest videos at the Wherehouse ("Your videos are out of this world!"). Superboy had his shirts pressed at Sally's Dry Cleaner ("You do a super job!"). Chuck Norris grazed the salad bar at Souplantation ("I get a kick out of your salads"). And Alec Baldwin liked the spaghetti at Filippo's, a narrow Italian restaurant tucked into the fold of a street corner minimall in the Valley.

So did Charlie, who wondered if Alec kept a stack of glossies with him at all times, ready to whip one out to any merchant who asked. Charlie speared his last meatball with his fork, and studying the wall of photos as he chewed, realized no one had ever asked him for his picture. He thought about offering one to Filippo, just for the fun of it, but decided he didn't want to risk having it refused.

Besides, the only photos he had of himself were a couple of Instamatic shots that Connie had taken, mostly of Charlie cooking at the BBQ grill or sleeping facedown in bed, twisted in the sheets, his butt exposed. Connie once spent an evening with a pair of scissors and Elmer's glue, making him a collage of BBQ and butt shots, which she proudly presented to him with great fanfare when he got home from patrol. The collage sparked a lot of laughs and lovemaking for a night or two, before it was put in the closet forever.

The bell above Filippo's door jangled as Detective Lou LeDoux blew into the restaurant, his pants clashing with the red-checked tablecloths and creating an instantaneous eyesore. He had always had that effect, sparking a violent conflict of pattern and color that assaulted the optic nerves of anyone within a glance. LeDoux felt one should stand out from the crowd, and dress accordingly. The least you could say was that he succeeded.

"Sorry I'm late," Lou said, settling into a seat opposite Charlie. "This old pervert was feeling up girls in the public pool out in Canoga Park. I was in the middle of arresting him and his brain exploded."

Charlie rubbed his temples. He could sympathize.

"Some vein just went pop," Lou added. "Is that what happened to you?"

"Could you please take off your jacket?" Charlie asked.

"Because that's the only explanation I can think of that explains why . . ." Lou continued, leaning close, his smile transforming into a tight grimace, ". . . you're being so *monumentally fucking stupid.*"

"I'll explain everything," Charlie said patiently, trying to not look at him. It gave him a headache. "If you'll just take off your jacket."

"That's it, isn't it? You've gone fucking nuts." Lou admired the fine cut of his blue-and-yellow-checked masterpiece. "This is a beautiful jacket, any sane person could see that."

"Take it off," Charlie implored. "Please."

"Let me guess." Lou took off his jacket and draped it over the back of his chair. "My jacket is sending messages to the mother ship."

"No, but I'm sure it can be seen from earth's orbit." Charlie was relieved that Lou LeDoux was wearing a plain white shirt underneath his hideous jacket. It was much easier on the eyes. He could think clearly again. "Lou, I need your help."

"I can't help you," Lou said. "You're too far gone. You need somebody who can prescribe drugs."

"I admit I may have stepped over the line—"

"Stepped over the line?" Lou interrupted incredulously. "You dug it up with a bulldozer. First you blow away some schmuck, then you go on national TV like some paranoid fuck and threaten to kill anyone who gets in your way. But is that enough? No, you got to go impersonate a police officer."

"That's what they pay me for," Charlie said wryly. LeDoux wasn't impressed with Charlie's wit.

"Do they pay you to ride along on a robbery-in-progress call?" Lou sneered. He had Charlie there. Charlie thought about explaining himself—that he stumbled into it only to avoid being recognized by Detective Emil Grubb, but that would only make things worse.

"The only reason I don't arrest you right now is that Flanek is taking credit for the bust," Lou LeDoux said, "and if I hauled your ass in, it would make the LAPD look like a bunch of clowns."

"And because I'm a brother to you," Charlie said.

"Brother-in-*law*," Lou shot back. "There's a big difference."

"Yeah," Charlie said. "For one thing, you couldn't sleep with my sister."

"Who says I am?" Lou said. "Thanks to you, not only is my career dying, so's my sex life."

"That'll change when you become a national hero," Charlie said. "Your career will soar and Zoe won't be able to keep her hands off you."

"Uh-huh." Lou leaned back in his chair. "And how does this miracle happen?"

Charlie reached into his pocket and pulled out the bag containing his bullet. He dangled it in his brother-in-law's face. "You take this bullet and solve a murder."

The truth about Charlie's transformation from real police officer to a fictional one was known only to a few agents, lawyers, Boyd Hartnell, Don DeBono and, of course, Esther Radcliffe. Lou LeDoux only knew that Charlie had been shot by some unidentified assailant, and that a casting agent, in the hospital for a boob job and tummy tuck, discovered him in the solarium, and immediately cast him in the *My Gun Has Bullets* pilot.

So Charlie began by telling Lou LeDoux the truth, that it was Esther Radcliffe who had gunned him down, and that his memory lapse was paid for with a television series. Then Charlie worked his way up to the good part.

"Esther Radcliffe switched my prop gun with her own, and this bullet proves it," Charlie said. "It matches the slugs pulled from Darren Clarke, the actor I shot. Now, all you have to do is arrest her for murder and grab all the glory."

Charlie waited to be forgiven, congratulated, and praised by his cynical brother-in-law. Instead, Lou LeDoux stared expressionlessly at Charlie for a long moment before speaking.

"Let me see if I got this straight," Lou said evenly. "You got shot by Esther Radcliffe, then you lied about it to get a TV series. So you're a lying fuck. Then this lady for reasons unknown—"

"I think she thinks I'm blackmailing her," Charlie interrupted. "But I'm not."

"Whatever," Lou continued. "She switches your prop gun for her gun, and you go and blow away your guest star. You stick your face in a news camera and tell the world you're gonna blow away whoever did this to you. That makes you a *crazy* lying fuck."

Charlie started to interrupt, as he didn't like where this conversation was going, but Lou held up his hand, as if stopping traffic. "Then you impersonate a police officer and tamper with police evidence."

"I had to compare my bullet with one from Darren Clarke," Charlie said, suddenly feeling on the defensive and angry about it. Why should he have to defend himself? He was bringing a murderer to justice and letting his brother-in-law take all the glory.

"And, as long as you were there, you went on a robbery call," Lou said. "That makes you a *felonious* crazy lying fuck."

Lou LeDoux started laughing. "And you expect me to arrest Esther Radcliffe based on that?"

"It's the truth," Charlie said desperately.

"Doesn't matter, it's a joke." Lou was still laughing. "Even if there was an incompetent D.A. who'd take it to court, and a brain-dead judge who'd hear the case, the bullet would be thrown out as inadmissible, now that you've tampered with the evidence. And as far as your accusations about Esther Radcliffe go, who's gonna corroborate your story? You? You're the least credible witness possible. So, who's the jury gonna believe? A sweet old lady loved by millions or you, a felonious crazy lying fuck?"

"She's guilty, Lou."

"Whoop-dee-doo," he said.

Charlie pocketed the bullet, feeling like a fool. Lou was right, he'd botched it. The whole case depended on a jury believing him, believing that Esther Radcliffe shot him in the stomach because she was late for a sale at Neiman Marcus.

Of course, that's not what he told the police then. No, he said he didn't remember anything. He couldn't possibly identify his attacker. But now, he goes and kills someone, and his memory miraculously returns.

Whoa, it's all coming back to me now. I know who shot me, it was Miss Agatha. And guess what, she killed this guy, too.

"You're right, Lou. But if this were television, it wouldn't be a problem," Charlie said. "The audience would buy it."

Lou studied his fuck-up brother-in-law, and took pity on him. He tossed Charlie a bone.

"You had some fun, made some money, and you're staying out of jail," Lou said. "It could be a lot worse."

Charlie was thinking about Esther Radcliffe passing out cookies while, somewhere in Los Angeles, Darren Clarke's family was grieving. He couldn't ignore what she had done, or let her get away with it just because he made some mistakes.

"Zoe loved your show, taped every single episode," Lou said, getting Charlie's attention.

"Really?" Charlie was surprised, and more than a bit touched. Charlie and his sister had fallen out of touch since he left home, escaped really, to go to the police academy. For a while she blamed him for leaving her alone; then when she got away, she replaced him with a cop of her own. They saw each other once or twice a year, but the closeness they had as children had become a distance that widened with each passing year.

"I think she believes you really are Derek Thorne," Lou said. "Then again, she thinks Lucy and Ricky Ricardo were a real couple."

"They were, Lou."

Lou LeDoux ignored the remark and fished in his jacket pocket for a card. He handed it to Charlie. "I got a friend, works for this outfit that handles mall security. He's always got a job for an ex-cop."

"That include ex-TV cops?" Charlie tossed the card back to Le-Doux. "I appreciate the thought, Lou, but I'm not ready to give up yet."

"Haven't you been listening? You're never gonna nail her for murder."

"No, probably not." Charlie said. "But I *will* bring her down. She's a killer, and if she gets away with this, eventually she's going to hurt someone else."

Suddenly, the image of Sabrina Bishop, in her tight leather outfit, flitted across his psyche. The poor girl was doomed. He had to stop Esther before she did anything to Sabrina.

"I don't want to hear it." Lou abruptly slipped on his jacket and got up. "I'm forced to be your brother-in-law, I don't have to be an accomplice."

"You have nothing to worry about," Charlie said. "I won't be breaking the law."

Esther Radcliffe had a secret, something so embarrassing she was willing to pay someone $50,000 to keep it quiet. Charlie was going to find out what that secret was.

"If it's anything like your brilliant moves so far, I'm sure I'll be hearing about it." Lou headed for the door, pausing for a moment before stepping outside. "Try to remember, Charlie, this is reality now."

Charlie watched his brother-in-law walk away and thought it was probably a good time for a commercial break.

Jack Blacke and Bobby Whyte were two irreverent cops who tackled crime with humor and rugged good looks. They were the Butch Cassidy and Sundance Kid of the LAPD, burning up the streets in their Mustang convertible, knocking bad guys senseless with a dizzying display of fast fists and even faster one-liners. And whether they were dodging bullets or bons mots, they always found time to seduce the beautiful women they inevitably encountered in their action-packed, carefree lives of heroic derring-do.

The on-screen chemistry and incredible pecs of the actors who played the two cops, Clive Martindale and Marc Thompson, accounted for what little appeal *Blacke and Whyte* had in its first thirteen episodes against *Frankencop* and *My Gun Has Bullets.* To capitalize on it, the network was going to send the two of them to Jamaica where, as *The Two Dicks,* they could banter and investigate shirtless and in shorts.

Perhaps as practice, the two dicks were bantering and investigating one another, naked in Clive Martindale's redwood hot tub, surrounded by the tall trees, complete darkness, and reassuring isolation of Topanga Canyon.

The same elements were working against them and in Delbert Skaggs's favor as he casually let himself in the front door of Martindale's rustic A-frame and quietly shut the door behind him. Plastic bags over his shoes and rubber gloves on his hands, he looked more comical than deadly, proving the old adage that looks could be deceiving.

As he strolled through the house, checking the rooms for other occupants, his mind was not on the two lovers frolicking in the burbling hot tub outside. They were going to be easy. So easy, in fact, he didn't bother to bring any tools of the trade—he'd just take 'em on the fly.

No, his mind was on the pleasures of delegating. It was a new experience for him, and he liked it. Because, in order to delegate, you had to have someone to delegate *to,* and that meant you had to have some kind of authority. He had never had authority before. Even if it was only over a moron like Eddie Planet, it was still a heady feeling for him.

For most of his career, Delbert had been a freelancer, never an executive. And in his experience, executives tended to get out of touch, so Delbert decided to delegate the easy stuff and keep his hand in by handling the tough assignments himself. Not that killing Martindale and Thompson would take much effort. But once an executive in his line of work lost his edge, or worse yet got soft, he became vulnerable, and didn't realize it until a guy like Delbert was slitting his throat.

Which was why he had let Eddie handle Boo Boo, and why Delbert decided to do the Two Dicks himself. Although Boo Boo was strategically the more important of the jobs, Delbert hated killing animals and, besides, if Eddie screwed it up, he could always take care of it personally later. And then reward himself by crushing Eddie's skull.

Satisfied that the house was empty, Delbert returned to the living room and glanced out on the deck. The Two Dicks were sipping champagne and nuzzling one another, ignoring the dangers of consuming alcoholic beverages in a Jacuzzi. Then again, they'd be dead long before the alcohol could pose any threat. Delbert would see to that.

He glanced around the room, with its high-beamed ceiling and hardwood floor. It was furnished like a Tahoe cabin, all woodsy and warm, with animal heads on the walls, wicker furniture, and afghans folded on the couches for those rare times when the temperature in L.A. dropped chillingly below 80.

That's when he heard the snap, crackle, and pop of an insect being electrocuted by a bug light. He looked outside and saw the bug light, artfully designed to look like an English coach lantern, hanging from a nail that had been hammered into a rafter a few feet away from the Jacuzzi. The blue fluorescent bulb cast a romantic glow over the Two Dicks, and lured insects into an electric grid that killed them cleanly and efficiently.

Delbert supposed it would work just as well on series stars. He studied the light more carefully. A long extension cord ran from the bug light along the rafter and then dropped to the floor, where it was plugged into an outdoor electrical outlet. All in all, pretty unsafe, especially if a professional hitman was around.

He opened the sliding glass doors without bothering to be quiet. The two men whirled around in surprise. But before they could say or do anything besides splash, Delbert reached up, carefully grabbed the bug light by its plastic base, and lobbed it into the hot tub.

He turned his back to look for a chair or stepladder, so he only heard the screams, the sizzle, and the splashing and missed the visual effects of his improvisation. Had he seen it, he would have admired the illusion of boiling water created by the combination of churning bubbles, smoke, and writhing bodies.

Delbert carefully lifted up a picnic table bench and set it down under the rafter, where the bug light had dangled. He found the nail the bug light had hung from and, using his hand, bent it downward to the point where the light fixture could have slid right off.

It was conceivable that bad hammering and the weight of the light fixture could have bent the nail, and caused the ill-placed bug light to slide right into the swirling water. A disaster waiting to happen.

When the police found the champagne, the semen, and the Two Dead Dicks in the hot tub, they wouldn't be thinking about murder. They'd be thinking what a couple of idiots Martindale and Thompson were. The accidental deaths would be the capper to a sordid scandal that would become Hollywood history.

Delbert liked the idea he was making history. This was only the beginning. He left, imagining vengeful bugs flying over the dead bodies, laughing to themselves.

ACT THREE

Chapter Fifteen

The next day, Charlie went to a newsstand and rummaged through the racks, looking for detective magazines and mercenary rags, snagging everything from *True Detective* and *Guns and Ammo* to *Soldier of Fortune* and *Covert Operations*. He didn't pay much attention to the newspaper headlines about the sordid, accidental deaths of the Two Dicks. His mind was on his mission. He took the magazines home and flipped through the classified sections in each of them until he found all the equipment he was looking for. He placed the orders, gladly paying extra for overnight delivery.

The demise of the Two Dicks was the furthest thing from Boyd Hartnell's mind. He lay strapped in to what must once have been a dental chair, because he doubted anyone made special seats for undergoing experimental hair technologies. As Dr. Desi slowly worked his magic, Boyd gritted his teeth in pain. At least Boyd had the pleasure of looking at Thor, pink and naked, shivering in the corner. Let's see if Sabrina finds you so cute now, Boyd thought.

Daddy Crofoot read the Hollywood trade papers while Mindy, a blackjack dealer, rubbed his pecker between her breasts. Judging from the headlines, he knew he had made the right decision sending Delbert Skaggs to Los Angeles. Delbert had always been a fine producer, that Delbert should excel in the same capacity in the television business didn't surprise Crofoot at all. The ratings for *Frankencop* were up, the competition was taking a beating, and Crofoot was beginning to think about expansion. He put down the *Hollywood Reporter* long enough to have his second orgasm of the day, and gave Delbert a call to congratulate him.

* * *

Sabrina Bishop read about the "bug-light Jacuzzi deaths" of Clive Martindale and Marc Thompson and wondered what Hollywood was coming to. It was an ugly business, and if it weren't for the incredible money, she'd find something else to do. She doubted anything paid as well, with the possible exception of drug dealing. Both involved entertaining the masses—the only real distinction was that making movies and TV shows was legal. There was nothing kind, gentle, or pleasant about the business, at least not that she had seen. Except for maybe Charlie Willis, the first nice guy she'd met since coming out here, and look what the business was doing to him. She went to the closet and pulled out his shirt, and surprised herself by putting it on. She was even more surprised when she realized how safe it made her feel.

Eddie Planet read the article in the bathroom, and from where he was sitting, he knew exactly where Hollywood was going. Right into his lap. At this rate, *Frankencop* would be a top-ten hit by the February sweeps, and he could parlay the success into a spin-off, maybe even a couple of new series. Just imagining what fate Delbert Skaggs had in mind for *Miss Agatha,* and the extra share points that would give his show, made his bowels sing.

Flint Westwood didn't like to read. He preferred to look at pictures. And when he saw the evening news, he remembered a hot-tub scene he had done in *Buck Naked in the 25th Century* where he fucked the Maiden of Mars while she gave the Titan of Saturn a blowjob. It was a fond memory, and it somehow made the horrible tragedy that befell Clive and Marc seem less ugly.

Don DeBono heard the news and, although the tragedy had struck a competing network, sought solace among the *TV Guide*s he'd saved since he was a boy. With his nose running from the dust, he flipped through the dog-eared pages and relived better days . . . when the Cartwrights ruled the Ponderosa, Kookie didn't lend his comb, and rugged TV detectives never killed anyone on the set or turned up parboiled in Jacuzzis in another man's arms.

* * *

Every television star with a secret was startled by the news. Better to die than to live with the humiliation of their true selves being revealed and eclipsing their fictional personas.

Only one celebrity thought it was better to get even. And her only regret was that the senile idiot Itchy Matthews had inadvertently given Charlie Willis the gun that was meant for his guest star. Now Charlie was alive to ask her for *another* $50,000.

Esther's only consolation was that it was the last mistake Itchy ever made. And it was going to be Charlie's last, too.

Chapter Sixteen

Anger was the first emotion Boo Boo felt whenever the sedation began to wear off. That's how Boo Boo knew he was returning to normal, because anger was the only emotion he knew. He was angry with the fleas on his body. He was angry with his silver food dish for being empty. He was angry that his shit and pee didn't smell stronger. He was angry at everything.

But what made him angriest was Lyle Spreen, his master, who he thought must be a dog, too. Spreen's butt smelled a lot like his own, he had fleas, he tasted like dog and was also angry most of the time. Boo Boo liked that. They were brothers. What he didn't like was that Spreen shot him with a dart every day and made the anger go away. Then everything became a blur of white lights, chubby children, raucous laughter, and hand signs from Spreen which, if obeyed, would result in getting a treat to eat. His anger dulled, he was overwhelmed with a sickening sense of complacency. He'd do anything, because it didn't matter—nothing did when he was that bored and disoriented, except maybe the mild excitement of getting a cookie.

Sometimes the heat of the lights and the intoxicating smell of sweaty human flesh would break through his narcotic haze and bring the anger back. And with it, the hunger. Then he really got a treat. A nice mouthful of human flesh. Yes, that was good.

That was the best.

He licked his balls and, in the comfort of his air-conditioned, carpeted doghouse, decided he wanted some right now. Boo Boo got up, shook, broke the electric beam that opened the sliding glass doors of his Tudor home, and walked outside. He paused to take in the view from his redwood deck.

Just beyond the cyclone fence that enclosed his quarter-acre domain, were the Pinnacle soundstages and office tower and, beyond them, the western street, the jungle, the Brooklyn neighborhood, and the studio tour.

And lots of tasty people.

Boo Boo had a genuine fire hydrant to pee on, a waterfall to soothe him, a fish pond to lie beside, a grassy knoll to roll down, even the shade of a $150,000 oak tree, hauled to the studio by truck and lowered into place by a crane, for him to relax under. But none of it pleased him. It pissed him off.

He wanted to be out there.

Where the food was.

Sure, twice a day someone came to feed him steak, and he appreciated that. But they all wore layers of protective padded clothing that tasted very bad. He knew, because he tried to bite them often. It was an insult. And it made him angrier.

But Boo Boo was a patient, persistent dog. He knew, someday, someone would open the gate and not have the dart gun or protective clothing. Oh, what a day that would be.

Maybe it would be today.

He lay down on the deck, licked his balls some more, and waited. Furiously.

Charlie sat in his Camaro across the street from Esther Radcliffe's favorite Rodeo Drive hair salon, waiting for her to come out with her new do.

She emerged looking as bad as when she'd entered, though her purse was probably lighter by a couple hundred bucks, a small price to pay for the pleasure of being told how beautiful she was for three straight hours.

Three hours that Charlie had spent with his bladder bursting. She clearly had no idea how hard it was to surreptitiously jam a Porto-potty shaped like a Dustbuster into his crotch and take a piss while parked on a busy street. There were at least two tourists Charlie knew of that wouldn't think Beverly Hills was quite so glamorous anymore.

He plugged a lot of quarters into the meter and prayed throughout the afternoon that none of the police officers he used to work with would recognize him. Thankfully, none of them did. But he was certain the Swedish couple would never forget him. It was during that time he became a strong supporter of the movement to have Paris-style, sidewalk pay toilets installed in Los Angeles.

He had started following Esther five days ago, which, as luck would have it, was right at the start of a killer heat wave. The air was thick, heavy, and 102 degrees by ten A.M. every day, meaning each breath was like sucking on a hot exhaust pipe. Charlie's back was damp and itchy with sweat, soaking through his shirt and gluing him to the hot vinyl seats.

It was like being a patrolman all over again. Only now, for the first time, he felt that life wasn't walking all over him. Even though he was just sitting in a parked car, watching Esther, he felt he was in charge.

Things had always happened *to* him. Rarely had he *made* things happen. Maybe a little Derek Thorne was rubbing off on him, and he decided it was a good thing. Maybe he, too, could become an active action hero like the character he portrayed. A take-charge guy, rather than a take-shit jerk. Right now, though, he'd settle for just salvaging what was left of his life. And making Esther pay.

The valet brought Esther's Rolls up to the curb and she got inside. When Charlie leaned forward, his back peeled off the seat like a big strip of masking tape. He started the car and slipped into traffic behind her.

He stayed a few car lengths away, but he was certain she wouldn't notice him if he was right on her bumper. She was completely self-absorbed—this much he had learned the first day he ever met her. Another thing he'd learned was that, when she wasn't shooting cops in the stomach, she was pretty boring. Most of her days were spent on the set, with a few forays to local restaurants and department stores. So far, nothing interesting had happened.

He had a high-speed camera and a telephoto lens under the seat, just in case. He also had night-vision goggles somewhere under the fast-food wrappers on the passenger side, a shotgun mike in the backseat, and a tiny listening device stashed in the glove compartment, all ordered from mercenary magazines and probably illegal. But there had been little to look at, and absolutely nothing worth eavesdropping on.

As far as he knew, if she had a lover, he, she, or it had to be out of town, or kept chained up in the basement of her house, far away from the sunlight.

It was a possibility.

He made a mental note to stop by the county assessor's office, check out the blueprints, and see if her house had a basement.

Whatever her secret, whatever her failing, he knew patience was the key to uncovering it. Eventually, he would stumble onto something. Esther was too big a psychopath not to do something Charlie could capitalize on. He only hoped he would recognize the opportunity when he saw it.

Charlie followed Esther down the Wilshire Corridor, a ribbon of asphalt winding through a canyon of vacant, high-rise, million-dollar condos. Built in the delirium of leveraged buyouts and junk bonds, it was a mile-long section of Wilshire Boulevard that now stood as a testament to the financial folly of the 1980s.

Esther turned left at Glendon, and into the parking structure of a mirrored-glass monolith. The building, which seemed to Charlie like a leftover prop from the prehistoric sequence of *2001*, towered over Westwood Village, a square-mile business district nestled comfortably between UCLA to the north, Wilshire Boulevard to the south, Brentwood to the west, and Beverly Hills to the east.

He stayed well behind Esther, following her down the corkscrew driveway six floors to the lowest, subterranean level of the parking structure. Charlie parked on the fifth level, grabbed his camera, and then crept on foot along the driveway to the bottom floor. He hid in the shadows as she got out of her car, her face obscured by sunglasses the size of a Chevy windshield and inspired by Liberace's candelabra. She might avoid recognition, but she wouldn't avoid being noticed.

Esther took the elevator, so Charlie was forced to jog up the stairs, stopping at each level to see if she emerged. It was a good thing he did, because instead of exiting into the lobby, she emerged at the first level, strode across the parking structure, and slipped out the back door into a residential street.

He followed her down Malcolm Avenue, a quiet, monied neighborhood of small, half-million-dollar, Spanish-style homes with perfectly manicured lawns. A European car was parked in every driveway, and street signs were so burdened with arcane restrictions they required two poles to get their indecipherable messages across.

Charlie saw her walk up to one house as if she owned it—and when she went through the front door with a key, he thought she might. But then he saw the black Porsche in the driveway and knew he'd discovered something big.

Flint Westwood's career was almost cut short the day he was born. His penis was so thick and long the doctor mistook it at first for the umbilical cord. The astonished doctor covered his mistake by performing an on-the-spot circumcision and no one was the wiser.

Of course, in those days Flint was just Huey Krupp, a well-hung baby from Brooklyn. But he was also the well-hung nephew of mobster Sonny Crofoot, who named his newborn son Daddy, his way of making sure *his* son started off life better than his father.

Huey knew before he could speak that he had something that set him apart from everyone else. He saw it in the way people looked at him whenever he was nude. Their eyes would widen, first in surprise, and then in embarrassment. At first this frightened him, but as time went on, he grew to like the special attention he got. No one else seemed to deserve those wonderful, shocked glances. He knew then that he must be special.

But as he got older, the other kids teased him mercilessly, treating him as if his unusually pronounced organ was some kind of hideous deformity.

Here comes Huey Dong.
Hey, Horse Dong, how's it hangin'?
Huey can run the three-legged race all by himself.
Mr. Ed is hung like a Huey.

It didn't help that Huey's intellectual wattage was far from electrifying. Thankfully, what Huey lacked in intellect, his cousin Daddy more than made up for in cunning. Daddy started charging a nickel for a peek at Huey's most unique feature, pocketing three cents for his efforts, and giving Huey the other two.

And whenever Huey performed for an audience, an amazing thing happened—his already enormous feature grew even bigger, which made it even more of an audience draw.

What had once been an object of shame for Huey became a source of tremendous pride, profit and, as he soon discovered, intense pleasure. And Daddy honed some of his business techniques. He beat up anyone, to the point of permanent disability, who dared threaten or insult Huey—because when Huey was down, so was his great gift, and so was the paying attendance at the peep show in Sonny Crofoot's basement.

Thus began a relationship between the two cousins that would continue into adulthood, as Daddy took his mob profits from drug dealing, grand theft, bookmaking, bone-breaking and arson-for-hire and bankrolled Huey's porno film career. Of course, Daddy took his customary sixty percent cut.

The first thing Daddy did was change Huey's name to something classy that also hinted at his wondrous endowment. Flint Westwood was born, first as a stand-in erection for lesser-gifted actors and later as a leading man himself.

But during all those years, one thing had never changed. Flint had to know he had an audience, or he literally couldn't rise to the occasion, whether for fun or profit.

Which was why now, as Flint lay on his back, his latest lusty conquest riding his livelihood like a pogo stick, three video cameras silently whirred behind the mirrors that lined the walls of his round bedroom.

The mirrors served a dual purpose. With them, he was always certain he could look out from his rotating bed and see at least one member of the audience enjoying the show—himself. And he could imagine that the cameras, hidden behind the mirrors, were the eyes for millions of adoring fans.

The woman atop him writhed and moaned, riding the fine edge between pleasure and pain. She wasn't the most beautiful woman he had ever screwed, but she was one of the most enthusiastic, and certainly the richest.

She was surfing on that rolling, building wave of pleasure, anticipating the mighty crash, the pounding against the shore, and the slow, tantalizing retreat back into the tranquil sea. The occasional jolt of pain she felt was an exciting riptide just below the turbulent surface of her ecstasy.

Although the beach was in sight, and the wave continued to grow in intensity, the shore never seemed to get any closer. The frustration was becoming a pain of its own, and not one she enjoyed. She needed that extra gust of wind to carry her forward.

That's when she imagined a fusillade of bullets pounding into Charlie Willis, jerking him across her psyche until he was blown apart into billions of bloody smithereens.

That was enough.

Esther Radcliffe shrieked, climaxing so hard and so loud Flint wondered if he'd inadvertently killed her. But luck was on his side tonight—the tragic event in Spokane was not repeating itself, which was good, because he had long since gotten rid of his chain saw.

Chapter Seventeen

●●●

Otto and Burt moved through the quiet, empty streets of Manhattan, across the dusty plains of the Old West, and finally past the shadow of soundstage 15 to Boo Boo's compound.

Otto was armed with bolt cutters and a syringe filled with sleeping pills dissolved in water. Burt carried an extra-large, swimming pool leaf net on an extendable pole in one hand, and a gunny sack in the other.

Tonight, they were on an important mission for Eddie Planet, one that would ultimately hurl them from obscurity into the national limelight as romantic leading men. Then their dreams would all come true. They could go into any airport nudie bar and the girls would let them put money into their panties. They could have a comic book made about them. They could become spokesmen for Swanson Dinners, and get all the Hungry Man Frozen Meals they could eat for free.

Eddie would see to that, because he was the most powerful man in television and the visionary who had discovered them. All they had to do was this one little favor, and it was easy. They had done the same thing a million times before.

"Ready for some takeout?" Burt snickered, thinking if they hurried, they could have Boo Boo on the grill in time to watch Suzanne Somers's Thighmaster infomercial.

"Yeah," Otto said, stopping at the gate to Boo Boo's domain and handily snapping the lock with his bolt cutters. He opened the gate wide and, with a grandiose wave of his arm, ushered Burt in. Burt stepped inside, bowed politely, and then the two of them launched into their ritual dance.

They got through their soft-shoe, their patty-cake, their jumping jacks, and were midway through their John Travolta spin when Boo

Boo leapt out of the darkness for Otto's neck. Burt saw the furious furball out of the corner of his eye. He swung his leaf net at Boo Boo, missed the dog, and smacked Otto in the head, knocking him off balance and inadvertently saving his life.

Instead of ripping apart Otto's neck, Boo Boo landed in Otto's crotch, clamping his teeth firmly on a mouthful of genitalia.

Otto considered this only a temporary setback. At least he had Boo Boo right where he wanted him. Otto took his syringe and prepared to jam it into Boo Boo.

Unfortunately, this was the exact moment Burt decided to help Otto, reaching for the dog at the same instant Otto brandished his needle. Instead of jamming it into Boo Boo, Otto injected Burt, who staggered backward and splashed into the canine reflecting pool.

Boo Boo, seeing a flash of the dreaded needle, immediately released Otto, scampered over his face, through the gate and into the night in search of less well-armed prey.

Otto reached down, relieved to find his testicles still attached to his blood-soaked crotch, and then picked up the leaf net to fish his comatose friend out of Boo Boo's pond.

Although Otto was a generally optimistic fellow, he was forced to admit this hadn't gone well.

Charlie emptied his Porto-potty into the perfectly manicured bushes of Flint Westwood's Spanish-style house, which was, appropriately enough, in Westwood.

He had been so stunned when he first recognized Flint's black Porsche parked out front that he snapped a roll of film just of Esther Radcliffe going inside the house. Why, he didn't know, but he had a feeling he'd be sorry if he didn't.

He then ran back and moved his car out of the parking structure. It was a good idea, because Esther had been inside with Flint for six hours, and Charlie didn't have the $50 in cash it would've taken to ransom the Camaro.

It took him half an hour to figure out how to use his shotgun mike, but once he did, he pointed it at the house. Whatever he might have heard was drowned out by someone watching *Oprah* next door.

So he crept up to the house for a closer look, and to empty his Porto-potty. Of course now, as he was standing right outside the house, was the moment Esther picked to leave. Thankfully, it was a dark night, and she walked past Charlie, crouched behind the bushes, without even noticing him, and strode back up Malcolm to the parking structure.

Charlie waited until she disappeared around the corner before he went to his car and drove to the parking structure, arriving just as Esther's Rolls was coming out.

Esther cruised west on Wilshire, got on the San Diego Freeway, and took it south to Jefferson Boulevard, which stretched across the city from the depths of South Central Los Angeles to the edge of the continent.

He stayed several cars behind her as she cruised Pacific-bound on Jefferson, across the wide-open marshland, the most valuable un-developed property in Los Angeles. The land had been earmarked for decades as the site of an ambitious, upscale neighborhood of tower-ing condos, exclusive beaches, swank shopping, and private marinas, but was mired in legal challenges, zoning ordinances, and politics. For now, the land was home to cancerous ducks, corpulent mos-quitoes, and chunks of sewage that dropped from incoming jets at LAX like shit from a pterodactyl.

Esther surprised him by heading out toward Playa Del Rey, an oceanfront village along the spit of beach between the airport run-ways and the Pacific Ocean.

Playa Del Rey was the ugly cousin of Marina Del Rey, where wealthy singles, stewardesses, and recent divorcées flocked looking for hard bodies, development deals, and tropical drinks.

Once, Charlie thought about moving to Marina Del Rey just to get laid, but took one look at the prices and decided he was better off celibate in Reseda.

Charlie couldn't imagine what Esther was doing in ramshackle Playa Del Rey, where departing aircraft rattled the shingles off half-million-dollar homes and choked the skies with exhaust fumes. No doubt the people who lived there stuck earplugs in their ears and cotton up their noses, admired their ocean views, and honestly thought they had it made.

The Rolls tooled down the coast on Vista Del Mar, the ocean on one side, the airport on the other. His car shook as a 747 roared overhead, so low Charlie half expected the retracting landing gear to scrape the roof of his car.

Esther turned left into a tiny, well-lighted picnic area on the airport side of the street, sliding her Rolls between a seaspray-corroded Econoline van and a couple of Mexicans necking in a '73 Impala. Charlie slowed to watch Esther walk quickly across the grass toward the cyclone fence that surrounded the floodlit oasis on three sides.

A tailgater behind Charlie leaned on his horn three or four times in rapid succession. Charlie could have shot the sonofabitch for drawing attention to him, but thankfully Esther didn't look back.

Charlie parked illegally across the street, ran across the busy thoroughfare, and strode into the park, his head low, his camera around his neck. He looked up just enough to see Esther slip through a hole in the cyclone fence and disappear into the darkness beyond.

As much as he hated Esther, the cop side of Charlie wanted to rush out and stop her. It was insanity for a woman her age, or any age for that matter, to walk into a vacant lot in the dark. No, it was suicide.

On the other hand, he knew she was insane, and was probably better armed than anyone she was likely to meet in the darkness. Besides, if anyone tried to attack her, he'd be there to rescue her. And he knew he would, too, even though Esther had shot him and framed him for murder.

What a chump, he thought.

Rather than go through the hole, Charlie climbed the fence nearest him and dropped over as quietly as he could on the other side.

Charlie crouched and spotted Esther moving along what looked like a path through the weeds. She seemed to know exactly where she was going, even though it was pitch black.

She's a lunatic, he thought, as if that was a big revelation.

He started after her and immediately tripped, landing on his side and scraping his elbow on a slab of cement.

The ground shook, and for a split second, the area was illuminated by the lights of an airplane taking off. In that moment, Charlie saw a snapshot of a dead neighborhood. Faded numbers on cracked curbs. Crumbled chimneys spilled across weed-choked foundations. Cracked driveways leading to nothing.

Charlie realized he was lying in the rubble of a house, and that Esther was walking down what had been a street. Now he remembered. Thirty years ago this dark wasteland had been the fashionable neighborhood of Vista Del Mar, demolished to make room for the airport expansion. Only the ruins remained of the ornate homes that once overlooked the sea.

What the hell was she doing here?

Charlie checked his camera and was relieved to find it in one piece. He carefully found his way to what remained of the curb and followed it in the direction Esther had taken. Blindly, he stumbled along for a few minutes, hoping he wouldn't collide with Esther, who had so confidently navigated the same street only minutes ago.

He instinctively ducked as another plane took off above him, shaking the ground and bathing the street in a flash of light. Esther was only a few yards ahead of him, kneeling in front of an old, rusted mailbox lying on the cracked rubble of a driveway.

Charlie slipped behind the debris of a brick flower box and snapped a few pictures. He was able to see her slipping a brown-wrapped package into the mailbox before the plane passed and the decaying skeleton of Vista Del Mar was once again shrouded in darkness.

He heard her footsteps approaching and lay flat on the ground. She marched confidently past him, as if the whole place were bathed in light and she could see every crack and stone in her path.

Instead of following her, Charlie stayed where he was, watching her make her way back to the parking lot. She got into her Rolls and drove off.

Charlie turned his attention back to the mailbox and was surprised to see something move in the gloom. He hunkered down and peered through his camera, but he didn't see anything until a moment later, when a plane passed overhead, its lights revealing a man standing over the battered mailbox, holding the package.

It was Flint Westwood.

Flint tore the package open to reveal a thick wad of cash. Charlie didn't have to count it to know it was $50,000.

Charlie snapped away, taking as many pictures as he could before the plane flew off and Esther's secret melted back into the night.

Chapter Eighteen

Long faces lined the long table in the long boardroom this morning, the start of the longest day in the long history of the United Broadcasting Company.

Its cash cow was missing.

Actually, its cash *dog*—the illustrious Boo Boo, beloved by millions, linchpin of Don DeBono's entire schedule.

For Don DeBono, nothing could be worse. A classic television sitcom was threatened. The entire UBC schedule hung in the balance. And UBC's position as the number one network was in grave peril.

How could a merchandising juggernaut worth more than $50 million annually in T-shirts, coffee cups, key chains, lunch boxes, and thousands of other overpriced trinkets *be gone?*

The season was becoming a disaster of legendary proportions, and all on Don DeBono's watch. As long as UBC dominated the schedule, DeBono felt whatever happened to primetime during the season, on whatever network, would be remembered as his legacy. He wouldn't be fondly remembered as the man who steered UBC into its fifth straight victorious season, as the man who introduced America to *Miss Agatha*. No, history wouldn't be so kind. The *TV Guide*s of the future would forever link him with the slaughter on *My Gun Has Bullets*, the parboiling of the Two Dicks, and the disappearance (or worse) of Boo Boo.

Don DeBono sat at the far end of the table, an Alka-Seltzer burbling in his glass of Evian, glaring at Boyd Hartnell, who sat with his head in a turban, a stupid smile on his face. Like fucking Boyd didn't realize what a monumental catastrophe this was. There was no sign of Boo Boo anywhere and, so far, no ransom demands had come in. The dog could be lost forever.

"How the fuck could you let this happen?" DeBono asked, every vein on his face visible, pulsing just under the skin. "Your incompetence could cost this network hundreds of millions of dollars."

"It's not *my* show or my problem," said Boyd, relishing the moment. Under his turban, his golden mane was taking hold, and as Don DeBono disintegrated, Boyd was growing stronger. What did he care if Boo Boo was gone? Most of Boyd's shows were on rival networks and were going to benefit from this amusing turn of events. And, more importantly, his scalp was tingling. If Dr. Desi's experiment worked, not only would he have Sabrina Bishop, but he'd have chest hair again to hide his scrawny pecs. He'd know very soon.

"The dog was on your fucking lot," DeBono said. "Boo Boo is worth more than your whole fucking studio, and where were your guards? In their damn shack, jerking off when they should have been protecting the dog."

"We only rent you studio space," Boyd replied. "Boo Boo's welfare was entirely your responsibility. If you wanted round-the-clock security guards on Boo Boo's compound, you should have put them there."

DeBono grabbed his glass of Alka-Seltzer, his hand shaking as he brought it to his mouth and downed the antacid.

Boyd couldn't believe how well this was going. DeBono was practically begging to be humiliated in front of his underlings, and Boyd gladly complied. He couldn't resist twisting the knife one more time.

"But I guess it wasn't worth twelve bucks an hour to you," Boyd said, getting up. He wanted to see Sabrina Bishop while he was at the peak of his power and manliness. "Now if you'll excuse me, I've got pressing business."

DeBono watched Boyd leave, and wanted badly to kill the man. He knew Boyd was right, and it made him sicker and angrier than he already was. If he couldn't find someone to blame, and fast, his career would be over. There wasn't a single person at the table who wouldn't slit his throat at the first opportunity.

His best shot at a scapegoat had just walked out of the room. His second choice, Boo Boo's trainer Lyle Spreen, got the news at his kennel. He was so shaken he forgot to watch where he was walking. Spreen slipped on a dog turd, cracked his skull open, and ended up in a coma at Cedars Sinai. There went DeBono's elaborate plan to blame Boo Boo's mysterious disappearance on the abusive techniques of his trainer.

DeBono glanced over at Buttonwillow McKittrick, vice president of current programming, always dressed in black, and saw her quickly lick her full, red lips. It was all she could do not to foam at the mouth. She was probably sharpening her icepick, waiting for the first opportunity to stab him in the back. *He* would be if he were in her position.

After all, that's how he got this job in the first place. Every executive knew the only way to step up in network television was on someone else's back.

If he fell, the network would be hers.

So DeBono had to think fast.

Until Boo Boo was found, it would take raw, programming genius to keep the schedule alive. And if Boo Boo *wasn't* found, DeBono would have to concoct a surefire hit overnight. Nothing short of a miracle.

"Who knows about this?" DeBono asked Gilbert Schlaye, the chicken-necked VP of publicity.

"Everybody everywhere," Schlaye replied. "CNN had it on the satellite two hours ago. Katie Couric burst into tears on the *Today* show. Three hundred kids broke into sobbing fits at a Chicago grade school—they had to call out the paramedics. They closed the school for the day, and they're offering psychological counseling to the panicked children." Schlaye was no threat, DeBono thought—the guy was a time-card puncher and nothing more.

"Our L.A. station is preempting programming for round-the-clock coverage on the search for Boo Boo," interjected Larry Sydes, VP of affiliate relations, and professional interjector. Unwilling to be the first into any fray, he always waited to speak until his voice could be lost among others. The sneaky little shit would go far in network television, DeBono thought. But not on my back.

"Sources tell me *Time* pulled their issue off the presses," Schlaye added. "Just to put Boo Boo on the cover. Cost 'em millions, but they figure it'll jack up sales so much it will more than make up for it."

It was a bigger disaster than DeBono thought. There wasn't a television viewer from Los Angeles to Peking who wouldn't know the news by lunch time. Everybody would be watching *Boo Boo's Dilemma* tonight, if only to pay their respects.

"How many *Boo Boo*s do we have in the can?" he asked Buttonwillow.

"Three," she replied, barely able to hide her smirk. He was fucked, and she knew it. They'd just reshuffled the schedule, the Thursday night lineup was too new to stand up on its own without *Boo Boo*. Three episodes was nothing, no time at all to build another show into a hit.

For five years, UBC had been a self-sustaining success, built on its continuing hit series, like *Boo Boo* and *Miss Agatha*. Each season, DeBono would place the half-dozen new series on the schedule between two established hits, virtually guaranteeing that the new show would also be a success. And once the new show was a hit, it would be moved to another night, where the process would be repeated. That way, when the established hits began to erode, like *Miss Agatha*, there were hits to take their place.

There was only one other show that had even a fraction of Boo Boo's popularity, and that was its spin-off, just moved to Sunday nights.

"How many *Rappy Scrappy*s do we have?"

"Thirteen," she said.

His lucky number. Half a season worth of episodes. In that instant, Don DeBono saw his salvation.

His heart pounded furiously. Blood and adrenaline surged through him, his throat went dry, and his prick turned to marble.

He wasn't desperate anymore. He was stoked.

He didn't realize it until that moment, but he had grown complacent, maybe even bored, in the safety of being number one, the numbing predictability of success. He hadn't looked over his shoulder in four years. Now his network was on the edge of disaster, and a roomful of executives were drooling over his job.

This was what television was all about.

Crisis scheduling. Kamikaze programming. Sheer terror.

Oh, how he missed it.

If this was how his career would end, so be it. He'd take the whole damn network with him.

"Pick 'em up for the back nine episodes," he told Buttonwillow, talking so fast he was practically spitting the words into her shocked face. That would bring *Rappy Scrappy* to a full season of twenty-two episodes.

"I want to see scripts on my desk Monday morning," he said. "Tell 'em to rewrite old *Boo Boo*s if they have to. Hell, tell 'em to do it anyway."

She nodded, shocked, like a woman who'd just seen a corpse suddenly sit up in its casket.

DeBono pointed at Schlaye, who jerked as if slapped. "On *Boo Boo* tonight, I want you to pump the shit out of *Rappy Scrappy* during every commercial break."

DeBono whirled, pointing at Clark Van Mitchell, the VP of variety shows and specials, who grabbed his armrests and sat bolt upright.

"I want you to slap together an hour-long salute to *Boo Boo* for next week, followed by an hour of new *Rappy Scrappy* episodes," DeBono demanded. "Get Carol Burnett to host the special, tell her to tug her ear and all that shit."

DeBono surprised himself with each word that came out of his mouth, making it up as he went along and knowing, intuitively, that it was right.

"But what do we put in *Rappy Scrappy*'s regular slot on Sunday?" Buttonwillow asked, dazed.

"A very special episode of *Rappy Scrappy*," he replied, prompting a rapid-fire flurry of guesses from around the table.

"AIDS?"

"Wife-beating?"

"Teen pregnancy?"

"Vivisection?"

"*Rappy's Boo Boo Memories*," he said, turning again to Clark Van Mitchell. "Go through the *Boo Boo* episodes, find all the scenes of the two animals together and build me something. *Rappy* is weak in rural areas, so drag Roy Clark out of mothballs to host and sing a catchy musical salute to *Boo Boo*."

DeBono stood up and walked around the long table, his executives craning their necks to keep him in sight. "Then, if the dog isn't found, we run all three episodes of *Boo Boo* on one night as a grand finale."

"All *three?*" Buttonwillow asked incredulously.

"All of 'em," he said.

She thought it was insanity. It was like drinking all the water you had left while you were still in the middle of the desert.

"What do we do the week after that?" she stammered.

"Who the fuck knows?" He grinned.

And with that, he abruptly left the room, happier than he'd been in years.

Eddie Planet couldn't remember the last time life was this good. He was enjoying three blistering orgasms and two effortless bowel movements each day. He had a show on the air, and it was getting better ratings every week. All that was missing was a corner office and a private bath.

Getting involved with Pinstripe Productions had turned out to be the shrewdest move of his illustrious career. Was it risky? Of course it was. But risk was Eddie Planet's middle name. If he wanted to play it safe, he wouldn't be in the TV business.

With *My Gun Has Bullets* gone, *Frankencop*'s ratings were climbing and now, with Boo Boo eliminated, the rug had been pulled from under *Miss Agatha. Frankencop* was poised for greatness.

Eddie was on his way out to Chatsworth in his leased Cadillac Eldorado to see Otto and Burt when his cellular trilled. Eddie answered it, and was surprised to hear Morrie Lustig, president of MBC, on the other end. They exchanged greetings, and Eddie slipped effortlessly into sales mode.

"Have you seen the *Frankencop* numbers, Morrie?" Eddie said. "They add up to a hit."

"I got a number for you, Eddie," Lustig replied. "Nine."

"You're picking us up for the back nine?" Eddie pulled over in front of a Taco Bell. They were getting a full season. No show of Eddie's had survived that long since *Hollywood and Vine.* More importantly, Morrie Lustig was calling Eddie personally to tell him.

"Consider this call the official order," Lustig said. "We're very encouraged by the ratings and the demographics. It's skewing across the board. If we can find a companion piece, we're thinking about moving it to another night."

"*Haight-Ashbury,*" Eddie said, without missing a beat. "Larry Haight is a conservative Frisco ex-cop who doesn't play by the rules. Carol Ashbury is a liberal Berkeley psychologist, a child of the sixties. Together, they're private eyes *with a difference.*"

Lustig had a poster in his office that consisted of just four words "*. . . and they're private eyes!*" It was a joke, aimed squarely at anachronisms like Eddie Planet. Since Morrie never let him in his office, Eddie had no way of knowing about it.

"We're not really looking for another P.I. show," Lustig said. "But there's an idea we've been kicking around over here. How do you feel about Peter Pan as a cop?"

"Excited," Eddie said.

"Really?" Lustig asked.

"I'm shaking," Eddie said. "It's breakthrough, ground-breaking, highly promotable television. He's young, so you get the kids. He's a fairy, so you get the women and the homos. And he can fly, so you get the Trekkies, the fat people, and the mentally retarded. All he needs is a gun, a badge, and an attitude, and we got the high-testosterone male audience. It's a natural, Morrie. I'm kicking myself for not thinking of it first."

"Tell you what, Eddie. Maybe you could give it some thought, develop the idea a bit, and we can talk about it."

"How about over lunch next week?" Eddie said.

"Lunch is for losers," Lustig said. "We'll have a predawn surf meeting."

"I'll wax my board." Eddie didn't have a board.

"Cowabunga," Lustig said and hung up.

Otto and Burt lived in a mobile home on a weedy patch of land in an industrial corner of Chatsworth. The rusted hulks of dozens of old cars dotted the field around their house. From a distance, they looked like cattle grazing on the tall, dry grass.

Eddie steered his Cadillac down the gravel drive leading up to their house and honked his horn twice. Otto and Burt were two people he never wanted to catch off guard.

He got out of his car and was immediately hit with the acrid aroma of burning meat. Eddie walked around the mobile home to find Otto and Burt, in matching checked BBQ aprons, standing over a fire in an oil drum, the flames licking at the blackened meat on the grill.

"Howdy, boys," Eddie said. "You wouldn't believe who I was just talking to on the phone."

"David Hasselhoff," Burt said.

"No," Eddie replied.

"Loni Anderson," Otto said.

"The network," Eddie snapped, then forced himself to relax, to put a smile on his face. "They're thrilled with the tremendous favor you did for them last night."

Otto and Burt shared a guilty look. Eddie took it for modesty.

"It was no biggie," Otto said quickly. "So do we get our own show now?"

"Let me tell you, things are really gonna start moving for you boys. Why, just driving over here, I was pitching ideas for you at the network."

"We want to do *Sunn of a Gunn,*" Otto said. "Burt and I, we've been working on a script."

"It's two thousand pages long," Burt said.

"But it's good stuff," Otto added.

"I'm sure it is," Eddie said, "but I don't think there's room on the schedule for that kind of sophisticated programming right now. Look, they are dying to work with you, it's just that we might have to go with something else first. I have this idea about cavemen that I think you two are perfect for."

"What's elegant about a caveman?" Otto asked.

"Animal skins are very classy," Eddie said. "Just look at alligator shoes. But we can discuss it over lunch sometime."

"How about now? We got lunch right here." Burt skewered the slab of meat with a screwdriver, turned it over, then dabbed brown sauce on it with a paintbrush. "It's a little well done, but it's the only way this grill cooks."

"You did clean the oil off the inside of that drum, didn't you?" Eddie asked.

"Hell no, how do you think we light the briquettes?" Otto said.

"Right," Eddie said. "Silly of me. We'll go out for lunch another time. But I am curious about something."

"The barbecue sauce is a secret," Burt said, "but one of the ingredients is Cap'n Crunch."

"Sounds tantalizing." Eddie guessed that was probably the only edible ingredient in the sauce. "Actually, what I was wondering was, well, what exactly did you do with Boo Boo?"

Otto and Burt shared another look. This time, Eddie could clearly see the fear in their eyes.

"Well?" Eddie asked.

Burt took the screwdriver and used it to lift something off the meat. When he held the screwdriver up in front of Eddie, a collar dangled from the end.

Dizziness swept over Eddie. He leaned against the mobile home for support, and took a deep breath.

"Good work," he gurgled, backing away. He gave them the high-five and hurried back to his car. It wasn't until Eddie drove off that Burt tossed the collar into the weeds.

"We're lucky he didn't read the tag." Burt let out a sigh of relief. "Or he would've seen it says Fifi."

"Wouldn't matter," Otto observed calmly. "I don't think he understands French."

Chapter Nineteen

Boo Boo Disappears, UBC Takes Severe Blow

The television landscape was shaken by a major temblor yesterday with news that Boo Boo the dog has disappeared from his Pinnacle Studios compound.

Studio security personnel have searched the studio grounds, while police and animal control officers have prowled the surrounding neighborhood, all to no avail. Authorities suspect foul play, but no evidence has turned up pointing to either a kidnapping plot or murder.

Boo Boo's trainer, Lyle Spreen, remains hospitalized in critical condition at Cedars Sinai after an undisclosed accident occurred at his Malibu ranch following news of the winsome pooch's disappearance.

The unexpected loss of the powerhouse Boo Boo's Dilemma *hits UBC at a particularly vulnerable moment. The web is still smarting from the abrupt cancellation of* My Gun Has Bullets, *due to the accidental shooting of actor Darren Clarke during filming. And the web recently shuffled its winning primetime skeds on Thursday and Sunday evenings. The loss of Boo Boo is expected to cripple the Thursday slate, and is sure to bring down the net's overall weekly averages.*

Pundits predict the likely winners will be DBC's sitcoms Adopted Family *and* My Wife Next Door *at 8 P.M., taking the charge from UBC's* Energizer Bunny *at 8:30. Meanwhile UBC's sitcoms* Broad Squad *and* The Anson Williams Show, *even without the benefit of the* Boo Boo *lead-in, are likely to beat DBC's lackluster* Young Hudson Hawk *and MBC's aging* Dedicated Doctors, *if only by a slim margin.*

The big slugfest will be 10 P.M., where the surprisingly strong Frankencop, *renewed for the full season and benefiting from the loss of* The Two Dicks *(due to the tragic death of its stars), will go up against the venerable* Miss Agatha.

The Esther Radcliffe *whodunit has been winning the slot in its initial outings, but with numbers far below those it was garnering on Sundays. Whether that can continue with the loss of audience flow from* Boo Boo *remains to be seen.*

Industry insiders believe Miss Agatha's *competitiveness against the high-concept actioner* Frankencop *will depend on the drawing power of Sabrina Bishop with men 18–45. Bishop, who won popularity in direct-to-video softcore thrillers, has a large following among men and younger viewers, the demographic groups seen as the core audience of* Frankencop.

Although UBC has yet to officially announce its plans, insiders report prexy Don DeBono will play out the remaining Boo Boo *episodes in the 8 p.m. slot, followed by specials . . .*

Charlie had turned his master bathroom into a makeshift darkroom and was now carefully developing the photos he took on his surveillance.

McGarrett lay curled up on the bathmat, sound asleep, his muffled barks and twitching legs showing that he had a far more active dream life than the one he led awake.

Charlie almost envied him. He pulled an eight-by-ten of Flint Westwood out of the chemicals in his sink, carefully stepped over his dog, and hung the picture up to dry in his shower, right next to several photos of Esther Radcliffe.

By themselves, the grainy photos didn't say much, but what they hinted at was tantalizing. Esther was convinced Charlie was blackmailing her, so convinced she tried to kill him, and yet her costly tormentor was actually the guy she'd spent six hours with yesterday afternoon.

And Charlie didn't think they spent the time playing checkers.

On the radio, propped on the top of the toilet bowl, KNX 1070 continued to report on the disappearance of Boo Boo, a dog kids who couldn't count or read a grocery list nevertheless knew was a reincarnated Catskills comic living with a typical American family. Bob Tur, in Air 1070, flew his chopper in circles over the Valley, improbably hoping to catch a peek of the elusive, superstar pooch from the sky.

If Charlie didn't know better, he'd think Esther was behind the disappearance. But there was no logical reason for Esther to kill the dog. Unless, perhaps, it had pissed on her Rolls, dumped a load outside her trailer, and had the audacity to bark at her. Those were all very real possibilities. He didn't put anything past Esther.

Charlie slipped the photographs and the negatives into a large manila envelope, which he carried with him into the bedroom. He put the envelope on his bureau and picked up a tiny transmitter that was about the size and shape of a coin.

The device could fit easily in a telephone handset and was powered by the phone itself. The bug could pick up anything spoken in its immediate vicinity. This technological wonder sent everything it heard, to be captured for posterity and extortion, on a small, voice-activated tape recorder that could be hidden anywhere within thirty feet.

Charlie admired the devices for a moment, thankful for the amazing stocking stuffers one could find in the classified pages of a mercenary magazine. He slipped the bug and recorder into his jacket pockets, along with a pocket screwdriver, wire cutter, and some black electrical tape.

Tonight he planned to put this charming little bug to work uncovering, once and for all, Esther's dirty secret. Then all he had to do was figure out how to use whatever it was he found out against her in the worst way possible.

He might not be able to get her for murder, but if he worked hard enough, he might be able to kill her career.

*　*　*

In another bathroom, ten miles east and thirty-two stories up, Boyd Hartnell knew he was ready. He looked at himself in the mirror, and a Greek god stared back at him.

It was unreal. He never imagined, in his wildest dreams, that he could have a head of hair that lush, that smooth, that abundant. It highlighted his sharp features, hinting at the strength of his spirit, the raw masculinity simmering beneath his sophisticated, urbane exterior.

Dr. Desi had outdone himself. Hell, he had probably made medical history. Boyd would be immortalized, not only in the souls of every red-blooded woman, but in medical textbooks throughout the world.

Boyd took a deep breath—and discovered even he wasn't immune to the powerful male pheromones his manly body exuded, a natural nerve gas. If it made *him* giddy, he could only imagine the power it would exert over others.

Now he had it all. The body. The money. The power. And finally, ultimately, the hair.

He carefully wrapped his golden locks back in the turban. What woman could resist him? More importantly, how could Sabrina?

Tonight Sabrina Bishop could not deny him. Tonight he would cast his manly spell over her, set her free of her inhibitions, and make her his, and his alone. She would want him, as she wanted no other man.

Boyd emerged from his private bathroom and strode across the office to his desk, where he had already packed his change of clothes in a Pinnacle Studios duffel bag.

His phone was ringing, and his calendar was scribbled full of appointments, but he didn't care. Some things in life transcended business. He had a pressing appointment with destiny.

Pinnacle Studios would still be here tomorrow, after he conquered his dream. Then Boyd would take the studio with him on his personal journey of rediscovery, making Pinnacle bigger and stronger as he himself grew in power and influence.

He grabbed his bag, slipped out the back door of his office and then, when he was certain no one was in the hall, crossed the corridor to the stairwell and slowly began his long descent.

* * *

With the all-important November ratings sweeps coming, the producers of *Johnny Wildlife* were resorting to stunt casting to draw in the
viewers.

Bob Barker, Tippi Hedron, and Doris Day—all animal lovers and
big draws with the Geritol demographic—were out in the Pinnacle
Studios forest, ready to do their cameos in return for a generous dona-
tion to an animal rights charity.

When Deborah Yelty, thirty-five-year-old former network programming exec turned cocaine freak, originally conceived *Johnny
Wildlife,* she sold it as a heat-seeking missile aimed right at the fe-
male, eighteen-to-thirty-five-year-old demographic. And she knew
what women wanted—strong, professional men who are also sensitive and cuddly. So she made him an ex–Texas Ranger turned fron-
tier veterinarian. What could be more strong, professional, and
sensitive than a veterinarian with his shirt off hugging lots of adorable animals to his sweaty, iron pecs? Even so, to hedge her bets she
cast Reed Roland, the twenty-five-year-old heartthrob from the soap
All Our Tomorrows.

Before the series was even in production, she was checking on the
availability of Michael Bolton, Fabio, and Clint Black for November
sweeps. The thought of Bob Barker would have sent her into gales of
laughter.

But here he was, in the makeup trailer, in spurs and a cowboy hat,
having fake trail dust carefully applied to his tanned face.

Turned out *Johnny Wildlife was* a draw for women. Unfortunately,
most of them were grandmothers. Deborah couldn't figure it out. But
ratings were ratings, and although the demographic wasn't the most
desirable one, she was determined to exploit whatever audience she
had to the fullest.

So it goes in television. Which was one reason why Deborah Yelty
was snorting up her royalties and would, five years hence, have her
cancerous nose amputated. But for now, her nose was intact as she
marched across the set, a cellular phone and a pager clipped to the
belt of her pleated slacks like guns in a holster. She was looking for
Reed Roland, who refused to do the scene in which the intrepid Dr.
Wildlife is forced to shoot a rabid dog.

"The dog is too cute," he told her when she found him in his canvas chair. "Furry, lovable, the kind of dog every family wants to have."

"That's the idea," she said.

"It's a bad idea, Deb," he yelled. "I'm not gonna shoot the family dog."

"You don't understand, Reed. We want people to see Little Bobby's dog as their own. That way, when you shoot him, sixty million people are going to break into tears."

"And hate *me*," Reed said. "Can't you make him ugly and mean? He's a rabid dog, for Christ's sake, can't I shoot him in self-defense?"

She wanted to slap him across the face and tell him to get his tight ass in front of the camera. What she said instead was, "We'd lose sympathy for the dog."

"Fuck the dog, Deb," he declared angrily. "The audience is supposed to sympathize with *me*. And they won't if I blow away an adorable furball. I want this dog to be a frothing, snarling beast."

"Didn't you ever see *Old Yeller?*"

"The guy who shot *Old Yeller* didn't have to come back next week."

If she couldn't reason with Reed, she'd just have to trick him. He could shoot whatever dog he wanted now—she'd replace it with another one in editing. When he saw how it worked on the air, he'd pretend they'd never had this discussion.

"You're right, Reed," Deborah said. "I don't know what I was thinking."

"You *weren't* thinking, that was the problem."

Deborah told an A.D. to ask the animal wrangler to find the ugliest dog he had, and to put some froth on his mouth. Satisfied at the power he wielded, Reed headed for the barn to do the scene. To his surprise, when he got there, the cute dog had already been replaced with the ugliest dog he had ever seen.

"Now that's a dog I can kill," he said to the director. "Nobody is gonna hate me for putting that sack of shit out of its misery."

Fact was, nobody knew what had happened to the dog that was there before, or where this one had come from. But their star was back, they were one shot away from lunch, and that was all that mattered.

"Are we ready to do this scene or what?" Reed asked.

Everyone got into position. The soundman balanced the boom mike just above Reed's head. The makeup lady dabbed a little fake sweat on Reed's face. And the dog drooled in big, thick rivulets, staring at Reed and growling.

Deborah knew the moment she saw the dog it could never stay in the show. Reed was right, the audience would be rooting for him to kill it, which would undermine the emotional integrity of the whole story.

She also wondered how the animal wrangler had switched dogs so quickly. Maybe the guy had been around long enough to know that when a star throws a tantrum, the star usually gets what he wants.

The propman checked out the gun to make sure it was loaded with blanks—you couldn't be too careful after what happened on *My Gun Has Bullets*—and handed it to Reed.

The director called for quiet on the set, and then yelled "Action!"

Dr. Wildlife approached the frightened, drooling animal slowly.

"Hello, Trigger. It's me, Doc Wildlife."

The dog growled, foam glistening on his sharp, bared fangs.

"I reckon you don't recognize me. Well, if there's any part of you still left behind all that hate, I want you to know that Little Bobby loves you, and wishes more than anything he could have you back." Dr. Wildlife stopped, wiping a tear from his cheek. "But we both know that ain't gonna happen. Rabies done took you long ago, Trigger. The best thing I can do for you now is put you out of your misery."

Dr. Wildlife took the gun out of his holster and aimed it at the dog, who suddenly lunged at him, tore the doctor's gun hand off at the wrist, and scurried away.

Reed staggered back, gripping his arm, spraying blood out of his wrist as if it were a hose. Three crew members tackled him to the ground, while everybody else ran off in terror, including Deborah, who dashed clear across the lot and out the gate, never to return. Her car had to be towed off the lot four weeks later.

In all the pandemonium, Boo Boo disappeared unrecognized into the forest, his jaws closed tight on the amputated hand, which still gripped the useless gun.

Chapter Twenty

Several hours had passed since a "rabid coyote" apparently strayed from the wilds of the Hollywood Hills onto the Pinnacle Studios lot and attacked Reed Roland, making off with his hand, a prop gun and, as it was later reported, a $10,000 Rolex.

Animal control officers and forest rangers were scouring the mountains behind the studio, looking for the beast and his gory prize. Studio executives scrambled to control the bad publicity, which lately was hemorrhaging from the studio faster than the blood from Reed Roland's severed limb.

It didn't help that in the midst of this great crisis, Boyd Hartnell was nowhere to be found. He was unreachable at home, in his car, even at Dr. Desi's. In his absence, writer/producer Jackson Burley filled the void, if only because he happened to be in Boyd's outer office, waiting for a meeting with him, when the crisis occurred.

Jackson was on the cellular with Chad Everett's agent before Reed Roland had even been carried off the lot.

Otherwise, it was business as usual on the unlucky Pinnacle Studios lot.

In Soundstage 3, Frankencop was getting emotional vibes from his pilfered pancreas, which was salvaged from another cop's corpse. In this particular episode, Frankencop felt compelled to help the organ donor's widow (Morgan Fairchild) and her young son fend off an evil land developer trying to grab the family's ranch. Flint felt he was really getting the chance to stretch as an actor, particularly since this was the first time his prick's motivation was to help someone.

In Soundstage 2, Adrian Zmed was making his triumphant return to series television in the pilot *Chippendale Cop*, police officer by day, male stripper by night. The studio flacks felt it would be a cinch to promote. *The only thing he doesn't take off is his badge.*

And in Soundstage 10, on a "very special episode" of *Miss Agatha*, Patty Duke was guest-starring as Ellen Neller, a blind, deaf woman who witnesses a murder. Esther was so upset at being upstaged by Patty Duke that she was fighting back by stealing as many of Sabrina's lines as she possibly could.

Sabrina watched helplessly as what had been her major scene was reduced to a single line. After each rehearsal, Esther would run over to the script supervisor, take a pen, and cross out entire chunks of Sabrina's dialogue.

"Your character would *never* say that, dear," Esther said, or "Honey, you just *know* that was meant to come out of Agatha's mouth."

Sabrina put in a desperate call to the writers, who said it didn't matter to them who said what as long as the pages got shot and the residual checks kept coming in. They had stopped caring about what they wrote for the show several years and hundreds of thousands of dollars ago.

So now Sabrina was relegated to nodding her head in agreement at the every brilliant deduction Miss Agatha came up with. Sabrina wasn't surprised to find out which line of hers remained untouched.

"Miss Agatha," Alexis Cole, Agatha's ninja-kicking, leather-clad niece said, "you're brilliant."

"Nonsense," Agatha replied. "Anyone can solve a murder if they pay attention to the details. Now come along, we mustn't be late for tea."

Sabrina was mad, and she was frustrated, and she was tired, but she had to admit it was better than those days spent shivering topless in front of the camera, waiting for her "nipple close-up."

She also had the added, personal satisfaction of knowing she was a big star around The Pool, the center of the universe at her grandmother's Palm Springs retirement villa.

She emerged from the soundstage to find that it was still dark. It was dark when she arrived at five A.M., and it was dark now when she was leaving. Somewhere, she was sure, a day of sunlight had passed, but she'd missed it again.

Sabrina trudged to her trailer, looking forward to peeling off her leather and slipping into a baggy, comfy pair of sweats and going home. When she opened the door, she was thinking about how good a hot bath would feel, so she was totally unprepared for what she saw after she turned on the light. Not that anything could have prepared her.

Boyd Hartnell sat on the edge of her bed, naked under a silk bathrobe, his head overwhelmed by a grotesque mane of golden retriever hair styled into an enormous, flowing pompadour that made him look like a canine Elvis.

The scream was barely out of Sabrina's mouth when Boyd lunged at her, tackling her to the floor and smothering her face with his lush, bouffant head of dog hair.

"Feel it, smell it, lose yourself in it," he whispered. "I'm yours."

"I don't want you," she said, choking on a mouthful of hair.

"You don't have to deny yourself any longer." He pinned her shoulders to the floor. "Give in to your wildest desires."

"Let me go." She tried to crawl out from under him, knowing she could kick the shit out of him if she could just get to her feet.

"Run your fingers through my silken hair," he said. "Revel in its softness."

Suddenly, someone yanked Boyd off of her and tossed him through the open doorway onto the pavement outside, slamming the trailer door shut in his face. She reached out to the stranger in front of her, who lifted her to her feet and clapped her hard on the back until she finished coughing the hair out of her windpipe.

Only after she caught her breath did she get a good look at her rescuer—lantern-jawed, tall, and dressed in Polo.

This was the second time Flint Westwood's prick had been motivated to help someone.

"I've never seen a dog like that before," Flint said.

"It wasn't an ordinary dog," Sabrina coughed. "It was a studio executive."

Flint nodded, as if he understood what she had just said, which he didn't. What he understood very clearly was that she had tremendous breasts, and began to rethink what had motivated him to action. He was getting tired of Esther's saggy, withered bags, even if he was getting $50,000 a pop to fondle them.

"It's a long story," she explained, thanking him and introducing herself. He reciprocated, and she was surprised to learn that he was the star of a TV series.

"Don't take this personally, Flint, but I've never heard of you," she said. "I've been so busy that I haven't had a chance, or really the desire, to watch any television."

Flint was elated. If she didn't know who he was, she had no reason to be suspicious of him and she certainly didn't know he was fucking Esther.

Sabrina coughed some more. "I can't seem to get his hair out of my throat."

It occurred to her then that the hair she was coughing up was important evidence in the sexual harassment suit she'd be filing tomorrow morning. Sabrina resolved not to settle for anything less than a million and a pilot deal.

"You need a drink," he said. "C'mon, I'll give you a ride home. We can stop someplace on the way."

Right now, a stiff drink sounded like a great idea. And she could use a little protection from Dogboy, though she was confident that once on her feet she had the advantage and could kick Boyd's ass. Still, she gladly accepted Flint's offer, and let him escort her to his Porsche.

Boyd cowered unseen in the shadows, tears streaming down his cheeks, and watched Flint Westwood drive away with his dream. He couldn't figure out how things had gone so horribly, terribly, nightmarishly wrong, how she could possibly have resisted the mix of manliness, power, and the ultimate head of hair.

What was the point of it all—of success, money, perfect hair—if a man couldn't have the woman he loved? Boyd staggered to his car, shaking with shame and disappointment. Nothing in his life had ever prepared him for such a monumental rejection. He was not sure if he could go on living knowing he'd be denied the true love he deserved.

He was reaching for his keys when the wind blew through his hair, sending his scent wafting into the night, carrying it across the lot and into the brush, where it was inhaled and savored by one who could truly appreciate it.

Boo Boo, his hunger for human flesh satisfied, suddenly froze, discovering a new hunger long suppressed by drugs. This new hunger was overpowering, undeniable. He spit out a piece of Reed Roland's pinkie and darted toward this new and wondrous smell.

Boyd pulled his car keys out of his pocket, but his hand was shaking so much he dropped them. He was reaching down to pick them up when Boo Boo saw him for the first time. And what a mightily attractive sight it was. Boo Boo couldn't control himself. He sprang gleefully through the air, colliding with Boyd's ass and knocking him headfirst into the door of his Mercedes. As thick as Boyd's pompadour was, it wasn't enough to cushion the skull-cracking blow.

Boyd thudded unconscious onto the pavement, blissfully unaware as lustful Boo Boo dragged him back to his cave, deep in the Pinnacle Studios jungle, for a night of endless passion, doggie style.

Chapter Twenty-One

The drug Flint slipped into Sabrina's drink knocked her out faster than a right hook. Flint knew this because he had used both techniques on women in the past when his inimitable charm failed him. Which was most of the time.

Not that women didn't yearn for a gander at his power tool, just that they usually weren't the women he wanted. And they usually weren't rich enough to pay for him not to care.

"She just can't hold her liquor," he said to nobody in particular, tossing her over his shoulder and carrying her out of the bar and back to his car.

It only took him twenty minutes to get back home, which he figured gave him more than enough time to do the deed and return Sabrina to her trailer before she knew what hit her.

And when she did find out, she'd be wide awake and on her way to the bank to make a sizable withdrawal. He still charged women for a look at his prick, whether they remembered seeing it or not, but the prices had gone up considerably with inflation.

Charlie Willis was asleep in his car across the street when Flint arrived, so at first he wasn't even aware there was someone with Flint. It was only as the garage door was closing that he caught a glimpse of Flint, and what looked like Sabrina Bishop over Flint's shoulder.

Then the garage door closed, and Charlie was left wondering if what he'd seen was real or the remnants of a very strange dream. Just to be sure, one way or the other, Charlie got out of his car and dashed over to the house for a closer look.

He slipped carefully through the kitchen door, the same one he'd broken into a few hours ago to install the listening device in Flint's phone. He'd felt vaguely guilty about breaking the law he'd sworn to uphold, but not so guilty that he denied himself a little tour of the place. He had seen nothing out of the ordinary, except for the circular bed in a mirror-lined round room.

Which was why he knew the sounds of movement he heard were coming from there, and why he was particularly worried. Somehow, he just couldn't imagine Sabrina spinning around on the bed with Flint, even if she did make love in a dental chair in *Torrid Embrace*. Then again, he told himself, she might not be here at all.

Charlie crept cautiously down the hall, disturbed by the sounds of heavy breathing, buttons popping, fabric ripping, and zippers unzipping. He was nearing the half-open, bedroom door when he heard the electric hum of the bed beginning to rotate.

He flattened his back against the wall and using the tip of his shoe, carefully nudged the door open and peered inside.

Sabrina Bishop was sprawled half conscious across the spinning bed, her shirt ripped open, Flint Westwood standing over her, struggling with her bra.

"Halt," Charlie said.

Flint whirled around, startled, as Charlie charged into him, knocking him backward into the mirrored wall. The two men crashed through the glass into a tiny room containing a professional video camera and shelves of boxed cassettes.

Charlie scrambled to his feet and, momentarily distracted by his discovery, gave Flint the opportunity to grab a wooden stool and throw it at him. Charlie ducked, and the stool sailed over his head and across the bedroom, smashing into the opposite side of the glass wall, revealing yet another camera and a video printer for producing still photos.

Enraged, Charlie turned and decked Flint with a powerhouse right hook that sent Frankencop tumbling into the shelves of cassettes, taking them down with him to the floor, where he slumped unconscious amid the hundreds of his video interludes.

Charlie was about to read Flint his rights when two things stopped him. One, the realization he wasn't a cop and two, the videocassettes. Charlie picked up a box and read the sticker.

Esther/Nov. 17.

A trickle of blood rolled down from his forehead and obscured his vision. He wiped the blood from his eyes with the back of his hand, and noticed that it, too, was pretty cut up.

He stuck a couple of cassettes in his torn shirt, climbed out of the little room and checked on Sabrina. She was still unconscious, tossing her head ever so slightly from side to side.

Charlie picked her up in his arms and carried her away.

Once again, Eddie Planet stood in Daddy Crofoot's suite at the Mirage, looking ten stories below at the fiery eruption of the fake volcano.

Same view, different Eddie.

He didn't fly up here coach on some rinky-dink, overbooked airline filled with sweaty, overweight pensioners with slot machine fever. This time, Eddie and Delbert Skaggs flew up to Las Vegas in Daddy Crofoot's private jet. And Eddie wasn't here this evening to beg for financing, his bowels tied in knots. He was here to be congratulated.

Frankencop was already guaranteed to play out the season and, with the way ratings were climbing, it had the potential to run for several years. If it did, it would make Eddie Planet rich, and Daddy Crofoot even richer. Throw in merchandising dollars and possible series spin-offs, and the profit potential was enormous.

In three years, Eddie figured he could conceivably walk away from *Frankencop* with $50 million in his pocket. If he played his cards right. And thanks to Delbert Skaggs, Eddie had learned a whole new way of playing the game.

Eddie glanced over at Delbert, who sat in a leather chair, his back ramrod straight, staring into space ahead of him as if watching a movie.

No doubt Delbert was seeing the future. And as Eddie glanced back into the synthetic pyre below, so was he. Eddie was already thinking about putting to work for himself the lessons he'd learned— with a little help from Otto and Burt.

Eddie foresaw a time when there'd be only one showrunner on *Frankencop*—and it wouldn't be Delbert Skaggs. If Otto and Burt could get rid of a dog, how much harder could a person be?

Oddly enough, Delbert's thoughts were on the same wavelength. He'd mastered the television game—no, he'd *re-created* it—and although Eddie had unexpectedly served him well, the pathetic little worm was outliving his usefulness.

Sure, Eddie had the pitch, but in the television future Delbert envisioned, the pitch wouldn't be necessary. In Delbert's mind, pitching was synonymous with pleading and Pinstripe Productions wouldn't pitch, or plead, to anyone.

The networks ruled by power and fear, qualities Delbert, or anyone who toiled in organized crime, understood. The networks had the power to buy shows, to turn a poor, struggling producer into a rich and influential one. The networks also had the power to take it all away, to kill shows and careers in an instant.

It was no different from the way the mob did business. Except the networks, those clowns, were soft. None of 'em had any real muscle. The only power they had was what the cowardly producers *gave* them. All that money just sitting there for the taking, and no one understood how easy it was to get it.

Until now.

First, Delbert planned to eliminate the competition and then, anyone at the network who dared influence the fate of *Frankencop*. No network would ever cancel a Pinstripe Productions series. Delbert would personally cancel anyone who tried. The series would end when Daddy Crofoot decided it would.

"Hello, gentlemen," Daddy Crofoot said as he emerged from behind the double doors of the master suite, looking happy and refreshed in his white terrycloth robe.

Eddie turned just in time to catch a fleeting glimpse of three naked women in the bed before Daddy Crofoot closed the doors behind him.

"Sorry to have kept you waiting," Crofoot said. "Delbert, looks like Los Angeles agrees with you."

"If it didn't, I'd have to kill it," Delbert said with a grin, rising to greet Crofoot, who pulled him into a hug.

"That's what I like about you," Crofoot said, clapping Delbert on the back. "Where others see an obstacle, you see an opportunity. I just hope you never think of me as an obstacle."

"Never, Daddy," Delbert said, knowing neither he nor Crofoot believed it for a second.

Crofoot moved past Delbert and strode over to Eddie, who flashed his biggest smile.

"Daddy, you look great," Eddie said, and then, at a loss for words, but feeling an uncontrollable urge to fill the silence, added, "Have you lost a few pounds or something?"

Crofoot shook Eddie's hand, gave him a perfunctory smile, and turned his chair back on him to face Delbert, who settled back into his chair.

"I want to tell you both how pleased I am with the progress you've made in Los Angeles. The ratings are up, and the competition is . . ." Crofoot searched for the right words. "How shall I say it?"

"Getting killed," Eddie said, without thinking, and instantly regretted it. But Crofoot didn't seem insulted. In fact, quite the opposite.

"Yes, exactly," Crofoot replied, turning around and offering him a quick, approving smile.

"I'm glad you're pleased, Daddy," Delbert said, his elbows resting on the armrests and making a steeple out of his fingers. That was probably as close as he ever got to a place of worship. "But we're just getting started."

"Yeah," Eddie said. "Morrie Lustig called me and personally invited me in to pitch some projects. Even lobbed an idea of his own over the plate. I think I can knock it out of the park."

Delbert Skaggs and Daddy Crofoot just stared at him. Eddie suddenly felt very uncomfortable.

"But if you've got some concepts you'd like to kick around, hey, I'm open to fresh ideas," Eddie said.

"We aren't going to the network to peddle any more series," Daddy Crofoot said. *"They* will be coming to *us."*

Now it was Eddie's turn to stare. Who did these guys think they were? Did they honestly think that just because *Frankencop* was getting some decent numbers, the networks would be crawling to them for shows?

"What are you gonna do," Eddie asked. "Kill 'em if they don't?"

"That's the idea," Delbert said coolly.

Daddy Crofoot slowly approached Eddie, who backed against the cold glass. For a moment, he thought Daddy was going to push him out the window into the volcano below. Crofoot slipped his arm around Eddie's shoulder and pulled him close enough to whisper in his ear.

"You know what I think, Eddie? I think you shouldn't be worrying about what to pitch," Crofoot said. "You should be worrying about the three hundred thousand an episode I'm losing."

"Daddy, you'll get it all back in syndication," Eddie said. "Forget about it."

"I can forget about a lot of things," Crofoot said. "Money isn't one of them. Let me explain something to you. My friends, like Delbert here, they make me money, earning my respect and admiration. My enemies, they cost me money, and disappear from my life completely. I want you to be my friend, Eddie."

"I want to be your friend," Eddie said, his throat suddenly so dry he could barely speak.

"Good," Crofoot led him toward the master suite. "Give it some thought. In the meantime, I know three beautiful ladies who can help you clear your head."

Crofoot opened the double doors for Eddie, revealing the three naked, voluptuous women, who beckoned to Eddie like hungry succubi. To Eddie, their heads could just as well have been covered with writhing, hissing snakes. He stumbled inside, like a man in a trance, the doors closing gently behind him as he fell onto the bed and into their arms.

"When can I kill him?" Delbert asked when Crofoot returned.

"Soon," Crofoot promised. "There may still be some things about this business we don't know."

"I'm concerned about *Miss Agatha*," Delbert began. "It was a success on Sundays, and now it has been—"

That's when the phone rang. Crofoot let it ring a second time before he picked up the receiver.

"Yes?"

"Where's Skaggs?" Flint shrieked, clearly in a panic on the other end of the line. "I've been looking all over the fucking planet for him."

"Calm down, Flint. He's right here with me. Now what's the problem?"

"Charlie Willis."

And as Crofoot listened to Flint tell his story, his face turned hard and cold, devoid of all humanity. It was an expression Delbert Skaggs recognized, because he had seen it before on his own face, on those rare occasions he'd happened to see his reflection before killing someone.

Chapter Twenty-Two

The first thing Sabrina noticed was his smell, then it was the feel of his shirt against her skin. Above all, it was the feeling that she was safe.

She lay there, her eyes closed, his shirt hugged to her body, and tried to piece together the images that flitted across her psyche. There was Boyd Hartnell, transformed into a hideous dogman, flying at her. There was Flint Westwood, lifting her toward him.

She remembered jukebox music, the taste of white wine, the odor of cigarette smoke, and the world spinning. Then everything dissolved into a kaleidoscope of images, her own reflection, Flint Westwood's leer, shards of broken glass. Somehow, she knew that something awful had happened, and that Charlie had saved her.

And now, her eyes closed, she could feel Charlie Willis near, his shirt around her, and it soothed her. She didn't know where she was, or what had happened, and yet she felt secure.

So when she opened her eyes, she was not surprised to see Charlie Willis in the darkness, sitting in a chair, watching her. So was McGarrett, who lifted his shaggy head from Charlie's feet to get a good look at her, then shuffled out of the room.

"Are you all right?" Charlie asked softly.

She held out her hand to him and whispered. "Hold me."

He didn't move. He seemed reluctant to take her hand. "Don't you want to know what happened?"

"Later," she said, gently wiggling her fingers, beckoning him to take her hand.

Charlie leaned forward, took her hand, and let himself be pulled to the bed, where he carefully slid beside her. She curled up against him, wrapping a leg around his waist, reaching her arm across his chest, nuzzling her face against his neck.

Charlie lay there, uncomfortable at first, every muscle in his body tense, but as she drifted off to sleep against him, he felt himself relax. It had been a long time since he had held anybody. It had been a long time since anybody had held *him*.

It felt good.

Ever since Esther Radcliffe had shot him, life seemed unreal. Fact and fiction blended into an absurd pseudo-reality that swept him up like a hurricane and spun him across the city. At times, he wondered whether he was, in fact, truly conscious or still lying in a hospital bed, confusing a bizarre, drug-induced dream with reality.

But now, being held, he suddenly felt grounded, as if certain for the first time since being shot that he was himself, and that while the world might be tilted on its axis, his balance, at least, was restored.

Charlie stroked her hair and realized as he, too, fell asleep, that he hadn't rescued her. She had rescued him.

Charlie didn't remember waking up, only the taste of her lips on his, the feel of her body atop his own. His heart was already pounding, his skin already damp with sweat, his body already hungry for her touch. He was caught up in it without ever knowing when it began.

And then she pulled him into her, squeezing him tight, thrusting herself against him, her face twisted with the ache of desire. He leaned up, taking her breast in his mouth, devouring it. She moved against him hard and quick, pumping her pelvis against his, her hands holding his head tight to her bosom, her breaths coming deep and fast.

He gripped her buttocks with his hands, forcing her to move even faster, and tugged on her stiff nipple with his lips, sucking it into his mouth, swirling his tongue around it. She let out a cry, and suddenly she came, jerking against him, her eyes squeezed tight, her lower lip quivering, every muscle and tendon in her neck jutting out, taut as piano wire.

Charlie felt his own orgasm burst free, his face pressed against her soft flesh, his hands digging deep into her ass, holding her against him.

And when it was over, he slowly fell back against the mattress, bringing her down with him. They lay there together, breathing hard, until their hearts stopped pounding, their bodies cooled, and they fell asleep again, safe in each other's arms.

Muck Thing's swamp looked even more ominous at night than it ever did on television.

It was here that Shayne Collier, idealistic young scientist, was conducting his controversial genetic experiments. But fate took sides against him. A bolt of lightning hit his laboratory during a critical stage in his experiment. In the cataclysmic explosion, the doctor was transformed into a sickening amalgamation of man, plant, earth, and beast.

Now Shayne Collier is Muck Thing, a towering half-insane pillar of slime who, as Peter Graves intoned during the opening titles each week, *is in a constant, bloody battle with himself for control of his soul.*

No one could ever be sure whose side he was on, and whom he would kill, friend or foe. Right now, as Otto and Burt trudged through the mud in this distant corner of Pinnacle Studios, they hoped it wouldn't be them.

If it were daylight, they'd know where the mechanical version of Muck Thing was buried in the slime. But now, sloshing around after Boo Boo, they were afraid they might accidentally bump into it and the crocodile it wrestled hourly to the glee of tramloads of tourists.

But if they didn't find Boo Boo before someone else did, their fate would be much worse. Eddie would never hire them again, and *Sunn of a Gunn* would remain a dream, surely never to be realized.

So here they lurked, hunting for a dog, an activity they ordinarily would have enjoyed. But a hobby stops being fun when it becomes work.

Otto and Burt were armed with crossbows, steel-tipped arrows, and a gunny sack for stowing Boo Boo's remains. This time they were taking no prisoners, an attitude best expressed by the way they were dressed—army camouflage gear, red headbands, and aviator shades.

It didn't matter that it was pitch black out. They looked bad, so they were bad. Dudes to be reckoned with.

Otto and Burt marched from the swamp and onto the bucolic grounds of the stately Windsor Manor, made famous in *Windswept*

Love, Pinnacle Pictures' forty-year-old ripoff of *Gone With the Wind.* Dozens of times each day, Atlanta and the Windsor Manor burned to the ground in a pyrotechnical extravaganza, thrilling tourists out of the nausea inflicted by riding the tram through *Inspector Infinity*'s Spinning Wheels of Time.

That's when Otto heard the tinkle of liquid. He naturally assumed it was Burt wetting himself. His daredevil buddy had been incontinent ever since a misguided stunt for Lee Horsley's *Dead Beat* involving a motorcycle, a moose, and the Dallas Cowboy cheerleaders went horribly awry.

But it wasn't Burt uncontrollably relieving himself that Otto heard. It was Boo Boo, leaving his mark on one of the Windsor Manor's portico pillars, a few short yards away.

Startled, Otto fired his crossbow in the dog's general direction. Although the arrow missed Boo Boo by a good ten feet, the little mutt got the sentiment. He bolted into the Windsor house.

Otto and Burt rushed after him, dashing across the tram tracks and storming into the house. They reacted so quickly, probably neither one of them gave any thought as to how, exactly, the Windsor Manor erupted into flames for each passing tram. If they had thought about it, perhaps they might have noticed the tiny sensors on either side of the tram track, and the beam of light which, when broken, activated the flames.

Behind the antebellum facade, in the pitch darkness amid the blackened pipe and hinged girders, the first realization Burt had that something was wrong was the smell of rotten eggs and a loud hissing sound. Otto assumed it was Burt again, and gave his friend a nasty look. Burt knew better.

"It's not me," Burt said, grabbing Otto and running toward the nearest window. They dived out just as the manor burst into flames, collapsing on itself in a premeditated pile of burning timbers.

The bad-ass dudes hit the ground aflame and ran screaming across the tracks into the swamp. With their clothes on fire, it's understandable why they didn't notice the other sensor beam they broke, the one designed to activate the next attraction on the tour.

Otto and Burt rose from the muddy water, their clothes steaming, their skin blackened and blistered, to see Boo Boo sitting at the edge of the swamp, riveted by something just beyond them.

"You don't think . . ." Otto began.

He would have finished, but his question was answered when the giant mechanical crocodile dragged Burt screaming under the water. Before Otto could react, Muck Thing rose up in front of him and grabbed him by the throat.

Boo Boo watched the furious Muck Thing and the vicious crocodile ripping each other apart, Otto and Burt caught between them. After a minute or two, Boo Boo pissed on a tree to let 'em all know who was boss, and moseyed back to his new home for a little loving.

It began like any other episode of *Miss Agatha*. There she was, in her trademark paisley dress and sweater, her hair neatly pinned in a matronly bun, confronting a suspect in his home.

Only this time, she began her questioning by pushing him on the bed, grabbing his cock, and wrapping her mouth around it.

McGarrett ambled up to the TV, sniffed the screen, and shuffled off to the kitchen for a good stiff drink from his water bowl.

That morning, as Charlie watched Esther Radcliffe sucking Flint Westwood's outrageously large dick, he was struck by a few things. One, he now was confident he knew Esther's secret, and two, he knew why she was willing to kill the person she thought was behind it. What he couldn't figure out was why she hadn't realized it was Flint from the start.

She had to have been blinded by her own vanity, lust, and her hatred for Charlie Willis to have overlooked the obvious. Then again, perhaps not all the photographs were taken from the videos Flint filmed in his bedroom. Quite possibly, he had photographed other clandestine meetings, and had blackmailed her with those as well.

Now that Charlie knew Esther's dark secret, and what lengths Flint would go to secure new victims, he wasn't sure quite how to handle his discovery.

Perhaps there was a way to take care of them both, and keep his hands clean at the same time. While he was thinking about that, he heard footsteps coming from the bedroom. He quickly flicked off the set and turned to see Sabrina Bishop standing in the hall, naked under one of his shirts, which hung down to her knees.

She looked comfortable, as if she had been living in the house and wearing his clothes for years.

"Somehow, I keep ending up with your shirts," she said, smiling.

"You can have 'em all," Charlie replied, moving aside so she could sit next to him on the couch.

She sat down, kissed him lightly on the lips, and motioned toward the TV. "What were you watching?"

"A very special episode of *Miss Agatha.*" He handed her the cassette box. "With special guest star Flint Westwood."

"The jerk who drugged my drink," she said, glancing at the box.

"Flint is blackmailing Esther with this stuff," he said, "and I think you were next on his list."

"Who'd give a damn if I was screwing Flint Westwood? Anybody can go down to Blockbuster, rent *Torrid Embrace,* and watch me give Andrew Stevens a blowjob." She shook her head. "I would have used the tape to nail the sonofabitch for raping me, which didn't happen, thanks to you."

"No thanks necessary," he replied, stopping himself before he said *Just doing my job, ma'am.*

Something suddenly occurred to Sabrina. She looked at Charlie, confusion on her face. "I don't want to sound inconsiderate, but what *were* you doing there?"

Charlie got up and smiled. "Fair question. Tell you what, you sit down at the table, and help yourself to some coffee. I'll explain everything while I make us some breakfast."

So she sat at the dining room table, scratching McGarrett behind the ears and sipping fresh brewed coffee, while Charlie told her the story from the kitchen. He repeated what he had already told her about Esther shooting him, and continued through the bugging of Flint's phone.

Sabrina listened intently, asking only a few questions, which surprised Charlie who, based on their past experiences, expected at least a little incredulity.

"What are you going to do next?" she asked.

Charlie emerged from the kitchen carrying two plates and some silverware. "I don't know. I was hoping you might have some suggestions."

He went back into the kitchen, returning a moment later with a platter of what looked like scrambled eggs, which he set down in the center of the table.

"It took you all that time to make scrambled eggs?" she asked.

"These aren't just scrambled eggs." Charlie proudly served her a big helping. "This is one of my mother's favorite recipes. Something she whipped together when we didn't have any money. She called it Dangerous Eggs."

"What's in them?"

"Whatever's left in the fridge."

She looked dubiously at the plate in front of her. "That could taste awful."

"That's why we call 'em Dangerous Eggs."

She glanced at Charlie and cautiously took a bite. She chewed it for a moment, her face lighting up with surprise. "Hey, it's not bad."

Charlie scooped a healthy forkful into his mouth and nodded with agreement. "Yeah, it's pretty good." He shot her a smile. "The pastrami doesn't overpower the macaroni and cheese the way I thought it would."

She shot him a playfully nasty look, and then they ate in silence. Sabrina plowing through three helpings of eggs and half a pot of coffee while Charlie watched, amused.

"What's so funny?" she asked. "It so happens I'm always hungry whenever I'm attacked by a dogman, drugged by a blackmailer, and rescued by a TV cop."

"Ex-TV cop," he replied, turning to McGarrett, who sat beside the table, drooling. He set the platter down in front of the dog, who devoured the remains, sliding the plate along the floor as he ate.

"Dangerous Eggs are his favorite dish," Charlie said.

"I'm afraid to ask why." Sabrina got up slowly from the table and started to wander around the room.

Charlie stayed where he was, content to watch her, to wait for what she had to say.

"This was inevitable."

"You mean getting kidnapped by Flint Westwood, or regretting that you ate my breakfast?"

"I mean us getting together."

She spoke with her back to him, like a bad TV show. Charlie knew, because he had starred in one. He had protested to the director that people never did that and, lo and behold, here was someone doing it. If he ever got back into series television, which was doubtful, he'd remember that.

"You and I are a lot alike," she said. "We're both new to television, we're both alone, and we've both been used by Pinnacle Studios. You're also the only sincere person I've met in this business."

"I sold out everything I believed in for fifteen thousand dollars an episode," Charlie said. "I don't feel so sincere."

"That's the other thing we have in common," she replied. "I sold out everything *I* believed in for fifty thousand, a Corvette, and direct-to-video stardom."

"So what you're saying is that we deserve each other."

"What I'm saying is that it's time we both acted on what we believe in," she said. "You believe Esther framed you for murder because she thought it was you who was blackmailing her. Me, I believe in you. So I guess that means you should kick her ass and I should help you."

Charlie got up from the table, walked over to her, and took her in his arms. "This isn't television. You can get hurt."

"Then I guess you'll just have to protect me," she said, pulling him close and giving him a kiss.

Chapter Twenty-three

Hartnell Missing, Burley Temping

While police investigate the baffling disappearance of Pinnacle Pictures Television topper Boyd Hartnell, veteran producer Jackson Burley will temporarily take command of the troubled studio.

"It's not often a creative type like myself gets to see what life is like in the executive suite," Burley said. "I have a great deal of respect for Boyd Hartnell, and until his return, I look forward to helping Pinnacle recover from its recent troubles."

The Pinnacle lot has been besieged lately with a string of tragedies, from the accidental shooting death of an actor on My Gun Has Bullets, *to the disappearance of Boo Boo and the maiming of* Johnny Wildlife's *Reed Roland by a wild animal.*

Burley brings with him a track record of series success, and has put several new projects into active development, including the return of Don Knotts to TV in Matt Jacob, *based on the books about a down-on-his-luck, substance-abusing P.I.*

Burley also revealed that James Arness will trade in his spurs for Soft Shoe, *a sitcom pilot about a retired song-and-dance man who moves in with his gay son, a Broadway chorus-line dancer. "People think they're lovers," Burley says, "and then the hijinks begin."*

At parties, director Dag Luthan would often regale everyone with hilarious stories about how difficult it was working with a monkey in *Me and the Chimp,* or coaxing a performance out of a Pontiac in *Knightrider.*

But now, getting chewed out by Esther Radcliffe, he longed for the days of working with obstinate simians and talking cars.

"Look at these cue cards," she said, practically hitting him with the placard. "The handwriting is absolutely unacceptable."

On Esther's orders, the woman who wrote cue cards had already been summarily escorted off the lot by a security guard for her offensive handwriting. Luthan had expected to see the cue cards defaced with unreadable cursive or ugly chicken scrawl.

That would have been too easy.

Instead, he saw Esther's lines written with a Magic Marker in big, simple, block letters that anyone, except perhaps the legally blind, could read with ease from twenty yards away. And he told her so.

"They couldn't be any straighter or more evenly spaced if she had done every letter with a ruler," he said.

"Exactly." Esther tore the placard in half. "The letters are lifeless, without character or emotion. It's throwing off my entire performance."

Luthan couldn't contain his dismay, even though he felt certain it would cost him his first steady job in years. "You want the cue cards written *in character?*"

"Is that so much to ask?" She tossed the shreds over her shoulder and marched off the set, leaving Luthan to stare after her, stunned, with absolutely no idea how to fulfill her outrageous demand.

Esther stormed out of the soundstage and started toward her trailer when Sabrina Bishop called out to her.

"Esther, could I talk to you for a moment? I could use your advice." Sabrina said, standing in the doorway of her trailer, which, as Esther had demanded, was a minimum of six feet shorter than her bus.

"Of course, sweetheart," Esther replied, eager to exacerbate any problem Sabrina might have, and to revel in whatever discomfort the unwelcome costar felt in her cramped trailer.

Sabrina stepped aside and let Esther in, closing the door behind her and discreetly locking it, not that Esther noticed. The geriatric star was taking in the place, relieved to see the trailer was every bit as cramped and gaudy as she had hoped.

"You've done wonderful things with your dressing room. It's so homey." Esther sat down in one of the matching swivel chairs and smiled at Sabrina. "You certainly don't need decorating tips from me, so it must be something else. Whatever it is, darling, I'm here to help."

"The other night, I was assaulted by Flint Westwood," Sabrina said bluntly. "He drugged my drink, took me to his house, tore off my clothes, and tried to rape me."

"Oh dear, how horrible." Esther reached out and took Sabrina's hand, giving it a comforting squeeze. "What a nightmare."

It was the most acting Esther had done in twenty years. While she was doing her best to exude concern, what she really wanted to do was slap the lying little bitch until she bled. Esther knew Flint Westwood didn't need to drug women for sex, and certainly not when he had an incredible fuck like herself more than satisfying his needs.

"I only hope you were able to escape with your virtue intact." Esther figured Sabrina's virtue was probably tarnished before the little slut was in her teens.

"I was rescued before Flint could do anything else to me."

"By whom?" Esther asked.

"By me," Charlie replied, emerging from the bedroom curtain behind her.

The sound of his voice caused an instantaneous reaction in Esther. In a nanosecond, her polite facade shattered, revealing the monster beneath. Sabrina could swear Esther actually snarled as she whirled around to face her foe.

Esther started to rise, but Charlie grabbed her by the shoulders and roughly shoved her back into her seat.

"Sit down, Esther," Charlie said sharply. "We have some things to discuss."

"So you two are in this plot together," Esther hissed. "I should have known. The sleazy parasite after my money and the filthy slut after my show. It's a perfect match."

"Shut up and listen," Sabrina snapped.

"Believe it or not," Charlie said, "we're going to do you a big favor."

Sabrina opened a drawer and pulled out a manila envelope. "Flint wanted to do to me what he was doing to you."

"You should be so lucky," Esther said to Sabrina, then motioned to Charlie, "but you sure as hell aren't if you're fucking *him.*"

"I'm not the one who's getting fucked," Sabrina said, spilling open the envelope on the table beside Esther. Out tumbled Charlie's photos of Esther making the drop in Playa Del Rey, and Flint picking up the money.

Esther slowly sorted through the pictures, her face reddening with each new shot.

"Flint Westwood was the one blackmailing you, Esther, not me," Charlie said. "You killed a man for nothing."

Esther stared at the pictures, hardly able to believe what she was seeing. It meant confronting the unthinkable notion that it wasn't her that Flint Westwood found attractive, it was her bank balance. And even more repulsive than that was the realization that if Charlie Willis wasn't blackmailing her now, he soon would be.

"I haven't killed anybody," Esther said evenly. "*Yet.*" She pushed the pictures away. "Are these the only pictures you have?"

Charlie smiled. "If you mean, have I seen you riding Flint's pogo stick? Yeah, I have."

Sabrina shot Charlie a scolding look, a glance that Esther didn't miss.

"So, you little bitch," Esther sneered, turning her chair to face Sabrina. "When do I get your bill?"

"We don't want your money," Sabrina said. "We aren't blackmailers."

"Then why are you telling me this?"

Charlie spun Esther's chair around to face him and leaned forward on her armrests until his face was an inch from hers, forcing her to rear back. "To give you a chance to do the right thing. You can either turn yourself in to the police, and take responsibility for the death you caused, or I can give all the photos and videos I have to the press and let them figure it out."

Esther glared at Charlie, her face screwed up in a scowl of hatred. "And you don't call that blackmail?"

"Think of us as your conscience," Charlie replied, straightening up. "If you have one, of course."

"Can I go now, or do you intend to beat mc, too?"

"I already have," Charlie said.

Esther stood, pushed Charlie aside, and squeezed past Sabrina to the door. "This isn't over. I'll see you both groveling at my feet, I promise you."

"You have two days to get your personal affairs in order," Charlie replied.

Esther shoved open the door and slammed it shut behind her. Sabrina let out a deep breath and turned to Charlie. "Now what?"

"She's probably going to kill Flint Westwood," he said. "Then us."

"What do we do?"

"My brother-in-law's a cop. I'll have him keep an eye on Flint." Charlie took Sabrina in his arms and gently pulled her close to him. "And I'll keep an eye on you."

She squeezed him even closer and whispered in his ear. "I want more of you on me than that."

What saved McGarrett's life was his keen sense of apathy. He simply lay on the kitchen floor, watching with vague curiosity as Delbert Skaggs picked the lock on the back door and slipped into the house.

Had McGarrett jumped and barked and snarled like other dogs, Delbert would have had to use the silenced gun in his hand. But it turned out well for both of them. McGarrett got to live, and Delbert didn't have to kill him, something he would have hated to do.

Instead, Delbert petted McGarrett with his gloved hand and proceeded through the house looking for Flint's videos. He didn't have to look far. Charlie had shrewdly hidden them on top of the VCR.

Delbert set down his gun and his briefcase and picked up the universal remote. He turned on the TV and the VCR, and hit Play. McGarrett ambled in and watched Esther having sex his way, then he returned to the kitchen, his mild curiosity satisfied. So was Delbert's. He switched off the VCR and left the tapes where they were—he'd take them on his way out.

When Delbert first heard about Flint's predicament, he was afraid it would complicate his strategy for dominating network television. But then, after giving it some thought, Delbert realized Flint's problem was actually a stroke of luck. Even Daddy Crofoot appreciated it once Delbert explained his plan to him.

Delbert picked up the briefcase and headed for Charlie's bedroom, where he opened the closet and looked for a suitcase or a tote bag. Delbert found a blue gym bag labeled *LAPD* and, attracted to the irony, stuffed it with the $50,000 in his briefcase, which he'd taken from Flint, who'd taken it from Esther.

That done, all that was left was finding Charlie's gun.

Robokillers, giant mechanical monsters from another world, stomped through the city, smashing buildings, crushing cars, and firing flame-streaking missiles from the massive cannons mounted on either side of their gleaming steel heads.

Below them, a small band of resistance fighters mounted a brave, if ill-equipped, defense against the towering invaders. They battled the otherworldly death machines with bazookas, land mines, and rebel tanks, jury-rigged cannons mounted on iron-plated jeeps.

It was here, amid the blackened girders of smoldering skyscrapers, that the last great battle for humanity would be fought. And a thousand tourists sat impatiently on metal bleachers, their Polaroids and camcorders aimed and ready, waiting for it to start.

No one was more expectant than Joel Metzger who, at thirty-three, still lived at home and slept in uniforms from *Star Trek*, *V*, *SeaQuest*, and *Logan's Run* that his mom made for him. On weekdays, he worked at a comic book store. Every weekend and holiday, however, his butt was planted right here.

The *Global Armageddon* action show was a pyrotechnical extravaganza based on the hugely successful movie of the same name. The one that changed Joel's life. Before the movie, Joel had been a Spacey, a diehard *Space: 1999* devotee who found himself constantly embroiled in the heated world of fan bigotry. In the world of fandom, Spaceys were a reviled minority, downtrodden by the ranks of Trekkies and followers of The Force. Spaceys just didn't get the respect they and *Space: 1999*, rightfully deserved in the science fiction community.

Tired of fighting against the narrow-mindedness of fandom, Joel sought respite in the opening day of the latest science fiction epic. Little did he know, standing outside the Mann Valley West on that fateful Friday evening three years ago, that the movie he was about to see would change his life forever. *Global Armageddon* wasn't just a movie, it was a rich, fascinating culture full of complexities and significance.

It was also a merchandising phenomenon for Pinnacle Studios, who depended on a steady stream of income from lunch boxes, hats, records, toys, T-shirts, canteens, videocassettes, candy bars and, of course, the *Global Armageddon* attraction at the tour, to finance lots of other, less successful movies.

Four times each day a dozen stuntmen reenacted a fiery battle between three towering Robokillers and the resistance. The entire fifteen-minute show consisted of the stuntmen taking spectacular falls, getting hurled through the air by explosives, and steering the rebel tanks over the rubble-strewn landscape, while all around them bombs exploded and buildings toppled, and Robokillers marched, shooting missiles.

Joel knew every move by heart, had analyzed the motivation of each character, scrutinized the battle strategy of both sides, and written a lengthy paper on the subject that was printed in the prestigious *Global Armageddon* fanzine. He'd sent copies of his treatise to the Pinnacle Pictures board of directors, offering himself as a consultant and proposing a complete redesign of the show based on his findings. Surprisingly, they had yet to respond.

Perhaps what eluded Joel was that a change in the program would cost millions even if, in the mythical world of *Global Armageddon,* it might give the resistance fighters a greater edge. All the staged action, from the hulking Robokillers knocking over buildings to an out-of-control jeep bursting into flame, unfolded according to an automated and precisely timed computer program activated by remote control. The show was, in essence, an updated version of a player piano, only instead of playing a ditty, it decimated a make-believe city.

The Robokillers and vehicles were on tracks, the buildings crumbled on cue, and each missile moved along a predestined course on barely visible filaments. Nothing was left to chance. It was all operated by remote radio control by the day's toothsome master of ceremonies, usually a wannabe actor hoping to break into the business by working on the tour.

Joel was one of the few who aspired to be just a *Global Armageddon* host, nothing more. No one cared about the characters, understood the enemy, or saw the show more than he did. But most of all, he dreamed of holding the remote control that brought the world of *Global Armageddon* to life. In fact, he could die happy if that was all he achieved in his life.

Sadly, this was as close to *Global Armageddon* as he was ever going to get. Because while the Robokillers marched through the city, a far more terrifying, and unbilled, studio attraction prowled beneath the bleachers.

Boo Boo was hungry.

It wasn't enough that *he* was hungry, he had a mate to feed now, too, back in his cave, deep in the backlot jungle. Boo Boo's drooling, moaning, prostrate lover, with her deep mane of golden hair, was everything Boo Boo had ever dreamed of. Life was good these days, spent mating, sleeping, marking, and hunting for food.

He brought his lover back half-eaten hamburgers, stale fries, anything he could scavenge. That was fine for mere sustenance. But what he craved, and his lover deserved, was the delicacy dangling above him right now—a big, juicy ass.

Which, unfortunately, happened to belong to Joel Metzger, who was about to experience his own personal Armageddon, thanks in large part to the fact that he'd sat in the same spot every time, week after week, show after show, for years. The bleacher beneath him had imperceptibly begun to sag under the stress of his excited bouncing and jumping, day in and day out.

At the exact moment when one of the Robokillers shot a missile seemingly into the audience, and hundreds screamed in surprise, Boo Boo leapt up and sank his fangs into Joel's butt.

Joel's scream was drowned out by those around him. When the bench broke, and he was pulled down under the bleachers, those who noticed thought it was part of the show.

He landed on the back of his head, snapping his neck and dying instantly, which was probably fortunate, because a moment later Boo Boo was tearing his flesh off in thick, bloody chunks.

Meanwhile, everyone in the bleachers above was too spellbound by the destruction in front of them to notice the carnage occurring under their feet.

In fact, Joel wouldn't be missed until three days later, when his mother returned from a slot machine tournament in Tahoe to find, to her horror, his *Deep Space Nine* bedsheets unwrinkled and the new box of Rice Krispies she'd left for him unopened, the free *Global Armageddon* action figure still buried inside.

Chapter Twenty-four

··

Flint Westwood was glad when Esther called him on the set and invited him to her house that evening. He figured it would give him a chance to do a quick appraisal of her personal property and see if maybe a price hike was in order. Besides, after the harrowing day he'd had, he was in the mood for some penile adulation.

So he left the set in his Porsche and sped along Mulholland Drive to her Beverly Hills estate, which was hidden behind a high stone wall and tall trees.

Esther's house resembled a French villa in Provence and, in fact, almost was. She'd bought a three-hundred-year-old stone mansion and had it dismantled and shipped to Beverly Hills to be reconstructed. Unfortunately, no one could decipher the dismantlers' French scrawls and crude drawings. And even if they could, the county's building codes and seismic regulations prevented her from rebuilding the house anyway.

So Esther's house became a *replica* of a French villa, while the *actual* French villa became the wall that surrounded Esther's property, the only imported wall in Beverly Hills.

Flint Westwood had no appreciation of French architecture or imported stones, but he understood what the folly must have cost her. And if she could still live well after that, then she had money to spare. To spare on him, that is.

If she had any servants, he figured she'd given them the night off, because she buzzed him through the gate herself. And she was there to meet him at the door, in a clinging silk robe, a crooked, lusty grin on her face.

Esther didn't say hello, didn't ask him why he was all bruised and cut, and didn't offer to give him a tour. She just grabbed him by the crotch and led him up the grand spiral staircase to her bedroom, which was dominated by a hand-carved four-poster bed and a crystal chandelier. She didn't want talk, she wanted action. Fine with him. He could peruse her belongings afterward.

She pushed him back on the bed, pulled off his pants, and began working his member into greatness without even taking out her dentures. Obviously, she worshiped his hard body. The way he figured it, the old bag was lucky to have him at twice the price, even if she knew it was him she was paying, which she didn't. And wouldn't. Daddy Crofoot would see to that. His endowment was worth as much to Daddy as it was to Flint.

Closing his eyes, imagining Sabrina Bishop writhing on top of him, he could almost forget it was Esther lapping up his awesome enormity and her ardent appreciation began to feel pretty good. He felt the blood surging downward, awakening the slumbering behemoth between his legs, making it rise in all its majesty.

She stopped for a moment, so he glanced down to take an admiring gander at himself, and was not disappointed. It was a landmark in its own right, the leaning tower of Los Angeles in all its engorged glory.

He was so entranced by his own erection, he didn't notice Esther reaching under the bed until it was too late.

In one swift motion, she whipped out a pair of hedge shears and pinched his giant boner between the gleaming, razor-sharp blades. He gasped in utter terror, unable to speak, unable to breathe, his eyes locked on his throbbing, hostage penis.

"It's a shame we don't have the cameras running, lover boy, because this would be a keeper. My best performance yet and your last." She grinned with malicious delight, her lips wet, her arms braced to Bobbitt. "After I cut it off, I'm gonna smoke it."

Esther was about to chop when her breast exploded in a sickening burst of silicone and blood. She jerked back, her hands still clinging to the shears, and then the top of her head flew off, knocking her to the floor and freeing Flint from the shears.

Unable to breathe, he watched his penis shrivel up like the Wicked Witch of the West, perhaps never to rise again.

Delbert Skaggs casually unscrewed the silencer from his gun and strode into the bedroom to glance at Esther. She was heaped in a clump on the floor, covered in blood and brains, her hands still gripping the hedge shears. He had planned to kill her, but he hadn't expected to find her with Flint, and he certainly didn't expect to find her about to chop his prick off.

"Don't worry about cleaning up the mess," Delbert said. "Leave that to me."

No problem at all, Flint Westwood would have said, if he'd been able to speak. He was still staring at his groin and still wondering if he'd remember how to breathe again. There was so much to comprehend. Esther with the shears. Delbert with the gun. Esther dead on the floor. His prick dead between his legs. How did she know about the pictures?

"Does anyone know you're here?" Delbert asked.

Flint tried to speak, but nothing came out. Delbert tossed Flint his pants and asked again. "This is very important, Flint. Does anyone know you're here?"

Flint shook his head no.

"Good," Delbert said. "That makes things much easier."

For a moment, Flint thought Delbert was going to kill him, too, and so did Delbert, who never let anyone witness a killing and survive.

Yet he let Flint live. It went against everything he believed in, but there was no way around it. He needed Flint alive at least until they had enough episodes of *Frankencop* for strip syndication. Then Delbert would kill Flint and, as the villains on *Frankencop* always said, make it look like an accident. He couldn't let a witness live, even if it was a member of Daddy Crofoot's family. In the meantime, Delbert had to make sure Flint got away clean.

There was nothing UBC could program against *Frankencop* now that could pose a serious threat. With Esther Radcliffe dead, *Miss Agatha* was finished. And with Boo Boo dead, UBC lost the one show they had that could provide a strong enough lead-in to a new series and make it a formidable competitor to *Frankencop*. Pinstripe Productions' dominance of Thursday nights, and soon the entire Nielsen rating, was assured. There were just a few more, final details to take care of first.

"There's a plainclothes police officer parked outside your house," Delbert said. "I want you to go home, change your clothes, and go to a movie or something. Can you do that?"

Flint slowly pulled on his pants and nodded.

"The cop is going to follow you, so obey the speed limit and make sure he doesn't lose you," Delbert said, watching Flint slip into his loafers and button up his shirt. "Enjoy the show, have a nice dinner, and when you get back home, all your troubles will be over."

We'll see if that's true next time I'm in bed, Flint thought, hurrying out the door without bothering to thank his guardian angel, or to ask himself what Delbert was doing there in the first place.

Charlie and Sabrina spent the night making love, hungrily, desperately, like two starving people given a shopping spree at Safeway.

They moved through Sabrina's condo like two Tasmanian devils, their wild, unrestrained lust upending tables, knocking over couch cushions, toppling chairs, and wiping dishes off the kitchen countertops. They finally ended up in her bed, clawing the sheets off the mattress as they writhed, wrestled, wriggled.

For the first time in months, Charlie felt he actually had some control over his life, even while completely letting go of his pent-up passions. Making love to Sabrina felt great, and not just physically. It made him feel he had come back to life, returning to the real world from that different dimension he'd been inhabiting since he was shot. Maybe even *before* he was shot.

Only now did he realize that losing Connie had hurt him far more deeply than he was willing to admit. Fact was, the day she walked out on him was the day he lost control of his life. All it took to get a grip on it again was an insane old woman, a bullet in the stomach, premature ejaculation, and pretending to be a man he wasn't. Not exactly a therapy he'd recommend to the lovelorn. But hey, it worked.

Charlie still had his problems, but at least he felt he was fighting back, maybe even winning a couple of battles along the way.

It was different for Sabrina. Being with Charlie, she felt secure for the first time since coming to Los Angeles. More than that, she didn't feel alone against it all anymore.

Ever since she arrived in Hollywood, she had been surrounded by mercenaries, lechers, sharks, and pigs. The only person that she could depend on, that she could trust, that she could *stand* to be with, was herself. Now she had Charlie. And she was going to hold on tight.

And that's what she did, wrapping herself around him in a myriad of different ways, in several different rooms, until they finally, ultimately lay exhausted in her bed, entwined in each other's arms, sticky with each other's sweat.

They stayed that way for that long, sweet hour between their last simultaneous orgasm and the moment when her alarm clock jangled at four A.M. Sabrina had an hour to shower and make a feeble attempt to study her script before the limo arrived to take her to the studio.

While she did that, Charlie lay tangled in the sheets, the room thick with the smell of sex and sweat. If Glade could bottle the aroma, he thought, they'd make a fortune.

The limo arrived promptly at five o'clock and whisked her away to Pinnacle Studios, where she'd have another hour or so for makeup and wardrobe before she was expected on the set for a thrilling episode of *Miss Agatha*.

Charlie figured she'd be safe from Esther on the lot, as long as Sabrina checked out her prop gun and any weapon a guest star might use against her. He also warned her to keep an eye open for runaway cars, falling lights, or unstable scenery. When shooting wrapped, he'd be waiting for her at her place. In the meantime, he had some work to do.

As soon as she was gone, he dressed and straggled out of the house, figuring he'd shower and shave when he got home, then knock off some copies of Flint's cassettes. He wanted to be prepared for a mass mailing tomorrow—he had very little faith that Esther would suddenly do the right thing.

The freeway heading north into the valley was practically empty, while the southbound lanes were already packed with puffy-eyed commuters heading into the city from the suburbs, jerking themselves into consciousness with cranked-up radios and jumbo jugs of coffee.

The sun was beginning to shine through the airborne sludge, which was churned by the spinning blades of countless helicopters as radio stations, police, and TV channels all vied for the best view of the awakening city.

Charlie tuned in KNX news radio to see if the world had changed drastically overnight. Boo Boo was still missing, but was sighted running down the aisles at a Wal-Mart in Sacramento, chewing on a bone in Yosemite, pissing on a shrub in New Jersey, and eating cherry pie with Jimmy Hoffa at a truck stop in North Platte. The less important news of the day—a presidential summit, a devastating earthquake in China, and a cure for the common cold—was promised after the commercials.

But by then Charlie was already pulling into his driveway. He snatched up his sprinkler-soaked edition of the *Los Angeles Times* and trudged to his door.

When he stepped inside, his mind was on breakfast, and whether or not he should have stopped for a McMuffin. So his first thought when he was slammed against the wall, and felt the gun jammed in his back, was that he should have eaten something before getting killed by Esther.

"Don't move," said a gruff, male voice behind him. Suddenly a half-dozen cops spilled in through the front and back doors, kneeing aside McGarrett in their rush to get in. Bringing up the rear was Spinoza, the forensics expert.

Charlie felt his arms being pulled behind his back, and a pair of handcuffs closed around his wrists. Then he was spun around to face Sergeant Emil Grubb.

"You're under arrest," Grubb said.

"What's the charge?"

"Murder," Grubb replied, holstering his gun and turning to the cops around the room. "Toss the place, catalog and note everything you find." The cops pulled on rubber gloves and got to work. Charlie glanced at the TV. The videocassettes were gone.

Grubb turned back to Charlie.

"You got the right to remain silent, and all that stuff," Grubb said. "Do I need to do the whole number?"

"No," Charlie replied. "Who did I kill?"

"You mean besides that actor?"

"There's someone else?" Charlie asked incredulously.

"Esther Radcliffe."

Whatever control Charlie fleetingly felt over his life abruptly disappeared.

ACT FOUR

Chapter Twenty-five

The situation was achingly familiar. A recalcitrant murder suspect questioned by the hard-nosed cop. It might as well have been a scene out of *My Gun Has Bullets*. In fact, Charlie was certain it was.

The interrogation room was just like the set, and the dialogue sounded like half a dozen scripts that still kicked around in his head. Only in those scripts, Charlie was Derek Thorne, supercop, crusader for justice, quick with a quip or a right hook. Now Charlie was playing the villain.

He heard actors say playing the bad guy was more fun than the hero, but Charlie wasn't enjoying the chance to stretch as an actor. Hands cuffed behind his back, Charlie was intentionally paraded down every corridor in the station before they finally took him into interrogation. For a cop, for a man who believed in the badge, there was nothing more humiliating. And Grubb knew it.

"Last time you killed someone, we had you, we had the gun, we even had the murder on film. All that was missing was the motive," Grubb said. "This time, you made it easy. All that's missing is the film."

Grubb held up an evidence bag containing a gun. "You recognize this?"

"It's a plastic bag," Charlie said, stealing a line from a bad guy in episode three. Or was it episode four?

"This is your gun, We found it in a storm drain a mile from Esther Radcliffe's house," Grubb said. "Your prints are all over it."

Grubb handed the bag to the silent, stone-faced cop standing by the door. Cop #1. That's what he would be called in a *My Gun Has Bullets* script. He was significant enough to be a presence, but not enough to actually deserve a name.

"Obviously, someone stole my gun and killed her with it," Charlie said, glancing at Cop #1. He even looked like the extra from episode three.

"Funny, I thought the obvious explanation was that *you* killed her." Grubb responded.

"That's why you're still in the North Hollywood division," Charlie said. "If I killed Esther, and was dumb enough not to wear gloves, why didn't you find any powder burns on me?"

"Because you were smart enough to wash your hands with Ajax before you came home."

"I was smart enough to do that, but so stupid I left my prints on the murder weapon and tossed it in a gutter a mile from the crime scene."

Grubb shrugged. "Maybe you underestimated my intelligence."

Charlie sighed. "I doubt it."

Grubb paced back and forth, collecting his thoughts. "You know what we found in your house?"

"The six hundred pairs of socks I've lost?"

"Fifty grand in cash," Grubb said.

Charlie didn't have to look too far ahead to see where this clumsy frame was going and who was behind it. Flint Westwood.

He never figured the guy for a killer, then again, he wouldn't have thought Esther was one, either. The only thing Charlie couldn't figure out was how the whole thing went down.

Maybe Esther was planning on killing Flint with Charlie's gun, and things went bad, and Esther ended up dead. Perhaps Flint framed Charlie as an afterthought. Or maybe a frame was Flint's idea all along, to get back at Charlie for ruining his little blackmail operation.

Whatever the explanation, Flint was at the center of it and Charlie was the fall guy.

"It's not my money." Charlie said.

"So you're telling me someone took your gun and left behind fifty grand to cover the loss?"

"I'm telling you someone stole the gun and planted the money," Charlie said.

"There you go, underestimating me again," Grubb said. "I got another theory, you want to hear it?"

"I don't know," Charlie said, turning to Cop #1. "Do you?"

Cop #1 said nothing. Of course he didn't. Extras usually don't, otherwise their price jumps from $50 to $500 a day, plus pension, health, and residuals. The show could only afford seven or eight speaking parts an episode. If Cop #1 had any lines, he'd have a name. So Grubb was probably getting that guy's dialogue, too. If Charlie's life was a TV show, he hoped Grubb was a recurring character who'd get written out real soon.

"It goes something like this," Grubb said. "You pull over this crazy old lady for speeding, and what does she do? She shoots you in the gut. The studio buys you off with a TV series, but you never really forgive the hag for popping you. So you blackmail her for fifty thousand."

Charlie sagged in his seat. *Lou LeDoux.* It had to be Lou. The sonofabitch sold him out. His own brother-in-law. Lou wouldn't take the story to the police when Charlie *wanted* him to, but now, when it meant saving his own ass, Lou tells everybody. Now the truth made a tidy motive for murder.

What was interesting, though, was what Lou apparently *didn't* tell—that he was following Flint Westwood for Charlie last night. Which meant Grubb probably knew nothing about Flint and Esther. Charlie wasn't sure if that was going to help him, but he decided not to volunteer it anyway. He could see now he would need every edge he could get if he was going to get himself out of this.

Grubb pulled out a chair and sat down at the table with Charlie. "She gets tired of paying you, so she loads your prop gun with live ammo. But her plan goes wrong. You don't get killed, some other poor schlub does."

At least I'm off the hook on *that* killing, Charlie thought, if only by virtue of being charged with another. He had no doubt about being charged. Even an idiot like Grubb could convince the D.A. to press forward with a ready-made case like this.

Flint had done a good job.

"So you hit Esther up for another fifty grand. When she won't pay, you go over and see her. Maybe you didn't plan to kill her, maybe you just lost your temper, and that's why you blew her brains out. Whatever the reason, you did it." Grubb looked at Charlie. "Did I leave anything out?"

Charlie decided to see just how much Grubb really knew. "If I was blackmailing her, what did I have on her that was worth so much money?"

Grubb took another evidence bag out of his pocket. The guy was singlehandedly keeping Ziploc in business. Inside the bag was a bullet. "You threatened to reveal she shot a cop."

So they didn't know about Flint and Esther, and they didn't have the tapes or the pictures Charlie took of Esther paying Flint off in Playa Del Rey. Flint must have taken everything, but Sabrina still had the photos that she showed to Esther.

Even so, Charlie had to admit, it was a hell of a case. He'd appreciate it more if *he* was the hard-nosed cop who put it together instead of the recalcitrant suspect going to prison.

"Now's your opportunity to shoot me down with your brilliant alibi," Grubb said.

Yeah, so it was. And Charlie would have one, too, if only there was a script to read it from.

Charlie thought about spilling the truth, telling Grubb he spent the night with Sabrina Bishop, but that would draw her into his mess. The press would go crazy. It wouldn't take much of an intellectual leap, not even for Grubb, to figure the two of them were in on the killing together, Charlie for revenge, Sabrina for her own show. He wasn't going to bring her down with him. Not that he planned on going down.

"I couldn't sleep, so I drove around all night," Charlie said.

"*That's* your alibi?" Grubb was surprised. Clearly, he'd been expecting better. "You got some witnesses, like a gas station attendant, a waitress, somebody?"

"Nope," replied Charlie.

"You want to call your lawyer?"

"Yeah, I think I should." Charlie glanced at Cop #1. "You want to bring me the Yellow Pages?"

Shooting came to a sudden halt on the *Frankencop* set right before Flint Westwood's first scene of the day.

For the last three hours, the crew had just been sitting around in the shade, eating from the craft services table and reading the trades.

The director was on his cell phone, whining to his agent. The actors were in their trailers, enjoying the air conditioning the below-the-line grunts didn't have.

It was bound to happen on any show. Eddie Planet had seen production shut down for a hundred different reasons. Faulty equipment, nervous breakdowns, bad weather, salary disputes, food poisoning, union problems, rattlesnakes, even a flood.

He could even understand the news about Esther Radcliffe's murder having such an emotional effect on some crew members that they couldn't get the first shot for an hour or two.

But never, *ever*, had he heard of a show shutting down because the lead actor's pecker couldn't get into character. And never before had a shutdown meant so much to Eddie personally. Each hour of inactivity was costing the production company tens of thousands of dollars. The losses would be added to the deficit. And the higher the deficit got, the fewer hours of life Eddie Planet had left. Daddy Crofoot had made that very clear.

So now Eddie was in Flint's trailer, standing in front of Flint, who sat in his bathrobe, doe-eyed and depressed.

"All you have to do in this scene is pick up the radio and call headquarters," Eddie said. "There's nothing to it."

"My cock doesn't want to call headquarters."

"Your cock isn't on camera," Eddie said.

"It doesn't matter." Flint stared forlornly at his groin. "It's part of me."

"Yes, I know that," Eddie said impatiently. "But if the rest of you doesn't call headquarters, you won't know that the Slime Devil escaped from Cryoprison."

"There's no cock motivation in that," Flint said. "I'm an actor, goddammit—there needs to be cock motivation."

"Okay, fine, *cock motivation.*" Eddie drummed his fingers on the countertop. "The desk sergeant, her name's Monique."

"I thought the desk sergeant was Harry."

"Well, now it's fucking Monique," Eddie snapped. "And she's not wearing underwear."

"She's not?"

"No, she's not," Eddie said. "She's waiting for your call, for *your cock* to call, and just hearing your voice, knowing that magnificent cock is part of you, turns her on."

"And what's in it for my cock?"

"It wants to fuck her." Eddie pounded his fist on the counter. "What else do you think it wants to do?"

Flint closed his eyes and concentrated. Eddie watched, drumming his fingers again on the counter. Flint opened his eyes and shook his head. "It's not working."

"Maybe it would work if you tried it outside, in character, in front of the camera," Eddie said.

"I don't think so," Flint said. "It's just not into it today." The fact was, his penis had retreated into his testicles and might not *ever* come out.

The trailer door opened, and there stood Delbert Skaggs. That, in itself, was a surprise, since this was the first time he had ever shown himself on the set. But he was about to do better than that.

"Hello, Eddie," Delbert said, closing the door softly behind him. "What's the problem here?"

"His cock lacks motivation," Eddie said.

Delbert nodded his head, took a seat beside Flint, and put his arm around him. "I think I have the solution." With his other hand, Delbert reached into his jacket, pulled out his gun, and jammed it into Flint's crotch.

Flint let out a little yelp, sitting straight up, his eyes glued on the gun. This was the second time in twenty-four hours his stupendous studliness had been threatened.

Eddie instinctively jerked back, pinching his knees together as if it were his own crotch Delbert was aiming at.

Delbert spoke very calmly. "Why don't I just blow it off and it won't trouble any of us again?"

"Daddy wouldn't like that," Flint stammered.

"Daddy has invested millions of dollars in this project. Usually, when something endangers Daddy's investments, he has me remove it." Delbert forced the gun deeper into Flint's groin, causing Flint to ride up in his seat. "*This* is endangering his investment."

"I think I found a motivation," Flint squeaked.

206

Delbert removed the gun. "I thought you would."

Flint quickly got up from his seat and hurried out of the trailer. Eddie watched Delbert slip the gun back into his jacket.

Eddie willed his knees to separate and reached into the refrigerator for an Evian. "You certainly know how to talk to actors," Eddie said, shielded by the refrigerator door.

When Delbert didn't respond with a hail of gunfire, Eddie figured it was safe to stick his head out again and close the door. Delbert just sat there, watching him. Eddie opened the plastic bottle, took a long drink, and forced a smile.

"You and I make a hell of a team," Eddie said. "I'm the idea man, the creative talent if you will, and you're . . ." Eddie looked into Delbert's dark, almost lifeless eyes, and it came out before he could stop himself. ". . . you're the killer."

Eddie's knees involuntarily clacked together, his testicles shriveled up, his back went rigid, expecting Delbert to whip out his gun and shoot. Instead, Delbert just smiled thinly. "You got something you want to say, Eddie?"

"Don't get me wrong, I think things are working out great," Eddie said, relaxing only slightly. "An actor gets killed on *My Gun Has Bullets*. The Two Dicks get parboiled. Boo Boo disappears and Miss Agatha gets snuffed. It's all good news for us."

Eddie finished his water and carefully set the plastic bottle down. "I was just thinking it's time to let the show compete creatively for a while."

"Creatively." Delbert wanted Eddie to get out on that limb, to give him another reason to want him dead.

"With compelling stories, strong characters, and interesting actors," Eddie said. "You know, maybe see how we do awhile the old-fashioned way."

Delbert slowly rose from his seat to stand in front of Eddie. "The old-fashioned way is dead, I thought you understood that."

"I do, of course I do," Eddie said quickly, realizing his next few words could mean the difference between life and death. "I was just thinking maybe it would be better for the show, for Daddy's investment, if our competition stopped having accidents for a couple weeks. We wouldn't want anyone else noticing all our good luck."

There was a long silence during which Eddie imagined Delbert trying to decide how to kill him. *Should I slit Eddie's throat? Shoot him in the gut? Or smash his head against the wall until his skull splits open?*

Eddie didn't know it, but it was probably as close as he would ever get to actually reading Delbert's mind.

Delbert motioned Eddie closer and then spoke quietly into his ear.

"Thinking can be hazardous to your health, Eddie," Delbert whispered. "I would advise against it."

"Say no more," Eddie whispered, giving Delbert the thumbs-up and stepping back, allowing his co–executive producer plenty of room to get to the door. The sooner the better.

"I always appreciate your sound advice," Eddie said, "because you know this business like you were born into it."

Delbert opened the door and stepped outside, but that didn't stop Eddie from talking.

"I said it from the moment we met, you're a natural," Eddie said. "More than that, you're a *visionary.*"

Delbert slammed the door and headed for his car. The fact was, Delbert envisioned at least two, possibly three more deaths in the future. One was Eddie Planet, the other was Sabrina Bishop. She knew about Flint's blackmail scheme, and also had the potential to carry on the *Miss Agatha* franchise. She had to go. And if the American justice system couldn't take care of Charlie Willis, Delbert would.

Back in the trailer, Eddie sat down carefully, breaking into an itchy, anxious sweat. *Frankencop* was on the verge of becoming a megahit, and he was thankful to Delbert for bringing them to the precipice. But Delbert's job was done. Eddie didn't need a co–executive producer anymore, certainly not one who jeopardized the success of the show. Surely, even Daddy Crofoot would appreciate that.

And if he didn't, well, maybe Eddie didn't need *him* anymore, either.

Chapter Twenty-six

Listening to television themes could usually lift Don DeBono out of the doldrums and energize him to action. Yet not even the throbbing rhythms of *Barnaby Jones* could stir him today.

DeBono sat behind his desk in an office that suddenly seemed too big, making insignificant everything that he was and aspired to achieve. All because some bloodthirsty, psycho-killer asshole murdered Esther Radcliffe. If he had any tears left, he'd start sobbing again.

He wasn't mourning Esther Radcliffe, it was the loss of *Miss Agatha* that he grieved for. Without it, he had no more hits left. His network was a wounded deer in cougar country.

And just outside his door the vultures were circling. Buttonwillow McKittrick was sharpening her talons, ready to pick on his rotting bones.

Esther's death wouldn't have mattered so much if he still had Boo Boo, the wonder dog, the hitmaker. Even Esther's sensational murder got second billing in the nation's newspapers to the burning question WHERE'S BOO BOO?

The whole country loved Boo Boo. The ugly mutt was bigger than Elvis—already he was being sighted more often than the King, Big Foot and the Loch Ness monster put together. He was being sighted everywhere but Thursdays at eight P.M. on UBC.

Gripped by a pang of anxiety, he aimed his remote at the stereo system and skipped forward to *Ironside*.

The theme's familiar strains conjured up a rush of reassuring images. The main title silhouettes. Robert Ironside. Lighting his cigarette. Enjoying that first puff. Then ka-blammo. Shot in the back. Finished.

But Ironside wasn't. Did he let a shattered spine stop him? Hell, no. He fought back. Even strapped in a wheelchair, no villain could best him.

Okay, DeBono thought, sitting up straight. So he had no hit shows. He'd been shot in the back by lady luck. He was down. What could he do now?

He zapped the CD player again. *The Six Million Dollar Man.* Steve Austin, astronaut, a man barely alive. Lost his arms and legs in a fiery crash. Did that stop him? No, it made him better than he was before.

Better. Stronger. Faster.

That's what his network was. Cut off at the knees. A cripple. What DeBono needed was bionic science. He got up from behind his desk, and walked toward the display case of *TV Guides.* There was wisdom here.

He zapped again while staring at it all, every minute in the history of television, bound and cataloged on the shelves in front of him.

Ratings and shares danced in his head. Series. Specials. Finales. *Rescue from Gilligan's Island.* The "Who Shot J.R.?" season premiere of *Dallas.* The final episode of *The Fugitive.*

What did they all have in common?

Popular characters. Everyone loved Gilligan, hated J.R., and rooted for Richard Kimble.

Big events. The castaways finally rescued. Loathsome J.R.'s attacker revealed. Dr. Richard Kimble finding the one-armed man.

But there was more to it than that. DeBono could feel it. He was missing that essential something that grabbed the nation by the throat and slammed them against their TV screens.

What the hell was it?

DeBono tapped the scan button on his CD remote. The themes from *Mary Tyler Moore, Lost in Space, Branded, Wonder Woman, Saddlesore, Time Tunnel, The Honeymooners,* and *Batman* shot past his head like bullets. He closed his eyes, paced, and tried to squeeze the answer out of his brain with sheer concentration.

It was no good. Nothing was coming. If he had the answer, he wouldn't need Boo Boo. And how could he concentrate when another, bigger question was tormenting him, just as it did an entire nation?

Where's Boo Boo?

DeBono suddenly froze, his heart pounding so loud it drowned out *F-Troop.*

Where's Boo Boo?

Could it be so simple? So obvious? He switched off the CD player and stood very still, holding the thought, caressing it.

He suddenly realized what each of those hit shows had in common. They answered a question, not just *any* question, but one that gripped the entire fucking country.

Will Gilligan and the castaways ever get off the island? Who shot J.R.? Would Richard Kimble catch the one-armed man and clear his name?

Where's Boo Boo?

Yes. That was it. He started to shake. Either it was the physical manifestation of a staggering intellectual epiphany, or he was having a nervous breakdown. Maybe it was a little bit of both.

Where's Boo Boo?

DeBono marched to his intercom and punched it. "I want every department head in my office now."

It was only an idea, half formed, yet Don Debono knew it could be the greatest success in the history of television. It might even put him on the cover of *TV Guide.* All he needed was a star, and he had the perfect person in mind.

"I don't have a lawyer, and I only had one call, so I'm calling you," Charlie said.

Sabrina sat in her limo, holding the cellular phone to her ear. Esther Radcliffe's murder was an enormous shock, Charlie being arrested for it was an even bigger one. Both her career and her love life had taken powerful blows.

"But you couldn't have done it," Sabrina said. "You were with me last night."

"They don't know that." Charlie stood at a pay phone just outside his holding cell. A police officer stood a few yards away, barely out of earshot, watching Charlie.

"Didn't you tell them?" Sabrina asked.

"No, I didn't."

"Why not?"

"Because I don't want to get you involved in this," Charlie replied.

Even in jail, charged with murder, he was trying to protect her. She wanted to reach out and hug him.

"I *am* involved, Charlie. If you won't tell them, I will. I'm on my way down there right now."

"Please don't, you'll only be making things worse for both of us." he replied.

"I want to help you," she said. "I don't want you going through this alone."

"If you want to help, you can find me a good lawyer," he said. "And could you feed McGarrett for me? I think they left him at the house."

He was worrying about *his dog*. She started to cry. Charlie was too good. She wasn't going to let anyone, not even the police, take him away from her.

"I want to see you," she said, wiping away a tear.

"No," Charlie replied firmly. "Promise me you'll stay away from the police station. It's going to be swarming with reporters and I don't want you sucked in to this. You don't know me, you've never even met me. Hell, you've never even *heard* of me. Okay?"

She didn't say anything.

"Hello? Sabrina? Are you there? Have I lost you?"

"You haven't lost me," she said. "And I'm not going to lose you."

There was a sudden burst of static on the line and then it went dead, the signal cut off. She held the silent phone against her ear for a moment, then set it back in its cradle.

Sabrina was reaching for the wet bar to make herself a drink, when the phone trilled. She snatched it up.

"Charlie?"

"No," said the voice on the other end, "this is Don DeBono."

Sabrina leaned back into her seat, preparing herself. Here it comes. The ax. "Mr. DeBono, what can I do for you?"

"I know you're still grieving, and believe me, I share your sorrow at this tragic time," he said softly, then added with urgency, "but I need you here at UBC in twenty minutes."

Couldn't he just tell her now that her TV career was over and save her the humiliation of being told face to face?

"Is that really necessary?"

"Necessary?" Debono sounded surprised. "Sabrina, I've got two hundred people in a soundstage right now building sets and setting up lights. I've got six film crews on the street shooting footage and twenty-five editors waiting to cut it all together. All we need is you."

"To do what?" she asked.

"Save our network."

Charlie spent the entire night trying to sleep and knowing he couldn't, not as long as he was in a jail cell.

Because he was once a cop, they couldn't stick him in with the usual tenants in the holding cells. If they did, they knew all they'd find was Charlie's corpse in the morning. So they stuck him in the drunk tank and let the intoxicated denizens of society sleep it off with the evening's pack of whores, killers, rapists, junkies, thieves, and pushers. That would sober the drunkards up quick.

Charlie was left to sit on a stone slab in a cell that reeked of piss and puke. The walls were stained and soaked with it. He figured they could dismantle the building, bury the slabs, and wait a thousand years, and future archeologists would still be able to figure out how much booze its inhabitants had imbibed and what they'd eaten for dinner.

Contemplating profound thoughts like that distracted him from his predicament and kept him up until morning, when he hoped to meet his lawyer, whoever he or she might be.

Sure enough, at 9 A.M. he was told he had a visitor. Charlie was led into a room, where he relished the recirculated air and basked in the warm glow of fluorescent light for a few minutes until his attorney arrived.

A police officer opened the door and in bounded a rotund man in a satin *Cop Rock* show jacket, his round face capped with an Amblin Entertainment baseball cap. If it weren't for the Armani shirt, slacks, and tie, Charlie would have figured him for an obsessed TV freak, arrested while stalking somebody like William Shatner. The man turned to the officer.

"That'll be all, friend," the man said, waiting for the officer to leave. Once the cop was gone, the man held out his pudgy hand to Charlie.

"Victor Ratliff," he said, giving Charlie an enthusiastic handshake. "It's a real thrill to meet you. I loved your show."

"Thanks," Charlie replied.

Ratliff set his briefcase down and sat on the edge of the table, presumably because the chair couldn't hold his weight or, Charlie guessed, because he saw Perry Mason do the same thing.

"I take it you're my attorney," Charlie asked.

"That's entirely up to you, Charlie," Ratliff said. "Rest assured, I'm a specialist in celebrity criminal law."

"Excuse me?"

"Celebrities are larger than life—the law doesn't apply to you the way it does to the average Joe. We understand that fame gives you a sort of diplomatic immunity."

Which is how Esther Radcliffes are born, Charlie thought. Now he knew how such a dangerous woman managed to stay out of jail. There were probably countless violent acts in her past that some "specialist in celebrity criminal law" had hushed up. Like the time she shot a police officer, who was given a series in return for his silence.

"When it isn't possible to get you off outright, our firm recognizes that our responsibility is twofold," Ratliff continued. "To defend our clients and, at all costs, maintain their bankability—or TVQ in your case."

Charlie couldn't believe that in his twelve years of law enforcement experience, he'd never encountered this particular beast before. "How exactly did Sabrina find you?"

"We're quite well known in certain circles. Let's just say we only represent people in the biz," Ratliff said. "Perhaps you heard about a certain sitcom father arrested at an orgy wearing women's lingerie?"

"No, I can't say that I have."

"Or the influential casting director who ran a call girl ring?"

"Must have missed it."

"How about the starlet who beat her boyfriend into a coma?"

"Never heard of her."

Ratliff smiled. "Then I've made my point."

Charlie gave him a dubious look. "You really think you can keep my name out of the papers?"

"No, but I *can* minimize the damage, maybe spin the story to your advantage, and I'm a hell of a fighter in court." Ratliff replied. "However, my services aren't cheap. I charge about the same as *Matlock.*"

"I can afford it." If I empty my bank account, sell my house, and hire McGarrett out for stud service, Charlie thought.

"Can you get me a *My Gun Has Bullets* jacket?"

"We weren't on long, we only had T-shirts."

"That'd be fine," Ratliff said. "I'm sort of in the biz myself, you know."

"No, I didn't."

"Sure, I dabble. I write scripts. Musicals, mostly. Maybe you'd like to see one?"

"Right now I'd like to see the outside of this jail," Charlie replied.

"No problem." Ratliff clicked open his briefcase. "We'll get you into court for an arraignment and have you bailed out. Figure bail is gonna be in the high six figures."

Charlie nodded. Ratliff pulled out a yellow legal pad and a pen.

"Before we go any further, I want to hear the whole story, from the top." Before Charlie could begin, or even decide how much of the truth to tell Ratliff, something occurred to the star-struck jurist. "Oh, Sabrina asked me to give this to you."

Ratliff reached into his briefcase, pulled out a neatly folded man's shirt, and handed it to him.

There was a handwritten note attached to the shirt. It read: *I'm returning the favor. I won't leave you exposed, either. Love, Sabrina.*

For the first time in twenty-four hours, Charlie felt he might just make it.

Chapter Twenty-seven

Otto and Burt were sitting in Eddie's living room, two briquettes leaving charcoal stains on his wife Shari's white couch. When she got home from her aura massage, Eddie was certain she'd kill him.

Let Shari throw a tantrum—it was nothing compared to the potential rewards of this little gathering. Eddie brought them their martinis, shaken not stirred, as they requested.

"What happened to you guys?" he asked, looking them over. Their clothes were scorched, and their hair was singed down to the roots. Their skin was blistered and red, slick with medicated cream and oils.

"We fell asleep in the sun," Burt said, always fast on his feet.

"Your clothes are burned," Eddie said.

"It's a style," Otto said. "It says to the world that you're so hot you set your own clothes on fire."

"I see." Eddie didn't, but for a brief moment, he actually found himself thinking their idea wasn't bad, and wondered if he should steal it.

Otto and Burt were too worried to realize they might have just come up with a new fashion fad. They were more concerned with what effect their charred flesh would have on their budding acting careers.

"You think our sunburns will make a difference?" Burt asked.

"In what?" Eddie was thoroughly bewildered.

"Our chances with *Sunn of a Gunn*," Otto replied. "I mean, do you think we're too tan for the parts?"

Eddie stared at them, dumbfounded. "I don't know."

"George Hamilton is tan," Otto observed. "And he's still suave."

"We're even tanner," Burt added. "So we're even suaver."

"Especially in that new fashion of yours." Eddie was unable to resist the jab, not that they'd notice. "No, your rich tans won't hurt the show. We've only got one obstacle, and it's a big one. In fact, that's why I asked you here today."

Otto and Burt were relieved—they thought he'd found out about Boo Boo or, maybe, about Twinkles, Shari's cat. When they were working on Eddie's house back in '88, Burt accidentally ran over Twinkles, so Otto poured the cement patio over her.

"What obstacle?" Burt asked.

"I'm really excited about *Sunn of a Gunn,* and I can't wait to get started on it," Eddie enthused. "You guys are natural-born stars. The Cary Grant and David Niven of our generation. Anybody could see that. Except Delbert Skaggs."

"Why not?" Otto asked.

"It boggles my mind, too," Eddie replied. "I've tried to convince him, but he just refuses to accept it. Frankly, I think it's jealousy, that he didn't discover you and your immense talent himself."

"Can't we do the show without him?" Burt asked.

"Unfortunately, no." Eddie sighed heavily and refilled his drink. "I'm under exclusive contract to Pinstripe Productions, and if he doesn't go for the idea, it's dead. It's a shame, because I know the networks would flip for this."

There was a long silence in the room, broken only by the occasional snap of Burt popping one of his blisters. Eddie pondered his drink. Otto stared at the television, the opening titles of *Sunn of a Gunn* playing out in his mind on the blank screen.

Otto and Burt in tuxes, flanked by babes. Otto and Burt leaping out of an airplane, holding babes. Otto and Burt in their Bentley, babes in the back. Otto and Burt in a gunfight, protecting babes.

Then the picture abruptly vanished, as if someone had pulled the plug on the TV.

Otto looked up from the TV at Eddie.

"So, if Delbert Skaggs, for some reason, weren't around," Otto asked, "then Pinstripe Productions would do the show?"

"In a flash," replied Eddie, pleased that Otto had made the intellectual leap himself. Now all he needed was a little push. "I just don't see how that's gonna happen."

Burt shared a glance with Otto and smiled. "The same way it happened to Boo Boo."

"Hey, there's an idea," Eddie said, as if it were the first time it had occurred to him.

Otto smiled back at his friend. "Great minds think alike."

The two burnt stuntmen clinked their martini glasses together in a toast to their future, something Eddie would have to make sure they never had.

Charlie spent the early evening handcuffed to a chair outside the holding cells, waiting for his bail to be processed and his release to come through.

He told Ratliff the same story he gave to Emil Grubb, and was careful to keep Sabrina out of it entirely. Charlie still wanted a chance to clean up the mess himself, and figured he could always tell Ratliff all the dirty details if things got desperate enough. Though Charlie had a hard time imagining things getting any worse than they already were.

It was Ratliff's idea to wait until nightfall to get out of jail. Ratliff thought it would make it easier to slip past the throng of reporters, who spent most of the day crowded outside the building, angling for the opportunity to corner Charlie Willis, suspected murderer of a television icon.

Which was why Charlie was surprised the tiny television set on the guard's desk wasn't blaring out news about his arrest for the heinous crime. Instead, the UBC network announcer told viewers to stay tuned for *an astonishing, live special!* . . .

Suddenly there was Sabrina Bishop, standing in the center of what looked like a high-tech command center, surrounded by computer terminals, television screens, and smart-looking people either talking on headsets or typing away at keyboards. She was dressed in a sharp, efficient Ellen Tracy suit, grim-faced and serious. On her lapel was an official looking ID badge with her photo on it.

"Hello, America. I'm Sabrina Bishop. Tonight, we join a nation-wide manhunt. We'll track the clues and follow the leads. We'll interview the witnesses, reenact their experiences and, with your help, we'll try to answer the painful question tormenting us all." She stared solemnly into the camera. *"Where's Boo Boo?"*

Those three words, in carved-granite letters, hurled into the camera, prompting a thunderous musical refrain, reminiscent of the *Dragnet* march.

An announcer's voiced intoned, "Everything you are about to see is true, up-to-the-instant facts in the search for Boo Boo as it unfolds, *live* from our Command Center with your host, Sabrina Bishop."

The theme played and the credits rolled over pictures of adorable Boo Boo, culled from his series. Charlie glanced at the guard, who was riveted to the screen.

Someone yelled from the holding cells, "Can you turn it up?"

It was a request from the alleged barbecue murderer. Earlier that day, he'd been arrested, standing over an outdoor barbecue, gently brushing hickory smoke sauce on the remains of his neighbor, whom he'd killed and chopped into bite-size pieces.

The guard silently obliged, cranking up the volume. Despite the gulf that separated law officer from criminal offender, the two men shared a common love deeper than the divisions that divided them.

Boo Boo.

Charlie looked over his shoulder and saw, to his surprise, that all the inmates were quiet, straining to catch a glimpse of the tiny screen. They actually gave a damn about a sitcom dog, almost as if the pooch were their own.

And that's when he came to a stunning realization: you don't have to be an actor in a TV show to confuse reality with television. Nobody can tell the difference. *Everybody* thinks these characters are real.

When he was growing up, he sought refuge on television, identifying with Reed and Malloy on *Adam-12,* and longing for the orderliness of their world. It affected his entire life.

Meanwhile, how many people felt like members of the Cartwright family? Or felt closer to Rob and Laura Petrie than they did to their own neighbors? How many people sent Rhoda Morgenstern a wedding present? Cried when Lucy Ricardo gave birth? Mourned when Henry Blake was killed? How had it affected their lives?

The enormity of television's power hit him for the first time. It was so strong it could even evoke sympathy from a psychopathic killer for a fictional dog. They actually *believed* that Lorne Greene was Ben

Cartwright, James Garner was Jim Rockford, and Esther Radcliffe was Miss Agatha, and that they had a close, personal relationship with each of them.

"Sabrina will find Boo Boo," a suspected drug pusher opined, as if reading Charlie's mind. "She worked with Miss Agatha."

The BBQ murderer nodded in agreement.

Now Charlie understood something else. Don DeBono wasn't just exploiting the popularity of Boo Boo, but *Miss Agatha* as well. Everything about television was a manipulation of viewers' sympathies.

The one thing he didn't understand was what Sabrina was doing hosting the show.

Where's Boo Boo? returned with an establishing shot of a Wal-Mart store. The camera pushed in on the store, while Sabrina narrated. "Yesterday, in Sacramento, California, Gladys Aufderbeck went to this store for toothpaste. What she got was a brush with destiny."

And there was Gladys, thirty-two years old going on ninety, re-creating her magic moment, heading down an aisle, pushing her rickety cart. Now it was Glady's voice narrating the action. "I was in aisle seven, where the toothpaste used to be, but apparently they moved it to aisle eight some time ago. As I rounded the corner, I got the surprise of my life."

She stiffly and self-consciously reenacted her look of surprise. The camera whip-panned down the aisle for a glimpse of what looked like a small dog, then cut to an extreme close-up of Boo Boo from an episode of *Boo Boo's Dilemma*. "It was Boo Boo," Gladys narrated. "Right there in Wal-Mart. The dog saw me and ran away."

The action cut back to the Command Center, where Sabrina now sat with Gladys at one of the computer consoles. "I was terrified," Gladys confided to Sabrina. "I was afraid whoever stole Boo Boo would come after me."

Sabrina gave Gladys a reassuring squeeze and a glance full of concern, then turned to the camera.

"Our team of investigators is in Sacramento at this moment, looking for clues," Sabrina said. "If you saw Boo Boo, call the nine hundred number on your screen. Each call costs $2.50 a minute, a portion of which will be used to continue our nationwide search for Boo Boo. In a moment, we'll visit a New Jersey front yard where Boo

Boo may have left his mark only hours after his disappearance . . ."

Charlie didn't get the chance to see the famous soiled shrub, because Ratliff arrived with his release papers. The guard reluctantly tore himself away from *Where's Boo Boo?* to unlock Charlie's cuffs.

Ratliff quickly led Charlie through the jail house, self-assuredly taking him through back corridors and secluded stairwells as if he'd designed the building himself. Finally, they emerged in an alley behind the building, where Charlie found a rented Chevy Lumina waiting for him.

Ratliff gave him a firm handshake and handed him the keys. "Stay away from the press. If they happen to find you, don't say a word and, whatever you do, don't hit any of them."

"I haven't heard the news," Charlie said. "What are they saying about me?"

"You don't want to know," Ratliff replied. "But we've leaked the section of the police report regarding your motive. When the truth comes out about Esther, and what she did to you, this is gonna look like justifiable homicide."

"I didn't do it."

"Whatever." Ratliff waved the thought aside. "If I do my job right, by the time this is over, your TVQ will be higher than ever."

"Of course, I may be on death row at the time."

"But think of the TV movie and publishing action we can get," he replied. "It could be enough to finance your appeals."

"What a reassuring thought." Charlie walked around the car to the driver's side.

"We always look at the bright side," Ratliff gave Charlie the thumbs-up. "I want to see you in my office the day after tomorrow. We have to start preparing your defense."

Charlie nodded and got in the car. Ratliff suddenly remembered something. As Charlie pulled out, Ratliff yelled after him.

"Don't forget my T-shirt!"

Charlie waved to him to show he'd heard, and steered the car onto a side street to avoid the reporters out front. He knew where he had to begin if he was going to find out the truth. With Flint Westwood.

It took him twenty minutes to get to Flint's place. He parked across the street and studied the house. There were no lights on, and Flint's car wasn't out front. Not that Charlie worried about running into Flint, but he wanted to know more before forcing an encounter.

Charlie got out of the car, crossed the street, and went straight for Flint's fuse box. He carefully lifted the panel to reveal the tiny tape recorder that he'd attached to the wiring several days ago. The miniature tape contained all the messages that had been sent from the voice-activated bug he'd planted in Flint's phone.

He pocketed the recorder, got in his car, and drove off, listening to the tape as he headed down Wilshire Boulevard toward Santa Monica, for lack of a better place.

There were several calls to Pinnacle Studios and to the set of *Frankencop* looking for either Eddie Planet or Delbert Skaggs. Charlie was familiar with Eddie Planet but had never heard of Delbert Skaggs, who, he gathered from the calls, was also a producer on the show.

The desperation in Flint's voice increased with each failure to reach Eddie or Delbert. Flint called their cars, their homes, and finally placed a call to the Mirage Hotel in Las Vegas, where he asked for Daddy Crofoot's suite.

Charlie pulled over at Bundy and clicked off the recorder so he could think where he had heard Crofoot's name before. It must have been ten years ago. There had been a shooting outside of a Beverly Hills restaurant, and he was assigned to traffic control. A bunch of guys had opened fire on the diners, gunning down a group of insurance salesmen they'd mistaken for an East Coast mobster and his cronies. The mobster they were after was Daddy Crofoot. The suspected shooters were later found floating in the Los Angeles River with their throats slit.

Why would Flint Westwood be calling a mobster?

Charlie switched on the recorder again and eased the Lumina back into traffic. Flint's call was put through to Crofoot's suite and someone, presumably Crofoot, answered.

"Yes?"

"Where's Skaggs?" Flint demanded desperately. "I've been looking all over the fucking planet for him."

"Calm down, Flint. He's right here with me. Now what's the problem?"

"Charlie Willis." Flint replied. *"He's an ex-cop."*

"I know who he is," Crofoot said.

That remark surprised Charlie, until he remembered the media attention the My Gun Has Bullets *shooting attracted.*

"Is it safe to talk on this line?"

"If it wasn't, we wouldn't be talking."

"Right," Flint said. *"Okay, here's the thing, Willis broke into my place, knocked me around, and found my home entertainment system."*

"What do you mean, your 'home entertainment system'?"

There was a moment of silence on the line. *"You know what I need to get it up. I had a babe with me, I was taking pictures, and he stormed in, kicked the shit out of me and took my film."*

"Delbert, there's an extension by the couch, get in on this," Crofoot said.

There was a click, and then a new voice entered the conversation. Charlie presumed it was Delbert Skaggs, who asked to be filled in on the details. Crofoot quickly summarized things for him.

"So you were filming your fuck with hidden cameras?" Delbert asked.

"Yeah."

"Who was the woman you were with?"

"Sabrina Bishop," Flint said. *"She's on Miss Agatha."*

"Our new competition," Delbert explained.

"Willis took the film of Flint doing her," Crofoot said. *"So what?"*

Flint cleared his throat. *"Actually, he stole the film of me and someone else."*

"Who?" Delbert asked.

Flint hesitated for a moment. *"Esther Radcliffe."*

Crofoot exploded, yelling into the phone. *"Why the hell were you fucking that withered old bag?"*

"For fifty grand a pop," Flint said.

"Are you out of your goddamn mind?" Crofoot yelled.

"Do you realize the position you've placed the show in?"

"I was doing it to help *the show,"* Flint said. *"It was gonna be a surprise."*

"Believe me, it is."

"You don't understand," Flint said. *"I was gonna bleed her for every cent she had, and then send out the pictures anyway. You know, cropped real tight so all you saw was her and my big dick. It would have ruined her show."*

"Miss Agatha was on Sundays," Delbert said. *"They just moved opposite us."*

"I was looking ahead," Flint said.

"Can we do something about this, Delbert?" Crofoot asked calmly.

"I think I can take care of it." Delbert said. *"It could even work out to our advantage."*

"I don't see how," Crofoot said, *"but do what you have to do. Flint, I'll talk to you later."*

Crofoot abruptly hung up.

Charlie twisted the steering wheel, forcing the car into a tight, screeching U-turn across Wilshire Boulevard. He slammed down on the gas, the tires smoking, and roared back toward the San Diego Freeway.

There was more to Esther's killing than covering up Flint's stupid blackmail scheme. Somehow the mob was involved in *Frankencop,* and Charlie had stumbled into it.

Who was Delbert Skaggs? Was *he* the one who planted the money on Charlie? Could *he* have killed Esther Radcliffe? And was she killed to frame Charlie or for some other reason?

Charlie weaved through the cars in front of him, then cut across Wilshire Boulevard traffic onto the freeway onramp, roaring up the shoulder and into the northbound lanes. His speedometer edged past 90 as he sped through the Sepulveda pass, using the shoulder as his own private lane, leaning on his horn to force cars out of his path.

He began to think back on the events of the last few weeks, and a disturbing trend began to emerge. All the tragedies that had befallen the industry had benefited *Frankencop.* The shooting death on *My*

Gun Has Bullets. The electrocution of the Two Dicks. The disappearance of Boo Boo. And now, the murder of Esther Radcliffe.

Was it a coincidence, or something more? Charlie knew his own future could depend on the answer to that question . . . and finding the proof to back it up. And he knew exactly where to start.

Pinnacle Studios.

Chapter Twenty-eight

The mistake most crazed fans made trying to break into the studio was that they went through the front gate. There were at least a hundred ways onto the lot. You could get in through the tour, the office tower, the two dozen buildings that ringed the perimeter, the employee parking structure, and the various service tunnels.

Or you could do what Charlie did, and just climb the fence where the security camera is blocked by a billboard advertising Pinnacle's latest, high-concept, over-budget, flop movie. Which, at the time, was another remake of *King Kong*, starring Shannen Doherty.

Charlie dropped over the other side of the fence somewhere in Spain. The famed Spanish street was part of Pinnacle Studios' "little Europe" section of the backlot, which gave so many of Pinnacle's 1960s espionage series their international production value.

He crept through villages in Italy, Germany, and France, then trudged through the jungles of Africa, which at times had also been the jungles of Vietnam, South America, and the planet Umgluck, among others.

Finally, after traversing half of the earth and some alien worlds, he found himself outside Eddie Planet's bungalow.

Because producers had such faith in the security of the lot itself, they didn't take many precautions with their own offices beyond a decent dead-bolt. Besides, what was there to steal, story ideas? No one would notice, or care.

Charlie didn't bother with the lock; instead he found an unlocked window, slid it open, and climbed in.

He found himself in the outer office, where the walls were adorned with publicity posters from Eddie Planet's shows.

He's the best deputy ever to wear the badge. And this town wants him, dead or alive. DEPUTY GHOST. Taming the West from beyond the grave.

What do you get when you take the best of a dozen dead cops? One incredible cop. FRANKENCOP. Coming this fall!

Charlie studied the *Frankencop* poster. In small print, he saw the words *Eddie Planet Films in association with Pinstripe Productions.* Perhaps that was where Daddy Crofoot and Delbert Skaggs fit in.

He continued on, passing a door that had *Executive Bathroom* written on it in Magic Marker, and stopped when he saw Delbert Skaggs's nameplate on a set of closed double doors.

Charlie opened the doors, expecting an opulent office. Instead, he saw the same basic furniture that Pinnacle provided in most of their offices and that almost all the high-profile producers tossed out in favor of something more stylish.

The corner office was dominated, however, by a giant schedule board. Already the magnetic placard for *Miss Agatha* had been removed, leaving two empty spaces opposite *Frankencop* where series should be.

The placards for *The Two Dicks, My Gun Has Bullets, Boo Boo's Dilemma, Johnny Wildlife* and *Miss Agatha* were being used as paperweights on Delbert's neatly organized desk.

Charlie sat down at Delbert's desk and examined the board for a moment. He remembered seeing one in Jackson Burley's office, too. It was almost as if the things were altars, symbolizing the religion this strange sect of people lived by. But what they did in front of it after genuflecting wasn't clear to him.

Burley had likened it to the chalkboard a football coach might use to illustrate plays to his team. This, Burley had told Charlie, is the playing field. The only thing you don't see is the ball or the goalposts, but they are there.

Charlie tried to understand the game that was in play on the board now, feeling that if he did, things might suddenly make sense. But the board seemed lifeless to him, hardly the strategy in motion.

He turned in his seat and scanned the desktop. In front of him he saw a yellow legal pad on which a very different schedule had been drawn. It was the original three-network lineup for Thursday night as it stood at the beginning of the season. The ratings of each show had been jotted down beside their listings.

Lifting the page revealed another sketch, this time of a schedule with *The Two Dicks* and *Boo Boo's Dilemma* X'd out. Beside each show that followed *Boo Boo's Dilemma* on UBC Delbert had written a "current rating" and a "probable rating." In each case, the probable ratings dived. Except for *Frankencop,* which dramatically increased. Obviously, Delbert was guessing what would happen to the performance of those shows if they lost Boo Boo's lead-in. Which Charlie knew couldn't conceivably happen, since *Boo Boo's Dilemma* was the highest-rated show in America, and there was no way Don DeBono was going to move it.

Unless someone else did.

It was a chilling thought. Charlie quickly flipped through the pad—on each page was another hypothetical schedule, each one anticipating what effect the loss of a particular competitor would have on *Frankencop*'s ratings.

Now they're all dead, Charlie thought, just like Delbert imagined. Lucky Delbert.

Finally, there was a page in which *Miss Agatha* was slotted against *Frankencop.* The "current rating" for *Frankencop* was far below the rating for *Miss Agatha.* On the next page, *Miss Agatha* had been X'd out, and the "probable rating" for *Frankencop* doubled.

Now it all made sense to Charlie. The accidents, the frame-up, Esther's murder.

The mob owned *Frankencop,* and they were killing anybody who got in the show's way. As long as it was on the air, people would die.

With the pictures of Flint taking Esther's money, and the secret recording of Flint's call to Las Vegas, Charlie figured he had enough evidence to clear himself and, possibly, stop Delbert Skaggs before anyone else got hurt. Especially Sabrina.

He took the notepad and left in a hurry.

* * *

Eddie Planet eased open the Executive Bathroom door and peeked out in time to see Charlie Willis slip out the window.

Earlier in the evening, Eddie had been in his office, punching up a particularly awful *Frankencop* script, when *Where's Boo Boo?* came on the air.

He watched it mesmerized, knowing deep in his gut that he was witnessing television history. *Where's Boo Boo?* was an inspired, brilliant conception on every commercial and creative level. His immediate gut reaction was the show would grab a minimum 30 share. His immediate gut reaction also sent him running to his Executive Bathroom.

If *Where's Boo Boo?* could knock out a 30 share or more, it could make hits out of whatever stupid sitcoms or lame action shows followed in its wake. Which translated into doom for *Frankencop*, and a lot more killing. And with Delbert Skaggs's imminent demise, the responsibility for murdering the competition would fall to Eddie.

That prospect was enough to send anyone scurrying to the nearest toilet, especially a man with as sensitive a digestive system as Eddie Planet.

So there he was, sitting on the toilet, pants around his ankles and Watchman on his lap, when he heard someone crawling through the window in the outer office. He turned off the mini-TV and listened to the footsteps move down the hall.

At first he was afraid it was someone coming to kill him, maybe Delbert, maybe someone else. But the intruder went straight for Delbert's office, spent a few minutes inside, and then hurried down the hall.

Eddie took a chance and opened the door a crack, enough to see that the intruder was Charlie Willis.

What was *he* doing here, in Eddie's bungalow, only a day after being arrested for murdering Esther Radcliffe?

Of course, Eddie knew Delbert had done it, but how could Charlie Willis possibly know?

Oh God, did he know?

Suddenly, Eddie's stomach was seized by the memory of Charlie Willis, the morning after the shooting on his show, staring out from Eddie's TV set, his gun aimed at his unknown adversary.

I don't know who set me up, but I got a message for you. My gun has bullets and I'm coming for you.

What if Charlie thought it was Eddie who had set him up? What if Charlie came gunning for him?

Eddie grabbed his cramping stomach and tried to think. Breaking into a studio had to be a violation of Charlie's release. If Eddie could get him thrown into jail, maybe Crofoot knew some people who could jam a shiv into Charlie or something. At least if Charlie was in jail, Eddie would be safe from him.

Eddie picked up his cellular phone and dialed.

"Hello, security? This is Eddie Planet. Somebody just broke into my bungalow. I don't know for sure, but I think he had a knife, maybe even a gun."

Charlie was walking down a snow-capped street in Copenhagen when he was caught in the glare of headlights. He whirled around to see a Pinnacle Studios security cart humming up behind him.

"Stop right there," the security guard ordered from his souped-up golf cart.

Charlie dashed into the nearest storefront, came out of a saloon in Dodge City on the other side, ran across the dusty street, through the Silver Dollar Hotel facade and emerged from the courthouse that dominated the square of Anytown, USA. The main street led off into a painted backdrop of a country road that seemed to meander off into the horizon.

For a moment, he stood in the town square, a bit disoriented, feeling like a hapless, time-traveling protagonist in a bad *Twilight Zone* episode. Then he heard the buzz of an approaching security cart and the crackle of a walkie-talkie. He crawled underneath the bandstand just as the high-powered floodlights around the square flashed on. Suddenly, the entire town was awash in light.

The security cart glided to a stop beside the bandstand, the guard pausing to look around. Charlie looked behind him and, through the slats in the bandstand, saw the security guard from Copenhagen arriving on the opposite end of the square.

The radio crackled on the cart beside the bandstand. "He's got to be in the square somewhere," said a voice Charlie recognized as the guard from Copenhagen. "Be careful, he's probably a wacko, and they say he's armed."

They say? Who the hell were *they?* Charlie wasn't going to stick around to find out, but he'd have to be very careful. Studio security guards were usually the guys who, for good reason, couldn't get into law enforcement. They spent most of their days sitting in the guard booth, or sitting in the security cart. Either way, their physical prowess was hardly honed to a sharp point. On the other hand, amateurs with guns scared him a lot more than an armed professional. Action was so rare for these guys they were likely to shoot the first person they saw, especially if they thought they were hunting a crazed psycho.

The guard got out of his cart, took out a flashlight, and walked up the courthouse steps to investigate inside. Charlie didn't waste a second. He crawled out from under the bandstand and slid into the cart, where he found the key still in the ignition.

Charlie twisted the key into drive, lowered his head, and sped off. The security guard whirled around and reached for his gun, which, thankfully, he had forgotten to unstrap. While the guard fumbled with his holster, his friend from Copenhagen gave chase, tooling after Charlie in his own wobbly cart.

Once outside the city limits of Anytown, USA, Charlie made a hard right, toward Muck Thing's swamp. The cart bounced onto the wide tram tracks, and continued along the predestined route. Charlie twisted the key to neutral and, as the cart entered the swamplands, he dived out into the brush. The cart continued on its own momentum along the tram tracks, disappearing around a curve. A moment later his pursuer followed, also disappearing around the bend, his cart zipping as fast as its batteries would allow.

Charlie waited until he heard the roar of Muck Thing and the collision of the two carts to emerge from hiding and dash into the dark, thick jungle. From here on, he'd be able to move virtually unseen, safe from another run-in with studio security.

He was nearly at the fence when something leapt out of the brush for his throat. He whirled around to his left, saw a glimpse of hair and fangs flying at him, and instinctively raised his arm across his face in self-defense.

Boo Boo buried his teeth deep in Charlie's thick arm, his jaws clamping tight on his prey. Charlie screamed in pain and anger, and swung his arm back furiously against a tree trunk, trying to knock the vicious beast off.

Whap! Whap! Whap!

He bashed the mud-caked terror repeatedly against the tree, but was unable to dislodge Boo Boo, who was beaten senseless, his jaws locked shut around Charlie's blood-soaked arm.

Charlie stared in horror at his arm, the filthy, drooling dog dangling from the bloody flesh. He couldn't believe what he was seeing, but he had no time to ponder the insanity of it. Behind him, he could hear footfalls in the brush, and could see flashlight beams cutting through the trees. His screams had drawn the security guards into the jungle.

Gritting his teeth against the pain, Charlie ran to the fence and scaled it, the dog still clamped on his arm. He staggered to his car, and whacked the dog a few more times against the grille, to no avail. With his right hand, he opened the driver's-side door and rolled down the window. Then he got in the car and, with the dog dangling above his wrist, propped his bloody arm on the window and sped off into the night.

Chapter Twenty-nine

The first thing Dr. Gaston Grospiron told Charlie Willis when they met years ago was that he was a Mensa. However, with his thick French accent, Charlie thought the verbose veterinarian had told him he was a matzo.

Mensa or matzo, he'd been McGarrett's vet ever since Charlie found the dog nosing through trash in an alley behind Rodeo Drive. Whenever Charlie brought McGarrett in for a checkup over the years, Dr. Grospiron would examine the dog while regaling Charlie with some long-winded diatribe about politics, women, medicine, taxes, or whatever else was on his mind.

It was no different when Charlie showed up at Dr. Grospiron's twenty-four-hour emergency clinic that evening, an unconscious dog clamped on his shredded arm. While the doctor carefully injected a muscle relaxant into the dog's jaws and gently pried the animal loose from Charlie's arm, he yammered authoritatively and, because of his accent, incomprehensibly, about the European common market. Oddly enough, the learned Dr. Grospiron was completely oblivious to Charlie's legal trouble, or showed rare discretion by not bringing it up.

All the while, Charlie stared at the hell beast hanging on his arm, still shocked that this could have happened to him. The thought distracted him from the pain, the trip he'd have to take to the emergency room for shots and stitches, the mob takeover of primetime television, and the murder charge he faced.

Perhaps that's also why it took Charlie a long hour in the veterinarian's operating room, watching him expertly remove the tranquilized dog from his arm, before he realized that the vicious mutt that had attacked him was . . . *Boo Boo.*

"As deese ees a strange dawg, it weel be necezary to test for zee babies," Charlie thought he heard Dr. Grospiron say.

"The dog bit me," Charlie said irritably, "it didn't fuck me."

"I sayed zee *rabies*," Dr. Grospiron stammered, faux furious, "not zee *babies*. I weel keep zees animal 'ere, but first I drive you to zee 'ospital."

That sounded like a good idea to Charlie, who was too tired, too dizzy, and in too much pain to mull the full ramifications of his discovery that the creature that had attacked him was America's favorite pooch. Keeping the monster in Dr. Grospiron's care until Charlie could figure out what to do about him seemed like the best decision.

Dr. Grospiron cleaned Charlie's wound, wrapped it lightly in clean gauze, then drove him to Tarzana Medical Center in Charlie's car, while one of the vet's nurses followed in the doctor's Mercedes.

Once they were confident Charlie would be all right, Dr. Grospiron and his nurse left Charlie in the waiting area, holding the gauze to his wound, watching reruns of *T.J. Hooker*.

Three hours, four shots, and twenty stitches later, Charlie left his car in the parking lot, walked across Reseda Boulevard to the Gaylord Motor Inn, and checked into a room for the night. He knocked back his codeine and antibiotics and went to sleep.

While Charlie slept, knocked out by exhaustion, tremendous stress, significant blood loss, and a strong painkiller, viewership numbers were being tabulated from the ten major markets around the country.

The numbers, upon which careers and fortunes would ride, were quickly analyzed, quantified, and categorized, then faxed, transmitted, or otherwise hustled to everyone whose livelihood depended on what people watched.

These statistics were the "overnights," and represented the feedback from the biggest population centers in the nation on the evening's primetime fare. The broader-based, national numbers would come later, usually only underscoring more dramatically the story foretold by the overnights.

Don DeBono never left his office after the closing credits of *Where's Boo Boo?* He sat behind his desk all night, waiting for the moment of truth, for the sheet of paper from the research department that would tell him if his outrageous gamble had worked.

Sabrina Bishop was up all night too, wondering if she had done the right thing accepting DeBono's offer, or if a decision made in a moment of panic and desperation had ruined her career. And she worried about Charlie Willis, asking herself why he hadn't called her since his release, and where he might be right now.

Flint Westwood wasn't up at all that night, at least not between his legs. He lay awake in bed, staring at his crotch, waiting for the night erection all men supposedly have, the one he *always* had, until that hell bitch tried to snip his magnificence off. Now the only thing that rose was his fear that he might be impotent forever.

Eddie Planet spent the night pacing around his bedroom, tormented by several unanswered questions that terrified him. Was *Where's Boo Boo* an enormous hit? If so, what did it mean for *Frankencop?* Did Charlie Willis know about the mob's involvement in Eddie's show? And if so, who would Delbert Skaggs kill when he found out?

Delbert Skaggs slept peacefully, and was behind his desk at Pinnacle Studios at dawn, when he noticed immediately that his notepad was gone. But Delbert was not one to panic. He remained in the darkness, waiting for the overnights, and Eddie Planet, to arrive.

Delbert never suspected that, just outside the studio gates, Otto and Burt sat in a rusted, dented heap of a GMC truck, stuffing Jack in the Box sourdough breakfast sandwiches down their throats, waiting for their chance to kill him.

Otto and Burt had also watched *Where's Boo Boo?* last night as they smeared Noxzema on their charred flesh, ate Doritos, and felt intellectually superior to the rest of the world. Unlike all the other poor jerks out there, they *knew* where Boo Boo was. Or at least they had a pretty good idea. But it was worth watching the show just to get a look at Sabrina Bishop's hooters. Maybe they'd let her do a *Sunn of a Gunn,* if she played her cards right. Before that could happen, though, they had to get rid of Delbert Skaggs, and that took top priority over everything, even capturing Boo Boo.

The overnights came in to Don DeBono's office at about nine A.M., hand delivered by Buttonwillow McKittrick, his VP of current programming. He could tell by the depressed look on her face that he'd scored big. The only thing that could make her look that sad was the realization that she wouldn't be getting his job.

He snatched the paper from her trembling hand and looked at the numbers. *Where's Boo Boo?* had scored a phenomenal 48 rating, becoming one of the most-watched shows in television history.

Broad Squad and the *Anson Williams Show,* benefiting from the powerhouse *Where's Boo Boo?* lead-in, each scored a 34 share, stellar numbers in their own right, leading into one of the last *Miss Agatha* episodes, which grabbed a 28 share to beat *Frankencop* by 10 share points.

"Congratulations, Don," Buttonwillow said. "You've made the record books."

"Again," he added.

"Again," she reluctantly conceded. "Too bad you can't pull that miracle off every week."

"Why not?" Don Debono admired the sheet of overnights as if it were a work of art.

"What do you mean?" She was confused, certain she had stated the obvious before.

"Exactly what I said. Why not? Tell me why I can't do *Where's Boo Boo?* every week." DeBono stared at her, waiting for the answer.

"Because," she stammered, completely taken by surprise. The suggestion of making *Where's Boo Boo?* a weekly series was patently ludicrous, he must know that, right? "Because, the audience will buy it *once.* The show was a special, a one-time fluke—maybe for one hour it relieved some of the anxiety they're feeling. But it'd be *ridiculous* to do it every week. Boo Boo can't possibly be in all those places. The audience isn't that desperate or stupid."

She was astonished to see that, by the look on his face, he wasn't swayed. "I mean, c'mon, Don, the people who claim to see Boo Boo are either lunatics or liars. We might as well make it up ourselves."

"So?"

"So!?" She couldn't believe this. Couldn't he see what he was talking about was crazy? "What are we going to do? Say one week he was snatched by aliens, the next by Big Foot, the week after that he's had a sex change and has become your cat?"

"Sure, why not?" DeBono said.

"Because it's *insane,*" she shouted.

"No, it's primetime television and a guaranteed number one hit." He stood up slowly. "If you can't see that, perhaps you belong in first-run syndication."

DeBono looked her in the eye. She was clearly not cut out for network television. She didn't have the necessary vision or low opinion of the viewing public.

"We're ordering twenty-two episodes immediately. I hope you'll watch them in your new job, wherever that may be."

Buttonwillow turned on her heel and marched out, her career at UBC finished. There was nothing she could do about it. From his new position of strength, there would be no undermining him this time, not even by sleeping with his boss.

As soon as she was out the door, DeBono called Buttonwillow's assistant and promoted her.

"It'll be your office by lunch time," he promised.

Across town, at the Pinnacle Studios lot, Eddie Planet carried the overnights into Delbert Skaggs's office, hoping that the old adage about shooting the messenger wouldn't apply.

Delbert glanced at the sheet of paper and analyzed the numbers. This was not good, Delbert thought. Obviously, he'd been going about this the wrong way. Instead of killing the soldiers on the street, the stars of the shows competing against him, he should have aimed his sights higher. You want to stomp out a crime family, you start with the leader, the Godfather.

Delbert had started small—that was his mistake—and had under-estimated the ingenuity and experience of Don DeBono. It was a mistake often made when a young upstart tried to invade a crime boss's territory.

However, it was a mistake that was easy to correct, as long as you had a loaded gun. Right after he killed Sabrina Bishop, to assure that neither *Where's Boo Boo?* or *Miss Agatha* could come back to haunt him, he'd eliminate Don DeBono. The UBC "family" dominance of "the business" would die with DeBono.

Killing him would be business as usual for Delbert. He'd killed so many crime family bosses, it had become his specialty. But first, there was another small matter to take care of.

He looked at Eddie, who didn't like what he was seeing in Delbert's eyes. It was a killer look.

"Who could've figured DeBono would come up with something like that?" Eddie shrugged. "That's the TV biz. You gotta love it."

"Where's my notepad, Eddie?" Delbert asked.

"You're missing something?"

"Yes, Eddie, I am. My notepad. Where is it?"

"Maybe you misplaced it," Eddie offered.

"I don't misplace things," Delbert said. "I do, occasionally, misplace people. Permanently."

"Come to think of it," Eddie replied quickly, "we did have a breakin last night."

Delbert grabbed Eddie by the throat and slammed him back against the wall. "Why wasn't I informed, *immediately?*"

"I didn't think the guy took anything," Eddie blathered. "I mean, who would've thought to look for a lousy notepad?"

"I want to know exactly what happened."

"It was no big deal," Eddie gurgled. "I walked in on him, scared him off. I called the guards, but they lost him."

"You saw him, didn't you?" Delbert squeezed Eddie's throat until he could feel Eddie's pulse pounding in his hand. Delbert had found that cutting off a person's air supply encouraged the truth. They were so desperate to breathe, they couldn't sustain an expression of innocence. It was no different with Eddie Planet. The fear in his bulging eyes told Delbert everything. Delbert loosened his grip just a bit. "Yes, I thought you did. Who was it, Eddie? Who broke into my office?"

"The guy looked like"—Eddie croaked, spitting out the name—"Charlie Willis."

Delbert abruptly released Eddie, who slid down the wall and slumped on the floor. He looked down at Eddie with disgust.

Charlie Willis.

It seemed Don DeBono wasn't the only person Delbert had underestimated. The time for subtlety was gone. It was going to be St. Valentine's Day in television land.

"I have some errands to run," Delbert said. "When I get back, you and I are going to have another little talk."

And with that, Delbert marched out. Eddie watched him go, and silently prayed Otto and Burt ran into him first.

Chapter Thirty

....

It was about ten A.M., and Sabrina was finally beginning to fall asleep when her phone rang. She grabbed it and heard a groggy, thick-tongued voice on the other end.

"Sabrina?"

"Who is it?" she asked.

"It's me, Charlie."

If it was, he had a sock in his mouth. "Are you drunk?"

"I wish I was, maybe I'd feel better." Charlie was still in his bed at the Gaylord Motor Inn, his left arm swollen and pounding with pain, his hand numb. The night before had seemed like some twisted nightmare, until he awoke on his back, the sweat-soaked sheets clinging to his skin, his bandaged arm propped up on pillows.

"I had a hell of a night," he said, "but I'll tell you about that when I see you."

"Where are you?"

"A dive motel off the Ventura Freeway, but never mind that. The important thing is, I'm out of jail and I think I found the solution to my problem."

"*Our* problem," she said. "We're in this together."

He couldn't help smiling to himself, despite the pain he was in. "Okay, our problem."

She hesitated, wondering whether this was the right time to bring up what she had done last night.

"I had a hell of a night myself," she ventured.

"I saw."

He said it so straightforwardly, she couldn't discern his attitude. "Do you think I made a mistake?"

Did he? he asked himself. Could he really condemn her for trying to salvage some small piece of her career while she had the chance?

"No, why should I?"

"Because I sold out, because I took part in a show that pandered to the lowest common denominator."

Charlie thought about it for a moment. "How is that different from doing *Miss Agatha* or *My Gun Has Bullets?*"

"I did it for the money," she said. "I did it to save my career. I did it because I was scared and alone."

"Hey, you couldn't have been alone," he replied. "We're in this together, remember?"

She laughed, feeling better already. "How soon can you get here?"

"Give me about an hour, I've got to wrap my arm up in a trash bag and take a shower."

"You have to *what?*"

"It'll all make sense when you see me."

After Sabrina hung up, she lay in bed, trying to decide whether to stay where she was and maybe catch a few minutes of sleep and be all warm and cuddly in bed when he arrived, or take an invigorating shower and greet Charlie awake and clean.

She opted for the shower and went into the bathroom to run the water, thereby proving it's the little choices in life that often have the biggest consequences. The sound of the shower running killed any chance she had of hearing her front door opening, and Delbert Skaggs slipping inside her house.

He took a moment to admire her colonial-style furnishings and her sharp eye for interior design as he screwed the silencer on his gun. The native pine dropleaf dining table went well with the open-beam ceilings. He'd try not to get too much blood on the walls—it would be a shame to soil the fine knotty pine cabinetry and moldings.

As he was making his way down the hall to her bedroom, outside the house and across the street Otto and Burt were sitting in their truck, the engine idling.

They had followed Delbert here, and watched him enter the house a moment ago. Now they were wrestling with the issue of just how to kill him. They were determined not to mess this up the way they had with Boo Boo.

"It has to look like an accident," Otto said.

Burt studied Sabrina's tiny, one-story, cottage-style house, with its bay window and small porch.

"What if a giant boulder fell from a cliff and smashed the house?"

Otto gave Burt a look. "We don't have a boulder."

"We could get one," Burt replied.

"We don't have a cliff," Otto said.

"Fine, shoot down my ideas. That's easy." Burt argued. "Let's see *you* come up with something."

"Okay, what if a runaway train veered off the tracks and plowed into the house?"

"We don't have a train," Burt said. "Or tracks. See how easy it is to be negative?"

"But we have a *truck*," Otto pointed out. "What if a drunk driver lost control of his car and smashed into the house?"

"We don't have a drunk driver," Burt grinned, just being difficult.

Otto grinned back. "Hand me a beer."

Burt reached under the seat for a beer, popped it open for his buddy, and handed it to him. Otto opened his mouth, tossed his head back, and poured the entire beer down his throat, crumpled the can, and threw it out the window.

"A buzz ought to do," Otto said.

With a deep belch, Otto revved the engine, jammed the car into drive, and floored it.

Sabrina Bishop was naked, about to step into the shower, when she suddenly had the overwhelming sensation that she was not alone. She stepped into the bedroom and saw a shadow in the hall.

"Charlie?" she said.

Delbert Skaggs stood in the hallway, about to answer her with a bullet, when he heard screeching tires outside. He looked back just as a truck burst through the living room window in an explosion of wood and glass.

The truck roared through the house, demolishing one wall after another, finally hurling through the sliding glass door and skidding to a halt in the backyard.

Otto and Burt jumped out of their crumpled truck and shook bits of the windshield off their bodies, then turned to admire their path of destruction. The gutted house barely stood, swaying and creaking, bits of plaster and glass raining down on the rubble. A geyser of water shot up where the shower used to be.

"Too cool," Burt declared.

"Let's check it out," Otto said.

They ran into the house, dodging falling rafters and shards of glass, looking for signs of carnage. They didn't have to look far. The hallway had collapsed on Delbert, all they could see was his bloody hand peeking out from under the rubble. Burt stomped on it for good measure.

"Maybe we should cut it off and take it with us as proof," Burt suggested.

The front wall suddenly collapsed, opening the interior of the house to the street. Any second now, neighbors and police would be showing up.

"Forget it." Otto sniffed the air. He could smell gas, and based on recent experience, he knew it wasn't Burt. "We better hustle our bustles."

They were turning to leave when Burt suddenly grabbed Otto by the arm. "Do you see what I see?"

Otto followed Burt's gaze into what remained of the bedroom. The walls had caved in on the bed, which propped them up just enough to save Sabrina's life. She lay unconscious on the floor, naked and bloody, covered with a thin layer of plaster dust.

"Yeah," Otto replied. "A fringe benefit."

Otto and Burt rushed over to her, slid her out from under the rubble, carried her to the truck, tossed her onto the bed, and covered her with an oily tarp.

Then they climbed into the truck, slammed their doors, and peeled out, smashing through the fence into the alley, their tires squealing as they charged off.

Charlie knew something was wrong as he turned the corner, steering the rental car with his good hand. People were standing on their lawns and sitting on their porches, staring up the street, where a section had been cordoned off with yellow police tape and officers were herding a crowd away.

He pulled over to the curb, got out of the car, and jogged up the sidewalk, dodging people going in the opposite direction.

Charlie ducked underneath the tape and ran down the center of the street, terrified that he'd see a coroner's wagon in front of Sabrina's house. Instead, he saw a lone police car, its lights flashing. Her house looked as if it had been hit by a hurricane.

He was heading for it when an officer grabbed him by the arm and spun him around.

"Where the hell do you think you're going?" the officer yelled.

Charlie shook free, but the officer blocked his path.

"Turn around," the officer demanded. "We're evacuating the area."

"I've got a friend in there," Charlie shouted.

"Not anymore you don't," the officer said. "The house is empty."

Charlie tried to push past him, but it wasn't easy with just one good arm. "I have to be sure."

The idea that Sabrina might be hurt because he hadn't anticipated she might be a target, because *he'd been too late,* was too much to stand.

"I'm sure." The officer pushed him back. "Now get the hell out of here, there's a gas leak and—"

Just then the house exploded, knocking them to the ground and belching a tremendous fireball into the air that showered the street in flaming debris.

Charlie scrambled out from under the dazed officer and stared at the burning house, the flames spreading to the homes on either side. Charlie was also burning, the rage inside him so strong it was all he could do not to strangle the first person he saw.

They had gone too far. It wasn't a question any more of keeping himself out of jail, it was all about making them pay. If Sabrina was hurt, they would pay with their lives, regardless of the law.

He was Derek Thorne now, a rogue cop meting out his own brand of justice, and it felt right. Charlie marched back to his car, oblivious to the crowds running to the flames, the sound of sirens in the distance. He had to save Sabrina. It was the only thing that mattered.

He got in the Chevy, jammed the car into reverse, and slammed on the brakes. The car fishtailed to face the opposite direction, then he sped off, weaving through the traffic until he found a pay phone.

The car jumped the curb and slammed into the phone booth, shattering the glass and nearly toppling it to the sidewalk. Charlie stomped through the broken glass, dropped a quarter in the slot, and dialed the studio. Eddie Planet wasn't there. Charlie dropped another quarter in the slot and called him at home.

Eddie answered the phone on the first ring, his voice cracking. "Hello?"

"I'm coming for you," Charlie said, "and if she's hurt, you're dead."

It was what Eddie had feared, but it was trivial in comparison to the gun a horribly disfigured Delbert held to Eddie's temple.

Eddie covered the phone, glanced desperately at Delbert, and stammered, "What do I say?"

Delbert stood next to him, his nose crushed and his forehead slashed open, wiping the blood out of his eyes with the back of his mangled left hand. His entire body was caked with blood and plaster, his right ear held in place by a clump of matted hair and one thin membrane. And yet, as bad as he looked, Eddie didn't doubt the killer's resolve, or his fury.

"Tell him to fuck off," Delbert demanded.

"But—"

Delbert cocked the trigger. Eddie wet his pants and quivered as he spoke.

"Fuck off," Eddie said unconvincingly into the phone, then covered it as he appealed to Delbert. "He's gonna kill me."

"Don't worry, I'll kill you first." Delbert wiped more blood out of his eyes.

Charlie gripped the receiver so tight it was beginning to crack.

"You've got one way to come out of this alive," Charlie said. "You'll bring me Sabrina Bishop."

Delbert grinned, tearing open his broken lips, blood dribbling from his mouth like saliva. "Tell him if he wants the woman, we want something in return."

"You got something to trade?" Eddie trembled as he spoke into the phone, the urine stinging his thighs.

Charlie took a deep breath. So that was how this was going down.

Fine. He could play by those rules. It was just a question of who would break them first, and who would die doing it.

"Tell Delbert I have Boo Boo," Charlie said. "The dog for Sabrina."

"Bullshit," Eddie screeched.

"I found the dog last night at the studio," Charlie said. "Makes you wonder about that 'wild animal' that attacked Reed Roland, doesn't it?"

"The whole fucking country thinks they've seen Boo Boo," Eddie yelled. "The dog is fucking dead."

If Charlie was telling the truth, Eddie feared Delbert would kill him right now. But it wasn't the truth. The dog was dead. Otto and Burt couldn't have blown it. It was a simple job, it couldn't have gone wrong.

Then Eddie remembered Otto and Burt didn't wear seat belts because they couldn't figure out how they worked.

"If you're so sure, then we have nothing to talk about," Charlie said.

Eddie covered the phone and mustered all the self-confidence he could find within himself, which wasn't easy, standing in soiled pants with a gun to his head.

"He's full of shit, Delbert."

"The idiots you sent to kill me"—Delbert spit blood out of his mouth with each word. "Were they the same ones you hired to kill the dog?"

"I never sent anyone to kill you, how could you even think—"

Delbert pistol-whipped him across the face. Eddie fell to the floor, dragging the phone off the table with him.

Eddie started to cry. "Yes, it was them."

Now Delbert *knew* Charlie had the dog. He shoved the gun into his shoulder holster and grabbed the phone. "All right, Willis. You have my attention."

It was the first time Charlie Willis had ever heard Delbert Skaggs's voice. And the first time they met face to face would be the last, one way or the other.

"We make the switch at ten o'clock tonight, Pinnacle Studios," Charlie said. "on the *Global Armageddon* stage."

"I don't like it," Delbert said.

"It's nonnegotiable."

If Charlie was going to have a chance, he would have to make sure they met in a place he could control, and on his terms.

"I'll kill the woman," Delbert retorted.

"Then the dog shows up at UBC, *Frankencop* dies, and so do you."

Delbert spit out a gob of blood and glared at Eddie, who was whimpering on the floor, his pants soaked in his own piss. Delbert liked everything clean and this wasn't just a mess, it was an incredible, ugly mess. He wasn't sure what bothered him more, his injuries, or the dirt, the blood, the drool, and the piss that surrounded him. Charlie Willis's proposal had the benefit of being quick and clean, and Delbert had to appreciate that. However it went down, it would be orderly.

"All right, Willis. Tonight."

Delbert hung up and grabbed Eddie by the throat, pulling the urine-soaked, sobbing executive producer to his feet.

"You're going to call them," Delbert said, "and they are going to bring her to the studio."

Eddie nodded, a simpering coward.

"You better hope she's alive, Eddie, because that's the only reason you still are."

Delbert threw Eddie back on the floor and went to clean himself up.

Charlie burst into Dr. Gaston Grospiron's clinic and searched all the examination rooms until he found the jabbering Frenchman looking down a wheezing St. Bernard's throat.

"Where's the dog?" Charlie demanded.

"Ah, my good friend, I 'ave bean looking for you," Dr. Grospiron excused himself from the St. Bernard and its owner, and led Charlie into the hallway. "I 'ave good news. Ze dawg does not 'ave ze rabies."

"Great, where is he?"

"What do you mean?"

"Where is the damn dog?"

Dr. Grospiron shrugged. "Most of 'eem is in a body bag in ze freezer, ze 'ed is steel in ze lab."

Charlie felt his heart skip a beat. "You decapitated the dog?"

"Of course," Dr. Grospiron replied. "I 'ad to exameen ze brain to determeen if 'e 'ad rabies."

Charlie slumped against the wall. Things only got worse. No matter what he did, he always ended up further and further behind.

Dr. Grospiron gave his friend a bewildered look. "You weren't planning on keeping 'eem, were you?"

"Actually, I was planning on giving him away," Charlie said.

"A vicious beast like zat?" Dr. Grospiron shook his head, confused. "You are deranged, my friend."

Dr. Grospiron walked away, shaking his head. Charlie, despondent, slid down to the floor and rested his head on his knees. What the hell was he going to do now?

The door beside Charlie opened and a woman covered in Givenchy emerged, her perfectly coiffed French poodle walking in time with her owner.

"You did a wonderful job, Emilia darling," the woman said to the groomer. "You're the Jose Eber of dogs."

Charlie lifted his head and glanced at the dog, who looked like a walking topiary, then peered into the room at the groomer, a petite Mexican woman who was already sweeping up the hair.

An idea occurred to Charlie. It was a long shot, but it might buy him a few precious minutes when it counted.

"Excuse me," Charlie asked the groomer, "but how good are you at making a dog look really pitiful?"

Chapter Thirty-one

Sabrina awoke to find herself in a black silk negligee, sitting on a couch, her hands bound behind her back with duct tape, her head resting on a tuxedo-clad man's shoulder. Her head pounded, and she felt like throwing up.

"Smile," Burt said.

She looked up, just long enough to see Burt in a tuxedo holding a Polaroid camera, and then she was blinded by the flashbulb.

"Who are you? Where am I?" She squinted, trying to focus her eyes and control the urge to vomit. The man she saw, in that brief moment, looked like he'd gone bobbing for apples in a french fryer.

Otto abruptly stood up and hurried over to Burt. Sabrina, losing her support, flopped down onto the couch cushions, which reeked of beer, Doritos, and body odor.

Ignoring her, Otto and Burt waited anxiously as the Polaroid slowly spit out the photo. When it was nearly out, Otto plucked it from the camera and held the photo in his hands, watching as the image of Sabrina resting her head on his shoulder began to appear.

Sabrina blinked several times, and her eyes focused on a dozen Polaroids spread out on the cushion beside her. Each photo showed her in various stages of undress, propped in a different adoring or suggestive position with either Otto or Burt, wearing their rented tuxedos, a stupid grin on their blistered, greasy, fire-seared faces.

That was too much. She vomited on the floor, her stomach heaving until she thought she might pass out again. But she regained control over her spasming muscles and opened her eyes.

Neither Otto or Burt seemed to have noticed her intestinal upset, they were so completely absorbed in the picture.

"This is the best one yet," Otto said. "I reek suave."

"You do," Burt agreed.

Her stomach purged, Sabrina suddenly felt better, her mind sharper, and she began to regain her bearings. The last thing she remembered was going to take a shower, and having the sensation someone else was in the house. Then there was an enormous crash, and she dived to the floor. The walls caved in on her and that was the last thing she saw before waking up here.

Wherever *here* was.

She took in her surroundings. It was a mobile home. Centerfolds were stapled to the walls, and the floors were littered with fast-food containers, beer cans, and potato chip bags. The furniture was ravaged, and the TV set looked like it was stolen from Ozzie and Harriet's living room.

Sabrina did a mental inventory of her body. She felt a little bruised, and there was a cut somewhere on her head, but she was certain she hadn't been raped or sodomized, which was a tremendous relief. She preferred not to imagine what else they might have done with her while she was unconscious. Her feet felt numb, and she couldn't move her legs. She glanced down to discover her ankles wrapped together in duct tape. She was a prisoner.

"Take a look at this." Otto held the picture in front of her face. "Don't I look debonair?"

Sabrina thought very carefully about what to say. "Yes, you do."

Otto seemed genuinely pleased. "We're on our way to the top," he predicted to Burt.

Sabrina concentrated on squeezing any fear out of her voice. "I don't mean to sound rude, but what am I doing here?"

"Promotion," Burt said.

"For *Sunn of a Gunn,*" Otto added. "We have to show the network we're twice as good as George Hamilton."

"I see." Sabrina realized she was being held by two dangerous lunatics. The good news was that so far she hadn't been hurt. Humiliated and degraded, yes, but she could live with that. After all, she was an actress. "So you're actors."

Otto and Burt shared a proud grin.

"Not yet," Burt said, "but soon."

"I'm an actress, so that makes us colleagues," Sabrina said.

Colleagues. Otto liked the way it sounded. Very classy. Very suave. "That's us, a couple colleagues," he said.

"Suave and debonair colleagues," Burt corrected.

"Well, since we're all members of the acting fraternity, do you think you could untie me?" Sabrina asked. "I sure would love to go home and clean up."

"We can't do that," Burt said.

"Why not?" Sabrina asked.

"For one thing, your home kind of fell down," Otto explained. "And we need you for rehearsals."

"We got to practice being classy dudes," Burt said to Sabrina, who was getting dizzy again from the sheer insanity of it all.

The phone rang. Otto shared a look with Burt. "This could be our future calling."

Otto excitedly answered the phone. Sure enough, it was Eddie Planet.

"Great work today," Eddie said. "Really exceptional job. I think we're on track."

Eddie was wearing clean clothes and was feeling a little better now that Delbert's gun wasn't pointed at his head anymore. But not much. Delbert was still in the house, dressing his wounds and finding some of Eddie's stuff to wear.

"Now we have to find a sophisticated writer," Otto said. "Someone who can capture all the nuances of our personalities."

"Stephen King," Burt suggested.

For once, Eddie had to agree. If anyone was going to capture their personalities, it would be him.

"Steve-o is on board, guaranteed," Eddie replied. "Look, guys, there is one little thing. You wouldn't have Sabrina Bishop over there, would you?"

"Yeah, she's been helping us get into character."

Eddie shuddered at the images *that* conjured up. "Bring her to the studio at nine o'clock tonight."

"Why?"

"Because she's going to be your costar in *Sunn of a Gunn*," Eddie vamped. "The network is wild about her and they are desperate to do a screen test with the three of you tonight, in Times Square."

"Cool," Otto said.

"A word of advice—you don't want to hurt or molest her in any way." Then Eddie remembered Otto's previous remark. "You haven't, have you?"

"No, all we did was take some promo shots."

"Good, your future in show business depends on it," Eddie said firmly. "I'll see you tonight. Don't be late."

Otto hung up and gave Burt the high-five. Sabrina watched, dumbfounded, as they did their little dance. A soft-shoe, a patty-cake, two jumping jacks, and then a quick spin into their *Saturday Night Fever* pose.

"Too cool for words," Otto and Burt said in unison, then turned and smiled at Sabrina. For the first time since she'd regained consciousness and retched her guts out, she feared for her life.

McGarrett lifted his leg on the Robokiller. The giant, alien soldier hid behind a scaled-down skyscraper, waiting for his remote control cue to smash the building, fire a few rockets from his head, and make the audience go wild.

But the audiences were long gone, and the only ones left were Charlie and McGarrett, who lurked behind the towering steel monster, killing time until the exchange. Charlie had arrived early to commit a burglary, and get comfortably settled in. His life, and Sabrina's, could depend on every move he made now.

He glanced down at McGarrett, who kicked some dirt over his mark and sniffed it to make sure it was sending a strong message. Charlie was pleased with McGarrett. Emilia the dog groomer had done a fantastic job. McGarrett had never looked worse. Mangy, smelly, ratty, everything that Boo Boo ever was, a dead ringer for the decapitated hell pooch. Unfortunately, McGarrett was also a lot bigger.

Charlie was banking on a few things being in his favor—darkness, distance, and the probability that Delbert Skaggs and Eddie Planet had never seen Boo Boo up close. If Charlie was wrong, he had one other option literally up his sleeve, stolen from the *Global Armageddon* control booth just a few minutes ago.

Now it was just a question of waiting.

* * *

Otto and Burt, carrying a trunk between them, emerged from the Pinnacle Studios service tunnel, up the subway station steps and into the center of Times Square.

They stood in the darkness for a moment, soaking up the elaborate illusion. The famous neon signs and diamond screens were off, but the place was still striking in its authenticity, despite being compressed into roughly two acres.

The first three floors of every building in Times Square had been reproduced in three-quarter scale, and had been used in just about every series Pinnacle Studios had ever made. The TV shows shot everything tight and low, while the feature films threw money into fancy matte photography to add the tops of the buildings, streets in the distance, and hundreds of cars.

Standing here brought fond memories to Otto and Burt. There wasn't a window here they hadn't crashed through, a rooftop they hadn't tumbled from, or a storefront they hadn't driven into.

But those days were gone. They were stars now. The two of them, and the woman in the trunk, were going to be America's favorite threesome.

Eddie Planet walked out of the Lindy's Deli facade, a nervous smile on his face, to see the two charred stuntmen standing in their tuxedos, the large wardrobe trunk between them.

"Glad you boys could make it. Love the tuxedos, very nice touch."

"Where's the camera crew?" Otto asked.

"They're running late." Eddie looked around anxiously. "Where's the girl?"

Otto and Burt unlatched the trunk and pulled it open. Sabrina tumbled out, disheveled and sweat-soaked in her negligee, gasping for breath. Her wrists were lashed together behind her with duct tape, and although her legs were free, Eddie could see bruises around her ankles where they had been bound.

"I see you've shown her your usual hospitality," Eddie remarked with disdain, but apparently Burt didn't pick up on it.

"We got some pictures," Burt replied excitedly, reaching into his jacket for them.

"No thanks." Eddie waved Burt off. "That won't be necessary."

Sabrina struggled to clear her head and catch her breath. There might be only one chance to make a break for it, and she wanted to be ready.

"So what are we gonna do first?" Otto asked.

"Find a new hand," said a voice behind them.

In that same instant, a bullet blew apart Otto's left hand, spraying his rented tuxedo with blood and bone fragments.

Eddie screamed and hit the ground, putting him eye to eye with Sabrina. When he saw the anger in her eyes, he wondered if he wasn't safer standing up.

Otto grabbed the remainder of his hand and whirled around to see Delbert Skaggs emerging from the darkness, holding his silenced gun.

Even cleaned up, Delbert wasn't pretty. His smashed nose hung over his scabby lips, and his head was so badly swollen, it looked lopsided.

"Now we're even." Delbert held up his gnarled hand to show them what he meant.

Otto was furious. "I didn't stomp on your hand." He motioned to Burt. "*He* did."

"My mistake." Delbert shrugged and shot Burt in the hand.

Burt yelped, the force of the bullet spinning him in a bloody pirouette.

The three men, standing there with their lopsided heads and maimed left hands, looked like brothers.

"Thanks a lot," Burt sneered at Otto, holding up his gushing stump. "How's this going to look on the screen test?"

"It's not *my* fault." Otto glared at Delbert. "These are rented tuxedos, asshole. Now they're going to make us buy them."

Their hands were blown off, and they were worried about staining their clothes. They didn't even seem to feel the pain. It was the most astounding thing Delbert had ever seen, but he had no time to think about it. With luck they'd bleed to death before he had to kill them.

"Shut up and step away from the girl." Delbert motioned them away with his gun. He was going to kill these two jerks right here, and Eddie, Sabrina, and Charlie before the evening was out. The only thing keeping Eddie alive right now was that Delbert needed an extra hand with Sabrina.

Otto and Burt reluctantly moved to one side. Eddie and Sabrina lay motionless on the ground, splattered with blood. Delbert pointed at Eddie with his gun.

Eddie immediately covered his head with his arms, but before he could start to beg, Delbert spoke.

"Get her on her feet."

Eddie was so grateful to be alive he almost squealed. "Yes sir, right away," he said, scrambling to his feet.

He grabbed Sabrina under the arms and lifted her up. She glared at Eddie with such loathing he had to look away, so she shifted her gaze to Delbert, who didn't shrink away at all. In fact, he liked it.

"Since I seem to be so goddamn important here," said Sabrina, her confusion long since overcome by her fury, "you mind telling me what the hell this is all about?"

"Ratings," Delbert replied, shifting his attention to Eddie. "Take her to *Global Armageddon*. I'll join you in a few minutes."

"Unhand her," someone shrieked, "or I'll kill you all."

Everyone turned toward the voice, and what they saw horrified them.

McGarrett suddenly stood up, alert, his entire body stiff.

"What is it?" Charlie asked, not expecting an answer.

McGarrett sniffed the air, the hair rising on his back, and took two strong steps forward. Charlie stuck his hand through the loop of the leash and wrapped it once around his wrist.

"Take it easy, McGarrett," Charlie said firmly. "Relax."

The dog bolted, yanking Charlie off his feet, dragging him along the ground behind him, the rough gravel tearing at his body like tiny knives.

"Stop," Charlie yelled, rolling on his stomach and grabbing the leash with both hands, trying to regain control. It was futile. McGarrett ran at full clip, showing reserves of strength Charlie never guessed he had.

"McGarrett!" Charlie roared. "Stop!"

The dog dragged him out of *Global Armageddon*, through the Champs Elysées, and into Dodge City. Charlie struggled, but his arm was hopelessly tangled in the leash, and he didn't have the strength in his other arm, ravaged by Boo Boo, to put up much of a fight.

McGarrett seemed oblivious to him, the sedentary dog using every ounce of his being to charge toward Times Square.

Just as they were leaving the Old West and entering midtown Manhattan, the leash snapped. Charlie rolled to a stop, dazed and bloody, glancing up in time to see McGarrett running down 42nd Street, the torn leash trailing behind him.

Boyd Hartnell rose up on his knees, mud-caked and naked, his once glorious mane a tangled haven for fleas and ticks. Drool spilled out of his mouth, landing in gobs on Reed Roland's gun, which he held in his claw and pointed at Delbert Skaggs.

"Drop your gun," Boyd screeched, scratching his balls with his free hand.

Delbert complied. He made it a rule never to argue with a frothing, armed man scratching his filthy balls with inch-long fingernails.

Otto and Burt, their injuries momentarily forgotten, stared at this beast in utter fascination.

"It's Boo Boo," declared Otto, certain the celebrity mutt had somehow evolved into this hideous creature. "The whole studio must be radioactive."

Boyd turned his wild gaze on Eddie.

"She's mine," Boyd screeched. "Give her to me now."

Eddie immediately unhanded Sabrina, who stood for a moment, uncertain which fate was worse—remaining with this motley bunch, or going with the dogman.

"If I can't have you, Sabrina, no one will," Boyd yelled, then howled at the moon.

That was enough incentive for Sabrina. She was staggering toward him when McGarrett tore out of the darkness and tackled Boyd, knocking the gun from him.

Sabrina dived for Boyd's gun. Delbert dived for his. Otto kicked the gun out of Delbert's reach and Burt stomped on his hand, then on his head for good measure. Eddie threw himself down the subway steps into the access tunnel. And McGarrett lustily ravaged Boyd, the two of them tumbling down the sidewalk, howling, hair flying.

Sabrina caught the gun against her chest, sliding the weapon along with her into a storefront doorway. In one smooth, lightning-fast move, she jumped into the air, tucked up her legs, and swung her arms underneath her feet, bringing her lashed wrists in front of her. She snatched the gun, whipped around, and fired off two shots at Otto and Burt, who leapt behind a park bench for cover.

Otto and Burt were entertainment professionals. They knew the sound of blanks when they heard them. So did Sabrina. She tossed the gun and ran through the door into the next street on the other side.

Otto and Burt weren't going to let their babe get away. They ran after her, leaving a trail of blood in their wake.

Charlie staggered to his feet and saw Sabrina run toward Europe, followed a moment later by Otto and Burt. Furious, he charged off after them, wishing he had a gun.

She ran blindly down the streets, hearing her pursuers behind her. None of this made any sense to her. Who were these people? Why were they killing each other? What did they want with her? The only thing she understood was that, for whatever reason, she was fighting for her life. That was really all that mattered anyway.

Sabrina ran around a corner into Florence, Italy, and jumped through the open window of a cafe. She hunkered down and held her breath. A moment later, Otto and Burt scrambled past, on their way to Rome.

She closed her eyes and exhaled slowly, relieved. That's when someone reached through the window and clamped a bloody hand over her mouth. She bit him as hard as she could, freeing herself, whirling around to confront . . . *Charlie!*

She was horrified, not only at having bit him, but by the way he looked. He'd obviously been through a terrible beating.

"I'm so sorry," she whispered. "I thought you were one of the bad guys."

"Don't worry about it," he said, clutching his hand and grimacing with pain.

Charlie climbed through the window and she pulled him into a big hug.

"It's so good to see you." She pressed her face into his chest. "I didn't think I ever would again."

"We aren't out of this yet." He reluctantly pushed her away. "But we'll have a much better chance if at least one of us has both hands."

Charlie found the sharp point of a rusty nail sticking out of the wall, and led her over to it. While she used the nail to cut the duct tape around her wrists, Charlie explained, as best he could, what was going on. By the time he was through, she was free and red-faced with anger.

"I'll kill 'em," she said.

"You can kill them later," Charlie said. "Right now, let's concentrate on getting out of the park alive."

He peered out the door and, satisfied they were alone, took her by the hand and led her out. They were in the middle of the street when they both heard the growl of an engine.

"Run," Charlie yelled.

Behind them, a bashed GMC truck whipped around the corner, smashed into a fountain, and screeched across the cobblestones toward them. Otto drove, Burt yee-hawed.

Charlie knew there was no way they were going to outrun a truck. He grabbed Sabrina's hand and dragged her with him into the nearest facade.

Otto saw them and wrenched the wheel, charging directly into the row of fake buildings. The truck decimated the thin facades, plowing through them in a spray of splintered wood and stucco.

Florence destroyed, Otto spun the truck around in a swirl of dust.

"I never liked Italy," Burt said.

When the dust settled, they saw Charlie and Sabrina dashing across Dodge City into the Silver Dollar Hotel. Otto pressed the pedal to the floor. The GMC shot forward, tires smoking, toward Dodge City.

Charlie and Sabrina raced out of the courthouse on the other side and hurried down the steps into the town square of Anytown, USA. Behind them, they could hear the roar of the truck closing in. They only had a few seconds until Otto and Burt blew through the courthouse behind them and found them in the open.

Charlie pointed to the end of the street, at the backdrop of a country road winding into the distance, which was painted onto the wall of soundstage 17.

"That way," he said, nearly out of breath.

"It's a dead end," she protested.

"I know."

And with that, he took her hand and they ran down Main Street to the country road backdrop. Charlie and Sabrina were barely across the square when the truck burst out of the courthouse, hurled into the fake columns, and crashed into the bandstand, flattening it.

Charlie looked back to see the truck closing in behind them, the courthouse crumbling in its wake. It would only be a second or two before the truck mowed them down. They were all running out of road.

"We'll get 'em before they reach the hills," Otto yelled, looking ahead at the long, winding road.

"What hills?" Burt asked.

Just as Otto realized his mistake, Charlie and Sabrina jumped into the brush on either side of the road. Otto stomped on the breaks, but it was too late.

The truck slammed into the painted wall of soundstage 17, hurling Otto and Burt across the crumpled hood like two tuxedoed crash dummies. An instant later the truck exploded, coughing their flaming bodies up into the air, which was as close as they would ever get to being stars.

Charlie and Sabrina straggled out of the bushes and stared at the burning truck, the flames licking the country road off the soundstage.

"Let's go," Charlie said. "We don't want to be here when the police arrive."

They slogged through Muck Thing's swamp lands, dashed down the Champs Elysées and cut across the postapocalyptic landscape of *Global Armageddon.*

They were winding through the rubble toward the bleachers when Delbert Skaggs popped up behind the burned-out car in front of them. He set his elbows on the charred hood, steadying the gun he held in his mangled hands.

"End of the line," Delbert croaked, aiming the gun at Charlie.

"Give up, Skaggs." Charlie stepped in front of Sabrina. "It's over."

"For you it is," Delbert said. "Of all the people I've killed, I'm going to enjoy killing you the most, and until a few days ago, I didn't even know you."

Charlie nervously shook his arm as if trying to get the blood circulating again. "I advise you to drop your gun."

Delbert flashed a toothless grin. "Give me one good reason."

The remote control dropped out of Charlie's sleeve into his hand. Charlie met Delbert's gaze. "Because my gun has bullets."

Delbert cocked the trigger. "You don't have a gun."

Charlie pressed a button. With a metallic roar, the Robokiller smashed through the skyscraper behind Delbert and fired two flaming missiles from his head-mounted cannons.

Charlie and Sabrina hit the ground.

Delbert whirled around to see the fake missiles streak past him on their thin wires, smacking harmlessly into the ground on either side of the burned-out car.

He was starting to turn, a derisive laugh rising in his throat, when the explosive charge hidden under his feet went off, blowing him and the car hulk into the air.

The car was rigged to a line that brought it back to earth. Delbert was not. The hitman cartwheeled through the air, smacked into the bleachers, and broke through the floor, his body landing atop the half-eaten, decomposed corpse of Joel Metzger, who had been missing for days.

As Charlie and Sabrina stood up, one of the resistance fighters' cannon-mounted jeeps burst through the debris behind them, firing rounds at the Robokiller. Charlie pulled Sabrina off the stage just as the Robokiller fired back, and the ground where they had been lying exploded.

The two of them climbed onto the first row of the bleachers and sat down, catching their breath, the pyrotechnical extravaganza continuing on in front of them. In the distance, they could hear approaching sirens and the chopping rhythm of a helicopter streaking their way.

Wincing, Charlie slid his dog-bitten arm around Sabrina's shoulder and drew her to him.

"I think I've had enough of the tour," he said. "How about you?"

Tag

....

Six Months Later

A fifty-year-old, cigar-chomping vaudeville comedian reincarnated as a French poodle—everyone knew *that* was *Boo Boo's Dilemma.* But when the dog is decapitated in a freak accident, and his head is attached to a malfunctioning robot, well, that's even funnier.

And it was also *Boo Boo's New Dilemma,* the breakout hit of the new television season. The phenomenal numbers generated by the wacky sitcom allowed UBC to sweep Thursday night, an evening capped off by *Agatha's Niece,* starring Sabrina Bishop.

On rival network MBC, Reed Roland made a triumphant return to television, turning *Johnny Wildlife* into *Dr. Hook,* who, in the premiere, captivated the nation by performing an emergency tracheotomy with his prosthesis on an ailing moose.

But nothing surprised Charlie nearly as much as the news that Eddie Planet was back on television, executive-producing *Sunn of a Gunn,* starring Erik Estrada and Chad Everett, in the old *Frankencop* slot.

Charlie Willis was cleared of all the charges against him, but it was a lengthy, excruciating process that cost him most of his *My Gun Has Bullets* earnings, and his show T-shirt, in attorney's fees.

But Eddie Planet came out of the scandal completely clean, even sympathetic. He never had to defend himself, his reputation was never in question, and as hard as Charlie tried, he couldn't come up with one piece of evidence to implicate Eddie in the plot.

Eddie claimed to be an innocent dupe, unaware that Pinstripe Productions was owned by the mob, or that Delbert Skaggs was a hitman. Anyone who could have testified otherwise was dead or, in Daddy Crofoot's case, missing.

It amazed Charlie even more now as he sat in Sabrina's trailer, feet up on the table, reading *Daily Variety.* Eddie took out a full-page

....

261

advertisement mourning the passing of "Hollywood legend" and "consummate showman" Flint Westwood, who died on the operating table during penile implant surgery.

So now the last person who could connect Eddie Planet to the scandal was dead, and Eddie couldn't resist using the event for self-promotion. He'd even taken out an ad praising Boyd Hartnell on the same day as his memorial service at Rolling Hills Pet Cemetery.

Eventually, Charlie knew he'd find a way to make Eddie Planet pay for all the trouble he had caused. In the meantime, Charlie was happy just to have survived the ordeal, though he'd been marked forever by it. The scars from the bullet wound and the mauling of his arm would always be there to remind him.

But he'd come out with his reputation intact and, more importantly, with the love of a beautiful woman, who just happened to be coming in the door.

Sabrina, exhausted, trudged into the trailer between takes, still wearing her black leather jumpsuit. She kissed him on the cheek and grabbed an Evian from the fridge.

"So, have you made a decision yet?" she asked.

He tossed the *Daily Variety* on an empty seat and, for the first time in hours, looked down at the three badges on the table.

One badge was from the Beverly Hills Police Department, offering him his old job back. One was from Pinnacle Pictures, offering him a job as the company's chief of worldwide security. The last one came from Jackson Burley and Don DeBono. It was Derek Thorne's badge, and if he pinned it on, they'd guarantee him twenty-two more episodes of *My Gun Has Bullets*.

"No," he groaned. "I'm trying not to think about it."

She set her Evian on the table, climbed into his lap, and straddled him. "Maybe I can help."

He smiled, took her zipper in his teeth and peeled her jumpsuit open. "Did I ever tell you I have verisimilitude coming out of my pores?"

She buried his face in her bosom, closed her eyes, and sighed. "I knew it was something."